I0742267

TENEKA WOODS

Hot August Nights

AMENITY PRESS
PO Box 654
Missouri City, Texas 77459

Copyright © 2019 by Teneka Woods
ISBN 978-1-7336787-0-4 (paperback)
ISBN 978-1-7336787-1-1 (ebook)

Cover design: Paper & Sage
Formatting: Polgarus Studio

ONE

"Well, you know how the saying goes. Everything happens for a reason."

Cynthia sighed and shifted in her seat, her tailbone numb from sitting nearly three hours as her friend, Tora, braided her hair in preparation for her summer getaway. "Maybe. But this is definitely the worst year ever."

"Or it could just be a sign that you need to start over in every way."

"It can only get better from here," Cynthia said, trying to sound optimistic even though she was reeling inside.

"So what do you plan to do at your grandmother's house?" Tora stepped back to take a sip from her soda, set the glass down hard on the kitchen counter, then popped her knuckles. She grabbed a section of Cynthia's hair to start the next braid.

Cynthia did not consider herself superstitious, but her grandmother liked to believe bad news came in threes, and she wondered if she was getting a taste of what she meant. The first came when her landlord announced he needed his rental townhome back to house his ailing mother and gave her just thirty days to vacate. Second, the charter school where she had been working as a Social Studies teacher for the past couple years was closing its doors due to someone's mismanagement of the funds. And just when she thought her situation could not get any more desperate, her longtime partner fell weak to temptation and tried someone new.

"Look for a job of course," she answered dryly.

Tora dropped the braid from her hand and walked around the chair to face Cynthia. "Wait. You're not planning to move there, are you?"

Cynthia reasoned her hair would have been completed an hour ago if her friend did not stop every few minutes to do something else: change the channel on the television, go to the bathroom, stop one of the cats from playing between the venetian blinds, make a sandwich, turn off the television to turn on the radio. But Tora was doing something free of charge that normally cost her upwards of two hundred dollars, so she had no mind to complain. "No, but I do have to search for a job every day you know. I can't just sit back and hope the few districts I've submitted my résumé to call me, although that would be nice. I hate the whole process. Completing those long-ass online applications. The waiting. Interviews. I don't even know if I really want to teach anymore."

"Really?" Tora sighed this time. "Sis, now don't go getting all discouraged and what-not. You've always loved teaching. Why the sudden change of heart just because of this layoff?"

"I don't know. Maybe it is time for a change like you said. I've been doing it for nine years. I'm open to trying something new. Maybe something in corporate. Who knows?"

Tora unraveled the braid she'd started only to braid it again. "Well, at least try to have some fun, even though I don't know how much fun there is to have out there in the country. Maybe you will meet a cowboy and he take you out to ride his horse or something."

Cynthia almost choked. "Oh lord, Tora." Their friendship was just a few years old. Tora had moved south from Pittsburgh seeking warmer weather year-round. A hurricane ran her out of Florida, icy winters ran her out of Georgia, snow ran her out of Tennessee, and so she settled in Houston, Texas where there would be only threats of excessive rain and flooding every one hundred years. They met at Cynthia's favorite local barbecue restaurant. She was passing time reading her book club's latest selection as she sat waiting for her order when Tora walked over, introduced herself, and to tell Cynthia Bernice L. McFadden was also one of her favorite authors. Over talk of McFadden's *Loving Donovan* and chopped beef sandwiches they became friends and Cynthia suggested Tora attend the next book club meeting.

"I'm just saying," Tora continued, "don't sit around and sulk. Didn't you say your grandmother is pretty active there in church events and bingo clubs?"

Cynthia sucked her teeth. "My grandma is in her seventies. Why would I want to hang out with her and her senior friends?"

"Hellooo?" Tora waved her hand in the air expecting Cynthia to see the obvious. "Some of those senior women may have sons. And I'm sure not all of them still drive themselves around. Who do you think is taking them to their church banquets and bingo games?"

"Tora, I need a job. A man is nowhere on the radar right now. And definitely not after what Jonath—" She didn't bother to continue.

Tora picked up her glass, taking a long swig to finish off the cola. She twirled a piece of ice around her teeth. "Well, you know what they say: the best way to get over a man is to get under another one."

"*What?!*"

It was a little after two in the morning when Cynthia finally settled down for bed. Her scalp tight and sore from the eight-hour braiding session, she eased down onto the air mattress, the soft pillow offering little comfort for her aching head. Days were so much easier to deal with than nighttime. The day held many distractions to keep her mind busy and off her current situation—mainly the sunken feeling in her chest that seemed to worsen with each passing day. She believed things would get easier, but Jonathan was always right around the corner of her thoughts, unfolding a chair and taking a seat. Jonathan Blackshire. The man she'd spent the past three years of her life with. The man who'd consumed most of her time. It was the type of love affair most girls dream about: the long courtship beginning with talks over the phone to get to know each other on a base level, then romantic dates to test compatibility, which led to conversations about the other's hopes and dreams for the future and for a deeper relationship, then the decision for exclusivity. Jonathan was kind, attentive, generous. Cynthia had no reason to believe their relationship stood on shaky ground. Sure, they had their share of quarrels in between as most couples do, but nothing significant to cause her to question their status. In him she saw the future. But while she stood rigid in her commitment, defying all the elements that seem to split couples apart, Jonathan got tripped up and fell face first into the lap of another woman.

Cynthia rolled over on her side, taking a deep breath as she did so, trying to ease the feeling in her chest. She could not close her eyes because closing her eyes would only bring forth visions of him. Of them. She considered turning on the music app on her phone, but she was not in the mood for a love song and too sad to be shaken by something more upbeat. The air mattress lay next to the floor-to-ceiling built-in bookcase and on the bottom shelf was Tora's grand collection of magazines—the spines of them face-out so Cynthia was able to see she subscribed to everything from those offering tips on clean eating to creating arts and crafts to how to snag and keep a man. With only slices of moonlight cutting through the blinds and across the bookshelf she lay there counting the number of magazines using only her eyes until the slow tick of the analog clock hanging on the far wall lulled her into a dreamless sleep.

* * *

Cynthia pulled her silver Toyota Corolla into the gas station to fill up. It was the only service station left before she made it to her grandmother's house. On the other side of the highway was the only supermarket within a 15-mile radius where the town could purchase groceries, some clothing, and get an auto oil change. As the gas pumped she pulled out her cell phone, pressing the quick key to dial her grandmother.

"Hello Mama Genie," she said when she heard her grandmother's voice on the other end.

"Oh, hey baby, so you're on your way now, huh?"

Cynthia left Tora's apartment earlier than she initially told her grandmother she would. She couldn't wait to be on the road and out of the city where everywhere she turned only reminded her of Jonathan. "I'm here getting some gas near the grocery store. Is there anything you need before I come?"

"Here?" her grandmother shrieked. "You told me you were gonna call me before you left. The food ain't near-bout done yet. You trying to sneak up on me?" Then she fell into her full-belly laugh, which made Cynthia smile.

"Well, I thought I'd surprise you."

"Good thing I put it on when I did or else I'm sure you would've been starving had I sat here and waited for you to call me." She laughed again. "But naw, I don't need nothing. Holiday come by here about a hour ago and he gon' bring back the salt-bacon for my greens. He should be back pretty soon."

Cynthia heard the snap of the gas pump signaling the tank was full. "Hold on a minute, Mama Genie." She set her cell phone in the passenger seat, hopped out the car to place the pump back in its slot, and grab her receipt. "Who is Holiday?" she asked, placing her key in the ignition and cranking up the car.

"Did I tell you the last time we talked I think some people getting ready to move in the house next door?"

"No, not that I remember," Cynthia said. She usually came down to visit at least three times a year: at Christmas, for Mother's day, and in the summer for her grandmother's birthday. But for the Christmas past Jonathan surprised her with a weekend ski trip to Colorado along with a few of their friends. By May Cynthia was heartbroken and trying to understand what hit her and could not fathom being around anyone—let alone her grandmother who believed Jonathan was the epitome of what she hoped for for her granddaughter and future grandson-in-law—so she conjured up an excuse of why she had to forgo their Mother's day celebration.

"Well him and his daddy been here every day near-bout working on the house. And he come by sometimes to see if I need anythang when they go to town for some supplies."

"Oh, that's really sweet of him."

"Unh-huh," her grandmother continued, "he a real nice young man. His daddy seem pretty nice too. I think his name Frank."

"Well I hope the people moving in are nice. I still miss Sister Dunham," Cynthia said, referring to the woman who occupied the home next to her grandmother throughout her childhood and teen years.

Mama Genie exhaled. "Me, too."

Cynthia finally pulled out of the parking lot and headed down the road she'd traveled so many times before. The road that led to the place where she could always find peace and solace.

TWO

A blast of heat along with the aroma of southern cooking greeted Cynthia as she opened the screen door to let herself in. "Mama Genie, that oven got it so hot in here! You've been cooking all morning or what?" She set her luggage next to the coffee table and stepped into the kitchen to give her grandmother a tight hug and kiss on her cheek, breathing in the familiar scent of Avon's Skin-so-Soft body oil and Charlie perfume powder. All four burners atop the stove were occupied: a big pot of greens on one of the eyes in the back, whole baby carrots with slices of butter on top and sprinkled with brown sugar simmered next to it, butter beans on one in the front, a skillet of cornbread ready to go into the oven on the other. A pecan pie sat on the counter next to the flour and sugar canisters.

"How you doing, sugar?" Mama Genie turned to smack two kisses on Cynthia's cheek too. "Everything should be ready in about another hour."

"No problem. I ate something before I came anyway, so I'm okay for now." She took a seat at the small table in the kitchen, but got right up because the heat was too much for her in the narrow space. "Why do you have the door open letting all the cool air out? Doesn't that make the A/C work harder or something?" Cynthia walked back to the living room to close the front door.

"The A/C ain't on," her grandmother said.

"Why not? You're not hot in here?" She could already feel sweat pooling in her cleavage.

"It ain't been cooling lately so I just leave it turned off during the day."

"What do you mean it's not cooling?" Cynthia went to the thermostat in the hallway even though she knew looking at the thermostat was not going to change anything. The dial noted it was eighty-three degrees inside. "How long has it been like this and why didn't you tell me? Did you call a repairman?"

"Not yet. It ain't been bothering me none. You know I'm cold-natured and I just turn my li'l fan on at night."

Cynthia pursed her lips. She knew this had more to do with the cost of the repair than her grandmother's preference for lukewarm temperatures—which only served as another reminder of her lack of disposable funds to help out. She decided the repair would be charged to her credit card if necessary and worry about the expense later, but there was no way she was going to let Mama Genie walk around in all this heat. "I'm calling someone to come out and take a look at it first thing tomorrow morning," she told her. "I'll be upstairs unpacking."

The air was even stuffier upstairs and Cynthia opened the two windows of her childhood room. One overlooked the backyard that was not really a backyard but a wide open field of grass and weeds. The other window was positioned on the side and faced the side of the house next door. She looked out at Sister Dunham's old house recalling the many sweet moments she spent sitting on the steps of her front porch as Sister Dunham and Mama Genie sat in the rocking chairs talking about many things. The porch now was built to extend from the front all the way around to the back of the house.

She emptied the clothing from her suitcase onto the floor, separating them into piles to be washed, wanting to get rid of any lingering cat hair picked up from Tora's apartment. Cynthia was draining her meager savings living in an extended-stay hotel when Tora offered her a place to stay in her apartment and set up an air mattress in the den slash home office. She was grateful for the hospitality, but the French doors of the den offered her little privacy, sleeping on an air mattress every day was a drab, Tora liked cats, and they were accustomed to going to the den to relieve themselves. So when Cynthia woke up many mornings to see the eyes of two Blue Point Siamese staring at her through the glass doors, she knew she had to get away for a while to figure out her next move. She'd called her grandmother to tell her she was coming for a month-long visit. Here, she would have a whole room, her own bed, and an environment fresh and free of cat litter.

She took off her clothes, bra and panties, and threw them on the piles, too. In a dresser drawer she found one of her old favorites—a green T-shirt dress—and pulled it over her head, then slipped into a pair of bikini briefs. The dress fit snugly around her hips now and fell just mid-thigh since she'd put on fifteen pounds in the past few months, placing her at an even 175 on her five-foot, four-inch frame. It was the harsh consequence of being an emotional eater. She gathered the braids as tenderly as she could without screaming out loud into a ball on the top of her head, wrapped them with a silk scarf, then descended the hardwood steps in her bare feet for the utility room just beneath the stairs and started her first load of laundry.

"Is there anything you need me to do?" She kissed her grandmother's cheek again just because. Her face was damp with perspiration and Cynthia pulled the strings of hair plastered near her grandmother's eye back behind her ear.

"Not really. Everything pretty much set. Unless you wanna make some lemonade. I think I got some mix in the pantry."

"Okay, I can do that." Cynthia rifled through the shelves of the small pantry until she came across the can of Country Time lemonade mix. She pulled the plastic pitcher from the top shelf, filled it with water from the sink, then grabbed a big mixing spoon from the dish rack sitting on the counter.

"So ain't nobody call you yet?" Mama Genie came over to take a seat at the table, letting out a puff of air as she sat down.

Cynthia scooped the powdered mix, then sugar, into the water and began to stir. She told Mama Genie often there was no need to buy lemonade in the can when the same brand is sold in liquid form, pre-sweetened and ready to serve, but there are many things Mama Genie just won't give up. "No, not yet," she answered.

"And what you plan on doing if they do call you? You got to drive all the way back for the interview? Or can they do that over the phone?"

"Most-likely I will have to drive back, but I don't mind. I don't expect them all to call me at the same time." Cynthia added a little more powder to the water.

Mama Genie peered at the pitcher. "Are you sure you measuring that stuff out right, girl?" The question seemed more rhetorical to Cynthia as she did not pause to give her time to answer, but continued, "You never know. Somebody is sure to call. They always need plenty teachers. How is that Tora doing?"

"She's fine. She was taking the cats out for a walk when I left this morning."

Mama Genie looked at Cynthia to make sure she heard her right. "Taking the cats out for a walk?"

Cynthia laughed. "Yes, she actually puts them on a leash and takes them out for a walk to get fresh air."

Mama Genie laughed at the image. "I ain't never heard of nobody walking a cat. That girl is still crazy I see."

"She does. Well… she does more carrying than walking them, but she takes them out all the time. Those cats are her babies." Cynthia braced herself because she knew what was coming next. Mama Genie'd asked about her job, her friendship, so it was only natural that she would want to know about the other aspect of her life.

"I'm surprised Jonathan let you come down for a whole month by yourself. I thought for sure y'all would've been headed off on another one of y'all's summer vacations."

Cynthia called Mama Genie several times a week to check on her, to chit-chat, and the conversation oftentimes led into talk about her and Jonathan. And over the past few months with the distance and phone line between them she was able to mask the truth and not reveal what was troubling her. She would quickly say things were fine, rehash something Jonathan had said or done in the past for good measure then lead the conversation on to another subject. But standing in front of Mama Genie now she still wasn't ready to talk about him. She didn't want to think about him. She had come to try to forget about him and that's what she intended to do.

"I just told him I wanted to come and spend some time with you since it's been a while. And he's fine with that."

A bashful smirk crossed Mama Genie's face. "Well don't I feel special," she groaned in her playful, sarcastic way.

"Yep," Cynthia said, "and I even brought a couple dresses so I can go to church with you."

Mama Genie sucked her teeth. "Now I know a storm must be coming soon if you're going to church with me. Reverend Moore still asks about you every now and then."

Cynthia grabbed two lemons from the produce basket and rinsed them to be cut into thin slices. "I like Reverend Moore, but he just goes on and on and on and on. Service starts at ten o' clock and don't end until three. That's just too long to be in church. It was fine back in the day, but I just can't deal with it anymore, Mama Genie. I'm sorry."

"You don't have to apologize to me," Mama Genie scoffed, "he is long-winded but he's letting the Lord use him. And that's just how you new-age folks are. Attention span ain't longer than a minute."

"Well, I just think one-and-a-half to two hours is good enough. That's how long our services are. Pastor Steward is just as thorough and gets it done in less than half the time. Then we have the rest of the day to do as we please." Cynthia dropped the lemon slices into the pitcher and walked over to the refrigerator, placing it in the freezer.

"And that's what's wrong with people today. Can't sit still long enough to reap the benefits of a good lesson. Something solid. Always in a hurry to move on to do something else." Mama Genie leaned heavily onto the table to assist herself to stand. "Girl, let me get to this bathroom before I wet myself. Listen at the door for Holiday," she said as she shuffled down the hall.

Cynthia pulled open the oven door and slid the skillet of cornbread onto the bottom rack. She grabbed the double-folded dish towel her grandmother used as an oven mitt to lift the lid on the roasting pan to peek inside: two Cornish hens surrounded by red onion and gold bell pepper halves sprinkled with thyme. Cynthia had said she wasn't hungry, but just the smell of it made her forget all about the breakfast taco she'd had. She flipped the oven door back up and walked over to the sink to run dish water and wash the dishes sitting there—anything to keep her hands and mind busy.

A feverish knock on the screen door and a gruff voice calling out for Ms. Genie made Cynthia realize she must have been daydreaming as she did not hear anyone pull into the driveway or footsteps across the porch. "Ms. Genie, you in there? I'm back with your bacon." He tapped on the screen door again.

Cynthia snatched the dish towel from the counter, drying her hands as she went to the living room. She pushed open the screen door and stepped out without a second thought.

"Oh," the man said, and Cynthia watched him as his eyes roved over her starting from the top of her head to her feet and then back to the top again. She was just as caught off guard as she was expecting a young teen, but there was nothing pubescent about this guy. He was thick and broad-shouldered. His hair a thick and short textured Afro—as if he just roughed his fingers through it every morning as a means of styling it. Gray sprinkled his goatee. His skin was smooth and as black and lovely as the sky at midnight. A tuft of hair peeked out near the bottom of the V in his T-shirt that stretched across his chest. Freckles of paint splattered his navy blue cargo pants and the tips of his work boots. He held the bacon wrapped in white butcher paper in one hand and a thin classifieds newspaper in the other.

"You must be Frank," Cynthia said.

He flashed a bright smile. "Uh, no, I'm—" He stuffed the newspaper under his left armpit and brushed his hand against his back pocket. "I'm sorry, ma'am," he said examining the palm of his hand, "I would shake your hand but I'm kinda filthy right now. I'm doing some work next door." He gestured his head towards Sister Dunham's old place.

Cynthia smiled. "That's okay."

"I picked this up for Ms. Genie," he said holding the bacon out to Cynthia. "Tell her I will be here for a while if she needs anything else."

Cynthia took the bacon and watched him descend the steps and get halfway across the grassy path before she stepped back into the living room.

"So he made it back, huh?" Mama Genie said, coming up behind her.

"I thought when you told me about Holiday you were talking about a young boy," Cynthia said and walked back into the kitchen. She removed the strip of tan masking tape from the white paper, unwrapping the mass of fatty meat. Mama Genie turned on the faucet and watched her rinse the bacon.

"He is a young man." She set a plate on the counter and Cynthia cut the meat into large chunks before putting them in a skillet to be fried and then dropped into the pot of greens.

"Not that young. I was thinking about a teenager or something when you said he works with his daddy."

Mama Genie waved her off and plopped down in her favorite kitchen chair. "Anybody younger than me is young."

THREE

Emerald greens, sepia browns, and burnt orange were the colors that swirled through Holiday's mind as he sat on the back porch, taking a break from his work. The lady next door was unexpected and he couldn't get the image of her out of his mind. Her doe eyes and full lips. The smooth brown legs underneath the short dress that hugged her curvy frame. He even noticed her toenails painted a warm orange color—a gold ring wrapped around the second toe. Then her nipples. Had he stared? He couldn't recall, but the way they pierced the thin fabric seemed to be reaching out to him. He took a cigarette out of his back pocket and lit it up. He chuckled at himself because he had not even told her his name, did not ask her for hers. He had been coming to the house doing work for several weeks and had never seen her before. Ms. Genie hadn't told him she had a daughter. But why would she? Their conversations were usually short with just exchanges of hellos and small talk about the weather if she happened to be sitting on her porch when Holiday pulled up, or needed something from the store when he pulled out.

FOUR

Cynthia woke up to the sounds of hammering and sawing against wood. She had lain down to take a nap, restless from the early morning three-and-a-half hour drive to her grandmother's house. The windows were open but there wasn't much of a breeze. Her T-shirt was damp with sweat underneath her arms, her thighs too. She flung the sheet to the side and got up, the hardwood floor surprisingly cool against her feet. She could hear dishes rattling in the kitchen and Mama Genie humming a tune when she opened her bedroom door and crossed the hall to go to the bathroom. Turning on the shower head she stepped right into the tub without waiting for the water to warm.

Mama Genie was sitting on the couch watching the four o' clock news when she made it downstairs. She went to the kitchen to make herself a plate—a full plate this time since she had helped herself only to a small portion of the butter beans and a slice of corn bread earlier, deciding to wait until later in the day to eat. But that's how Mama Genie did her Sunday-style cooking. Cynthia called it Sunday-style because, even though it was Friday, and just the two of them, Mama Genie always made a feast early in the afternoon and they would nibble at the food throughout the day and still have enough left over to last a couple days.

"Sister Nash is coming by to pick me up at five. She want me to go by the nursery with her and want me to see her new flower bed she got. She say she got it fixed up real nice but want some yellow flowers to go with that red brick. Yellow is her favorite color y'know."

Cynthia did not know, but she pretended she did. "Mmm-hmm. But doesn't Sister Nash live in Douglass County? Why is she driving way out here?"

"Chile, I ask her that all the time, but she insist on us riding together. I tell her it make more sense for me to meet her there, but she say she'll come by and get me so I just let her. It save me from driving anyhow. And I think she just like driving. You know she only been driving for about three years."

"Three years?!"

Mama Genie laughed, slapping her knee as she did. "Yeah, I told her I ain't never knowed nobody to wait until they almost seventy to wanna learn how to drive."

Cynthia took a seat at the table, noticing two plates wrapped in foil. "What took her so long?"

"She just say she never really needed to. They always just had one car and her husband did all the driving whenever they went somewhere. She didn't work y'know. And when them children grew up they just drove her around after the husband passed. But she say they got tired of doing that and she got tired of having to depend on them. But ain't that something? Got her license at this age."

"It is."

"See them two plates right there," Mama Genie said. "I want you to take them next door to Holiday and his daddy. I meant to ask him earlier if he said his daddy's name was Frank. Did he say his name was Frank?"

Cynthia shook her head no, her mouth full of carrots so sweet they tasted like candied yams. "He didn't say anything about his dad. He just gave me the bacon."

Mama Genie offered no response and instead squint her eyes at the television and turned the volume up to hear what the news reporter was saying.

* * *

Cynthia heard the music as she walked the short path to the sea green color house next door. She walked up the three concrete steps to the porch and rapped on the screen. There was a white wood rocking bench on one side of the porch, and two navy blue shell-backed chairs on the other side, rusted with water stains in the seats. The hammering inside appeared to be coming from the back of the house. She cupped a hand around her eye and pressed her face to the glass to peer inside when there was no answer. Prince was loudly proclaiming from radio speakers that there was no particular sign he was more compatible with and all he wanted was some woman's extra time and kiss.

She twisted the handle on the door and stepped in.

It smelled like fresh paint. Plastic covered the wood floors and a variety of tools were strewn about. The small boom box sat on the kitchen counter.

She had not been inside the home since the repast dinner following Sister Dunham's funeral nearly a decade ago. Sister Dunham never married and did not have any children and her only brother had come down from South Carolina to lay her to rest. Cynthia realized now how similar the layout of the house was to her grandmother's except this one was a single story. The combined kitchen and dining room set to the left, the living room on the right. One could see straight to the back of the house from the front door via a long, narrow hallway. The front rooms seemed so spacious now that they were empty of all those plants Sister Dunham had. Plants and owls were her favorite things. Cynthia looked around the rooms as though the pots of palms and Birds of Paradise were still there sitting on the floor next to the sofas, snake plants on the coffee table and kitchen counters, baskets of ferns hanging from the high ceilings, ivies in cages with stems that coiled up the walls. She remembered only the plants with names she could pronounce even though Sister Dunham delighted in teaching her the names of the most exotic-sounding ones. And then the owls. She could still see them everywhere. Colorful ceramic ones. Crystal ones. In artwork all over the house. Wall clocks and whatnots. On Sister Dunham's apron and kitchen towels, her tablecloth where her head lay the day she and Mama Genie discovered her slumped over.

He appeared out of the bathroom and stopped short in the hallway when he saw her standing there.

"I'm sorry, but I knocked on the door several times. I guess you couldn't hear me over the music," Cynthia told him.

"Oh. I didn't know," and he took a step forward then stopped again. Cynthia found it charming as he suddenly tried to cover his chest with his hand. He was shirtless.

"Umm, I'm sorry. Had I known you were coming I wouldn't've been walking around like this."

Cynthia shook her head. "It's no problem. I'm the one who just helped myself and walked right on in, so what could I expect?" She noticed his T-shirt then draped over a short step-ladder in the living room. "My grandma sent you and your dad a plate."

He laughed and walked over to the step-ladder, his boots heavy against the wood floor, and swiftly put on the shirt, then to the kitchen counter to lower the volume on the radio. "Oh okay, so Ms. Genie is your grandmother? She is something else," he said taking the grocery bag with the two plates in it from Cynthia. "I can already tell it's something that'll put me to sleep if I eat it now." He bounced the bag in his hand as if he was calculating the weight of it. Pop is not here with me today, but I sure will take it to him later. Tell her I really appreciate this and thank you."

"You're welcome."

"Oh," he said and stuck out his hand towards Cynthia. "I'm sorry I couldn't do this earlier. And I didn't get your name."

She took his hand and smiled. "Cynthia."

"Cynthia," he repeated.

"And I know you're Holiday."

He nodded. "Yeah, well, it's Mason, but most call me Holiday. It's our last name." He looked at her now noticing the fitted green dress was gone and she was donning something that looked more like a fancy potato sack and wore beach thong sandals on her feet.

"Is it okay if I look back there," she asked him.

"Oh yeah. Go right ahead. I'm just going to put these plates in my cooler here." He walked over to the kitchen and Cynthia walked up the hallway. She looked into the small bathroom. The pink tiles on the countertop and shower walls were being replaced with a light gray marble; the white cabinets replaced with light gray ones. Sister Dunham's old room and the guest bedrooms had been painted white. They used to be shell pink. Then she walked out to the back porch.

"My grandma told me some people were finally moving in here," Cynthia said when she heard him step out onto the porch. "It's been vacant for a long time."

"My Pop's friend bought this a few months back and is getting it fixed up for his daughter he told me. As a graduation gift. She's graduating from college in December I think."

"Oh wow. Talk about a great gift. All I got was a bunch of cards from the ladies at the church—some with a few dollars in them— and my grandmother cooked a big dinner and those same ladies came over to the house and we ate." She laughed.

"Yeah, and he's upgrading everything, too. We just finished this porch here last weekend." He stood beside her and gave the banister a firm shake as if to test its sturdiness.

"It looks nice. Well, I don't want to keep you from your work," she said and descended the steps.

"Oh, it's not a problem at all. It was a welcomed break. Thanks again for the lunch."

Cynthia nodded and waved. And she didn't have to look back to notice that, instead of entering the house through the back door, Holiday rounded the porch on the side and watched her until she disappeared.

FIVE

"Hey, Pop." Holiday called out to his dad as he entered the house. Frank Holiday was sitting on his recliner, his feet propped up with one of his ankles bandaged. He'd stepped in a grassy hole while out giving an estimate on another job site somewhere and twisted it.

Holiday took a seat on the coffee table opposite him. The strong smell of BENGAY was in the air. "So it's not feeling any better today," he asked him, gesturing towards his foot.

"Naw, still pretty sore when I try to walk."

"So you've just been sitting here all day doing nothing?"

"Sitting right here." He looked at Holiday, flashing him a sly smile.

"And you're sure you don't want me to take you to have the doctor look at it?"

Frank shook his head stubbornly. "Nope."

"Ms. Genie sent over a plate for you. She thought you were working today."

"Oh yeah?"

"Yeah, she had her granddaughter bring it. I didn't even know she had a granddaughter. I thought she lived alone. Fine, too."

"Oh yeah?" Frank said again.

"Yep. A beautiful sistah."

"Well, that shouldn't be too surprising. Just look at Ms. Genie. She got a little weight on her, but you can tell she was something tough back in the day. Li'l ol' waistline. Wide hips. Big legs. I can believe it."

Holiday chuckled at this.

"They say the apple don't fall—"

"Too far from the tree," Holiday finished for him, and they laughed.

Holiday stood up and stretched. "Pop, you need anything? I'm about to take a shower then head over to Jesse Lee's. You know it's tournament night. Spades and dominoes."

"It's the last Friday of the month already? Man, time just keep flying."

"Yeah, so I'll be all night. The jackpot's coming home with me this time."

"Oh, that's what I meant to tell you. Annette called and told me to tell you to pick up the boy from his Auntie Roxy's house. She said she had something to do tonight and couldn't."

"She did? Why didn't she call me?"

Frank looked up at him. "She said she called you, but you didn't answer."

"I didn't get a phone call from her." Holiday walked over to the dining table where he'd set his phone and keys. He looked at the phone screen. "No missed calls."

"Hey," Frank said, "I'm just telling you what she told me."

"She did this on purpose. She knew where I was going tonight." He pressed the key to dial Annette. When there was no answer, he hung up and dialed again, this time leaving her a message to call him as soon as she received it. He shook his head and sighed. "Ain't no kids gonna be at the tournament. She know that."

"Son, just bring him by here. I'll look after him and you go on to your tournament."

Holiday dropped his phone back on the table. "Naw, Pop. I'm not going to put him off on you. Especially with your bad ankle."

Frank said, "It's all right. We can sit here and watch TV. Play a few games. Maybe I can teach him how to play spades, too."

"It's cool. She wants me to watch him, so I'll watch him.

* * *

Roxy opened the door—a can of Miller Lite in one hand and her twelve-month-old balanced on her hip. "Hey Brother-in-Law," she said and leaned into him for a hug. "Long-time no see. Where you been hiding?"

Holiday walked past her into the front room, over-stepping toys that littered the floor. Her seven-year-old was sitting on the couch sucking his thumb and watching cartoons. He flashed Holiday a silver-tooth smile and waved before turning back to the TV. "I've just been working hard. You know me and Pop stay busy out here. If we don't work we don't get paid."

"Uhn huh." Roxy closed the door. "It ain't that much work in the world. Why you didn't come to my birthday party last month? And don't say you was working 'cause the party didn't end 'til damn-near four in the morning. So you still had plenty time to show your face even if your lying-ass really did have to work."

Holiday just looked at her, wondering why she felt the need to talk to him this way and question his whereabouts as if he was obligated to her. "I just didn't think it would've been appropriate."

"Appropriate? Look, just because you and my sister ain't together no more don't mean you ain't family. You can still come around y'know? Hell, we ain't mad at you. Well, Nette is, but that's—"

He cut her off. "Where is Christian?"

Roxy set the toddler in her crib and she immediately began to cry. "Him and Max just left here riding them bikes somewhere. You know how Max is. He can't wait to get somebody over here he can actually play with." She pointed at her son on the couch. "His ass is just like his daddy was. Lazy. All he wanna do is eat and watch TV all day. I have to *make him* go outside."

"I'm not lazy," the boy said innocently without turning his eyes away from the television.

Roxy sat down on the green sofa, brushed Cheetos crumbs to the floor, and patted the spot next to her. "Have a seat, Brother-in-Law. Why you still standing up? Them boys'll be back soon enough. You want a beer?" She snapped her fingers, "Solone, go get your sister a bottle and Uncle Holiday a beer. Make yourself useful."

"Naw, I don't need a beer and I can't stay," Holiday told her. "Where-bout did they go? I can just go and pick them up and bring Max back here. I'm in my truck."

Roxy slapped the couch again. "*Sit down*, Holiday. Damn. Have a beer with me. Let them kids play. You ain't got nowhere to be. Tell me what's good."

After a six-pack of beer and half a pack of Benson & Hedges shared between them, Holiday left Roxy's around ten with Christian in tow. Roxy just wanted to talk and would not let him leave. She'd put baby Genesis down for bed, made the boys go to their room to play, and turned the television to the oldies music station. For nearly three hours she talked nonstop and Holiday couldn't remember a fourth of what she'd said. Annette had come up in the conversation a few times and Roxy'd tried to convince him that her sister was still very much in love with him, but just had a funny way of showing it sometimes. Holiday decided it was time to leave when Roxy told him he should reconsider and not give up on their marriage. By then Annette still had not returned his calls and forwarded him to voicemail just now as he tried to call her for the seventh time to find out if she wanted him to drop Christian off at her place on his way home.

"So I guess you're spending the night with me, Champ," Holiday said to Christian as he pulled into the driveway.

"Yes!" Christian jumped out of the truck and ran ahead of him into the house.

SIX

Cynthia flipped through the business pages phone book under A/C repair. There was no way to differentiate one good repair service from another, and she figured the ones listed with a big colorful ad were probably the most expensive, so she dialed the first one with only the business name and telephone number listed. She got a busy signal. She hung up and dialed the next one. It rang and rang. She tried another number and the line whirred and buzzed in her ear; it was the business fax number.

Finally her next call was answered.

"Hello, my air conditioner is not cooling. Is it possible to have someone come out and take a look at it today?"

"Hello?"

"My A/C is not cooling," Cynthia said again. "Can someone come out today?"

There were scratching sounds on the other end then the receiver dropped.

"Hello," a woman yelled into the phone. "What you say, honey?"

"Ma'am, can you hear me?"

"Yes, yes, I can hear you now."

"I was wondering if you can send somebody out to check my A/C."

"Check your A/C you said?"

Cynthia said, "Yes, today if possible."

"Okay, sure. What's it doing?"

"Huh?"

"The A/C, dear. What's it doing?"

"It's not cooling."

"Hold on a minute, honey. Let me call my nephew Josh. He's the technician and I don't know what his schedule is like today. He don't like for me to do the scheduling for him no more since he say I overbook him. Hold on a minute."

Cynthia pulled the phone away from her ear as the woman screamed for Josh.

A couple minutes passed before a male voice entered the line. "How can I help you?"

"I was wondering if you can come and take a look at my air conditioner. It's not cooling."

"Yeah? What's it doing," he asked.

Cynthia hung up.

Sister Nash had come by earlier to pick up Mama Genie after she decided the yellow flowers she'd bought yesterday were not enough to spruce up her entire yard and she needed more décor.

So Cynthia had the house to herself again.

She'd brought plenty of things along with her to keep occupied on quiet days like this: word search and Sudoku puzzles, a shoebox full of DVDs she had been intending to watch since last year, the adult coloring book she snagged from Tora's bookshelf even though she did not have anything to color the pages with, and her book club's next pick. She selected the word search book—something light that would not require much concentration—and went out to the porch. It was nearly three o' clock in the afternoon. The sun was bright and high in the sky, the wind nonexistent. Only the hissing and buzz of cicada bugs could be heard since the main road was several hundred feet away and only one car would pass every hour or so breaking the silence.

Sometimes Cynthia missed the simplicity of country life. The spacious solitude. The laid-back friendliness of the townspeople when they came together. Mostly being close to her grandmother. It was her senior year in high school when she decided she wanted to do something different and attend college in the next big city even though she was just miles away from Texas A&M—one of the most celebrated universities in the U.S. She settled in Houston where she attended Texas Southern University's business school, but was soon bored with the classes, yet too far in the curriculum to change majors, so she earned the business degree then decided to try teaching and sought certification through an alternative program. She'd been in Houston ever since and considered herself a city girl now.

But in this still moment it felt like the good old times when there wasn't much to do but she still found joy in doing nothing.

She opened the book to the next empty puzzle and searched for the first word. By her sixth word search she was thinking about him. His smooth dark skin, his wide back, the way sweat glistened on his shoulders, down his chest and stomach. She couldn't resist glancing to her left expecting to see the dark green truck parked in front of the house.

She supposed he took Saturdays off since he had not shown up next door and the afternoon was half-way over. It would make Tora's day if she called to tell her there was a sexy carpenter working on the house next door. Tora would definitely say it was a sign and opportunity for her to forget about Jonathan. Cynthia quickly pushed the thought out of her mind because there was no reason for her to even be thinking about Holiday in that way, or anyone for that matter. It was just a few months ago when her heart was torn in two. The day when she came face to face with what their relationship meant to Jonathan—what *she* really meant to him.

It was the last week in April and, following two days of continuous rain and area flooding, the city was under warning to remain inside unless it was absolutely necessary to be out on the streets. The need to satisfy her craving for Blue Bell's buttered pecan ice cream was necessary enough to be out on the streets after being cooped up in the house for two straight days and she decided as soon as the rain cleared she would go out and feed her sweet tooth. Once inside the store she picked up a half-gallon of ice cream and a few of Jonathan's favorite snacks. When she'd called to tell him she was on her way to see him—because that is how they'd always done it although both had a key to the other's place, they would call to announce their visit and ask if there was anything the other needed—he'd said the area surrounding his house was clear, but the main street at the entrance to the subdivision was blocked due to standing water and she should not try to come—that her 'little Corolla' might get stuck and swept away. And she had laughed and agreed and said she would just go home and see him soon before they hung up. But when he called her back to ensure she was not coming is when Cynthia felt it. That feeling in the gut called intuition. She knew then something was off and so, instead of turning left out of the parking lot of H-E-B to go home, she turned right and headed towards Jonathan's house. There was high water at the entrance just as he'd said and she waited a few minutes until she saw another car make it through the wave before she tried her luck.

Cynthia recognized the SUV as soon as she approached the house. Davina was Jonathan's co-worker and a mutual acquaintance —one that was part of their Christmas ski trip. She stood at the front door to listen for voices on the other side, hoping her intuition was wrong and that there was more than just one coworker inside since it was not unusual for them to get together to watch a game at his place or just sit out on the patio for drinks and chat. Maybe they'd all gotten drunk and ended up having to stay the night to recover but then the storm came.

All was quiet except for the TV.

She contemplated a few seconds whether she should ring the door bell or pull out her cell phone to surprise him and say she was able to make it through the neighborhood. But it was just her way of stalling. Stalling because she needed an answer ready for the question Jonathan was sure to ask, for her reasoning for showing up at his place as if she didn't trust him. Did she trust him? She was sure she did. And it was that trust that made her use the key to let herself in. That trust that made her believe that, despite the opened take-out containers on the coffee table, half bottles of Patrón and wine on the coffee bar, a woman's blouse strewn across the back of the love seat, sandals on the floor, it was all a misconception and Jonathan was just in the office on the computer and Davina was in the bathroom. And Davina would be wearing a tank or undershirt when she emerged because that would be the only purpose for her blouse being on the sofa Cynthia reasoned—a blouse too cute to risk being stained with hot wings sauce.

But Jonathan was not in the office and Davina was not using the toilet. It was the sounds of pleasure that pulled Cynthia towards Jonathan's bedroom. Davina was on her back, her eyes closed and her mouth opened as she hissed and moaned while Jonathan's tongue cleaned her torso.

Cynthia did not shout. She did not scream. She turned and walked out as calmly and as quietly as she'd walked in. But Houston's flooded streets were no match to the tears that poured from her eyes as she drove all the way home.

A set of love bugs floated across Cynthia's view and landed on the page of her magazine, bringing her back to the present. She looked down at them joined together and just as quickly flicked them off with her middle finger. This was the time for her to forget about love and relationships for a while and get used to being free to do what she wanted—to enjoy her own company again. Besides, fine, handsome guys like Holiday usually were either married or had a harem of women.

Cynthia set the Seek-n-Find magazine down and went into the house for the business pages again. She decided she would try one more time for the day to call and schedule for A/C repair in the hopes someone could come out Monday morning.

SEVEN

"I'm sorry, Champ, but I wasn't expecting you here this weekend so ain't no milk for your favorite cereal this morning." Holiday was standing in the kitchen pulling things out of the refrigerator trying to figure out what he could throw together for breakfast. "I can make you a omelet or a grilled cheese sandwich."

Christian was sitting at the dining table, his hand under his chin, trying to decide. "Grilled cheese sandwich, please," he answered, "with mayo."

"Mayo? Since when do you want your grilled cheese with mayo?" Holiday frowned at the thought.

"Since Solone showed me."

"That boy is something else," Holiday smiled. He put the sandwich in a skillet then pulled out another one to make an omelet for himself. Once done, he carried the two plates to the table and sat in the chair next to Christian.

"I still haven't heard from your mama, so I'm not sure what time she wants me to take you home. I had planned on going to this house I'm working on and do a bit of work, but it'll be just my luck she call as soon as we get there and I have to drive all the way back on this side. So we may have to just hang around here until we hear from her."

Christian smacked his lips as he licked butter off his fingers. "Okay. I challenge you to a game of Mortal Kombat."

"Oh I see you begging for another butt-whooping," Holiday swatted at him playfully. "Ready for Kitana to put it on you again."

"No, I'm playing with Kitana this time," Christian said.

"Naw, you can't choose my player just because she's undefeated. You have to play with your own until you become as great as me." Holiday changed his mind when he saw the sunken look on Christian's face. "Alright, I tell you what. You can have Kitana, and I will choose somebody else."

"Okay, good," Christian said, smiling big.

"But, I'm still going to beat you. You know why?"

Christian shook his head apprehensively.

"Just to prove to you that it's not about the player, but about the skills." He patted Christian on the head as he got up from the table to get them something to drink. "You want orange juice or fruit punch?"

"Fruit punch."

Frank entered the room then, walking with a cane. "Whatcha say, *Chris*," he said, squeezing Christian's shoulder as he limped past him to a seat at the table. "You must've snuck in here because I don't remember seeing you last night."

Christian giggled. "*Christian*, Grandpa. You know you have to call me by my whole name. And you was already in the bed."

"Uhn-huh," Frank snorted. "I been calling you Chris since I first laid eyes on you and I ain't about to change just 'cause your mama wanna be acting funny now. You been Chris all your life, but since she going through this change—or whatever it is she claim—she wanna act brand new."

Holiday placed the cup of fruit punch in front of Christian. "C'mon, Pop," he said to Frank. "Don't say things like that. She just want people to call him the name she gave him. She hates nicknames. That's all. She's the same way with her own sister's kids. She tell Roxy all the time what was the purpose of naming the kids what she named them if she wasn't gonna call them that."

Frank said, "Yeah, well, them kids got crazy names anyway, so I would call them something else, too. What are their names? Genevieve? Stallone? Millionaire? What?"

Christian threw his head back in laughter. "Ha! Nooo, Grandpa. It's *Solone* and *Genesis* and *Maximillion*."

Frank shook his head and laughed. "Exactly. Crazy. Just like I said."

Holiday laughed too. "Pop, you want a omelet? I can fix it for you right quick."

"Naw, I want my plate Ms. Genie sent for me. That's what I want."

"Oh, man," Holiday said. "That was some good eating right there. Wasn't it, Christian?"

"Yep! Real good," Christian beamed.

Frank said, "Is that right?"

"We tore into that when we made it here last night. She sure can cook."

"Ain't nothing like a woman that can cook," Frank agreed. "And you say she got a granddaughter? Is she about your age? Maybe she can cook too." Frank wiggled his eyebrows at Holiday.

Holiday chuckled. "Pop, there you go. Don't even start that."

"What?" Frank said innocently. "I'm just wondering for your sake."

"My sake?"

"Yeah, you been here for several months now. You say you ain't going ba—" He stopped when he saw Holiday shift his eyes towards Christian.

"C'mon," Holiday mumbled. There were a few things Holiday

refused to talk about in front of Christian no matter how relaxed and brash in their conversations he and Frank could sometimes get, and his relationship with Annette was one of them.

"I'm just asking for a friend," Frank then said.

"A friend, huh?" Holiday pulled the plate from Ms. Genie out of the refrigerator, removed the foil, and popped it into the microwave.

"Yeah. He seem kinda lonely to me lately and I think he could use a good lady friend. Somebody to talk to sometimes. Spend some time with."

"What makes you think he's lonely?"

"Oh, uh… well, he just don't do too much anymore. Just sit around the house if he ain't at work. Or down at the lake. But that ain't nothing if you ask me. 'Specially for a man his age. How he expect to meet a nice young lady if he don't go out sometimes?"

"How do you know that's what he's looking for though? A lady friend? Maybe he don't have a problem being single?"

Christian said, "Daddy, can I have another grilled cheese sandwich, please?"

"One wasn't enough for you?" Holiday grinned.

Christian shook his head. "I eat two sandwiches now."

"Two?! I just think you're trying to compete with Solone. Keep it up and you will be as big as Solone, too."

"And then I can play football and run over everybody on the team," Christian said.

"No," Frank said, "at the rate you going you won't be able to run at all," and he gently poked Christian in his side with the butt of his cane.

"Yes I will!"

Holiday turned the gas pilot on to warm the skillet again. "Back to this friend though, Pop. Like I was saying, maybe he's enjoying the single life. You know women are hard sometimes."

"Yeah, they can be. But it ain't nothing like having someone by your side. 'Specially a good one. And you're— I mean my buddy is a good guy, and I think he'd make somebody real happy one day. Only if he would give somebody a chance."

Holiday shrugged his shoulders. "You never know. I'm sure he's open to it if a good one come along."

The microwave beeped and Holiday grabbed a fork from the drawer. "Tell me if it's hot enough for you."

Frank dug his fork right into the greens as soon as the plate was in front of him. "It don't even matter. I'm gonna eat it just like this here."

*　*　*

Holiday pulled into the driveway of the house he used to know as home. It was nearly nine o'clock when Annette had finally texted him that she'd made it home and wanted him to drop Christian off. She opened the door wearing a thick blue bathrobe tied tightly across her waist, her hair pulled back into a sleek ponytail.

"Hey, Mama," Christian said and skipped past her.

Holiday and Annette stared at each other a few seconds, one waiting for the other to say something.

"Annette, what's going on," Holiday finally said, his voice steady and low. "Why are you acting like this?"

She raised a brow, looking up at him. "Acting like what?"

"Come on," Holiday said, disinterested in her mock ignorance. "Why would you do that? Why wouldn't you answer my calls? You know Jesse Lee have the tournament on the last Fridays."

"Mason, I forgot all about that."

He shook his head in disbelief. "You forgot?"

"Yeah. I forgot."

"Okay, even if you did forget why wouldn't you answer my calls,

Annette? You know I wouldn't do something like that to you." Holiday slid his hands into his pockets.

"Look, I just needed to get out and have some fun for a while. And you needed to spend some time with him," she said, pulling the robe belt even tighter.

"I have no problem keeping Christian," he told her. "You know that. But how much longer do we have to go on like this?"

"Like what?"

"You just act like you hate me or something."

"Please. Don't start that tonight. You're the one who moved out."

"Well, yeah," he said, "you left me no choice. After what happened with Laila we wasn't even talking to each other. That's no way to live. Christian don't need to be around that."

She raised her voice now. "Don't you even try to act like this was all my fault! I wasn't in this marriage by myself! And what happened to Laila never would have happened if you had just—"

Holiday reached behind her to pull the door close. "Annette, it's been a long time now. We can't keep going through this every time we see each other. I'm living with the pain of losing Laila every day just like you are. But we have to acknowledge the relationship was broke long before that. So can we put all this aside and be friends at least? For Christian?"

Annette stood still, not looking at him, but past his shoulder into the darkness.

It seemed like several minutes passed before she finally said, "I don't have a problem, Mason. Just be there for Christian, okay?" She backed up into the house, closed the door, and locked it.

EIGHT

"Amen, Amen. Sister Cynthia, let me look at you. It's been a long time. A long time." Cynthia was standing outside Saint Emmanuel Baptist Church with Mama Genie as she did her usual small talk and recap of the day's sermon with the other sisters of the church when Reverend Moore walked up and wrapped Cynthia into a bear-tight hug. "It is so good to see you," he said to her. "So good to see you."

Cynthia stumbled back a little from the pressure once he let her loose. "Good to see you, too, Reverend Moore. How have you been?"

"Ah, Sister, you know I am blessed and highly favored. Can't complain about nothing. God has been so good to me. So good." He dabbed at the sweat that beaded his mouth with his signature white silk handkerchief and Cynthia couldn't help thinking of how, when she attended the church as a teen, the boys joked around and started referring to Reverend Moore as Reverend Catfish, saying his mouth resembled that of a pink-lipped catfish. "Sister Genie told me you was in town and so I made sure to pull out my best sermon just for you. Didn't that sermon touch you, Sister?"

"Of course, Reverend Moore," Cynthia quickly said even though she couldn't even remember the scripture he had been teaching from. She zoned out once he got worked up. And Reverend Moore loved to get worked up. He would strut back and forth behind the pulpit shouting his praises, lean way back and scream his thanks, pause for confirmation from the twenty-three members that his teachings were reaching them as they jumped to their feet and shouted and screamed right back at him to *'Teach, Reverend!'* and *'Say that, Reverend!'*. Tambourines jingled and the organ groaned, which only motivated him to preach some more. Hours more. It wasn't long before Cynthia was tense with a burgeoning headache and just wanted for it all to be over.

"Amen," he said. "You know it wouldn't be right if I didn't spread the good news. The good news!" He leaned back on his heels and Cynthia was sure he was ready to break out into a parking lot sermon, but Mama Genie walked up just in time.

"Cynthia, Reverend Moore is gonna follow us to the house so he can get a plate and take something for Lady Moore since she not feeling well and couldn't make it to church today. Sister Nash is coming, too."

"Amen," Reverend Moore agreed. "I will be right behind you, Sister Genie."

Cynthia said, "Okay, I will go and start up the car."

* * *

Since Cynthia had nothing to add to the conversation regarding the church's upcoming summer revival she retreated to her room upstairs, leaving Mama Genie, Reverend Moore, and Sister Nash in the living room. She changed out of her clothes and lay in bed for a while just staring at the ceiling, then Holiday entered her mind. She was surprised by the jolt of excitement that rushed through her when she noticed his green Chevrolet parked out front as they were driving up the road towards the house. And then she saw him as she pulled into the yard. He was rounding the truck from the other side, his heavy toolbox in one hand. He set the toolbox down and waited as they exited the car before he greeted all of them and thanked Mama Genie on his and Frank's behalf for her generosity and good food. Cynthia had noticed how his gaze lingered on her as Mama Genie told him he was welcomed to come over later for dessert. She could not deny she found him highly attractive as he stood there in the sun, his skin as smooth and rich as a piece of Hershey's Special Dark chocolate.

She shook her head and sighed as if to shake the image from her brain. She picked up the novel sitting on the nightstand. The book club's reading for next month's meeting was a fantasy romance suggested by Tora since it was her time to host. Cynthia figured her imagination didn't stretch far enough to be able to appreciate a tale about a woman wanting to fall in love with a dragon. By chapter three the heroine was dreaming about making love with it.

Cynthia put the book down.

She grabbed her cell phone to check if there were any missed calls or voice mail messages—if a school district had called offering her an interview. Sometimes the mobile signal was poor and the phone would not ring at all, but then she'd notice a missed call when she checked it later. There were none. She then scrolled through the text conversations between her and Jonathan. She scrolled to find the older exchanges. Simple messages like *Babe, let's go to the movies tonight; Me and the crew will be at Julien's after work. You can come if you want; I love you; Do you mind picking up some ice cream on your way; Where did you put the bank card when you came back last night? It's not on the bar.* A few sexy photos were exchanged in between: Jonathan standing in front of the bathroom mirror wearing only a dimpled smile; a teaser of her legs only; a picture of his early-morning erection; a selfie of her lying topless on her back in bed per Jonathan's request. None of it mattered anymore, she thought. He probably had photos of Davina in his phone, too. And God knows what other women. Davina was the project coordinator at National Oilwell Varco where Jonathan worked as a data engineer. She was the only female in their crew and they got together often after work for drinks or sometimes when Jonathan had a backyard barbecue at his house. Davina was tall—taller than Jonathan and all his friends—and model-slim. A brown-skinned, twenty-something from Canada with long, curly black hair. Cynthia had heard the guys joking one time that Davina wasn't much of a looker in the face, but she had a beautiful personality. Even for Cynthia, she was a lot of fun. Davina loved to laugh and she was a major flirt wherever they went. There was never a bar tender or a doorman or a waiter Davina didn't like. Still, for Cynthia she was never a threat. She would see her make playful passes at Jonathan's friends—never Jonathan—and they would just brush her off, blame it on the alcohol, and declare coworkers were off limits. Cynthia tried to think back now if there had been any signs. If there was something she should have seen before that day when she saw Jonathan in bed with someone she knew. Davina wasn't considered a friend per se, but they all hung out together. Davina would sit next to her at these outings or across from her at the table and look Cynthia in the face just the same.

But it wasn't so much that she knew Davina than it was about the boldness of Jonathan. Cynthia could not wrap her mind around his carelessness. She had a key to his place and was free to show up anytime she wanted to unannounced. She could not understand how he could be so relaxed and risk being caught. Did their relationship mean anything to him, she'd wondered that night. Apparently not. Because only a man that didn't give a damn about her would do such a thing. This is what she'd told herself for days after. This is what made her dismiss his phone calls, ignore the knocks on her door for weeks, reject him when he showed up to the school needing to talk and apologize. Cynthia felt there was nothing that needed to be said.

Everything she thought she meant to him was void when she stood at his bedroom door and watched him give another woman the same pleasure he'd give her.

Cynthia got up and went to the window when she heard voices outside. She pulled back the curtain to see Holiday standing on the porch next door. He leaned on the banister, resting on his forearms, a cigarette between the fingers of his left hand. Cynthia studied him, watching as he took languid drags of it. *Damn.* Smoking was such an ugly habit, but he was sexy just posed there relaxed and nonchalant. In spite of herself she wondered what was his story. How many women did he have strung along after him? Or was he married? Did he have women strung along while being married? She squint her eyes trying to focus in on his ring finger. It was empty, but maybe he just didn't wear it while working she thought. Reverend Moore and Sister Nash were leaving and he waved goodbye to them. And then, as if he sensed her watching him, he looked right up to her window.

Cynthia jumped back. She stood still a few seconds, holding her breath. Then laughed at the silliness of her reaction. She slid her finger through the split of the curtains and peered out.

He was looking right at her. "Did I scare you?"

Cynthia was caught red-handed. She pushed the window pane all the way up and leaned out. "What you say?"

"I said I hope I didn't scare you."

"No, you didn't scare me. I thought this bug was going to fly in here." She fanned her hand in front of her face to shoo the imaginary pest. It was the best she could come up with.

He smiled, his teeth a brilliant white against his dark skin. Cynthia watched as he stubbed the cigarette out on the porch banister and then walked a few paces over to be even with her window. He didn't just walk, he strolled. His movements were slow and easy, as if there was never a need to rush about anything ever in life. She realized now he even talked slow. Not in a boring, drawn-out way, but a calm and laid-back way. "How was church service," he asked.

Cynthia couldn't bring herself to speak bad about Mama Genie's favorite pastor, so she nodded her head and said, "It was good. Reverend Moore is a special one."

"I liked that dress you had on. You looked really nice. I just didn't wanna say nothing like that in front of Ms. Genie or the reverend."

She blushed. The dress was a two-tone sheath: red at the top, pink on the bottom, a skinny pink belt wrapped around her waist. "Thanks." She waved her hand. "Mama Genie doesn't care about things like that. And the reverend, well, he's dished out his share of compliments, too."

"Oh yeah?" Holiday chuckled.

"Yeah." He leaned down on his forearms again just looking at her. The silence unnerving, so she finally said, "I'm surprised y'all are working today. On a Sunday of all days."

Holiday glanced over his shoulder. "It's just me here today. Pop is at the house resting again. He hurt his ankle so he wouldn't've been able to do too much anyway."

"Oh," Cynthia said. "I hope he's all right."

"Yeah, he say he is. He won't let me take him to have the doctor do a X-ray though. So we'll see how it's doing tomorrow. I'll tie him up and throw him on the back of my truck if I have to to get him there."

Cynthia laughed. "That's a shame."

"He's something else. But that's Pop."

"So you have to do all the work yourself today, huh?" she asked, just making conversation.

He stood up now. "Yeah, the day does go by faster when he's here. He like to goof around, so he's always trying to make me laugh."

Cynthia said, "That's good. Sounds like y'all have a good time working together."

He nodded, "Yeah, we do."

Cynthia cleared her throat, at a loss for what to say next.

"You can come over if you want to," he said.

She blinked. "Come over?"

He spread his hands over the railing. "That's if you want to. I don't mind the company. I won't even put you to work. I promise."

A nervous laugh escaped her throat. "Umm… I don't know about that." She looked over her shoulder, inspecting the room to see if there was some cleaning she needed to do instead, if the furniture needed dusting. She looked back at him and he was smiling his charming smile.

He said, "Just thought I'd ask. You never know what you can get unless you ask for it, right?"

Cynthia cocked her head. "And what exactly are you trying to get?" she asked him.

"Some company. That's all. You seem to be as sweet as Ms. Genie. I'm sure you will make painting these rooms a lot more fun for me."

Now she rested her elbows on the window sill. "So, that's it? You want me to come and watch you paint? Sounds about as exciting as watching it dry." She laughed at her own corny joke.

He dropped his head to hide his own laughter, and then nodded. "Yeah. I'm being honest."

She considered it for a few seconds. Here it is just day two of being home at her grandmother's house where she'd planned to come and escape the heartbreak she'd left back in Houston. This was her time to focus on herself and finally let go and move on from the relationship with Jonathan, but this guy was interrupting her plans. Yet, just looking at him made her feel giddy like a little girl experiencing her first crush with her next door neighbor.

"I may stop by for five minutes once I finish up what I need to do." She didn't have a damn thing to do, but she couldn't tell him that.

"Just five minutes?"

"Hey," she said, "truth is, I don't know you. All I know is you're the guy my grandma says picks up things she needs from time to time when you go to town. So, I probably shouldn't even give you five minutes. Not behind closed doors. All it takes is one minute for—"

He raised his hands in surrender. "You're right, you're right. You don't know me. I don't know what I was thinking."

"Uhn-huh," she said, offering a wry smile. "We'll see."

NINE

Holiday knew she would not come. He chided himself now wondering what made him so daring to even entertain the thought that she would just accept his invitation to spend some time with him. Cynthia was beautiful, no doubt, and he could not help himself, but the reality was just as she had said: he was a stranger to her and there was no way she would just enclose herself in a vacant house with him just because he wanted her to.

He popped the top on a can of Budweiser and waited until the hiss and fizzing subsided before he put the ice-cold can to his lips. Birds chirped and crickets tweeted around him as he sat on the tailgate of his truck looking out over the lake. Kids hooted and giggled in the distance and he watched a lone man in a canoe, his rod poised in the blue-green water, trying to catch something.

Holiday came to his favorite spot at least twice a week. He came to relax after long days working, to bring Christian out so they could play rounds of catch football or Frisbee, or to just sit and remember Laila. It had been two years since his baby girl passed away and the pain of losing her was still fresh. He missed her bubbly laughter and the squeals of "Da-dee" as she rushed to greet him whenever he walked through the door.

He tapped a cigarette out of its pack. Trying to quit was much harder than he thought it would be as he'd made the decision to smoke no more than three a day, but he was on his fifth one and he hadn't even had dinner yet.

48

TEN

Cynthia rolled her eyes as the air conditioner repairman explained over the phone he would not be able to make it for the ten o'clock appointment he promised her, but she could rest assured he'd be there between two and four instead. She could have still been lying in bed in her pajamas, but she rose up early because he'd promised to be there between eight and ten. She gave a terse "Okay," and hung up.

She walked over to the window and looked out. She'd heard Holiday's truck come in around seven and she'd jumped out of bed to peek without being seen. He got out of the truck and grabbed his tool box from the back and went inside. A few seconds later he came out and got the cooler. He moved about as casually as he always did, but he didn't even glance her way. *Probably feeling dejected,* she'd thought to herself.

Truth is, she'd wanted to go over, but knew it would be against her better judgment. Her heart needed to heal and it was best she steered clear of any relations with the opposite sex—especially when they gave her good feelings like Holiday did. If he had her all tingly at the sight of him from a second-story window two days after meeting, she knew it would be even more challenging on her senses to be in close proximity. Still, she stretched her neck against the window searching for sight of him on the back porch. Then Tora's words sprang in her mind: *The best way to get over one is to get under another…*

She sighed. There was no chance she would be getting under, over, around, through anyone. However, she'd solved half of the Seek-n-Find magazine, she couldn't care less about some woman's bestiality fetish, and she wasn't in the mood to watch TV. Holiday appeared kind enough and just wanted to be friendly. Plus, Mama Genie seemed to approve of him. What could it hurt to sit and talk with him for an hour or two? And she could use the distraction.

* * *

"Oh, so you're trying to sneak up on me again," Holiday said when Cynthia walked in. He was standing in the kitchen measuring the counter.

She smiled at him. "No, I just figured you'd have paint all over your hands so I didn't want you to bother trying to open the door."

"Naw, I didn't even get to that yesterday since you didn't come to help me. You must've had a lot to do."

"Huh?" Then she remembered the lie she'd told him. "Well, yeah, it took longer than I thought." He wasn't buying it, she knew, but he didn't let on.

"I'm glad you came." He leaned against the counter looking at her. And just like he did on Mama Genie's porch, his eyes took her in from head to toe. She had on a navy racer-back maxi dress and flat sandals. The dress was a little snug around her hips but not at all as fitted as the T-shirt dress, but he looked at her with the same intensity.

"I brought you some banana pudding."

He walked over to her, taking it from her hand. "So this is your way of apologizing for standing me up?"

She looked up at him. His eyes, a deep brown, framed by thick brows and eyelashes that were full and long with a slight curl—the type of lashes women pay money for to achieve the same look. He was lovely. "What are you talking about? I told you I was busy." She couldn't keep a straight face.

He chuckled. "I'm just messing with you. It's cool. Thank you for this. Let me get you a chair." He walked down the hall and came back seconds later with a green metal fold-up chair and set it in the space where the dining room ended and the living room began.

"Thanks," she said and sat down. He picked up the measuring tape again and stretched it along the counter near the sink.

"So tell me again," he said, "you're Ms. Genie's granddaughter? I don't remember seeing you around."

"Yeah. I live in Houston now, so I just came down for a visit."

"Oh okay. H-town. I've only been there a few times. To the rodeo."

"Oh yeah? You ride?"

He shook his head. "Naw. Some of my buddies do, but I don't. I went for a concert. Where-bout in H-town?"

"The northwest side. Like Highway Six and Little York area."

"Hmm… I'm not too familiar with that side. I had a friend move out there to Champions I think is where he told me. Is it near there?"

"Not really. That's closer to Forty-five. I'm near the I-Ten freeway."

He shrugged his shoulders. "I don't know. Most of my family's in Bryan and we have a few in Fort Worth, so I'm not familiar with Houston at all." He wrote something down on a mini notepad, and then he went to the small stretch of counter near the space where a stove should be.

He asked, "So what made you move to Houston?"

She crossed her legs and flattened the dress around her knee. "I went to college there and just decided to stay once I graduated. I got a job teaching."

He let the tape snap back into its holder and he turned to look at her. "You're a teacher? I never would've guessed that."

"And what's that supposed to mean?"

"Nothing, just that I wouldn't've thought you were a teacher. But now that you said it, I can see it."

She put her hands on her hips. "Oh really? Why is that?"

"I'm just saying, none of my teachers when I was in school looked like you."

She rolled her eyes playfully. "That is the lamest line in the book." He smiled at Cynthia and she had to look away because it made her blush.

"I'm just being honest. I know if you were my teacher I wouldn't be able to concentrate, so it was probably best mine were all old, wearing those white nurse shoes and tan stockings, and sweaters tied across their shoulders."

"Please stop," Cynthia said, laughing. "You are not right."

"So you're here relaxing on summer break until it's back to school time?"

"Pretty much." She didn't want to go into the topic of her employment status. "What about you," she asked to take the attention off her. "Which high school did you go to? I don't remember you either."

"I grew up in Bryan."

"Ah, okay," she nodded. *Because your face is definitely the kind that would linger in one's memory.*

He continued, "And my daddy has always done construction, carpentry. He made me help him a lot when I was younger, so it was just natural for me to start working with him after high school." He walked over to the cooler and lifted the top. "You want something to drink? I got tea, lemonade, water."

"A water is fine." He pulled the bottle from the cooler. Water and ice dripped all over the floor as he walked towards her.

"Wait a minute," he turned back to the counter. "I think I got some paper towels in my bag." He pulled one out and wrapped it around the bottle before handing it to her.

"Holiday Fixings? I noticed the decal for the first time when I walked up."

"Oh yeah," he whistled out a breath. "I'm not sure what Pop was thinking. He said it was Ma's idea, but she always denied it. Said he came up with that name. But you wouldn't believe how many people call us for quotes to cater their holiday meals."

"Oh my god. That's funny. But I'd probably think the same thing." She twisted the cap on the water bottle and took a sip. She looked around. "Hey, where is your dad? His ankle's still bothering him?"

Holiday leaned against the counter, crossing his legs at the ankle. "Yeah, we got an appointment tomorrow morning to have it checked out. I told him it was only going to get worse since he said the BENGAY and ice packs ain't working."

"Good," she said and took another sip because he was staring at her. She set the bottle on the floor at her feet just to have something to do and not have to look at him look at her so openly, so unapologetically. It seemed a minute passed and she couldn't take the scrutiny anymore so she ran her fingers through her braids and looked right back in his eyes, "What?"

"I can see the resemblance," he said. "Between you and Ms. Genie. Especially your lips."

She licked them nervously. "Hmm… I don't know. I never really thought about it."

"And your figure, too."

"Okay, you know what… you asked me to come over here and keep you company while you work. What's with all this— this—" She couldn't find the words because he had her in a brain fog.

"What? I just think you're a beautiful woman. There's no harm in me saying so, right?" Cynthia just looked up at him. "I don't mean to offend you, it's just that from the moment I saw you, I was like 'Wow.' I needed to know who you were and where'd you come from."

She shook her head, smiling up at him. "Well, thank you for the compliments. I really do appreciate them. And you're not too bad yourself." Which was a bold-face lie. He was much more than *not too bad.* He was gorgeous—the kind you definitely wanted to tell everyone you know about.

Cynthia did not realize how much time had passed until she heard Mama Genie calling her name. She had relaxed some sitting and talking to Holiday and their conversation had moved into a light and friendly banter. Holiday was putting an extra coat of paint on one of the living room walls.

She hopped up out of the chair just as Mama Genie opened the screen door.

"How you doing, Ms. Genie," Holiday said.

"Fine. How you, Holiday?"

"I'm doing good."

"I come by to see about my granddaughter. It's been a while and I know it don't take that long to bring over no banana pudding." She looked at Cynthia.

Cynthia laughed. "We were just sitting here talking, Mama Genie. That's all."

Holiday nodded in agreement.

Mama Genie said, "I started to bring my baseball bat with me just in case."

"Oh no, that won't be necessary, ma'am. Believe me. I wouldn't do anything to hurt your granddaughter."

"I know that's right 'cause this the only grandbaby I got."

Cynthia said, "There's nothing to worry about, Mama Genie, because if he'd tried anything there would've been a whole lot of screaming going on. And I wouldn't have been the one doing the screaming." She raised a brow at him then laughed when shock crossed his face.

"I know that's right," Mama Genie said again, and they both laughed.

"Oh man," Holiday shook his head.

"But Cynthia, the air conditioner man called and said he on his way. He about fifteen minutes away he said."

"Oh okay." Cynthia picked up her water bottle from the floor.

"See you later, Holiday," Mama Genie said. "It's coming along real nice in here, too." She looked around the rooms.

"Alright, Ms. Genie. Thanks again for the pudding."

"Oh, you're welcome."

Cynthia looked at him as she exited. "See you later."

He smiled. "Thanks for the company."

ELEVEN

"So," the doctor said as he entered the room—a short and scrawny man with glasses too small for his head and a doctors coat too big for his frame. "Everything looks good. It's just a really bad sprain. I'm going to give you an anti-inflammatory for the swelling, and just advise you to continue to stay off it as much as possible for the next two or three days." He scribbled the prescription on a carbon notepad then ripped off the top sheet.

"Aw, naw. I can't be down for three more days, Doc. I got to go out dancing this weekend," Frank said.

The doctor bobbed his head up and down, grinning. "Ah, so you still enjoy a little dancing from time to time at your age? That's good."

"Yeah, I gots to stay active, y'know. Somebody once said we don't stop playing because we get old; we get old because we stop playing."

"Ah! I see. That's a good one. Very good motto to live by." He looked over at Holiday who was sitting in the chair next to the patient table.

Holiday just shook his head. He took the note with the prescription from the doctor's outstretched hand.

The doctor patted Frank on the back. "Frank, you be careful, okay? I don't want to see you back here next week because you broke your hip out there trying to dance on an afflicted ankle."

Frank's whole body shook as he laughed. "Alright, Doc. You probably right about that one. So I guess I will stay put until it gets better."

"That's what I want to hear. Take care of yourself." Doctor opened the door to lead them out.

* * *

"Son, whatcha say we get some lunch," Frank said when they reached the parking lot. "I sure could use some of Nell's chili. You hungry?"

Holiday gave him a sideways look. "Didn't you just tell Doctor Gilbert you were gonna get off your feet?"

"What? Last time I checked Nell had plenty seats for me to sit down. You planning on standing up to eat?"

Holiday looked at his watch. It was eleven-thirty. "I guess we can stop for a bite. This lady called for me to come and give her a estimate. She wanna replace her kitchen tiles. Said anytime before two is fine."

"Well, well, well. If it isn't my two favorite customers. How y'all doing today," the waitress asked as they took a seat in Nell's Diner. She set silverware and straws in front of them.

"Ms. Bree! Doing good, dear," Frank said. "Just bring me a bowl of that chili. I don't need no menu. And a iced tea. Unsweetened. The biggest bowl you got, too."

"Now, Mr. Frank you know it only comes in small or large."

"Put it in one of them bowls y'all use for the salads. I see how big they are. Just don't tell nobody. I'll give you a little extra on the tip." He winked at her.

Holiday ordered the fried eggs and pork chop platter and she walked away. "You just can't go a day without messing with somebody, huh Pop?"

"Hey, I don't mean no harm. I'm just having a little fun."

"I know. All the time."

They were quiet for several minutes just watching the news showing on the television mounted in a top corner of the room. "Did you get those back rooms painted," Frank asked, breaking Holiday's attention.

"Yeah, I finished that up before I left." Then he thought about Cynthia. How she seemed so comfortable talking to him yesterday. The way she smiled at him. "Cynthia came over."

Bree set their drinks on the table.

"Cynthia?" Frank said.

"Ms. Genie's granddaughter."

"Oh, oh okay. That's her name, huh? Cynthia. What she come over for?"

"Just to talk. Well, I asked her to," Holiday replied.

Frank raised his eyebrows. "You asked her to?"

"Pop, she's a good-looking lady. I had to."

Frank laughed. "Look at you, son. I ain't missed but two days' work and you already got somebody to replace me. And just because she good-looking." He picked up his tea.

Holiday clasped his hands in front of him. "You're crazy, Pop. You know you can't be replaced. But, yeah. She just sat with me while I painted. Real sweet."

"Well, there you go. Didn't I say you needed somebody to get you back to your old self? And look what happened. She showed up."

"Naw, it's nothing like that. She's here visiting. I just think she's fine. That's all." He drank from his glass of water.

"Oh, I see," Frank said. "So she'll be leaving soon. Well, you just have to keep searching. You'll find her."

"I told you I'm not searching. I'm just enjoying life as it is right now. Y'know?"

Frank waved his hand. "Yeah, yeah. That's what everybody that ain't got nobody say."

Holiday laughed. Frank was half right because, although he wasn't down about his situation, he did miss having a woman around sometimes—even if it was just to talk. And he missed the intimacy. It had been several months since he'd been with a woman and his body ached with need. Seeing Cynthia—the roundness of her breasts and the way her lower back curved into a perfectly-round bottom— seemed to make him more aware of what he was lacking.

Bree placed their meals in front of them. "Let me know if y'all need anything else," she said smiling, and then walked off.

They ate in silence. Frank had his mind on the television while Holiday had his mind on Cynthia. He wondered if her lips were as soft as they looked. He wondered what she would feel like wrapped around him.

TWELVE

Cynthia had her laptop with her as she sat on the porch checking her emails. Only two of the positions she'd applied for showed her application status as 'under review.' She pulled up a site to search for other jobs. She had no idea what type of work she could be interested in since she had been teaching for so long. She believed teaching was her calling, but after years of dealing with unmotivated kids, uncooperative parents, and too many weekends spent grading papers, she was ready to try something new.

Most of the postings required some type of degree, but in the very next line noted several years' experience in the field was also necessary. And she never understood how a person was supposed to gain experience before they're given a chance to apply.

A vehicle coming down the road made her look up from the screen. At the sight of his green truck a rush of excitement came over her. She quickly looked back down at the computer screen:

Entry Level Sales/Marketing

Management Assistant I

Quality Assurance Technician

The driver's door slammed shut.

Sr. Administrative Assistant

Entry Level Finance Associate

A couple minutes passed, and she wondered if he'd gone in the house, so she looked up but was greeted by his sultry grin. "How you doing," he said.

Geez, that smile can melt dry ice. "Good. How you doing today?"

He walked towards her with the grace of a lion. She closed the laptop.

Climbing the four steps to the porch, he said, "I'm good. Especially now that I'm here and get to see you." He stood directly in front of her, his lower back resting on the porch banister.

She crossed her arms over her chest. "The lines. They just fall right out of your mouth every time."

"What *lines*? You think I'm giving you lines?"

"Yes, I do."

"Why you say that?

"*I'm good now that I'm here and get to see you,*" she mocked him.

He chuckled. "How is that a line? I'm just being honest."

She sucked her teeth.

"Is Ms. Genie in there? I can't be standing out here on her porch and not speak."

"Yeah, but she's taking a nap."

"Oh okay. So you think I'm lying about being excited to see you? That doesn't make sense."

"Yeah, well, how many others have you said that to today?"

He shook his head and sighed. "C'mon now, you're just giving me a hard time. Would you rather I pretend I don't see you?"

A furtive smile curved her lips.

"I enjoyed your company and—I don't know about you—but when I enjoy something I like to do it again."

She raised her brow at him now. "Is that right?"

"That's right."

"Hmm…" was all she could muster. He had that effect on her.

His dark eyes. The way he looked at her with such intensity, such curiosity. She was hot with nerves.

"So, you're just out here getting you some fresh air, huh?"

"Yeah, it's much cooler out here than it is inside since the A/C is out." She stood up and put her laptop in the adjacent rocking chair just so she could put some space between them.

"I thought the repairman came yesterday," he said.

"He did. He said it needed Freon, but it seems to be taking a long time for the house to cool down."

"Oh yeah? Well, I'm sure I can call a buddy of mine. He know somebody that can look at it for you."

"That's okay. We've already paid him, so he just needs to come back and look at it again. Thank you though." She started to gather her computer and notebook she had been using to jot down job postings she considered applying for.

"So what do you have planned for today other than waiting for the repairman?"

"Nothing. Just relaxing as usual. I may drive to town later. My car's been parked there since Friday," she motioned towards the driveway. She looked at him. "Why?"

"Oh, I was just asking. Wondering if you would like to come and keep me company again."

"I take it you don't like to be alone?"

"Not if I don't have to."

"Oh, so you think you've got options here?"

He laughed. "You are something else. I like that though."

She couldn't help smiling herself. She fronted, but she was enjoying him as much as he was enjoying her. "Sure, just give me a minute to do these dishes, then I'll be over."

* * *

"You can put on something else if you want to," Holiday said. He gestured towards the kitchen counter. "The CDs are right there."

"CDs? I thought I was the only one that still used them." She grabbed the small case from the counter and brought it back to her chair. She flipped through the pages. He had several albums for the same artists. Stevie Wonder. Frankie Beverly and Maze. D'Angelo. Ledisi. Jill Scott. Prince. Johnnie Taylor. Boney James. Teena Marie. Minnie Riperton. "You are very old school in your tastes," she said.

"Oh yeah, I like it classic."

She put in Boney James's *Ride,* and quickly pressed the button to skip track one for a song more appropriate for the occasion. "This album used to get me through those last-minute, late-night study sessions when I was in college."

"Really? I like it after work to relax. I'd've thought it would put you to sleep. A few of those songs anyway."

"No. It was just background noise, really."

"Boney kills that sax, though."

"Yeah, I like him too."

Holiday took a seat on the living room floor, his back against the wall, his legs outstretched in front of him.

"Are you sure that paint's dry all the way?" she asked, laughing.

He leaned forward quickly, brushing his hand lightly against the wall. "Oh yeah. It's cool. It was hot enough last night."

"Oh okay. Wouldn't want you to have to paint that a third time." She flipped through the CD holder again.

"So… Ms. Cynthia…"

"Hmm?" she said without looking up.

"How is it that your old man let you be away from him for so long? School doesn't start in…what? Another four weeks, right?"

She closed the case in her lap. "Is that your way of asking me if I have a man?"

He chuckled in his usual, unassuming way. "Well—"

"Tell me this," she continued, "do you think I would be sitting here entertaining you if I was involved with someone? Is that the type of women you're used to? Better yet, why would you be saying the types of things you've been saying to me if you assumed I had a man? You see, unlike some people who don't respect themselves or other people's relationships, I would *never* do something like—" She stopped when she noticed the confused look on his face. She was headed off on a tangent without realizing it and her rant had nothing to do with him but everything to do with Jonathan.

Embarrassed, she smiled and looked at him. "No, I'm not seeing anyone." Then she got up to return the CDs to the counter. "So, what is it that you're working on today?" she asked, needing to change the subject.

"I think I'll start on the kitchen" he replied. "He want us to replace the counters and re-paint the cabinets, too."

"Oh."

He uncrossed his legs at the ankle and crossed them again. "I can't believe a woman like you is single though."

She should have known there was no escaping the questions. She leaned against the kitchen counter. "Why is that hard to believe? Not everyone is lucky in love."

"You've been unlucky in love?"

She crossed her arms. There had been only four relationships in her thirty-one years. There was Tommy, the guy she lost her virginity to her sophomore year in high school. They dated until she left for Houston—and he left for Florida—following their graduation. It was a typical puppy-love affair throughout the courtship, but they agreed there was no way they would try to maintain a long-distance relationship while attending college thousands of miles away from each other; they parted ways amicably after the first year of college.

Dorian was the night-shift security guard assigned to patrol her college dorm. She fell for his boyish charm and incredible humor. Being with him was a non-stop comedy show, and she loved every minute of it. For nineteen months they shared great laughs and made great love. She thought she was his only girlfriend—he told her she was his only girlfriend—but one day she woke up after having spent a weekend in his apartment to find three of her tires slashed. Vince was eight years her senior when she met him at the age of twenty-three while working her first year as a teacher. He taught art history. It was an intense relationship and the first time she felt truly respected, wanted, and loved by someone. Vince asked her to move in with him. He wanted a wife and kids, but she felt she was too young and definitely not ready for that level of commitment. One night as they sat on the couch full and satisfied after he'd cooked her a delicious steak dinner, he patted her thigh gently and told her they could be friends. It took three years to get over him and she often wondered what could have been had she said yes. And then there was Jonathan.

Cynthia shrugged, and without going into specifics she said, "Even if it was just once, once is too many. Nobody likes that feeling."

"I hear you," he said. "I know there are a lot of no-good chumps out there. But only a fool would let you get away."

"Hey, don't you have work to do?"

He chuckled and got up from his spot on the floor. "Alright, Ms. Cynthia. I can take a hint."

THIRTEEN

Holiday wrapped up another day's work and was getting into his truck when a call came in from Annette. "Hello, Annette," he answered.

"Mason, I need you to come and pick up Christian for me. There is something I need to do and I will be gone for about three or four hours."

"Annette, how you doing?"

Silence. "Fine," she said. "How are you?"

"Doing good."

She blew out a breath. "I need you to come and pick up Christian."

"Not a problem. I'm on my way now."

She hung up.

* * *

"Go long," Holiday said and waited for Christian to run out before he threw the football.

"Got it!" The ball bounced in Christian's hands then slipped through his fingers. "Aww, man!" He threw it back to Holiday, slow and wobbly.

Holiday snatched it from the air, and without delay hurled it right back to Christian.

"Oomph!" he caught it with his stomach.

"Good," Holiday laughed. And for thirty minutes Holiday

watched Christian run, jump, fall down, get back up to run and fall some more, grass staining his shorts and socks, as they threw the football back and forth to each other.

"I need some water now," Christian said and they headed for the truck. He hopped on the tailgate and Holiday sat next to him.

Christian guzzled down half the bottle before he spoke again. "At first Mama said she would let me try out, but then she changed her mind."

"Oh yeah?"

"Yeah. She say she don't want me to get hurt."

"Well, you know how your mama is. She always been that way about you."

"But Maximillion play football and he don't get hurt."

"Not yet anyway. But there's always that possibility. Your mama just worry a lot."

Christian began swinging his legs out and back over the tailgate. "Naw, because she also told me it's already enough of us in sports and I should try to join the science club or something. Or think about being a engineer. But that sounds boring. And you can make millions of dollars in football!"

"You can make a lot of money as a scientist or engineer, too. Maybe even more money than a football player as a matter of fact."

"How so? Ain't no famous scientists. And I don't know no engineers neither."

Holiday chuckled. "Son, just because you don't know them by name don't mean they're not famous. Everything we use every day was invented or discovered by somebody. You can be the one to help find a cure for some disease, or a new medicine, or create a new famous toy."

"Wait... scientists make toys?" His eyes grew big.

"Sure they can. Engineers too. Matter-fact, them big water guns y'all like so much… them Super Soakers? A man named Lonnie Johnson came up with that. He invented that toy years ago—way before you were born—and kids still ask their mama and daddy to buy them one every summer to this day."

"Whoa! I didn't know that. I can invent my own toys, too!"

Holiday laughed again. "You just have to find something you like to do and work hard at it."

"But I like to play football too. Mama just don't want me to."

"Well, she may change her mind again. You never know. I just think she want you to think about other ways to be a success."

Christian hopped down off the tailgate. "Daddy! I just remembered… tomorrow is the first night for Hot August Nights! Can we go?"

Holiday frowned. "It's that time again? Already? You sure, son?"

"Yeeesss," Christian squealed. "I saw the commercial on TV yesterday. You can buy tickets online and print them out at home. They said it on the commercial. Can you get them now, Daddy?" Christian jumped around excitedly in the grass.

Holiday pulled out his mobile phone to check the calendar. Tomorrow was the first of August—also a Friday—which was the start of the town's big fair and festival. It began as a small summer back-to-school fair, but over the years with more and more people attending from surrounding cities, it expanded from a single weekend celebration to every Friday and Saturday the entire month of August and was later branded *Hot August Nights*.

"Yeah, we can go," Holiday told him. "But you have to ask your mama first."

"Okay, but she already said I can go."

"I'll be sure to buy the tickets tonight before I go to bed then."

FOURTEEN

"Cynthia," Mama Genie called to her from the bottom of the stairs, "Sister Nash is here."

She hit the switch to turn the fan off and grabbed her cross-body purse, slinging it over her head.

"Y'all want me to drive," she asked Mama Genie as she descended the stairs.

"I told you Sister Nash ain't gonna let nobody drive her."

Cynthia laughed. "Oh yeah, that's right." She locked the front door and followed Mama Genie to Sister Nash's idling Buick. She climbed in the back seat as Mama Genie took the front. They exchanged hellos and Sister Nash started down the road.

Cynthia stared out the window as the plains went by. Large open fields of cotton, the abandoned gins, a few wood frame houses—some dilapidated—here and there.

"Cynthia," Sister Nash began after they had been driving a while. "Sister Genie told me about your job situation. I'm sorry you got laid off."

"Oh, I'm trying not to worry too much about it. Thank you though. I've been looking around in the meantime."

Sister Nash glanced at her through the rearview mirror. "I put in a prayer request for you to Reverend Moore. We're all praying for you that you find something soon."

"Yeah, that's right," Mama Genie chimed in.

Cynthia said, "Thank you. I appreciate it."

"What about Jonathan? Is he doing all right? Sister Genie told me you left him back home while you came down to visit."

Cynthia stared at the back of Mama Genie's head, hoping she could feel her silently questioning why she felt the need to tell Sister Nash everything. "He's doing fine," Cynthia replied. "Working hard as usual."

"That's a good thing. He's a smart young man, Sister Genie tells me all the time. Make a lot of money, too, don't he?"

"Yeah, he makes pretty good money. I don't keep up with his salary though. It's never been my thing."

Mama Genie looked at Sister Nash. "She one of them new-age women, y'know? She worry about her own money."

Sister Nash said, "Well, ain't nothing wrong with that, but you still want a man to be able to take care of you. And he ain't proposed to you yet?"

Cynthia wished there was a partition she could roll up to close herself off from Sister Nash's questions. More than that, she wished she had stayed home. She contemplated whether she should just come out and admit she and Jonathan were no longer together, but that would only incite another barrage of questions, and she just didn't want to go there. Especially not in front of Sister Nash. And now that she knew Mama Genie was sharing all of her business with her friend, she wondered if it was even worth Mama Genie knowing.

"Not yet, Sister Nash, but I'm sure you will be one of the first ones to know when it's time for me to jump the broom."

"I can't wait. I'm looking forward to it."

* * *

The door chime clinked as they entered *LuAnn's Fine Fabrics*. There was a sale on select designs and Sister Nash wanted to see what they had to offer since she was bored with her old window drapes and wanted to replace them. Cynthia followed her and Mama Genie around the store like an obedient child as Sister Nash seemed to want to examine each and every piece of fabric on the long tables, running her hands over one, picking up another and holding it above her head towards the light to gauge its thickness, asking Mama Genie if the one she had an eye for would mesh well with the décor already in her living room. After thirty minutes had passed—and Sister Nash still couldn't make up her mind—Cynthia ventured off on her own. She could use a new hobby she thought to herself when a bright turquoise blue silk fabric with white calla lilies on it caught her attention. It would make for great throw pillows for her chocolate brown couch. Then she quickly put the fabric down. Her furniture was locked up in storage, and it would not make sense to buy something now that couldn't be used right away, especially since it was $23.99 per yard.

She glanced out of the shop window and noticed TCBY Yogurt was across the plaza. Mama Genie had given her a coupon she'd clipped out of the weekend newspaper promising a free cup of the day's flavor with the purchase of a small drink. Cynthia had a couple dollars to spare and she was bored already amongst the piles of fabrics. She found Mama Genie and Sister Nash to tell them where they could find her when they were done and she walked out.

The day's flavor was a strawberry mango sorbet, which Cynthia didn't care too much for, but she ate it anyway as she sat at one of the three wrought-iron tables fronting the store. There was no canopy so the sun beat directly down the front of her sundress and she knew it would be a matter of time before the sorbet and lemonade drink wouldn't be enough to keep cool. The plaza was bustling with people out getting a head-start to the weekend sales or just to be out and browse the dozen or so stores that lined the plaza. Most of them were the same stores that had always been there: LuAnn's Fabrics, Antiques & Things, The Sandwich Shop, Floyd's Appliances and Repairs, Brothers' Hardware, Elva's Vintage Clothing. Family-owned shops that the townspeople frequented out of personal commitment just to keep the business open.

She pulled the sunglasses sitting atop her head down to her eyes. She wondered what Holiday was up to now. His truck was parked next door when they left. It was parked there yesterday, too, but she did not go over. And he did not invite her to come over. He simply said 'hello' when he arrived and saw her sitting on the porch. She believed it was necessary to keep her distance, but at the same time, she wanted to see him. From her bedroom window she still peeked out from time to time, searching for him somewhere on the porch. And he would be there on the back, only his legs visible from the knees down as he had them propped up on the porch banister, smoke filtering the air around him. Or she saw him moving about inside the kitchen later as night fell.

A dark shadow suddenly blocked her view and she looked up.

"Cynthia," he said, his voice as smooth as the sorbet that slid down her throat.

"Wha— I mean… hey," she said, completely caught off guard but amused that her thoughts seemed to conjure up the man himself, in the flesh.

"What's going on? You mind if I sit down with you?"

"No, go right ahead." She moved her purse from the extra chair.

"I spotted you right away."

"Yeah?"

"It's hard to miss you in that bright yellow dress and the braids at the top of your head."

She laughed and was glad she had the shades to hide behind. She hated that he made her bubbly and giddy inside like some star-struck teenager, but that's what he did to her, and there wasn't much she could do about it. Then, for a brief moment, she remembered experiencing the same bubbly feelings for Jonathan in the beginning—and for a long time afterwards.

"What are you doing down here?" she asked him.

"Oh, I just came to see if I can find a match for this." He pulled a small brass handle out of his pocket. "For one of the cabinets."

She nodded.

"What about you? You came down to grab some lunch?" He looked at the empty bowl of sorbet in front of her.

"I'm with Mama Genie and Sister Nash. They're over there looking at fabrics. I just came out to enjoy the view. People watch."

"Oh, I see." He leaned back in the chair. Cynthia's eyes immediately wandered over his body. His skin was amazing—not a blemish or a pore in sight. They wandered over his wide back, taut biceps, and she noticed there was only a smidgen of fat around his stomach, which she didn't mind. She appreciated a little meat around the middle on a man. The cargo jeans he wore were not too big, but just right around his thighs. His was a body not made in the gym, but a product of manual labor.

And then her eyes settled on it. Right there inside his jeans it lay against his thigh, like a concealed zucchini.

She took a sip of her lemonade.

"What you got? About ten bracelets on each arm?" he said, looking at the many bangles and slim bracelets circling her wrists.

She held her arms out and they clanked and jingled. "Yeah, I love them. I think they look so much better mixed and stacked. Why? You think it's too much?"

"Naw, it looks good on you. It looks right with the dress. I like your style."

"Thanks."

His cell phone rang. He reached in his pocket and looked at the screen before he got up. "Excuse me while I take this." He walked several feet away before he answered and Cynthia shook her head.

Just fine for no reason.

"How long you gonna be here?" he asked after ending his call and returning to the table.

"I have no idea. We're riding with Sister Nash, so whenever she's ready I guess."

"Okay, I'm going to run into the store to see if I can find this right quick. Hopefully you're still here when I come back."

Sister Nash had chosen her fabric by the time he disappeared into Brothers' Hardware.

FIFTEEN

"I see you just been enjoying having this week off," Holiday said to Frank. He was home early after working only a half-day. Frank sat in his recliner, opened snack containers and packages all around him as he watched an old episode of *The Jeffersons*.

"Yep, but I'll be ripe and ready to get back at it Monday." He hoisted his leg up in the air to showcase his bandaged-free ankle. "It's good now," he smiled at Holiday.

"Good, because Ms. Washington down on Edloe said she want to replace the linoleum in her kitchen, dining, and bathrooms. I figure we can do that real quick on Monday."

"Old Ms. Washington, huh?" Frank grinned at Holiday. "You know she been trying to get you for a while now. She looking for husband number six I heard."

Holiday laughed. "Naw, Pop. She a little bit too old for me. She might be right for you though."

Frank shook his head. "Naw, that's how she like 'em. You know her last two husbands was not much older than her own sons. She don't want no old man like me. She say she need somebody with some spunk." He laughed.

"Don't get me wrong, she still look good for her age, but married five times? I may not be up to her standards."

Frank nodded. "Oh, you're up to her standards alright: young, good-looking, single, hard-working. That's what she want. I hear she like to take care of her men, too. Buy them anything they want, let 'em lay around the house doing nothing while she cater to them. She could be a good fit for you."

Holiday scratched his chin. "You can't be serious, Pop."

"What? She the one that wants you. I'm just letting you know."

Holiday chuckled. "I don't see it. I may want more kids one day, and I think she's done with all that. It wouldn't work."

"Hey, you never know. Technology is letting these women have babies in their fifties and sixties now."

He gave a sideways glance at his dad. "Why are we even having this discussion? I told you I'm just taking it easy right now, Pop. No need to rush into anything."

Frank raised his palms. "Alright, alright. But you know these women out here are waiting to scoop you up. As soon as word got around that you and Annette split up."

Holiday shook his head. It was no secret he was one of the most-wanted men by the women in town, but he didn't let the notion go to his head. While he wasn't actively seeking a relationship with anyone, he also wasn't a man to play with women's hearts. Sure, he could have any woman he wanted—there had been plenty to tell him so, and a few he was tempted to give in to—but he preferred to keep his distance until the time came where he believed he was ready to be available completely for the right one.

Wanting to move the subject away from Ms. Washington, Holiday said, "We should be able to do that job in no time."

"Sound good to me," Frank replied.

"Well, Pop," Holiday said, "I'm gonna head out for a while. I'm going to pick up Christian and take him down to the festival."

"Oh okay, that's right. All that starts today, huh?"

"Yeah, I got us a couple tickets."

"Alright, well, y'all have fun. I'll still be here. I can't do them crowds no more."

Holiday dialed Annette as he entered his truck. "Hello, Annette," he said when she answered. "Tell Christian I will be there around five-thirty to pick him up. I just have a few errands to run right now. Is he at Roxy's house or at the neighbors'?"

"What do you mean you're picking him up?"

"To take him to the festival. He asked me yesterday to take him, so I bought us some tickets."

"Why would you do that without talking to me first?"

Holiday sighed. "Annette, he told me you said I can take him. I didn't think it would be a problem. I mean… you telling me I need to spend time with him, right?"

"Yeah, but you don't know what I have planned. Paula at work invited us over for her son's birthday party. Christian just doesn't want to go because the party is for a three-year-old."

"A party on a Friday night for a three-year-old?"

"Her parents are leaving tomorrow afternoon for their anniversary trip out of the country and wanted to celebrate with him before they go, so Paula's giving him a little dinner party. But still… that's neither here nor there. The point is Christian knew what our plans were."

"You're right. But he had me thinking it was all right with you."

"Always, always consult me first. I will remind Christian of this, too."

Holiday completed his errands after ending the call with Annette. The festival tickets could be used only for the date of purchase and he had no reason to attend without Christian. He considered taking them to Roxy, but she would still need an additional ticket for herself and would most-likely ask to borrow money from him to purchase it, so he dismissed that idea. Then he thought of just going up to a random couple and their children to offer them the tickets free of charge. But a greater idea hit him.

* * *

"Well, hello there, Holiday," Ms. Genie said pushing the screen door open.

"How you doing, Ms. Genie?"

"Doing good. I didn't know you were still working today. I thought you had already gone. You need something to drink or something?"

"Oh, no ma'am. I came by to speak with Ms. Cynthia. Is she here?" he asked even though he was glad to see her car parked in the driveway when he pulled up.

"Yeah, she up there in her room." Ms. Genie called for Cynthia and within a minute she was standing in front of Holiday.

"Hey," she said.

"Hey, can I talk to you for a minute?"

"Uhh… okay," she said, a slight look of confusion across her face as he led her away from the screen door and down the porch steps.

"Listen, I know this is last-minute, but I was wondering if you had any plans for tonight. I got a couple tickets to the festival if you want to go." It surprised him when she quickly agreed. Then she laughed.

"You had me nervous for a minute there. I thought something was wrong," she said.

"Well, I didn't want Ms. Genie to hear you turn me down."

"Oh, okay," she laughed again. "No, I would love to go."

"My son couldn't go with me and I didn't want to waste my money so…"

"Alright, just give me about twenty minutes to throw something on," she said and hurried into the house.

Warm air blew on their faces through the opened windows as they drove down County Road 12. Temperatures were in the upper 80s, but the low heat index offered a comfortable atmosphere. D'Angelo's *Alright* wafted through the sound system.

"How old is your son," Cynthia asked him.

"He's eleven."

"Is that him?" She pointed to the wallet photo propped on the dashboard next to the odometer.

Holiday nodded. "Yeah, that's him. Christian. And his sister, Laila." He picked up the photo and handed it to her.

"Oh, there's two kids on here? I couldn't see the little girl from here. Wow! She looks just like you. How old is she?"

"She was three there, going on four. She passed away a couple of summers ago."

"Oh," Cynthia said. "I'm sorry to hear that."

Holiday blew out a slow breath. "Yep, that's my baby girl. Miss her every day."

Cynthia handed the picture back to him. She looked out the window. A few minutes of silence fell between them before she finally said, "I can't remember the last time I've been to this festival. Maybe when I was fifteen, sixteen years old."

"Oh yeah? We usually go every year. I think we've only skipped it maybe three times. But Christian loves it."

"That's cool."

He asked, "You have any kids?"

"Nope. No kids."

"Hmm… Teaching them every day hasn't turned you off to the idea of having your own one day has it?"

"No, not at all," she laughed. "I just haven't been in a situation yet that's made me seriously consider having some."

"So you never been married?"

She looked at him. "You don't have to be married to have kids. Especially these days. Well, that's what a lot of people seem to think anyway."

He chuckled. "You're right about that."

"But, no. Not yet."

"See, I knew you were special when I first saw you. How could I be this lucky to meet someone like you?"

"What are you talking about?" she grinned sheepishly.

He raised a hand. "Well, I don't even wanna say nothing else about it since you say I'm just feeding you lines." Then he reached over, gently touching her knee, "It's just been a while since I've been around a woman as cool as you."

A wave of heat rushed to the center of him when she covered his hand with hers.

SIXTEEN

"Oh yeah. They really have expanded," Cynthia said as they pulled into the county fairgrounds. The huge Ferris wheel rotated slowly in the distance. Small roller coasters dipped and whooshed through the air full of screaming kids and teens, some with their arms stretched high above their heads. A rocket-shaped ride hung upside down a few seconds, then barreled down towards the ground only to rush back into the air, suspending the passengers upside down again, while nearby giant swings twirled round and round. "The last time I came all they had was the Ferris wheel and one of those swings."

Holiday circled the grass lot two times searching for a parking space. He finally found one and backed into the space. "I told you. It just seems to get bigger and better every year. There are even more rides towards the back on the other side. I got your door," he said and got out, going around to her side of the truck. He held her hand as she hopped down.

"Thanks."

They walked around for a half-hour just taking in the sights and sounds: moms pushing strollers, kids rushing dads along to the next ride, couples walking hand-in-hand, lines of people waiting for buttery popcorn, cotton candy, nachos, sausages on sticks. Or to try their luck and win a game prize.

They were stopped several times as many people recognized and wanted to speak to Holiday. Cynthia noticed the quizzical looks by a few of the women as well as the men. Holiday didn't bother introducing her to any of them, and she didn't mind it one bit.

"So which game you wanna play first?" he asked.

"Oh, you're really gonna play?"

Nodding his head he said, "Yeah. What? You don't wanna play? The concert don't start until seven. Or you wanna just walk around?"

She hadn't planned on spending any money, and she didn't consider it a date (or was it a date?), so she'd packed a bottle of water in her cross-body bag, and a package of mixed nuts taken from Mama Genie's church-snacks stash. She was grateful for the invite and would just enjoy her time with him.

"I'll just watch you play," she told him.

"Ah. Okay."

So she watched him attempt to shoot basketballs in hoops, throw bean bags through baseball-sized holes, toss dimes onto glass plates, squirt water guns to race mini tug boats along a stream, only to end up with one prize after it was all over and done—a stuffed elephant no bigger than the palm of his hand.

She laughed and kissed the elephant's head when he gave it to her. "I will cherish it always."

"You're something else," he said and, with his hand on the small of her back, led her towards the concert stage.

For nearly three hours they stood watching the live bands—one was a local Zydeco band, the other a mix of rock and country—before they shuffled through the slow-moving crowd making their way back to the truck.

"Thank you so much for this. I had a really good time," Cynthia said.

Holiday threw his arm around her shoulder and squeezed her to him. "Naw, thank *you* for coming with me. I had a good time, too. We have to do this again though."

She looked up at him. "You want to come again?"

"Yeah, why not? What you doing tomorrow? It'll be a different band, too."

"Hmm… nothing, really."

"Alright, well I will come and pick you up at…" He hesitated. "Wait, I'm sorry. I might be bringing my son since he couldn't come today."

"Oh okay. That's right. No problem. We can come back another time."

He held the passenger door open as she hopped into the truck. "I'm gonna hold you to that."

* * *

"So… Ms. Cynthia…" Holiday stood on the bottom step of Mama Genie's porch.

"Hmm?" she said, looking down at him from the second step. It was a little after midnight and, with the exception of the low glow from the porch lamp, pitch black surrounded them and the croaking of crickets.

"When can I hang out with you again?"

She cocked her head and folded her arms. Being so close to him, his handsome face, the manly scent of him after a day spent in the sun, made her heart thud in her chest. "Didn't we just discuss this? I thought we planned to go to the festival again when you have some free time."

"Yeah, I thought about it, but that's too long." He propped one foot on the step where she stood.

The voice in her head was screaming: *No! This is not a good idea. Steer clear! Nothing good can come of this. Casual relationships only bring heartache. You have a life in Houston.*

But she couldn't deny the good feelings she got being in his company. "Well, what day do you have in mind?"

"Today."

"Today?" she asked, confused.

"Yeah."

"Aren't you spending time with your son today?"

"I am," he said. "But not right now."

She frowned. "Right now?"

"Yeah, Nell's Diner stays open until three during Hot August Nights. I figure we can go and have breakfast."

She considered it for a few seconds. "Oh, I really shouldn't. I'm on a tight budget this summer. You know us teachers don't make much and I d—"

"Don't worry about it. It's on me. It's the least I can do after all the good food you and Ms. Genie hooked me up with."

"Hmm…"

"I'm just not ready to go home."

She knew Mama Genie would be in a deep sleep by now and would not know if she'd come home at midnight or five in the morning. "Alright," she said.

SEVENTEEN

Holiday sat in the garage drinking a cold beer, his shirt drenched with sweat and plastered against his chest and back. He'd just given his truck a full detail wash and was waiting to let the wax settle in a while before wiping it off. If he could have his way he would still be sitting across the table from Cynthia, staring into those chocolate brown doe eyes. Watching her mouth part and her lips fold around her fork as she took a bite from her country skillet platter. The diner was crowded and noisy with mostly teens who'd just come in from the festival, so they ate the majority of their meal in silence since it was difficult to hear each other. Still, the way she smiled at him across the table had him wishing to see that smile again this afternoon.

"Y'all must've had a really good time since you didn't make it in 'til early this morning." Frank walked up behind him and grabbed a folding chair from the rack against the wall. "I bet Chris was wore out when you dropped him off."

"Yeah, it was cool," Holiday replied. "But I didn't take Christian."

Frank set his chair a few feet away from Holiday's. "What you mean?"

Holiday took a sip from the Budweiser. "He couldn't go. He didn't tell me Annette had a party planned for him to go to."

Frank shook his head. "Oooh."

"So I took Cynthia with me."

"You took Cynthia?"

"Yeah."

Frank chuckled. "Now, I know I may be a little old, son, but weren't you just saying a few days ago you wasn't worrying about keeping company with no woman? Wasn't that you? I could've sworn that was you."

Holiday chuckled too. "Pop, what's wrong with taking the lady out for a fun day in the park? Who else could I have invited? You said you didn't wanna go."

"I'm just trying to understand. I'm trying to figure out what it is about this woman that got you going in to work earlier, coming home later. Especially since you say relationships are complicated."

Holiday waved his hand. "There you go, exaggerating like you always do."

"I'm gonna have to meet this Cynthia. See if she all you think she cracked up to be."

"I told you she's just a sweet person. We just hanging out while she's here in town."

"Well, that's good, son. I told you it's good to have a sweet lady around you. Shoot, I miss your mama every day, but I sometimes wish I could get me a nice lady friend."

Holiday looked at him. "Really, Pop?"

"Oh yeaahh. I hear they got this social club for seniors now down in Douglass County. They have nights out where they go bowling and to the movies, catch a few plays. I should probably join to see if I can meet me somebody."

Holiday said, "I didn't know you would be into something like that. Especially at your age."

"Like what? Meeting some nice ladies?"

"Getting into another relationship. Marriage. Whatever."

He snorted. "I may move a little slower, but everything still works y'know?" He winked.

Holiday just shook his head.

"Seriously though, son. I'm never ashamed about my feelings. And you know I taught you to be the same way. I know some of you guys like to say you don't need no woman, women are too much work, yadda yadda yadda. But I don't have a problem saying I need a woman. I like having somebody with me."

Holiday nodded. "I know, Pop. I know."

Frank continued, "Your mama got me spoiled, and I know I probably won't meet somebody to give me what she gave me, to have what we had, but I'd like to think I could meet somebody to spend the rest of my days with."

"Yeah, I can understand that." He swallowed the last of his beer and tossed the can into the recycling bin.

EIGHTEEN

"I'm gonna be honest about it with you. It looks like you just need a whole new unit."

Cynthia and Mama Genie stood watching as the repairman examined the air conditioner. Sweat streamed down from underneath his baseball cap into his eyes, down his sideburns and pooled around his shirt collar. He pulled the cap off, pushed the sweat up from his forehead through his dusty blonde hair twice, and flung the excess sweat off his calloused fingers before putting the cap back on.

"And how much is that gonna cost us?" Mama Genie asked.

He coughed into his hand. "Well, uh, it can be anywhere from about eleven hundred to about twenty-five hundred dollars. But that depends on if there ain't nothing else wrong. Then it'll run you up to as much as four thousand. Depending."

"Oh, mercy!" Mama Genie said.

He looked from Mama Genie to Cynthia. "I can call the shop right now and have them place you on the schedule and we can get this installed for you next week."

Cynthia said, "Thanks, but we'll have to think about it and call you."

"Well, you don't wanna wait too long. May as well replace it now and forget about it for the next twenty years. Besides, y'all don't wanna be settin' around in all this heat."

Mama Genie said, "We'll make do for now. We wasn't born in air condition."

The repairman looked as if he had no clue what Mama Genie was talking about.

Cynthia said, "We'll call."

He nodded. "Alright. Welp, let me go to the truck and write up your receipt. It'll be seventy-five dollars today."

"Seventy-five dollars?" Cynthia exclaimed.

"For the trip charge, ma'am."

Mama Genie snorted. "Cynthia, you should've known they were gonna charge you again."

Cynthia sighed and turned towards the house to go and get her checkbook.

"I knew it was gonna cost us a arm and a leg," Mama Genie said, pouring iced water into her cup from the pitcher sitting on the small table between them as they sat on the porch.

Cynthia looked up from her Sudoku magazine. "Yeah, but I wasn't expecting it to be that much. I don't know why I expected eight-hundred, nine-hundred dollars. That seems more reasonable."

"Sister Nash say hers cost about twelve-hundred, so.... You reckon you should call Jonathan and have him call somebody to see if he can get us a cheaper price? Remember he was able to talk down that man that fixed the roof."

Cynthia froze at the mention of Jonathan's name. He was the last person she would call for anything she needed even if Mama Genie continued to praise him for his generosity. It was Jonathan who footed the bill when a huge branch fell from the tree on the side of the house, knocking a hole in Mama Genie's ceiling. It was a sign of a generous heart Mama Genie had said to Cynthia that day. There were not too many men around that would do something that kind for the relative of a woman he wasn't married to.

"I'm sure he's too busy and I don't want to bother him with this," Cynthia said. Holiday told me he knows someone, so maybe I will have him come and give us a quote."

Mama Genie said, "Well okay. That's fine by me."

NINETEEN

Ms. Washington lived in a triple wide mobile home that, from outside appearances, was less of a mobile home in the traditional sense, but a stately structure with its white column porch, sun room and double front door. The yard with its immaculately-trimmed grass, rose bushes and hedges resembled something on a page in *Better Homes & Gardens* magazine.

Holiday knocked on the door.

"It's open," Ms. Washington called from inside.

He turned the gold handle and he and Frank stepped into the entryway then stopped short at the sight just a few feet ahead of them. Ms. Washington was positioned on a yoga mat, her back to them, her legs splayed on either side of her in a perfect horizontal split with her torso flush with the floor. She wore a leopard thong leotard over a pair of white tights so thin they were almost translucent.

Holiday and Frank exchanged looks.

"I'm just stretching it all out. Be with y'all in a minute," Ms. Washington said. She slowly pulled her torso upright and brought her legs together in front of her, rolling her shoulders as she did so. Then she stood up, spread her legs wide again, then swiftly bent forward, looking at them through the V of her legs as she grabbed her left ankle to stretch her hamstring, and then her right ankle. She winked, smiling brightly.

"My lord," Frank said under a breath.

"Whew!" She stood and finally faced them. "I had to get my workout out of the way. Gotta keep the body fit and pliable."

"I heard that," Frank said.

She grabbed a towel from the back of the sectional sofa and dabbed at her forehead and neck. She walked up to Frank and air kissed both his cheeks. "Hey, Frank. You been staying out of trouble?"

Frank blushed. "I do the best I can, Ms. Washington."

She swatted him with her towel. She walked over to Holiday and stood so close to him he could smell the peppermint on her breath. "Holiday," she said in a low, raspy voice. "It's been a long time, sweetheart. You know I'm happy to see you." Then she leaned into him, her breasts smashing into his chest, and kissed his cheek.

"Hello, Ms. Washington," he said. "Good to see you, too."

She turned around and twisted off towards her kitchen. "Can I get y'all something to drink?"

"No, ma'am," Holiday said. "We're good for right now. We just wanna go ahead and get started so we can knock this out for you. We don't wanna take up too much of your time."

"Oh Holiday, sweetheart, don't worry about that. My whole day is free so you can take all the time you need. As a matter of fact, come to the back with me. I need to have you look at something." Then she turned to Frank. "Frank, the boxes are stacked in the sun room. I'm gonna borrow Holiday for a few minutes."

Frank slowly shook his head, giving Holiday a sly smile as Ms. Washington led Holiday to the back of the house.

"I heard about the nice shelf you built for Annette back when y'all were married," Ms. Washington said as she stepped into a room Holiday guessed was her home office. The only furnishings were a small desk and two filing cabinets. She closed the door behind them.

Holiday walked to the center of the room. "Oh yeah, we do that too. Shelves, entertainment centers, custom bed frames and headboards. We've pretty much done a little of everything."

"That's wonderful because I'm thinking about turning this into a library and I want wall-to-wall shelving."

"Then we can definitely do that for you. That won't be a problem at all. We can get together and draw up a few sketches for the design and measurements and go from there."

"Yeah, I'm glad you said that because that's what I was going to ask you. When can we get together?"

"Well, we got something else lined up later this evening, so me and Pop would have to come back later this week sometime if that's okay with you."

"No, I mean when can *we* get together, Holiday?" She reached up and pulled the twist-tie out of her hair, letting the thick voluminous auburn mane fall down to her shoulders. "You and me."

Holiday chuckled and put his hands in his pockets. "Say what?"

Ms. Washington closed the space between them. Licking her lips, she said, "Come on, baby. You're a free man now. Why don't you let a nice woman take you out on a date, hmm?" She slid her hand up Holiday's arm to his shoulder.

"Oh… umm… I don't know if I would have time for anything like that. I work a lot and when I'm not working, I try to spend as much time with my son as I can." He had to let her down softly.

"You're just saying that, I know. What's two or three hours out of your day? Surely you have time for some fun sometime." She brought her other hand up his arm and started to encircle his neck, but he gently grabbed her wrists and brought them back down to her sides.

"Ms. Washington, with all due respect, I'm just saying I can't commit to a date with you. Or anybody to be honest. Maybe if I was in another headspace and time. Being divorced yourself I'm sure you understand how it is afterwards. You're just trying to get through it."

"Oh, I know. And you don't have to get through it alone. We can be good for each other." She caressed his arms again. "So how about it, sweetheart? Why don't you come and get you some of th—"

Just then Frank opened the door to the room. Ms. Washington flashed him a heated look. "My goodness, Frank! Don't you know you're supposed to knock before you open a closed door?"

Holiday grinned at Frank over Ms. Washington's shoulder.

"Excuse me, Ms. Washington. I apologize. It didn't even cross my mind that anything personal could've been going on in here. I just thought y'all were talking business."

"We *were* talking business, but it's still common courtesy to knock before you enter."

Frank nodded. "You're right. And I apologize again. I just come to get the keys to the truck." He looked at Holiday. "I wanna see if we got another box cutter. This one kinda dull now."

"Sure thing, Pop. I'll check for you," he said, brushing past Ms. Washington to follow Frank out of the room. He was just past the doorway when he heard Ms. Washington mutter *Shit*.

TWENTY

"I'll be next door with Holiday," Cynthia said to Mama Genie as she breezed past her grandmother standing in the kitchen. It had been two days since she and Holiday spent the day at the festival and then at Nell's diner and she couldn't deny the excitement moving inside her to see him again. She quickly crossed the path and waltzed up the steps to the house and let herself in as she had become accustomed to doing. The voices coming from the bathroom stopped her and she decided not to go any farther.

"Hello?" she called.

Holiday emerged from the bathroom with the smile that made Cynthia feel weak. "Hey, hey." He walked up to her and squeezed her shoulder. "What's going on, Ms. Cynthia?"

"Nothing. I just came to see what you were up to. But since you got company I'll just go."

He shook his head. "Naw, that's just Pop. You don't have to go." His hand slid down from her shoulder to the small of her back. "Pop, come out here real quick," he called down the hall.

Seconds later Frank came around the corner. Cynthia looked expectantly at the man coming up the hallway eager to catch a glimpse of the one that bestowed such good looks to his son. It surprised her to see there wasn't much of a resemblance to Holiday at all in his features or stature. While he was just a couple inches shorter than Holiday, where Holiday was broad and tight, this man was stout with a bit of a pot belly. His skin—albeit just as smooth as Holiday's—was a cocoa brown compared to the inky hue of his son's.

But when he smiled at Cynthia it was like having a double dose of Holiday's charm.

"This is Ms. Genie's granddaughter Cynthia," Holiday told him. "Cynthia, this is my dad. Frank."

"Oh, so this is the one I've heard so much about." Frank proffered his hand.

"Good to meet you," Cynthia said as he squeezed her hand firmly.

"You were right about everything you said, son. Sure was," Frank nodded approvingly.

Cynthia laughed nervously. "Well I hope they were good things."

"Oh yeah," Frank said. "He told me Ms. Genie had a granddaughter just as beautiful as she is, so good looks must run in y'all's family."

Cynthia blushed and looked at Holiday. "Well… I can say the same about his family too."

This time Frank laughed nervously. "He is a handsome fella if I do say so myself. He got them looks from his mama though. She was a real-life beauty queen."

"Oh yeah?" She noticed he spoke of her in the past tense.

"Sure was."

Holiday said, "Let me get the chair for you, Cynthia."

She shook her head. "No, no. I don't wanna keep you from your work. I was just stopping by to say hi."

"Well let me walk you home."

"What? It's just right next door."

"I know, but I still want to walk you home." He placed his hand on the space of her lower back, just before the curve of her butt, causing a shiver in her at his gentle touch. "I'll be right back, Pop," he said to Frank as they headed out.

"It was good meeting you, Mr. Frank," Cynthia said.

"You too, dear. And call me Frank. I ain't for all that Mister stuff."

Cynthia laughed. "Okay, Frank. See you later."

"Your dad seems really cool," Cynthia said after they descended the steps.

Holiday nodded. "He is. The coolest cat I know."

"You have any siblings?"

"I have a brother in Fort Worth."

"Older?"

"Yeah, he's six years older than me. He's thirty-nine."

"Oh. You and him close?"

"Yeah, we are. He's married. Got five kids. We usually see each other for Thanksgiving since his wife's family is from Oklahoma and they go there for Christmas. And we always get together for Pop's birthday."

They were walking at a turtle's pace. "Are you trying to get out of working?" she asked playfully.

He chuckled. "No, I just needed this break. Plus, I really didn't want you to leave, but I can understand if you don't want to be there since he's there. He probably wouldn't get anything done hisself. Too busy trying to be a clown."

"He likes to have fun. There's nothing wrong with that."

"For sure. But I have to remind him to be serious sometimes."

"Well, thanks for seeing that I made it home safely," she said when they reached the porch. "I guess anything can happen within this three-hundred feet of path."

"I had to make sure you were safe. Didn't want no stray dogs to chase you home."

"Please, there are no stray dogs around here," she laughed.

"You are something else."

"So I will see you again this weekend for the festival?"

He smiled. "I was thinking maybe we can do something sooner."

She looked down at him from the top step as she did a couple nights ago. "Why does this feel like déjà vu?"

"We're not gonna be over there too much longer and once I drop Pop off at home I'm free for the night if you want to do something."

"Like what?"

He took a seat on the bottom step. "I don't know. Is there anything in particular you wanna do?"

Cynthia followed suit and took a seat on her step too. It wasn't supposed to be this way. She was not supposed to be this relaxed, this comfortable with a guy she'd only known for a little over a week. She wasn't even supposed to be spending time with anyone. This summer was supposed to be about getting Cynthia healed. "There's nothing to do here on a Monday night. It's one of the reasons why I moved to the city."

"Well... I'll think of something." He looked at his watch. "Is six-thirty okay?"

"Yeah, six-thirty is good," she answered without hesitation.

He stood up and reached for her hand. "Alright, I'll be back for you soon."

TWENTY-ONE

"I hope you like Chinese food," Holiday said as he shut the passenger door behind Cynthia. "I stopped and picked up some on the way here and figured we can drive down to the lake and eat there."

"I love Chinese food," she replied. "The lake sounds cool."

Fifteen minutes later Holiday backed into a grassy spot near the edge of the lake—the side less frequented by visitors unless it was a group of teens seeking a hideout to smoke their drug of choice or makeout in their cars. Holiday grabbed the food from the backseat and they got out of the truck. He lowered the tailgate, spreading a thick blanket across it for cushioning. Cynthia sat down and he placed the three big to-go containers between them.

"You think you got enough?" she asked, eyeing the stuffed trays oozing with the likes of chow mein and sweet and sour pork.

"I wanted to make sure you had a variety to choose from in case you don't like something." He handed her a paper plate and plastic utensils.

"Thank you. And I pretty much eat anything. I'm not picky at all."

"Well that's good to know. It makes planning a lot easier. What do you want to drink? Do you drink beer? I got a few of those left in here too." He pulled the cooler closer to them.

She scrunched her nose. "Now that is something I don't do. Beer is nasty. I'm more of a wine person."

He nodded. "Oh okay. I will remember that for next time. I got the usual: tea, water, lemonade."

"Lemonade, please."

She wasted no time digging into the containers and he was delighted with the fact that she was not shy about her portions. They were quiet for the first several minutes as they ate. Holiday thought about how, just a few hours ago, he turned down Ms. Washington's offer, claiming he was not capable of being good company for anybody for now. Yet here he was spending time with Cynthia. But he couldn't help himself. He knew from their first meeting she was something different. Or maybe it wasn't even about being different, but just that she was easy to be around because she hadn't lived in the town for many years and did not know who he was. Unlike Ms. Washington and the other single and lonely women around he could just enjoy the company of a woman without their pretenses.

"So what do you teach? Elementary? High School?" he asked, breaking the silence.

"Middle School. Seventh-grade Social Studies."

"Man, that teaching is a tough job to have. I can't imagine doing something like that. You like it?"

She set her can of lemonade on top of the cooler. "Well… can I be honest?"

He looked at her curiously. "Yeah, of course. Why wouldn't you be?"

"I used to love it. In the beginning. I went in with the mindset like many first-year teachers do: I'm gonna work with kids and motivate them and make learning fun for them and they are going to love me and study hard and do all their work and pass every test and they're going to give a speech at the end of the school year about how

I was the teacher who inspired them to be their best and they will remember me as the one who really cared."

"But what happened?"

"The truth happened."

Holiday laughed at the defeated look on her face. "Did they run you over?"

"It wasn't so much that they ran over me. But after a few years, I just *felt* run over mentally. The majority of these kids today are not motivated. It's really like babysitting. They just want to text back and forth on their phones, take and send selfies, and talk about the latest fashion trends or celebrity gossip. I pleaded with them to do the work. To think about their futures, et cetera, but they couldn't care less. I would get home at the end of the day and wonder what is the point of it all."

"Well… that seems to be what teachers say about each new generation though."

"And the parents don't care, either," she continued, "which makes it worse. How can we expect kids to care if their own parents don't care?"

"I tip my hat to y'all. It takes some serious patience."

She sighed. "A helluva lot of patience."

"And you only got a few more weeks before you're back in the lion's den again."

"Don't remind me. I'm here to forget."

"What else do you do in Houston? Since you say you had to get away from this boring town?"

She laughed. "Don't get me wrong. This is where I'm from, so my heart is always in this place. I was just seeking something different after high school. But it's just like living in any other big city I guess. Just the convenience of nearby entertainment. More people to look at. I like the museums, the restaurants. I go to the parks a lot. We go to different bars. There's pretty much something to do every weekend. There's always a comedy show or a concert to attend somewhere. We love small venues like the House of Blues."

"So you and your girlfriends get together and just have a good time. That's cool."

Suddenly there was a look that crossed her face he couldn't make out what it could have meant. Was it sadness? Then she let out a breath. "Yeah, it was always fun."

"Was?" he looked at her curiously.

"I mean… yeah, we have fun. Me and my friend Tora." He knew she was thinking about something, but he wouldn't pressure her to talk about anything she didn't want to talk about. She opened one of the containers and grabbed another Spring roll. She said between bites, "This is some good Chinese food. You see I can't stop eating it."

"Go ahead. Have as much as you want. Whatever is left I can take to Pop if you don't want it." He had finished eating and crumpled his plate and put it in one of the emptied plastic bags.

"No, I need to stop or you may end up having to carry me upstairs when you take me home.

He grunted at the thought. "Oh don't worry about that. I would do what I have to," he grinned slyly.

"Hmm…"

He got up from the tailgate, took a cigarette out of the pack in his pocket, and walked a few steps away from the truck to light it. "What makes you happy?" he asked, blowing smoke out the corner of his mouth.

"Huh?"

He gestured towards her top: a screen tee the colors of a Jamaican Rastacap. "Your shirt says 'Do what makes you happy'."

She looked down as if she'd forgotten she had it on. "Oh. That's right," she smiled. "Well… traveling makes me happy. I like to visit new places. Shopping of course. Good food. Old movies. Thunderstorms."

"Thunderstorms?" he frowned.

"I love stormy weather." She scooted back on the tailgate, pulling her knees up to her chest, crossing her ankles. The denim cut-off shorts with frayed edges she wore left a generous part of her thigh exposed.

Holiday could not look away. "That's the first time I heard somebody say that."

She laughed. "Sunny days are cool, but there's nothing like a good storm forcing you to stay inside and just…" she faded.

"Just what?" The devilish look she gave him sent his mind to a place he knew it didn't need to go. She knew exactly what she was doing, he was sure of it. "Just what?" he prodded again.

"Just… chill," she sighed and looked out over the lake.

He chuckled. "I hear you. So where do you like to go when you travel?"

"Oh, anywhere I can. Now that is one thing I love about working for the school district. Those long summers off. I'm still waiting to take a month-long trip to somewhere. My dream is one of those two-week long Mediterranean cruises. Or maybe rent a beach cottage on an island for a whole month."

"What's stopping you?"

"It's not something I want to do alone. And nobody I know has the vacation time to spend."

"Oh, I see." He could see the vision clearly in his mind: the two of them relaxing on a beach somewhere in the Caribbean, sunbathing in the tropical heat before cooling off in the sheer blue water. Then they would go back to the cottage, shower together, and…. But his thoughts were far-fetched. She was only here for a few more weeks and was just indulging him before heading back home to her life—a life that did not involve him. He decided in the meantime he would enjoy however much of her time she allowed him to have.

He put out his cigarette. "You wanna play a game?"

TWENTY-TWO

"Uno?" she laughed when he retrieved the deck of cards from the truck cabin. "You're taking me way back."

"I couldn't find the other cards, and I thought we could play some spades, but ain't no telling where Christian put them. So I got these."

"I'm not too good at spades anyway, so this is good."

"For real? Then you need to come with me sometime. Me and my buddies get together all the time for a few games. And we always have a big tournament at the end of the month. Food, drinks, music. Some of them bring their wives and girlfriends too. It's a big party."

It didn't blow over Cynthia that he seemed to make plans to spend more and more time with her. He was a smooth one. "I may have to come and check y'all out." She crossed her legs Indian-style and sat back waiting as he shuffled and dealt the cards. He flipped over the first one from the deck: a red six.

"Now you need to tell me something about you," she said.

"What do you wanna know?"

"What you would like to tell me."

"Hmm… wouldn't it be better if you just ask?" He played a Skip card and then made her draw two.

"No, because I'm curious to see what you think I'm worthy of knowing."

"Anything?"

"Yeah."

"Well… you probably don't want to hear this again, but I think you're very beautiful."

She crossed her eyes, making him laugh. "Really?"

He nodded.

"I was hoping you would come with something better than that. Something about *you*, not me. She threw out a blue Reverse and then a Wild card. "The color is yellow."

"You don't think that's good enough?" He pulled a card from the deck.

"Every girl likes a compliment every now and then, but I'm asking about you now. Tell me something about you." She waited for him to place a card on the pile.

"I still can't play."

"Then you have to keep pulling until you can."

"Nooo, that makes the game too long. Just one card."

"Alright," she groaned playfully.

"I want to kiss you."

Cynthia looked up from her hand. "What?"

"That's what I want you to know." He was dead serious. It was all in those piercing eyes the way he looked at her; a smirk was not included. Cynthia felt the heat.

"Umm… I'm not sure what you want me to say to that. Okay?"

"You don't have to say nothing. I just wanted you to know that. It's your play."

She looked at the cards in her hand again, the colors suddenly blending all together like the emotions stirring inside her: anxiousness, hesitation, anticipation. She shook her head trying to refocus. "Now you got me all discombobulated," she laughed.

"Discom-what?"

"Nothing. I think I ate too much."

"Then let's go walk for a little bit." He threw his cards down face up. "Besides, I would've won the game anyway." He had two Draw Fours.

"Clearly you didn't shuffle the cards right."

"Oh naw, I'm not a cheater at all."

Cynthia was grateful for the getaway because she didn't have to sit across from him trying to hide the way he made her feel. She walked beside him at his easy-going pace. The crushed-gravel path crunched beneath their feet as they strolled underneath a canopy of oak trees towards the pavilion. The sun was setting but that didn't stop the people that were out picnicking, exercising, and playing sports from packing up their things and heading home.

"Well?" she nudged his arm, looking up at him. "You prefer to remain a mystery?"

He told her he was from a close-knit family mostly of hard-working small business owners in Bryan, Texas. There were barbers and beauticians, mechanics, a day care and night club owner, a florist, and a convenience store owner. It was instilled and passed down from generation to generation the importance of striving to go into business for one's self. His big brother, Avery, and his wife Dawn, ran a youth center in the Dallas/Fort Worth area. Most of his days were spent working, and if he wasn't working, he was looking for work. He often drove through the town, and as far as the next town, to see where he could offer his services. He would stop at a residence if he saw a porch in need of a paint touch-up or a set of steps with weather-worn planks. If they shook their heads to say they were not interested, he would offer to do the job for free. Then they would smile—albeit with skepticism—until he showed up a few days later to complete the task as promised. As a result, they sought him when they needed repairs in the future or recommended his services to their family and friends.

He and his daddy would sometimes go fishing in Lake Conroe. He and his buddies got together to play dominoes and cards and drink beer and talk shit. He spoke only briefly about his seven-year marriage to Annette and said keeping Christian happy was his main focus. Then they stopped and watched several minutes of a group of kids playing touch football. He made no mention of his daughter or his mother.

They walked the entire perimeter of the lake—a distance of 3.1 miles—and made it back to the truck a little over an hour later. Cynthia's feet were covered in red dust. "I see you love your sandals," he said looking down at them.

"They're easy, but I definitely should have worn tennis shoes." She hopped on the passenger seat, slapped the sandals together and removed the rock fragments caught between her toes before putting her feet in the truck.

"Well, I hope you had a good time," he said when he pulled into Mama Genie's driveway.

"I really did. Thank you again."

"This just makes me look forward to the festival with you this weekend."

"Mmm-hmm…"

"You still wanna go, don't you? I hope what I said tonight didn't put you off."

She shook her head. "No, you didn't put me off. You were just being honest. I respect that," she smiled at him. The butterflies in her stomach danced wildly. She wanted to kiss him, too, but what would be the purpose beyond that one-second moment of bliss? There could never be anything between them, and she definitely wasn't one up for a one-night stand.

Holiday walked her to the porch.

"See you later," she said. He reached for her hand and she gently squeezed his, then she felt his reluctance to let go as she tried to pull away.

"I don't expect a kiss from you, but I would like to give you a hug."

Cynthia weakened under his gaze, his eyes boring into her. "I guess I can take that," she answered.

He took one step up and slid his arms around her waist as she circled his neck with her arms. He pulled her body into his, his embrace as tight as it was gentle. Cynthia closed her eyes as he ran his strong hands up and down her back. Despite what her mind warned her, it felt damn good to be held.

He released her. "Thank you. Have a good night, okay?"

"You too." She turned and went into the house as he descended the steps.

Mama Genie had fallen asleep in front of the TV, so Cynthia went upstairs without a peep, got out of her clothes, and showered. She lay in bed hours later still wearing a smile the day spent with Holiday put on her face.

TWENTY-THREE

Holiday stood in the kitchen loading the dishwasher. He had just eaten breakfast and was trying his best to resist going outside to smoke a cigarette as he waited for Frank to get dressed so they could be on their way to work for the day. Holiday went to bed thinking about Cynthia, about having her in his arms, the unexpectedly sweet scent of her braids as he held her close, the way her body fitted against him, and he wanted to see her again.

"Mornin', son," Frank said, shuffling into the kitchen and straight to the coffee pot to start it up.

"Hey, Pop. I'll be out your way in a minute so you can fix you something. I just had me a bowl of cereal. I wasn't too hungry after all that Chinese food I ate yesterday."

"I just may have me a bowl of cereal too, then," Frank said. "We still got that Raisin Bran up there? 'Cause I don't like that mess Chris eats. That ain't nothing but candy."

"Yeah, that's what I had," Holiday pulled the box of bran down from the top of the refrigerator and set it on the counter next to Frank. He put the final dish in the dishwasher and closed the door, deciding to wait until after Frank finished his breakfast before he started the machine.

Frank said, "Howie say he gonna stop by sometime this week to take a look at the house. To see how we doing."

"Oh yeah?" Holiday took a seat at the dining table and began to flip through the week's classifieds newspaper. "He back in town?"

"Not yet, but he say he will be. Just for a day, so he's gonna swing by. He called me yesterday and told me. We talked for a good while, too. He just having fun. Say his old lady got him headed to Mexico next. He say she start planning their next trip even before they're off the other vacation." Frank laughed, bringing his bowl of cereal, a banana, and cup of coffee to the table and sitting across from Holiday. He used his spoon to slice the banana, dropping them into the bowl of Raisin Bran.

"Sounds about right," Holiday said, smiling. Then he thought about Cynthia and her love for travel. It had been a long while since he took an extended vacation and he realized he could use some time off, but, as Cynthia had said, it was not something he wanted to do by himself. Family vacations were the norm in his house growing up. His mom and dad would take him and his brother Avery someplace every summer: Disneyworld, Disneyland, Sea World, the San Diego Zoo, a road trip to Tennessee or Chicago. So when he and Annette were married—and Avery met Dawn—the tradition continued and they all traveled together as one big family. But, as the years passed, Annette grew tired of traveling with his family and wanted just the two of them, along with Christian, to spend their summer getaways together, which soon created a rift between his mother and his wife that lasted for years.

"I miss those days. Me and your mama had a lot of fun before y'all came along," Frank said. "We knew we had to do all we could before we decided to have kids, so we did a lot."

"You saying y'all stopped having fun once me and Avery came?"

"Of course not. We loved taking y'all places, seeing y'all's face light up when we told y'all what we had planned for you that summer. But when it was just me and your mama… man, we had no worries, no sense of time or money. Whatever we wanted to do, we did it. Vegas. D.C. Atlantic City. Cancun. Miami."

Holiday watched his dad's eyes glaze over at the memory.

"So when we had y'all, it just added to the fun. She loved being able to take her family on vacation because she didn't get to do that when she was a kid, y'know? And we didn't get to do too much in my family, either. Too many of us. Then when Christian came along, and Avery's boys… aww man. When we all got together, it was like reliving those times with just the four of us."

Holiday nodded. "We need to get back to that. Maybe we can call Avery and see if he wanna plan something for next summer."

Frank grinned. "You want to?"

"Yeah, why not? Maybe even as early as Thanksgiving. A Thanksgiving vacation instead of just dinner. We can switch it up."

"That would be so nice. Me, you, Chris, Avery, the boys, and Dawn."

Holiday closed the classifieds. "Well, don't be so quick to count Christian in until I talk to Annette."

Frank looked at him over the rim of his coffee cup as he sipped. "Son, I thought I'd never have to say this to you, but I'm kinda glad you finally left her alone. You know I'm all about keeping your family together, but Annette was just downright mean a lot of times, and I didn't like it. And you know I was through after the way she acted towards your mama."

"I know, Pop," Holiday replied solemnly.

"You know all of us been close all your lives, always doing things together, but here she come saying she wanna do stuff with her own family. We understood what she was saying, and me and Savannah had no problem with y'all vacationing alone, but to just give up on the family tradition altogether? It broke Savannah's heart."

Holiday sat quiet, stroking his goatee.

"And now she want you to bend over backwards and be at her beck and call. Blaming you for what happened to Laila and using it against you."

Guilt filled Holiday at the mention of his daughter. "Pop, she just—"

Frank cut him off. "Now… that Cynthia girl. You seem to be really into her. Maybe you can bring her along with us on the trip." He wiggled his eyebrows.

Holiday exhaled, glad Frank wanted to talk about something else already. "You are something else, Pop. How many times do I have to tell you? She's only here for the summer. She's going back home in a few weeks."

Frank pushed his empty bowl of cereal to the side. "So what? She can't come back in November?"

Holiday shook his head. "It ain't even like that. I can't just ask this woman to go on vacation with us. We barely know each other. We're only getting to know each other since she's here."

"November is three months away. I'm sure you'll know each other good enough by then. Shoot, I may even have me a lady friend by that time and I can bring her with us, too."

Holiday chuckled. "Pop, let's not make any plans to invite extra people until we talk to Avery first. We need to make sure him and Dawn are even interested in a family trip with us." He got up from the table to put Frank's bowl in the dishwasher to start the clean cycle. "Are you ready so we can go now?"

Frank shook his head. "Wait. I wanna drink me one more cup of coffee."

TWENTY-FOUR

Cynthia smelled the biscuits as soon as she opened her eyes. She could hear Mama Genie closing cabinets and moving pots around in the kitchen and her stomach immediately began to growl at the thought of the big, country breakfast she knew would be waiting for her downstairs. She picked up her phone from the bedside table. It was a little after eight a.m. There were no missed calls, no voice mail messages. She got out of bed and pulled back the curtains. The sky was overcast. *No wonder I slept so good,* she thought. His green truck wasn't parked in the yard next door, but she smiled anyway at the thought that it might soon be there. She walked across the hall to take a shower and brush her teeth. Back in her room, she opened a drawer and decided on a pair of black capri leggings and red sleeveless tunic to wear. She unfastened the tie around her braids, letting them cascade down her shoulders and back, and then slipped her feet into some flat sandals.

"Hey, Mama Genie," she said once she entered the living room. Mama Genie was sitting in her favorite wingback chair, the television on the morning news.

"Hey yourself," she said, smiling.

Cynthia walked over and kissed her on the forehead. "You sleep good last night?" She sat down on the sofa next to Mama Genie's chair.

"Yeah, I slept pretty good."

"I did, too."

"I'm trying to listen at this weatherman now 'cause it look like it's gonna rain out there today."

"Yeah, I know," Cynthia said. "It wasn't too hot last night though."

"What did Holiday say about the A/C man?"

Cynthia's eyes grew big. "Oh lord, Mama Genie! I totally forgot to ask him about it."

Mama Genie frowned. "I thought that was the whole purpose for you going over there yesterday."

"I know, but it must've slipped my mind once I got there. His daddy was there. He introduced me to him. Mr. Frank seems nice."

"And then y'all hung out all yesterday evening and you still forgot?"

Cynthia shook her head. "I completely forgot, Mama Genie. Sorry. But I promise to ask him about it today if he comes by."

"What's that all about anyway?" Mama Genie looked at her.

"What?"

"You wanting to hang out with him. You was gone near-bout the whole day yesterday."

"Mama Genie, we just went down to the lake. It's nothing."

"Nothing, huh? I'm sure Jonathan would be pretty upset if he knowed about it," her grandmother laughed.

Cynthia folded her arms across her chest. "Jonathan has female friends. Him and his coworkers hang out all the time. He trusts me just like I…trust…him," she said, the bold lie like lead on her tongue.

"Uhn-huh," Mama Genie said dismissively. "Your breakfast is on the stove."

"Thanks," Cynthia said, getting up from the couch and going to the kitchen. There were biscuits just as she had thought, grits, scrambled eggs, and an Eckrich smoked sausage split down the middle and fried to a scorched crisp on the skinned side. She poured a glass of grape juice and took a seat at the table.

"What you and Sister Nash got planned for today?"

"Chile, we don't know yet. But she call me early this morning and told me she gonna stop by later. Probably do some more shopping. Well… she'll be doing the shopping, while I'll be doing the watching. She can shop every day. I told her she ain't gonna have too much house left to live in with all that stuff she buy."

Cynthia pulled the skin off the sausage since it was too tough to cut with her fork. "I came down thinking I was gonna spend some time with my grandma, but here you are leaving me to be by myself almost every day," Cynthia said playfully.

"Oh, don't you even try it," Mama Genie cackled. "You the one been leaving me, going out all day and all hours of the night, hanging out with Holiday."

Cynthia tried not to blush, but Holiday was all in her head. "Well… maybe we can do something when you and Sister Nash get back. If you're not gone too long. You wanna go to the movies?"

Her grandmother's face lit up. "Chile, I can't remember the last time I been to the movies. Sister Nash would probably love that. You reckon she can come with us?"

"Sure, she can come with us," Cynthia said, hoping the reluctance she felt didn't resonate in her reply. She could hear the one-hundred-and-one questions sure to come from Sister Nash now.

"We should probably go early before the rain catch us. What you think?"

"That's all right with me. I don't have anything else to do."

"Alright. I'll call her now and see if she can come sooner," Mama Genie said excitedly and picked up the cordless phone from its cradle on the end table next to her.

The gray sky outside cast a gloomy hue over the room, but she didn't want to turn on the bright overhead light, so Cynthia pulled the small wooden chair over to the window. She powered up her laptop to check the application status again for all the school districts she applied to. Nothing had changed. She checked her email. Having never applied for a corporate job, she was not sure how the application process worked. She half-expected there to at least be a confirmation of receipt of her résumé for the positions she'd been interested in. Still nothing. She logged on to review her bank account. The checks for the Freon and trip charge had already cleared, putting her balance just one purchase away from the triple-digit zone. She'd underestimated how much an A/C repair would cost, so her initial plan to charge it to her credit card and think about the cost later went out the window as soon as the repairman quoted a four-digit price. But she didn't think it was fair for Mama Genie to try to foot the total bill on her small, fixed income.

Cynthia sat up straighter when she heard a vehicle door close. She looked out and, just like that, the butterflies began to flutter in her stomach at the sight of him. He got out of the truck and went to the bed to remove material and supplies. She watched him enter and exit the house, taking in slabs of granite, buckets of something, his toolbox, the cooler. *So damn fine.*

Frank eventually got out of the truck but stood with his phone at his ear, laughing and babbling away with someone.

Holiday looked towards Mama Genie's front porch and then right up to her window as if he just knew she would be sitting there.

His smile thrilled Cynthia as much as the impending rain.

"How you doing?" he said.

"Good. How are you?" He laid the step ladder down in the grass and started towards her window. *That walk. I could watch it all day.*

"I'm cool. What you up to this morning? Were you sitting there waiting for me?" A sly grin crossed his lips.

"Yeah," she said. "I was, actually." She set her laptop on the bed and stood up, pushing the curtains to the side.

"Well you just made my day already, because I couldn't wait to get over here to see you too."

"I need the telephone number for the A/C repairman you were telling me about."

"Oh," he said. "That's it?"

"Yeah."

"Well I thought it was because you were excited to see me."

"You don't strike me as a man of arrogance. What would make you think that?" she asked, teasing him.

He appeared caught off guard by the question and just stood looking up at her. "Well… I mean… I thought we enjoyed each other's company. So I look forward to coming over here every day now for the chance to spend some time with you. I just thought you might've felt the same way."

She nodded. "I was thinking about that. We have been spending a lot of time together, but now I'm not so sure that's a good thing."

"And why is that," he asked, disappointment in his face.

"Because I don't even know if you have a girlfriend or not. Or if you're married."

"You think that's the type of man I am?"

Cynthia shrugged. "Well… it's not like we've really talked about it, so I don't know." She had only meant to tease him, but now that the questions were in the air she realized it should have been one of the first things she asked him the first time he invited her over to talk. But then, why would his relationship status have mattered if they were just two adults sitting and talking?

Holiday shook his head as if in disbelief.

"For all I know you could be going home to your woman at the end of the day after being with me."

"That's cold."

When he didn't offer anything else, Cynthia said, "The other guy told us we need a whole new unit, but I want a second opinion. So I would like to talk to the guy you know if you don't mind giving me his number."

Holiday placed his hands loosely on his hips. "So you saying we can't hang out together no more?"

"Honestly, I think you're a sweet guy, but why are we doing this?"

"Hey there, Cynthia," Frank called out to her.

She waved. "How you doing, Mister Fr— I mean… Frank."

Frank chuckled. "Doing good, dear. You all right?"

"Yeah, just relaxing today."

"What my son begging you for now?"

She grinned and looked at Holiday shaking his head.

"Go on in the house. I'll be there in a minute, Pop," Holiday told him.

"See… that's the response of a guilty man," Frank laughed and went into the house.

"He is hilarious," Cynthia said.

"He's crazy. Now back to what we were saying though…"

"Mmm-hmm?"

"I'm a little hurt you think I would do something like that."

Cynthia arched a brow. "Well… you haven't even denied it yet, either, so…"

He grinned at her, licking his lips, making her scream inside her head because he was the sexiest. "Come down here."

"For what?"

"Because we need to talk."

"No, I don't need to come down there. Your response—or lack thereof—just told me all I need to know."

"Are you messing with me right now?"

"No, I'm being serious," she said.

He clasped his hands behind his back and Cynthia tried not to stare at the way his shirt stretched across his chest. She tried to stop her eyes from traveling the length of his leg from his waist on down to his scuffed work boot.

"Cynthia."

And the way he said her name almost made her forget what it was she needed to hear.

She looked at him.

"I don't have a girlfriend. And I'm not married."

She waved her hand, sucking her teeth. "Then why didn't you just say that?"

"Because I can't believe you would think that about me. If I wasn't a single man I wouldn't be asking you out. I wouldn't've told you I wanna kiss you."

"Yeah, yeah. That's what they all say."

"Oh, man. You're killing me," he said, rubbing his hand up and down his chest.

She rolled her eyes. "Please stop the dramatics. You're not very good at it," she laughed.

"Cynthia. Come down here."

At the way he said her name again, she couldn't hide her blush. "Here I come."

* * *

"I feel like I should make you sign a promissory note so you don't try to skip out on me this weekend for the festival."

"Hey, I just need to know I'm not spending time with somebody else's husband."

Holiday chuckled. "I hear you."

They sat on the back porch—Cynthia in a chair and he on the steps with his back against the railing. Frank was inside whistling loudly along to Stevie Wonder's *Master Blaster*.

"So… are you going to give me the guy's number or are you going to call him for me?"

"Oh! That's right." He pulled his cell phone out of his pocket. "See, that's how distracted I get when I'm around you. I forget what I'm supposed to be doing sometimes."

She shook her head and smiled.

"And, really… it's my buddy Jesse Lee I'm calling. He's the one that knows the HVAC guy." He dialed his friend and after several seconds he left a voicemail message for Jesse Lee to return his call.

"I will let you know as soon as I hear back from him," he said.

"Okay."

"You look nice today," he said, slipping the phone back in his pocket. "Well… you always do, but you look good in red."

There he goes again, looking at me with those sultry eyes. "Do you ever comb your hair?" she asked him.

He laughed, his head falling back against the railing.

She loved it, though. The kinky curliness of his hair. His edges lined with precision.

"I do. But then I just let it do its own thing sometimes."

"I like it," she smiled.

"Thanks."

Cynthia crossed her legs as his gaze fell on her orange-painted toes.

"Is that your experience with men though?" he looked up at her.

"What?"

"Married men."

"No, I've never been with a married man."

"Then why did you say 'that's what they all say'? You pretty much accused me of lying to you."

"I just know some men are not completely honest about what they are doing sometimes. And I don't want to be caught up in the crossfire." She thought about what she went through with Dorian. She thought about Jonathan.

"Did somebody do you wrong?"

She gathered the braids to lift them off her neck, wondering why she thought wearing them down her back was a good idea now that he was making her nervous and hot. "It's not something I like to think about, but yeah. I'll be honest with you and tell you I have." She let the braids fall.

"That's messed up. So… what? You found out he was already involved with somebody else after y'all got together?"

"No," she said. "The other women came *after* we were together."

"It was more than one woman?"

She shook her head. "No, this was different men."

"Wow. So you've come across more than a few players? That's sad."

"It is sad, but it is what it is. I'm over it."

"Over what?"

"What do you mean 'what'? I'm over those relationships."

"Oh. I thought you were saying you were over men. I know women like to cut everybody off after they've been through a few bad experiences."

"Can you blame them? Get burned once or twice and you learn to not play with fire."

"But that's not fair. You can't put everybody down for the actions of a few."

"I'm not putting everybody down, but I know now everything is not what it seems. Even when you think things are going good."

"Well I hope you don't get rid of me. I have nothing to hide from you."

Cynthia smiled, raising an eyebrow at him.

"You want me to get you a drink?"

"No, I'm gonna head back over now. Me and my grandma are hanging out today. We may go to the movies."

"That's cool. What're y'all going to see?"

Cynthia stood up from her chair, prompting him to stand up too. "I don't even know what's showing, but I'm sure we'll find something. Mama Genie is just excited to be going. She's already invited Sister Nash to come with us."

"Nice."

"So, I will see you later," she said, moving towards the steps. He reached for her hand as she passed him.

"Have fun."

TWENTY-FIVE

The crackle and rumble of thunder vibrating the whole house woke Holiday out of his sleep. Yesterday's gray skies only brought a light drizzle towards the evening, but now torrential rain beat heavily on the roof and slapped his window. He rolled over on his back, stretched, and immediately thought about Cynthia. She loved thunderstorms and he wondered if she was the type of person crazy enough to be sitting outside on the porch watching as the lightning flashed all around her.

He wished he could be there with her, to see what she found so special about a thunderstorm. He had no aversions to stormy weather, but he'd just never heard of anybody admitting to preferring rain over sunshine. The notion was new to him.

He picked up his cell phone to call her, but realized he didn't even have her telephone number. Jesse Lee had not called him back, either, so he dialed him again, knowing he was an early riser.

"Holiday man, I was just about to call you," Jesse Lee said as soon as he picked up.

"Yeah right."

"Hey, you know I be busy around here, but this rain got me feeling lazy as hell right now. What's up?"

"I need you to call your partner—the guy that does HVAC—and

see if he can take a look at this A/C for me."

"Y'all's A/C ain't running right?"

"Naw, it's for a lady friend."

"Lady friend? Who? Annette?"

Holiday shook his head. "No, it's not Annette. Just a friend of mine."

"Why haven't I heard about this friend? Hell, I thought your ass was celibate the way you been walking around here lately. I thought you gave up women altogether."

Holiday laughed and threw the covers off, sitting up on the edge of the bed. He should have taken a bathroom break before he called Jesse Lee. "I just met her a few weeks ago. She live next door to that house down in Madison we been working on."

"Oh, so you trying to make something happen? What's her name? I might know her."

"Man, you crazy. Her name's Cynthia."

"Cynthia what?"

"I don't even know myself. I told you I just met the woman. And I doubt you might know her. She don't live here."

"I thought you just said she live next door to the house?"

"I meant her grandmother lives next door. She's just here for the summer. We hung out a few times."

"Oh *really now*? Well, is she fine or what?"

"Oh yeah, she fine. Fine as hell. Beautiful. Sweet. All that." He stood up and headed towards the bathroom, his bladder feeling like it was going to explode.

"Well, shit," Jesse Lee said, "why don't you bring her by the house Friday night? Yoauna just got a promotion on her job and she having a few of her girlfriends over to celebrate. Around six-thirty, seven o'clock. She want me to be there to throw some stuff on the grill, but I ain't trying to be the only man there with all them women. You know how that shit can go," he laughed.

Holiday balanced the phone between his head and shoulder as he used the bathroom. "Well, I'll have to ask her if she wanna come," he replied, recalling what Cynthia had said to him about them spending too much time together. "But it ain't no problem for me to come and hang with you a couple of hours. I can do that. But are you gonna call your partner?" He flushed the toilet and went to the sink to wash his hands.

"Oh yeah, I'll call him real quick and call you right back."

Frank was already awake and sitting at the dining table with his cup of coffee when Holiday entered the kitchen. He hadn't bothered to get dressed yet for the day since he knew Frank would not be interested in leaving the house until the rain slacked up. "Hey, Pop."

"Mornin', son."

"That thunder woke you up too, huh?"

"Yeah, it's pretty bad out there, and it don't look like it's gonna stop anytime soon."

Holiday decided on cereal again and poured himself a bowl and a glass of orange juice. "So I guess that means you're not trying to go anywhere anytime soon, either."

"And you guessed right."

Holiday chuckled and sat down. "I'll work on the billing and account reconciliation then. Is all your receipts in the drawer?"

"Yeah, I put what I had in there."

"Good. I just remembered I need to deposit Ms. Washington's check."

"Oh yeah," Frank said. "You might wanna hurry up and do that, son. She probably put a stop payment on it after what you did."

"Don't start that this morning, Pop. I did nothing to Ms. Washington."

"And that's the point. You hurt that woman's feelings. You see she went out to work in her garden and didn't say another word to us until it was time for us to leave." Frank laughed.

Holiday shook his head, didn't bother responding.

"She just knew she had you. Got all dressed up real nice for you, showing you she still flexible at her age. Imagine that."

Holiday raised his hand. "Go on with that, Pop. This is crazy."

Frank got up from the table to put his dishes away. "Old Ms. Washington. You know she over there scheming right now, figuring out how to get you when we go back to do her shelves."

"I'm not even trying to think about that this morning."

* * *

Holiday sat down at the computer desk to begin the dull task of recording their expenses and balancing the business account—something he was still not used to since his mother was the family bookkeeper and was better at organizing and keeping records. He opened the drawer and pulled out the lump of half-folded, half-crumpled, grease-stained receipts Frank left behind, shaking his head because he knew probably half of them were no longer legible.

He worked for nearly an hour before Cynthia crept into his thoughts. Single. No kids. Never been married. Passionate. Likes to have fun.

So what is her story?

He thought of her revelation to him that she had been betrayed—more than once.

What type of man would cheat on a woman like that?

TWENTY-SIX

On Friday morning Holiday got up thankful the stormy weather had passed. The rain lasted for two days, forcing him and Frank to stay inside most of the time. He took the opportunity to relax and watch television until he fell asleep on the living room sofa. He had to pick up Christian for the festival, but he also needed to see Cynthia about the party at Jesse Lee's.

And it didn't dawn on him that Jessie Lee did not call him back as he said he would until he pulled into Mama Genie's driveway.

Cynthia appeared at the screen door before he could even knock, and it took all the strength he had within him to not pull her into his arms. She was clad in one of those fitted T-shirt dress things again. This time white, this time thinner—like she was still dressed for bed. Those pretty toes had been re-painted an electric blue. To him, they looked good enough to lick.

"Well this is the earliest I've ever seen you over here," she said. "Did your friend call you back? What did he say?"

"Yeah, about that. He never did get back with me, so I had to call him. He told me he would get in touch with the guy, but he still haven't called me back yet."

"Oh."

"I'm sorry about that, but I'm definitely getting in touch with him today."

"Alright, because if not, I guess I will just have to call somebody else to take a look at it."

"Naw, this guy Jesse Lee knows is pretty good. But that's not the only reason why I came over here."

"What now?"

"Jesse Lee told me his wife is having some of her friends over tonight. They're gonna have a little get-together, and he told me I should bring you with me."

She raised her brow. "What does this Jesse Lee know about me?"

"Well, I told him I needed the guy's number for my lady friend. And that's when he started asking me about you."

She folded her arms across her chest, leaning into the door frame, her lips forming into a playful smirk. "Lady friend, huh? Is that what I am to you?"

"I know it's been a short while, but yeah, I consider you a friend."

"Hmm…"

"I'm headed now to pick up Christian so we can spend a few hours at the festival, but I'll be back tonight. And I know you said I'm taking up too much of your time, but honestly, I can't help it. I'm gonna just keep asking for a little of your time until you flat-out tell me *'no'*."

She laughed and he knew he had her.

"What time should I be ready?"

"I need your telephone number to call you. I wanted to talk to you the other day during the storm and didn't even have your number to call. You enjoyed these days of rain didn't you?"

"Mmm-hmm… You know I did."

Holiday wondered if she was offering a little innuendo underneath that innocent grin. He saved her number in his phone as she called it out to him.

"I just dialed it so you have mine," he said before he left, and was already looking forward to seeing her again when he got into his truck.

* * *

"Mason, try not to feed him a bunch of junk food today, okay? I'm moving towards a vegetarian—possibly vegan—diet and going to start weaning Christian off all that crap he likes too."

"Vegetarian diet? C'mon, Annette. What are you talking about?"

"Paula's been vegan for almost two years now, and she said it's changed her life. She feels better, she looks better. So it just may help me, too. I will be less stressed. Have more mental clarity."

"Annette, he's just a kid. He doesn't need to be on no vegetarian diet. That's crazy."

"Crazy? It's not crazy at all. I want my son to take his health seriously. It's never too early to start teaching him healthy habits."

"He's still growing. Eating junk food is part of being a kid."

"No, he needs to know now eating all that unhealthy food can lead to problems later."

"That's understandable, but why vegetarian? Why not just teach him to eat more good foods than bad foods?"

"I just want him to be health-conscious, Mason. I'm just letting you know the lifestyle we're leaning towards. This wasn't meant to seek your approval."

Holiday shook his head. He stood on the front portico with Annette as he waited for Christian to change his clothes at his mother's request for something more decent than the tank top and basketball shorts he'd initially worn.

"Well… if that's what you want, then, hey…. I just don't think it's fair to him. What will it look like for him to have to eat vegetables and stuff when his friends are sitting around him eating hamburgers, and pizza, and stuff like that? How you think that's gonna make him feel? C'mon, Annette. He already told me you won't let him tryout for football. You gotta let him do something he wanna do. He's a kid."

"That's right, he is a kid. And we need to guide him to where he needs to go. Football is too physical. You see how some of those men turn out. They get concussions, but don't see the effects until later in life when they're trying to figure out why they're depressed and suicidal."

"Annette, you can't think like that. If that's the case, we shouldn't do anything in life if we're scared about what could happen."

"Mason, I want the best for my son. I want him to think beyond what he sees Maximillion do. And those entertainers on TV."

"I want the best for him, too, but this—"

"I'm ready now, Daddy," Christian appeared at the door wearing cargo shorts and a polo style shirt.

Annette threw her arms around his shoulders. "Yeah, this is what I'm talking about. Basketball shorts are for playing basketball, right? That's not something you wear when going out." She kissed his forehead. "Have fun, okay, baby?"

"Yes, ma'am."

"And remember what I told you, Christian," she called after him as he ran off towards the truck.

Holiday said, "We won't be too long."

"Call me before you come," she replied.

* * *

"I think we pretty much rode every ride now, son. And I know you're tired of carrying that big ol' thing around."

Christian hefted the oversized gorilla he'd won in his arms as they strolled aimlessly through the park. "Yeah, but can we come back tomorrow?"

"Come back tomorrow? Why didn't you tell me you wanted to come more than once? I could've got the monthly pass. Last year you said just one day was good enough."

"I know, but it was more fun this time I guess."

"Well, I wish you would've told me sooner, but I got something to do tomorrow, son. We can't."

"Oh okay," Christian said sadly.

Holiday rubbed the top of his head. He pulled out his mobile phone to check the time. It was only three o'clock. "You wanna go to The Game Room for a little while?"

Christian's face lit up. "Alright!"

Fifteen minutes later they arrived at the town's arcade. It was nearly empty and a tall and lanky teen with severe pock acne promptly approached them to say pizzas were buy one get one half off for the day. But Christian told him he was still stuffed from the festival food and Holiday was not in the mood for pizza that had been sitting under a heat lamp for hours. Holiday purchased some tokens and they headed straight for the air hockey table.

"Your mama told me y'all about to go on a serious diet change."

"Yeah."

"How do you feel about that?" Holiday pushed the puck towards Christian, giving him first advantage.

Christian shrugged. "She say it's gonna make me healthy. I don't know."

"Do you know what a vegetarian is?"

"Uhn-huh. It means I can't eat meat."

"Yeah, and so are you gonna be able to give that up? That means no more good food with me and Grandpa. And Max and Solone. Your friends at school. You'll be eating salads and fruit while everybody else is eating pizza and hot dogs."

A swift flick of Christian's wrist sent the puck into Holiday's goal, earning Christian one point.

"Oh! You got me already!"

Christian laughed. "I can eat cheese pizza," he said. "That's vegetarian. And Ramen noodles. I can just eat that every day."

"Well, your mama may have you give up dairy, too, so no cheese either. And I don't know about those Ramen noodles every day. Too much salt."

"No cheese?!"

Holiday rushed the puck across the table, slamming it into Christian's goal. "Caught you slipping," he teased him.

"Don't worry. I'll get you back." They volleyed the puck back and forth between them, both safely guarding their goals, until Holiday relaxed and let Christian win so they could move on to something else.

"I just want you to know how hard it might be for you to get used to eating like that. I'm hoping she'll change her mind, but... since she's the one cooking your meals every night, I can't help you."

"I know. But maybe it won't be so hard. So long as I can still eat Lucky Charms I'm good, Daddy."

Holiday laughed and followed him to the hoops basketball machine.

TWENTY-SEVEN

"So *now* where you going?"

Cynthia laughed and plopped down on the sofa next to Mama Genie's chair. "Just to a backyard barbecue."

"With Holiday I suppose?"

"Yeah, his friends are having a party and he asked me to go with him."

"Uhn-huh. Like I said… you really been hanging out with him a lot."

"It's just something to do while I'm here. I may as well get out and have some kind of fun since nobody's calling me for a job, my funds are low, and we still gotta get this A/C fixed."

Mama Genie sighed. "Yeah, I know. But don't you worry yourself too much. We're doing just fine without it. And I'm sure somebody gonna call you eventually. You know you can always come back here for a little while if you need to until you find something."

"Yeah, I know," she said wearily.

It wasn't long before she heard his truck pull up outside and she quickly got up, deciding to meet Holiday before he had the chance to make it to the porch because she knew he would want to say hello to Mama Genie and Mama Genie would want to hold a conversation, and ask questions, and all that. "We shouldn't be out too late, I'm guessing, but I'm riding with him, so…." Cynthia kissed Mama Genie's cheek. "See you later."

"Uhn-huh." Mama Genie waved her off.

"You just snatch my breath away every time I see you," Holiday said, assisting her into the truck. "You definitely know what colors look good on you."

"Thank you," she smiled. "I try." He closed the passenger door and she reached to turn the air vents on her side of the dashboard directly on her. She was a ball of nerves already and she didn't understand why. Was it because she was about to meet some of his friends? Or was it because these outings with him were beginning to feel more like date nights than just two friends hanging out? As she dressed she attempted to convince herself she was not trying to look extra special for him—that the multicolor, tribal print maxi dress she'd chosen just happened to be the one she was in the mood for this evening. Something long, something flowy. Something offering just a hint of sexiness with its cutout detail around the waist.

She took a *Mentos Fresh Mint Gum* from the pack sitting in his cup holder and popped it into her mouth.

"I'm warning you now… my buddy Jesse Lee is kinda crazy. He got a mouth on him," he said when he sat in the driver's seat.

"Oh yeah?"

"Yeah, say anything that come to mind. I don't know how his wife been putting up with him all these years, but she loves that fool to death."

Cynthia laughed. "Is she like him?"

"Not really. I mean… she can get just as rowdy with him, but for the most part, she's more chill. You'll see."

After a mostly silent ride with a jazz radio station playing as their background noise they pulled up to a beautiful ranch style home with a long double driveway already packed with cars. Holiday parked at the edge of the driveway and got out to open her door. Music and high-pitched laughter filled the air as Cynthia followed him along a pebble stoned sidewalk to the backyard.

"Sounds like they're already in full party mode," Cynthia said.

The backyard was even more beautiful with its cabana style patio and charming, modern rustic décor. The low-wattage landscape lamps throughout lent a sexy ambience. Cynthia noticed right away there were nearly a dozen or so women in attendance and only one man, who was twirling a Jada Pinkett-Smith look-alike around as they danced near the grill. An immediate hush fell over the women sitting around cross-legged, fruity drinks in their hands, as Holiday greeted them all at once before guiding Cynthia over to the lovely dancing couple.

"Holiday!" the woman grinned, dropping her partner's hands, and opened her arms to hug Holiday. "I didn't know you were coming. How you doing, sweetie?"

"Doing good." He gently nudged Cynthia forward. "This is Cynthia. Cynthia, this is Yoauna."

Cynthia held out her hand for a shake, but Yoauna pulled her in for a hug. "Nice to meet you, Cynthia," and she stepped back, looking at Cynthia's dress. "Oh I *love* this dress. Turn around, let me see."

It was awkward and Cynthia knew the other women were staring her down, but she turned around as requested to give Yoauna a full view of the dress.

"Oh, sister, *you are wearing that*. Umph!"

"Thank you," she smiled.

"My turn," the man said, and stepped up to Cynthia to give her a hug, too.

Holiday said, "And this is Jesse Lee."

Jesse Lee squeezed Cynthia, taking in a deep breath before he let her go. "Damn, you smell good! What's that you wearing? I need to buy that shit for my wife."

Cynthia laughed.

"Nevermind him," Yoauna grabbed Cynthia's arm. "Come on. Let me introduce you to my girlfriends. These two will probably disappear into the house in a minute," she said about Jesse Lee and Holiday.

A few of the women gave a tight-lipped 'hello' as Yoauna rattled off their names—names Cynthia knew she would not remember and would have to be reminded of the remainder of the night.

"Can I get you something to drink?" Yoauna asked her.

"What do you have? You have any wine?"

"Yeah, we do. We got appetizers over there on the table, too. If you want some. Better yet, why don't you just sit down and I'll bring it over to you?"

"Thanks." Cynthia took a seat and the women eased back into their chatter, not bothering to include her in the sisterhood conversations.

A few minutes passed and she watched Yoauna talking to another lady as she filled a small plate, and Cynthia considered going over to get her own wine when the woman sitting next to her said, "I hope you don't mind me asking, but are you two together?"

Here we go. Cynthia turned towards the woman—a pale-skinned lady with hazel cat eyes and plump lips colored fire-engine red. Her hair pulled back into a very tight bun only accentuated her generous forehead even more. The gold loops in her ears were big enough to wear as bracelets. She was a beauty. "We rode here together, yes."

"No, I mean… as in *together, together*. Y'know? A couple?"

Cynthia prepared herself for the worst. She knew how gossipy a lot of women could be, but if there was something that could affect her view of Holiday and the little she knew about him, she was curious. "Uh… no, we're just friends."

The woman stuck her hand out to Cynthia. "I'm Chanel."

Surprisingly, it was one of the names she remembered because it suited her perfectly. She *looked like* a Chanel. "Nice to meet you again," Cynthia laughed anxiously.

The woman cleared her throat. "Me and him dated for a little while."

"Oh," was all Cynthia could say. *Are congratulations in order or…?*

"But I had to let him go. I couldn't do it no more."

Cynthia nodded, wondering where this was going.

"He's a good man, but won't open up. Won't let nobody get too close to him."

"Oh… okay."

"Is he still running behind his wife?"

Cynthia's breath caught in her throat. "Umm… I'm not sure what you mean." *Yoauna, please bring the damn wine already!*

"Y'know…" Chanel continued, "what happened to his daughter was sad and all, but I told him he can't keep beating hisself up about it. You got to move on at some point. Move on with your life."

Cynthia looked over at Holiday. His back was to her as Jesse Lee held the grill top open showing him what he had cooking. He hadn't told her much about his daughter at all other than she'd passed away. "Yeah, it is sad."

"How long y'all been friends? I don't think I've ever seen you around here."

"Not long at all. Actually, we just met this summer. I'm here visiting family."

"Oh, so y'all just hooking up while you're here in town?"

She didn't wait for Cynthia to answer, and said, "That's how he is though. He makes every woman he come in contact with feel special. He try to wine and dine you, make you feel like y'all going somewhere, but then you figure out he's just using you to pass time while he work through his feelings."

"Hunh," Cynthia huffed.

Chanel raised her margarita glass—complete with a cute little umbrella—to her lips, sucking slowly from the straw. She set the glass down on the table in front of them. "I told him I would be happy to give him another baby so he can get over the one he lost, but…"

Get over the one he lost? What kind of insensitive mess is that?

"He just couldn't make up his mind where he wanted to be so…"

"I'm sorry, I think Yoauna forgot about my drink and I'm dying of thirst right now," Cynthia said and got up to head towards the appetizer table.

Yoauna met her halfway, that mega-watt smile of hers on full blast. "Here you go, sweetie. Sorry it took me so long."

"No problem." Cynthia took the wine and plate of finger foods from her and immediately took a sip of the chilled drink. "I heard you got a promotion. Congratulations."

"Oh, thank you. It's been a long time coming, but I worked my ass off to finally earn my degree. I had to so I could move up to something else. It was definitely time to make some improvements."

"What do you do if you don't mind me asking?"

"I'm a sales rep now. In home healthcare."

"Oh, okay. That sounds fun."

"I went from answering their phones and filing their paperwork to selling their services," she beamed proudly.

"That's great."

"What type of work you do?"

"I teach," Cynthia said, "but I don't think I'll be doing that too much longer. I'm looking for a career change."

"Oh. It's that bad, huh?" Yoauna smiled. "I heard that. A couple of my girlfriends over there are teachers, too. One loves it, though.

But Trish? She said we might hear about her on the news one day for strangling somebody's child."

Cynthia laughed and took a bite of a strawberry from her plate. "I love this patio. It's beautiful."

"Thank you, girl. Me and my husband entertain a lot and I told him I wanted it to look real good back here so we can hang out when it's nice outside. Holiday did a damn good job. We get compliments all the time." At the blank look on Cynthia's face, Yoauna said, "Oh, he didn't tell you? Chile, Holiday did this patio."

Cynthia looked around again. *Of course he did.*

"That man knows he's talented. Hands of magic." Jesse Lee and Holiday were going into the house when Yoauna yelled out to them. "Hey! Y'all supposed to be the hosts. Have y'all checked to make sure these ladies' glasses are filled? If they need another round of appetizers?"

"Shit, I thought I was just supposed to cook the damn food. I didn't know I had to serve it too," Jesse Lee said, and everyone laughed.

"Yeah, baby. It would be nice if you can do that. I don't want my ladies to have to lift a finger tonight."

"I don't know why not. They came here to celebrate you. They should be the ones getting off they asses and serving you if you ask me. And these steaks wasn't cheap," Jesse Lee chuckled.

"Whatever, Jesse!" somebody yelled.

"It won't hurt y'all to cater to us tonight," another one said.

Jesse Lee walked over and put his arms around his wife. "Whatever you want me to do, baby."

Yoauna stuck her tongue out at him and he licked it before pulling her away to go dance. "Girl, this our song," she said over her shoulder as she sashayed away with him.

"They are too cute," Cynthia said when Holiday came to stand beside her.

"Yeah. That's real love between those two. You enjoying yourself?"

"Mmm-hmm. This is cool." She wouldn't mention the standoffish attitudes of some of the ladies. Or ask him about Chanel—not yet anyway. She swallowed down the remainder of the red wine and he took her glass.

"You want some more?"

"Thank you," she said when he returned and they took a seat on the loveseat behind them. "How long have they been married?" Cynthia asked, watching Jesse Lee and Yoauna all but grind on each other.

Holiday blew out a breath. "I couldn't even tell you, but it's been some years. They were high school sweethearts."

"That's cool. They look like they still have a lot of fun together. Do they have any kids?"

"A son. He's in college somewhere up north. He's a brainiac kid too. Real smart. Ivy League school, but I forget which one. I mess with Jesse all the time and tell him ain't no way that boy is his son. He's too smart to be."

Cynthia laughed. "Well, maybe he gets his smarts from his mama."

Holiday shook his head. "I don't know. Maybe. You should see him though. They embarrass him because of how crazy they are sometimes."

Cynthia looked at the good-looking couple. Jesse Lee had his back to Yoauna as he shook his hips, while she playfully slapped at them like a cowgirl. "I love it," Cynthia laughed again.

Just then Yoauna looked around, "Uhn-uhn! Ladies, y'all gotta get up. This is a party! Come on up here with us!" and she went to her girlfriends sitting down and pulled them up one by one to go to the dance floor, and then walked over to Cynthia and grabbed her by the hand. "You too, Ms. Sexy Dress. Come on, Holiday," she said, but he declined, so Cynthia handed him her glass and plate and followed Yoauna.

They danced through three songs before Yoauna let the ladies shuffle back to their seats to be served.

Jesse Lee said, "Alright, put a fist in the air if you want steak, two fingers if you want salmon."

"What if we don't eat red meat or like fish?" one of the ladies asked.

"Then you shit outta luck 'cause that's all we got!" An eruption of laughter followed.

"Can we have both?" another one asked.

"Baby, you better handle your girlfriends or I will take my ass in the house and sit down," he said to Yoauna, laughing.

Holiday got up from his seat. "Let me help out with the drinks."

It wasn't long before they were all served: grilled steak or salmon or both, with wild rice, mixed vegetables, and melt-in-your-mouth croissants. Mini fruit tarts for dessert. An hour later Yoauna was pulling everybody back to the dance floor where she and Jesse Lee led them all in back-to-back line dances. Yoauna was even able to convince Holiday to get up for one song, and Cynthia told herself she wouldn't be bothered by it when Chanel slithered up next to him. As the hours passed Cynthia lost count of how many songs they danced to and how many glasses of wine she'd had.

More than half of the women had already left when she and Holiday approached Jesse Lee and Yoauna to say their goodbyes.

"Y'all need us to help you with the cleanup?" Holiday asked.

"Naw, we got it," Yoauna said, and slapped her hand over Jesse Lee's mouth as he began to protest. "Thank y'all so much for coming." She hugged Holiday and then Cynthia. "And it was so nice meeting you, girl. I hope you come back to visit us again."

Cynthia smiled. "Me too. I had a lot of fun tonight. Thank y'all."

"Good night. Drive carefully."

TWENTY-EIGHT

"You mind if we roll the windows down? My dress is damp from sweating and this A/C is killing me," Cynthia said.

"Alright." Holiday switched the air conditioner off and lowered the windows.

"Mmm… now this is what I miss. Fresh, country night air." She inhaled deeply. "No exhaust and other fumes to choke you up or have you smelling like gas when you go somewhere."

Holiday chuckled and watched her as she reclined the seat and relaxed into the soft leather. He lowered the radio so only the faintest of jazz playing could be heard. They were the only vehicle on the road as his high-beams pierced the pitch black night.

"Did you really have a good time?"

"I did. Yoauna seems like a true sweetheart. And I loved watching her and Jesse Lee together."

"Yeah, they love to party. The spades and dominoes tournaments are pretty much like that, too. Except more men of course."

"Hmm…." Cynthia closed her eyes. Several minutes of silence settled between them before she said, "You could've told me your ex-girlfriend was gonna be there."

Holiday looked over at her. "My what?"

"Ex-girlfriend."

"Who you talking about? Chanel?"

She opened her eyes. "So there was another ex there, too?"

Holiday shook his head. "No. No. And she's not my ex-girlfriend."

"That's not what she said. She told me y'all dated for a while."

"Well… we went out a few times, but I don't think you can call that dating." He could see her fold her arms out the corner of his eye as he looked straight ahead to maneuver the curving road.

"It had to be something if she was willing to have your baby."

He took his foot off the accelerator. "She said that?"

"Yeah."

"And you believe what she told you?" he asked.

"I mean… like I said… you could be telling me anything. You could have a whole family at home and I would be none the wiser."

"Are you serious?"

"Very."

He slowed the truck and made a U-turn.

She sat up in her seat. "What are you doing?"

"Taking you to my place."

"For what?"

"To show you where I live. So you can see that the only person waiting for me at home is Pop."

She chuckled. "You don't have to do that. I take your word for it."

"Naw, I want you to see."

Cynthia reclined back in the seat. "This is crazy."

* * *

The low hum of the refrigerator and the ticking of a nearby wall clock were the only sounds inside as they entered the house. Cynthia followed close behind Holiday's heels as he went to the dining room

144

wall to turn on the light, dropping his keys on the table.

"You really didn't have to do this," she whispered.

He shook his head and grabbed her hand, leading her through the living room to the hallway. "You wanted to know."

He stopped at one room and flipped on the light switch. "This is the home office. Or computer room as Christian likes to call it." Cynthia peeked in and nodded. A couple steps away was another room. "This is where Christian sleeps when he's here."

"Okay."

They crossed the hall to the next room and he opened the door. "This is my room."

She giggled as she peered inside.

"You can go in if you want to. Look in the closet. Under the bed."

She rolled her eyes. "I get it. Geez."

"Naw, there's one more room," he said and they doubled-back to the front of the house. Frank's snoring was loud and clear as they stepped into the short hallway off the living room.

Cynthia pulled her hand away. "*Do not* open his door. I get it, like I said. I don't need to look in there."

"Yes you do. Just to confirm that that's not a woman in there sounding like a Grizzly bear."

A hand flew to her mouth as she tried to stifle a laugh. Holiday grabbed her wrist, tugging her forward. He turned the doorknob, his hand sliding up the wall for the light.

"Don't turn on the light!" Cynthia whispered harshly.

Holiday turned on the light anyway. "See. It's just Pop."

Cynthia shook her head as she looked in on Frank sleeping under the covers with his feet exposed at the end of the bed. "This is so wrong." She smiled as he turned off the light and softly closed the door.

"So this is where we live," Holiday said when they stepped back into the living room. "In case you ever need to stop by."

"Whatever," she rolled her eyes again and walked over to the long table against the wall. She bent down to look at the collection of family photos. Holiday turned on the ceiling fan to give her more light.

"Oh my god. Is this your mom?"

"Yeah."

She stood up to look at him in the face. "Frank was right. You look just like her." She looked back at the photo. "She is striking. Her eyes. Her eyelashes look three-D. I feel like I can touch them."

Holiday chuckled and watched her as she moved on to another photo.

"And she really was a beauty queen as Frank said."

"Yeah, she loved doing those pageants too."

She grinned as she looked at another. "Look at her looking like a young Cicely Tyson."

"Oh yeah. With them cornrows going up her head like that."

Cynthia laughed. "And this must be your brother and his wife."

"Yeah. That's Avery and Dawn."

"They have all boys?"

"Yep. All boys." He slipped his hands into his pockets. "That's why it was such a big deal for Ma and Pop when Laila came along."

Shaking her head again, she said, "It's uncanny how much y'all look like her. I've never seen that before."

Holiday took a seat on the sofa as she moved on, looking at every single photo on the table. The walls. At the ones on the stands next to the TV. And then down the hallway.

"Your kids are beautiful."

"Thanks," he said standing as she reentered the living room, thinking she would be ready to leave, but she sat down next to him on the sofa.

"Your daughter was you and your mom all over again."

He nodded. "Everybody say that."

"Gorgeous family."

"You want anything? Something to drink?"

"Oh yeah. Water, please. I think I had way too much wine." She kicked off her sandals and leaned back into the couch.

Holiday smiled and went to the kitchen.

He turned off the dining room light on his way back, turned on a lamp next to the sofa, and pulled the switch to turn off the light on the ceiling fan before handing her the bottle of water and reclaiming his seat.

"You're not feeling sick are you?"

"No. None of that." She took a long drink of water before twisting the cap back on.

It pleased him to see her get comfortable around him as he watched her pull one of her legs beneath her into the couch. "You didn't tell me how the day at the movies went," he said.

"It was all right, I guess."

"Yeah? What did y'all end up seeing?"

"I couldn't even tell you. Sister Nash bought the tickets and I followed them into a theater. I fell asleep soon afterwards."

He chuckled. "Really?"

"Yeah. Sister Nash didn't wanna see anything with any violence or cussing in it, so there wasn't much to choose from of course."

"Right."

"But... it was still nice. Sister Nash is still cool. They crack me up sometimes."

"I never hear you talk about your folks. Are they still around?" he asked her.

"Who? My parents?"

"Yeah."

"Yeah. They are. Somewhere here on earth."

"What you mean?"

She rested her head on the back of the sofa and laughed. "My parents. Uhh... they're a couple of buskers."

"Buskers? What's that?"

"Traveling musicians."

"Oh. So they're in a band."

"Not exactly. Well... it's just the two of them and they travel and perform."

"Oh okay."

"Street performers," she said, and then laughed when it finally registered with him. "I'm serious."

"So they just stand on the street corner and sing and people drop money in their bucket?"

She nodded.

"Nooo."

"Yes. They've been doing that as long as I can remember."

"You being serious?"

"I really am. I traveled along with them for like the first four-and-a-half years of my life."

"Wow. So you play music too, then?"

"I can shake a maraca. Or beat a conga. Whether or not it sounds any good though is up to interpretation."

He chuckled. "You're wild. I never would have imagined that. So they had you as a little girl standing on the streets singing with them?"

She nodded, turning those pretty eyes on him. "Mmm-hmm... they both play guitar and my mom also plays violin and harmonica. She's a beautiful vocalist, too."

"Wow."

"And to see them is to travel back in time. They're real hippie-like. My daddy is like a Jimi Hendrix with the fringed shirts and jeans and ribbons and scarves tied around his whole head. My mama with the long tunics and bell bottoms. They're a sight to see."

"You're blowing my mind right now."

"It's the truth."

"So how did you end up with Ms. Genie?"

"Oh, Mama Genie wasn't having it. She told my daddy they could do whatever they wanted to do, but they were *not* going to have her grandbaby out on no street corners singing for money."

Holiday laughed. "I heard that."

"So I ended up with my grandma and been there ever since. Until I went away for college."

"But you don't see your parents at all?"

"Not much. They always wrote to me though, and still call every now and then, whenever they're settled in one place long enough. Mama Genie scared them off I think. I have a box full of letters from them. From California. Minnesota. New York. New Orleans. Belize. Haiti. Wherever they were at at the time."

"You seem to not be bothered by it."

She shook her head. "I'm not. Mama Genie is the one upset with them. She told them it was irresponsible for them to be living like that—from pillar to post—when they had a little girl to raise. But I never felt like they neglected me. If you can believe that. Like I said… they sent me letters. Sometimes with little gifts in them: leaves, flower petals, money, pretty stationery and post cards, charm bracelets. That was exciting to me as a kid. And with Mama Genie, I never wanted for anything."

"I think you got a little bit of them in you," he said.

She raised her head from the sofa. "What do you mean?"

"The way you wear your hair. The hundreds of bracelets. Your style. Walking around barefoot. Or in flip flops."

"What? Braids are not hippie. I think you forgot. My style is not hippie. And I only go barefoot in the house."

"You are something else."

She took another drink of water. "What if Mr. Frank wakes up," she said, smiling.

Holiday shrugged. "He won't. But even if he did, he would be glad to see you here."

"I've been wanting to do this for a while now," she said, and leaned towards him, pushing her hand through the thick black kinkiness that was his hair, but she might as well been stroking his penis because that's where the sensation hit him as soon as her fingers reached his scalp. "I love this."

He licked his lips and smiled. "Yeah?"

And then she scooted closer to him, lifting his arm to rest across her shoulders as she rested her head on his chest. "What happened to Laila?" she asked quietly.

He cleared his throat. "Oh… uhh… she drowned."

She lifted her head to look at him. "Really?"

"Yeah. In the lake."

"I'm sorry to hear that."

He blew out a slow breath. "Yep."

"How did that happen?"

"We still don't know the whole story. But they were there in the park for a party and she went off with a few of her older cousins. Somebody wasn't watching her like they said they would. We don't know."

"So you weren't there?"

"No. Unfortunately no. She was with her mama."

"Oh."

They sat in silence with the whir of the ceiling fan above them. Holiday looked down to see she'd closed her eyes. He caressed the cool and silky smoothness of her shoulder, thinking, as she had said,

I've been wanting to do this for a while now, too. To be this close to her. To have her in his arms.

It seemed as if she could hear his thoughts because she looked up at him, raised her head, and kissed him.

Her lips were pillow soft. And she was slow to remove them, held them there on his mouth for several seconds instead, before pulling away and nestling against his shoulder, closing her eyes again.

Damn.

* * *

Holiday did not realize he had dozed off until he opened his eyes much later. He looked at the digital clock on the front of the cable box. It was well after three in the morning. He nudged Cynthia to wake her up so he could take her home although what he really wanted to do was pull her into his bedroom. That sweet kiss of hers was still fresh on his lips.

She stirred, moaned a little, but did not open her eyes.

He chuckled and shook her again. "You're gonna have Ms. Genie cussing me out for getting you home so late."

Her eyes blinked open. "What time is it?"

"About a quarter to four."

She sat up, stretching her back, then slid her feet into her sandals.

And as soon as she was in the passenger seat of his truck she closed her eyes for more sleep.

TWENTY-NINE

"Cynthia. Cynthia. Cynthi-aaaaaa."

She thought she was dreaming until three quick knocks on her wall made her realize the person calling her name and making the noise was right inside her bedroom. She opened her eyes, rolling over on her side, to find Mama Genie standing at the door.

"It's near-bout twelve o'clock and you *still* in the bed? Chile, you sick or something?"

"No, I'm not sick, Mama Genie. Just tired."

"Uhn-huh, I bet. What time you get in last night? Or this morning, rather?" she laughed.

Cynthia rolled onto her back and stretched. Yawning, she said, "It was late. The party was still going."

"So y'all had a good time, huh?"

"It was really nice." She thought about Holiday. About him taking her to see where he lived. About kissing him.

"Well, that's good. I was just coming to check on you to make sure you were all right since you didn't come down for breakfast and I didn't hear no movement going on up here."

"Alright. I'll be down in a minute."

Mama Genie closed the door and Cynthia rolled back over onto her side.

I kissed him. Lord, what have I done?

* * *

Cynthia picked up her cell phone for the third time, only to put it back down again. A stomach ache? Headache? Too much wine last night? Forgotten plans with Mama Genie? She needed an excuse to tell Holiday for why she would not be able to attend the festival and concert with him. Kissing him was a mistake. There was no way they could go beyond that kiss and she did not intend to have him believing that they could.

She scrolled through her contact list and pressed the button to dial him.

"Cynthia," he answered.

My god.

"I was thinking about you, too," he said, his voice as soothing as hot chocolate on a winter day.

"Oh yeah?"

"I wanted to call you as soon as I got up this morning, but I figured you would probably be sleeping in and I didn't wanna disturb you. How you doing?"

Oh why must you sound so good and be so kind? "I'm fine," she said. "Just sitting here."

She had showered, eaten the breakfast Mama Genie'd cooked for her as her lunch, and gone back to her room to decide what to do about tonight's plans.

"You ready for tonight?" he asked. "I hear one of the bands is gonna be this blues cover band that's supposed to be really good. So I'm looking forward to that with you."

"Actually, that's why I was calling."

He remained quiet, waiting for her to continue.

"I don't think… I'm not gonna be able to go."

"Aww, c'mon. I knew you were going to let me down."

"I'm sorr—"

"What made you change your mind?"

She sat up in bed with her back against the headboard. "Listen… I think you're a great guy, and I really do enjoy being with you, but I don't want to lead you on. After what I did last night I just—"

"Is that what you're worried about? When you kissed me?"

She nodded. "Well, yeah."

"I see." He was quiet for a moment and then, "Well… hey… if you don't want to go you don't have to. I wish you would though."

Why do I feel sooo bad? "How much do I owe you for the ticket?"

"Nothing. It's cool."

"No, it's the least I can do."

"Don't even worry about that, okay?"

She closed her eyes, pinching the bridge of her nose. "Look, I just don't think it's right… I mean… I'm only here for a few weeks and will be going back home soon, and I can't make you feel like this could lead to something when I know—"

"Then it won't lead to something."

She sighed, conflicted in her feelings, wanting to run to him and run away at the same time.

He said, "Cynthia, I enjoyed that kiss last night just as much as you did. And I won't even lie and say I don't want another one. More than that, I think about doing something else to you when I see you."

"What," she said nervously, a statement rather than a question.

"You're a gorgeous woman, and I want you—"

Cynthia wanted to slide underneath her sheets.

"But I definitely understand what you saying," he said. "This don't have to be anything you don't want it to be."

Damn you.

"So maybe I'll see you next time, alright?" he said.

Cynthia bit her bottom lip. "Okay," and he hung up.

THIRTY

Showing up unannounced wasn't his style, but he figured since he was in the area he would stop by because it appeared that was the only way he was going to get the information he needed.

He pulled into the driveway, got out, and rang the doorbell.

The door opened after the third ring. "Man, you lucky it's you, 'cause I'm like 'who the hell is this ringing my goddamn door on a Saturday afternoon'," Jesse Lee laughed, shaking Holiday's hand and pulling him in for a quick hug. "What's up with you?"

"I came to talk to you about the A/C man. Since you keep forgetting to get back with me, I figured I would come by and get his number from you myself."

"Aww man, shit. He ain't called me back yet." Jesse Lee turned away from the door and Holiday followed him inside.

"That's cool, but give me the number and I can call him myself so I don't have to keeping bothering you."

"The thing about it is he be funny-acting sometimes and don't want everybody to have his number. His ass be hiding from folks and shit." Jesse Lee went to his recliner and sat down. Holiday took a seat on the couch.

"Hiding?" Holiday said. "From who?"

"Shit. The IRS. Women. Men."

Holiday laughed. "That's crazy."

"Hell yeah. Let me call him right now," Jesse Lee said. He got up to go to the kitchen to use the phone and came back a few minutes later. "See… he don't have a voicemail set up, so I can't even leave a damn message. You want a beer, man?"

"Yeah, I'll take one," Holiday nodded. "Where is Yoauna?"

"Hell if I know," Jesse Lee said from the kitchen. "Probably out shopping. She just got the damn promotion, ain't even got her first paycheck yet with her new salary, and she already out spending money."

Holiday chuckled as he took the bottle from Jesse Lee. "You already know."

"I told her ass she gon' start contributing more towards these bills too," he laughed. "I ain't playing."

"Man, you crazy."

Then Jesse Lee grinned. "That's my baby though. She know I'll always take care of her. She can keep her money. Just take care of *my needs*."

"Hey, I hear you."

Jesse Lee slapped the arm of the recliner. "Man, you gotta tell me about this chick you brought to the party last night though! Where you say you meet her at?"

Holiday shook his head at the thought of Cynthia. "Over in Madison. Her grandmother lives next door to the house me and Pop working on."

"Oh, that's right. You did tell me that." Jesse Lee whistled. "You wasn't lyin'. Her ass was wearing that dress. I seen you looking at her while she was up gettin' her dance on."

Holiday laughed. He had been watching her dance. The way she moved with such ease and grace, her hips swaying left and right to the music.

"We was supposed to go down to the festival tonight, but she pulled out on me." He took a swig of the beer, wishing he had a cigarette to go with it.

"No shit? I knew it. She found out about Chanel didn't she?" Jesse Lee threw his head back onto the recliner.

Holiday waved his hand, shaking his head.

"As soon as I saw y'all walk in here, I told Yoauna, 'baby, we don't know shit, don't see shit, and we ain't involved in *nothing*'."

"Naw, it was nothing like that, but she did tell me Chanel told her we used to date and she was trying to have my baby."

"Oh for real? Damn, that's messy. Yoauna told me she had about fifteen messages when she checked her phone late last night. They telling her how wrong she was for inviting you to the party and you showing up with somebody else, knowing you and Chanel used to go together. I didn't even know Chanel was gonna be here! And Yoauna didn't even invite you! But still, it wasn't none of my business who you brought with you. But these women are crazy."

Holiday grunted. "Man, me and Chanel went out maybe five times. We didn't go together."

"Hey, that's how it is with them though, man." Jesse Lee shrugged and put the bottle to his lips. "And now Cynthia don't want nothing to do with you? See what I'm saying?" he laughed.

"Yeah, she told me it don't make sense for us to be going out and doing all this since she going back home soon."

"She got a man at home or what?"

He shook his head. "She told me she was single."

"Then what's the problem?"

"Your guess is as good as mine. I can't leave her alone though."

"Hell, I wouldn't be able to leave her ass alone, either. She fine," Jesse Lee laughed again.

Holiday chuckled. "Man, it's more than that. I like her whole attitude. And she's just so damn chill. We can sit and talk for hours about… about nothing really."

"Man, I hear you," Jesse Lee said. "But it still don't make sense to me why y'all can't be friends just because she going back home. Where she live at anyway?"

"Houston."

"Houston?! Man, that ain't but a few hours away."

"I know."

Jesse Lee sucked his teeth and picked up the remote to change the channel on the TV.

"Back to this A/C though, man," Holiday said. "Her and her grandmother been without it for a minute now, so if your partner can't come through by Monday, we'll have to go with somebody else. She was just hoping to get somebody that could do it for cheap."

"If I don't hear back from him by this evening I'll let you know."

Holiday looked at him. "You better call me back, too."

Laughing, Jesse Lee said, "Look at you, man. The woman don't even want you and you worrying about getting her grandmama's A/C fixed."

"Hey, you know I'm a man of my word."

"Yeah, and I'm just fucking with you," Jesse Lee said, standing up. "Come on, man. Let me whoop your ass in a game of dominoes right quick. You got time."

THIRTY-ONE

Cynthia lay on the couch half-watching, half-listening to the movie she'd put in the DVD player. Mama Genie had left to go and meet with a few of the ladies at the church to plan the Revival's menu—something that definitely could not be discussed over the phone according to Sister Nash Mama Genie had said.

She was already bored out of her mind and missing Holiday. She considered calling him back, to tell him she was only joking, that she still wanted to go to the festival with him.

He probably called somebody else as soon as he hung up the phone with me, she thought, and got up to go to the kitchen, searching for something to snack on. She wasn't hungry at all, but she grabbed the bag of corn chips from the pantry and Mama Genie's leftover bean dip from the refrigerator.

An hour later she was still lying there staring at the ceiling when she heard a vehicle pull up in the driveway. She sat up on the couch just in case Sister Nash had come back with Mama Genie, turned off the DVD movie, and switched the television to a regular channel. No violence or foul language allowed in the presence of Sister Nash. She laughed to herself at the thought.

But she did not hear voices outside, and then there was that familiar sound of slow footsteps across the porch. She would recognize that gait anywhere.

Butterflies took flight in her stomach followed by the ringing in her ears as excitement rushed to her heart and head.

He tapped on the screen door.

She hesitated a minute before she got up.

"Hello, Ms. Cynthia," he said when she appeared at the screen door.

"Hey," she replied sheepishly.

"I came by to get my money for the ticket."

She opened the screen door. "What?"

He leaned back on the banister. "Yeah, I thought about it, and you were right. The least you can do is pay me for the ticket since you decided not to go."

She blinked. "Oh. Okay. Let me go and get my purse. How much do I owe you?"

"Thirty-five dollars. Twenty-five for the ticket. Ten for the cancellation fee."

"Cancellation fee?"

He licked his lips. "Yeah."

I don't know if I should laugh at your sexy ass or be mad. "Alright. I'll be right back."

"Cool," he said, crossing his arms and ankles.

Cynthia opened her wallet once upstairs in her bedroom and pulled out the cash and counted it. She had only twelve dollars—a five dollar bill and seven ones.

Back on the porch, she handed the bills to him. "This is all the cash I have on me right now, so I will give the rest to you later if you come to work next door Monday."

He counted them, and then looked at her. "I can wait for you to go to the ATM."

Is he serious? She searched his face looking for a sign that he was teasing her. "Oh. Well, give me a minute to put something on," she said, flustered now. It wasn't about the fact that he was asking for his money back—she intended to repay him anyway—but it was the way he was acting. Cold. Unsmiling. She didn't think her canceling on him would have affected him this much.

His eyes traveled down, looking at the bleach-stained T-shirt and the lounge shorts she had on.

"If you gotta do all that then you may as well just come with me to the festival." Then that lady-killing smile spread across his face and Cynthia thought her panties might melt and slide down her legs.

She laughed. "Did you come over here just to mess with me?"

He chuckled. "Yeah. And to get my money, too."

"You are crazy."

"Crazy for you."

She shook her head, smiling.

"For real though. Go change. Let's just have fun."

She could only shake her head again at him as she turned to go upstairs.

This man. This man.

* * *

"I know you're gonna play a few games with me this time, right?" Holiday asked. They strolled amongst the throng of carnival-goers. It was much more crowded than it had been when they attended last weekend.

"Sure, I'll play with you. But let's ride a few rides first. It's been a while since I've been on an amusement ride," she smiled up at him.

"Alright, cool." They searched for a ride with the shortest wait time, but all of them appeared to be equal in length.

"Let's just ride this one," she said and they stood in line.

"I can't believe you were gonna stand me up," he said after they had been standing in silence for several minutes, slowly inching forward as the line dwindled.

"Oooh, don't rub it in, okay? I'm here now."

"Yeah, but now I don't know if it's because you're doing me a favor."

She groaned playfully. "Are we really gonna talk about this again? I already told you what it is. But you said we're here to have fun, so let's have fun, okay?"

"Okay, Ms. Cynthia," he replied with a smirk.

They were finally ahead in the line minutes later when one of three rowdy young boys exiting the ride noticed Holiday and shouted, "Hey, Uncle Holiday," as he ran up to him.

Holiday stuck his hand out to him, "Hey, Max, what's up, man?"

"What you doing here?" the boy asked, but before Holiday could answer, the other boys were pulling their friend away, telling him they needed to hurry up to get to the next ride—that they didn't have time to talk to people.

Cynthia laughed.

Holiday shook his head. "That's Christian's cousin."

"Oh okay."

Several rides, games, a shared smoked turkey leg and funnel cake later, they were lucky and found an empty bench underneath a scrawny tree and sat down.

"How much longer do we have before the concert starts?" Cynthia asked after they had been sitting for a while people-watching.

Holiday looked at his watch. "About another thirty minutes."

"Hmm…. So you like blues, huh? Are you sure you're thirty-three and not fifty-three?"

Laughing, he said, "Yeah, I do. I mean… I just like the music I heard my parents playing when I was a kid. Not hating on today's artists because there are some good ones out there, but naw… most of this new stuff is not my style."

"I see."

"See, Mama, I told you I saw Uncle Holiday," a young voice came over their shoulder.

They turned around and Cynthia noticed a woman pushing a stroller with a girl toddler in it and four young boys walking beside her—one of them Max—and headed towards them.

"Hey, Brother-in-Law," the woman said, looking at Holiday and then to Cynthia.

Holiday stood up. "How you doing, Roxy?"

"I'm all right. Just hanging out with these kids today so they can stop worrying me, talking about they bored at the house. What you been up to?" Her eyes shifted to Cynthia again.

"Not too much. I'm here just to enjoy myself, too. Waiting for the concert to start."

"Oh."

Cynthia wondered if she should introduce herself since Holiday made no effort to do so, but then he said, "Roxy, this is Cynthia. Cynthia, this is Christian's auntie."

"Hello," Cynthia said to her and Roxy nodded a hello too, but her hands remained wrapped around the handles of the stroller.

"Max thought you had Christian with you," Roxy said to Holiday. "They wanted him to come and get on these rides with them. They keep riding the same damn rides over and over."

"Naw, I brought him out here yesterday."

A round of sucking teeth noises and 'Aww, man' came from the boys.

"I may bring him back next weekend though, but we'll see," Holiday told her.

Roxy shook her head, "Oh, this is the only time we coming. These boys already know I don't have no money to bring them to this every weekend. And they mamas paid for them," she said pointing at two of the boys.

"I hear you. Well… we're gonna go ahead and head over to the stage," Holiday said and put a hand to Cynthia's shoulder, prompting her to stand. "See you later, Roxy," he said and gave each of the boys a low-five before they walked away.

He stopped and bought drinks—a beer for him, a pineapple slush for her—and they moved on to the stage area. It was already packed with people crowding around the stage while others sat further back on beach towels or camping chairs.

"You wanna stand up close or is back here okay?"

Cynthia shrugged. "It doesn't matter to me." Holiday led her further into the crowd, closer to the stage.

It wasn't long before the band took their places and went right into a blues number that had the crowd singing right along with them. Cynthia wasn't much of a blues music person, but she did recognize a few of the songs they covered. She was just happy to be in the midst of the feel-good vibes the crowd emitted as hands raised in the air, fingers snapped, eyes closed, and lips moved in song as couples—and singles—danced around them. Holiday stood beside her, nodding his head, taking his time with his beer, and at one point, wrapped his free arm around her waist, pulling her into his side.

And Cynthia loved it.

After the last song, they made their way back to the front of the park. And it took a long while to make it through the crowd before they were at the carnival section again. "You good? Or you want something else before we leave?" Holiday asked.

"Hmm… I'll take some cotton candy to go," she said.

They found a stand and, even though she insisted on paying for it herself, Holiday shook his head and said the treat was on him.

"Then you have to let me treat you to lunch sometime."

"Oh now you wanna hang out with me again, huh?"

She squint her eyes, looking up at him. "Don't start."

"Well, what you expect? One minute you telling me I'm asking for too much of your time, and the next you wanna take me out."

She nudged his arm. "I'm just saying… because you've been so nice to me. I owe you *something* at least," she smiled.

He looked down at her with a sly grin and she realized immediately it was probably not the best choice of words. "Oh yeah?"

She pushed him. "Don't you even think nothi— Ah!" she yelped as she stumbled forward. Holiday's hands were immediately on her to break her fall.

"Whoa. You all right?"

They looked down and noticed the buckle in the pavement she'd tripped over.

"Oh great," she said, slipping her foot back into the sandal. "The strap is broken."

"For real? Let me see," Holiday said and kneeled down to her feet. He pulled off the sandal as she stood, trying to balance herself on one leg. "Yep, sure is," he said standing back up.

Cynthia placed her hand on his arm for support. "I guess I have to hop all the way back to the truck," she said laughing even though she wanted to scream.

"Are you gonna be able to do that?" He looked ahead in the crowd. "We still got a ways to go."

She shook her head, groaning in frustration.

"And I doubt you'll find something in one of these stands. I don't think they sell shoes. T-shirts maybe, but not shoes."

Cynthia stood not knowing what to do, but she was for sure not going to walk barefoot on that germ-ridden pavement.

Holiday laughed. "I told you about them shoes anyway."

She rolled her eyes. "Whatever."

"I'll just carry you back to the truck."

She looked at him. "What? No way."

"What you mean? How else you planning on getting there?"

Cynthia looked around. "I don't know, but you cannot carry me. I am too heavy for you."

"Just get on my back," he said and kneeled down again.

She laughed. "No! Get up."

Looking up at her, "Cynthia," he said, "come on."

"I'm much heavier than I look. And with all the good eating I've been doing these past few weeks, I've probably put on another ten pounds."

He shook his head. "Stop. It ain't like I can drive the truck through here to get you, so come on now."

Passersby shot them questioning looks.

Reluctantly, Cynthia eased onto his back and Holiday stood right up as if she was merely a backpack on his back with three school textbooks in it.

She giggled nervously and wrapped her arms around his shoulders, the bag of cotton candy and broken sandal clutched tightly in her hand.

"See... you were all worried for nothing," he said.

"Hey, I was just warning you. I didn't want you to be caught off guard, causing embarrassment for the both of us."

"Naw, I already knew I could handle you."

"Hmm..." she smiled, and rested her chin on his shoulder.

She breathed in the clean, masculine scent of him and she couldn't help herself. She kissed him. On the soft spot just below his earlobe.

Cynthia felt his shoulders tense and his pace slowed a beat. She squeezed her arms tighter around him, nestling her head further into his neck.

Holiday offered no verbal response but resumed his normal pace and moved with the crowd towards the fairgrounds exit.

THIRTY-TWO

"I'm glad you decided to come with me," Holiday said as they sat in his truck in Mama Genie's driveway. He'd rolled down the windows and turned off the engine.

"Well, you pretty much gave me no choice," Cynthia smiled at him from the passenger seat.

He chuckled. "Naw, I couldn't let you off that easy. I wanted to show you a good time, paid money for the ticket. That wasn't cool to cancel."

"I know. I just… I'm having a hard time with this."

He looked at her. "With what?"

She waved her hand. "This. What we're doing. My feelings. I'm so confused."

"What is it that you're feeling?"

She sighed heavily. "I think you know I'm feeling you as much as you're feeling me. I have fun with you, but where is it going? And for what?"

"Well… I thought this was understood earlier when we talked on the phone."

Suddenly his phone began to vibrate in his pocket. He took it out, looked at the screen, and set it in the cup holder.

He continued, "I know you'll be going back home to your life in the city. Still, I don't think we can't have fun while you're here."

"Yeah, but at what cost though?" she asked him. "I'm not one for the whole one-night stand thing. That's what I'm trying to tell you."

He frowned. "Who said anything about a one-night stand? Whatever we do or don't do is up to you at this point. But…" he said, looking out the window as a truck sped by on the road—a bunch of teens riding in the truck bed, hooting and hollering into the night air.

She looked at him expectantly. "But what?"

"But that kiss just a few minutes ago… at the festival? How do you expect me to take that? The kiss from last night was a mistake you said. Are you gonna tell me tomorrow this one was a mistake, too?"

Cynthia chuckled, throwing her head back on the headrest. "No," she said, shaking her head. "No, it was not."

"Okay, so you meant what you did?"

She nodded. "Yes."

Holiday grunted and rested his head on the headrest.

"And I mean this too," Cynthia said quietly and leaned over towards him. She pulled his face to hers, pressing her lips to his. Slowly. Gently.

Holiday parted his lips to receive her tongue. It tasted of sweet pineapple.

Already he felt himself rising. He wished for more.

Her hand moved from his chin to the back of his neck, bringing him even closer to her. Over and over and over her tongue slipped in and out of his mouth until she gave him one final kiss on the lips and pulled away.

Holiday licked his lips, beaming. "Mmm…"

Cynthia smiled and gathered her cotton candy and sandals off the floor. "I need one more back ride. To the porch, please."

"Oh, is that what that was for?"

She laughed. "No."

He got out of the truck and went around to her side. Sliding one arm underneath her legs and the other around her back, he lifted her right up and carried her all the way to the front door where she was able to set her feet on the welcome mat.

"Thank you," she said and fished inside her purse for the keys.

"What you doing tomorrow?" he asked.

She unlocked the door and turned, looking up at him. "Just church. Since I didn't go last Sunday."

He nodded. "Oh, okay."

"Why?"

"Just asking."

"Mmm-hmm," she smirked, and stepped inside.

"See you later," he grinned at her.

"Good night."

THIRTY-THREE

Whatever we do or don't do is up to you.

Cynthia sat between Mama Genie and Sister Nash as they clapped and rocked and sang along with the congregation of Saint Emmanuel Baptist Church, led in a list of praise songs by the five-member choir.

But Holiday was all Cynthia could day dream about in the midst of the cacophony surrounding her.

She didn't sleep much last night for thinking about him. There was no turning back now after that body-tingling kiss she'd given him. She knew it.

And she couldn't deny she wanted to kiss him again.

And again.

Cynthia didn't realize she was blushing until Sister Nash leaned into her, whispering loudly, "You enjoyed that sermon, too, I know. It's all over your face, child."

She nodded. "Yes. Yes I did."

* * *

Reverend Moore—along with Lady Moore—had followed Mama Genie home again under the pretense of finalizing the logistics of the Revival, but everyone knew Lady Moore wasn't too skilled in the kitchen and this was the Reverend's way of getting a decent meal for once after a long while. Sister Nash had come along too.

Cynthia sat near the window in her room, her laptop running hot on her thighs as she browsed the Internet, searching for more job postings she would possibly qualify for.

If they would give me a chance. I can learn anything, she thought and decided to search the non-profit sectors.

Volunteer Coordinator

Community Outreach Facilitator

Donor Services Associate

Within a couple hours' time she'd typed up a new résumé and letter of interest more suitable for non-profit jobs and submitted them for nearly a dozen positions.

She powered down the laptop and lay across her bed. She was tempted to call Holiday, but she didn't want him to feel he had to entertain her every single day, although she knew now it was what he wanted.

She decided she would just go for a drive to town and walk around the plaza until the shops closed for the evening. After yesterday's fiasco she thought it wise to forgo the flip flops for a day or two and pulled on her neon orange and green walking shoes. They didn't match anything she had on, but it was the only pair of tennis shoes she'd brought with her since she didn't think she would need any during her stay. Her plan had been to come and detox from the sour situation with Jonathan, not to meet a handsome man that wanted to take her out and be seen.

"I'm gonna step out for a while," she said to Mama Genie once downstairs. "I won't be gone too long."

"Hanging with Holiday again?" Mama Genie smirked.

Cynthia wouldn't dare roll her eyes at Mama Genie, but that's exactly what she felt like doing as everyone's attention was on her.

Sister Nash said, "Holiday? The young man working on Sister

Dunham's place next door?

Mama Genie nodded. "Yeah, that's him. He been taking her to some of everywhere since she been here. Been showing her a real good time. Which is good, I told her. That way she won't be settin' around here worrying about when somebody gonna call her for a job."

Reverend Moore wiped his mouth with his handkerchief. "That's right, Sister Cynthia, I heard from the other sisters here that you lost your job."

Cynthia smiled tightly, wishing she had the nerve to wish them all a good day and run out the door. "Yes. I was just upstairs spending some time looking and applying for a few. Someone is sure to call eventually. I'm being patient."

"Well… here …let me pray for you right now. Real quick," he stood up.

Oh boy.

He motioned for the other ladies to stand. "Come on here, y'all. Let us pray for our Sister Cynthia. She needs to know that *GOD* has a plan for her. GOD!"

"Mmm-hmm."

"That's right."

"Amen. Sure he do."

Reverend Moore reached out for Cynthia's hand. "Come over here right next to me, Sister."

Cynthia squeezed past Lady Moore to stand beside the Reverend between the coffee table and the sofa.

"This won't be long," Reverend Moore said. "Let us bow."

Cynthia knew it was a lie as soon as she closed her eyes, but all she could do was stand there and receive it.

That prayer went well beyond ten minutes and Cynthia's left hand was dripping with Reverend Moore's sweat while her right was numb from Lady Moore's squeezing at every inflection of the

Reverend's coarse voice.

Cynthia was grateful to hear the final Amen fall from Reverend Moore's lips and opened her eyes, easing her hand away from his. "Thank you so much, Reverend Moore," and she looked at Mama Genie and Sister Nash and Lady Moore. "Thank y'all."

"Don't you worry about nothing, darling," Lady Moore said, giving Cynthia's hand a final squeeze. "This just means there's something better out there for you. In every way."

"I hope so," she nodded and moved towards the door. "I will be back soon, Mama Genie. See y'all later." And she hurried towards her car hoping she still had a bottle of hand sanitizer in her glove compartment.

* * *

An hour-and-a-half later she took a seat on a bench in the plaza after browsing Elva's Vintage Clothing and Antiques & Things. A flock of pigeons were having a joyous time bathing in the bird bath and just as Cynthia reached in her purse for her cell phone to capture them on camera it rang.

She quickly touched the screen to answer when she saw his name. "Cynthia."

No one before could make her blush so hard at the calling of her name. "How are you?"

"Missing you," he said.

She scanned the plaza. "Are you watching me?"

He chuckled. "Uh…no. Where are you?"

"The plaza."

"You and your grandmother shopping again?"

"No, it's just me. Bird watching. She had company, so I left."

"You wanna come over here? You can watch the ducks where I am."

She laughed. "The lake?"

"Yeah."

* * *

He was sitting on the tailgate dressed casually in khaki shorts and a maroon T-shirt. A warm smile spread across his face as she pulled up.

"Must you be sexy all the time?" she asked when she approached him.

He stood up and she stepped into his outstretched arms. "I'm being sexy?"

"Yes, with these fitted V-neck T-shirts all the time." She squeezed him, the fresh scent of fabric softener filling her nose. She wanted to run her tongue across the hair there, but thought better of it.

That cool laugh of his was music to her ears now. "How you doing today?"

"Good," she replied, pulling away and hopping on the tailgate next to him.

"Church service was all right?"

"Yeah, as can be expected."

The air was warm, but not too humid. And, like the plaza, there weren't many people out since Sundays were still regarded as the day to just attend church, enjoy a big dinner with family, and relax until evening services or prepare for the workweek ahead.

"Do you go at all?" she asked him.

"No," he shook his head. "Well… it's been a while. Since me and my ex-wife split."

"Oh, I see." Curiosity got the best of her. "You said y'all were married for seven years? What happened with that?"

He sighed. "I just think we were too young. I mean… not that people marrying young don't last sometimes, because my parents were a prime example of that, but I wanted a family. And we were in love, so we figured why not? Everything was cool in the beginning, but after a while it just seemed like nothing was making her happy anymore. I was working too much. Her friend's husband bought her friend a fancier car. She needed more time away from the kids. More Me-Time she used to always say. Then she and my mama had their own issues with each other. It was a lot to deal with. And once… after our daughter passed away… she shut down completely."

Cynthia nodded. "That's sad."

He waved a hand. "But that's life. All you can do is keep moving forward."

"Do you hope to marry again?"

He frowned as if the question was the silliest he'd ever heard. "Without a doubt. I loved being married. I would do it again in a heartbeat once I meet the right one."

"That's refreshing to hear," she said. "Especially in this day and age."

"What about you though?" He rubbed a hand across her back. "I still can't believe nobody's tried to make you his forever. You must be hiding something. Are you really a witch underneath that pretty face and sexy body?"

She laughed out loud. "What?!"

"Yeah, it's gotta be something you not telling me."

"*Nothing's* wrong with me. I just haven't met him yet."

"Will you know him when you see him?"

"I don't think it happens that way. You have to get to know the person."

He shrugged. "I don't know. Some people say they do. Avery told me he knew as soon as he saw Dawn she was going to be his wife. Pop said the same thing about Ma. He said she was the prettiest girl at their school and he didn't want no ugly kids, so she was the one."

Cynthia threw her head back laughing. "I can believe it. That sounds like something Mr. Frank would say. But that's just basing things on the physical. And they got lucky."

He nodded. "Well… they say it was their spirit too."

"Hmm…. I don't know. I figure marriage will happen for me in due time, and it will take a *very* special person. Someone truly trustworthy. So there's no rush, because when I do, it will be only once. None of this second or third or fifth marriage."

He chuckled. "I hear you. You wanna walk? I see you put on some real shoes today."

She leaned into him. "Whatever," and hopped off the tailgate.

He threw his arm around her shoulder as they strolled towards the graveled trail.

And hours later Cynthia had lost count of how many times they'd circled the three-mile loop, walking and talking until the sun set.

THIRTY-FOUR

Holiday pulled into the driveway and cut the engine, deciding to make the phone call before he went inside the house since he did not want Frank to overhear the conversation. She had already called him several times and left two voice mail messages. He knew exactly what her call was about and he'd decided to take his time returning it.

"That was a very fucked up thing to do, Mason," she said as soon as she answered. And her choice word surprised him because she'd made it known after her decision to adopt a physically and mentally healthful lifestyle that she was removing all negativity from her life, which included profane language. "So this is what you do now? Lying to Christian?"

"Annette, what are you talking about?" There was no doubt when he saw Roxy at the festival word would quickly get back to her sister, but he didn't understand what it had to do with Christian and lying.

"He told me you said you didn't want to go to the festival again. That you bought tickets for only one day. But you end up going the very next day? And you brought some whore with you instead?"

"That is not what I told him. And she's not a whore. I told hi—"

"Oh, so now you're defending her?! Over Christian?"

"Annette, let me finish."

"No, if you didn't want to take him you should've just told him that! Or I could've made some arrangements with Roxy to let him go with her and the boys since you had *someone better* to spend your time with."

"I didn't say I didn't wanna take him, I said we couldn't go because I had something to do."

"Right, but you went anyway. It's just that you took your whore instead!"

Holiday shook his head. "Annette, there's no need to be disrespectful about this. You don't know her and the way you're talking is just crazy. Come on now."

At this, and the calm way in which he said it, she went off.

He pulled the phone down from his ear to his jaw, picking up only bits and pieces of phrases as she screamed and yelled: didn't care... promised to be there... heartless... changing my mind... protect Christian... our marriage... selfish... about Laila... stopped trying and walked away ... moved on.

And he let her vent. She knew he would. He always did.

He prided himself that he'd almost made it through the entire day without one, but after the call to Annette, he needed a cigarette to calm his nerves. She knew just the things to say to push his buttons and she went there every time. And every time he would take the heat, believing that he owed it to her for not being there when she needed him on that dreadful day.

He finally walked into the house an hour later to find Frank sitting at the dining room table, a clean dinner plate in front of him, laughing loudly with someone on the phone. He nodded his greeting and went to his room to undress and take a shower.

"Where you been," Frank asked when he entered the living room after his shower, heading towards the kitchen. "I tried to wait for you before I had supper, but you was taking too long."

Holiday took a bottle of water from the refrigerator and came back to sit on the sofa. He was already feeling the effects of the long walk. "I was just down at the lake. Me and Cynthia."

Frank raised his eyebrows. "What this make? Seven days and nights in a row y'all been hanging out?"

"Who's keeping count?"

"I'm just saying… sound more like courtin' to me," Frank laughed.

Holiday waved his hand, smiling.

"Howie called me. And you ain't gon' believe this."

"What's that?"

"His daughter don't like the white walls."

"Huh?" Holiday said, frowning.

Frank nodded. "Yep, Howie told me he came by and took pictures and videos to send to her, and she said she didn't want no white walls in the house."

"Pop, you kidding."

"Nope," Frank laughed.

"And Howie didn't know this beforehand?"

"He say he didn't. But I sure told him there will be a extra fee. Just 'cause he my friend don't mean he get no special treatment. So she had him running around town trying to find the right shade of gray before he left for Mexico."

Holiday shook his head.

"She love how the bathrooms came out though. And the kitchen. He say the bathroom is what made her wanna do the rest of the house with a gray color scheme."

"That's cool."

"He said he'll be gone almost two weeks, but we can take our time."

"We were pretty much done anyway. Just had to do the cleanup and wax the floor."

"Yep," Frank said and turned the television to his favorite channel airing all the classic shows. *Good Times* was on.

He lay in bed later that night still going over in his head the things Annette had said. She never failed to remind him that it was his fault their marriage fell apart. That he was the reason their daughter was no longer here.

And he knew deep down she would never forgive him. It was in her eyes every time she saw him.

He sighed and folded his arms under his head as he lay staring at the ceiling. He never would have imagined that the love he once had for the woman he'd married, vowed to spend the rest of his life with, could trickle down to nothing. Annette would always be in his heart because they had history together, because they were a family. But he realized she intended to make the rest of his life a miserable one.

He picked up his cell phone to check the time. It was eleven o' clock. He wanted to call Cynthia just to hear her voice and to make him forget about the phone call with Annette.

His mood lifted as soon as she answered. "Cynthia."

"Yes?"

"What you doing still up?"

"Umm… it's not even midnight?"

"I thought you went to bed early."

She laughed. "It depends. Sometimes I do. Why? What are you doing?"

"Thinking about you of course. I needed to hear your voice so I can get a good night's sleep."

"Oh yeah? What are you thinking?"

He smiled. "You really wanna know?"

She was silent.

"Is Ms. Genie around?"

"No. She's asleep downstairs in her room. What you got on?"

"Huh?"

"I said… what are you wearing?"

He wasn't prepared for how she'd flipped the script on him. "Uhh… just my pajama bottoms and a T-shirt."

"Is that what you usually sleep in?" she asked.

"Yeah."

"That's too much clothing. Take them off."

He chuckled. When he was with Annette and they were still in love he went to bed as naked as the day he was born. But then, when things began to change between them, she'd said he should know it was time for them to grow up and be more decent and responsible. That they had children and shouldn't risk being caught nude should one of them come into their room in the middle of the night.

And he was still in the habit of sleeping that way.

"What?"

"You said you wanted me to put you to sleep, so come on."

Holiday got up from the bed and did as he was told, amused by her boldness. He loved it.

"Alright," he said, waiting for more direction.

"Now come to me," she said, her voice low.

"Huh?"

"To bed. Right here next to me."

"Cynthia. What do you mean?"

"You're ruining the mood. *Lay down in the bed,*" she said, sucking her teeth.

"Oh. In *my* bed? I see what we're doing now. I get it," he laughed and lay down in the bed. He and Annette had never done anything like this.

Cynthia sighed. "Here, come closer. Put your head on my chest."

"Alright."

"You know I can't resist putting my fingers through your hair, right?"

"Yeah."

"How was your day?" Her voice was in full sultry mode now and Holiday was already feeling a tingle in his body.

"Good. Especially once I saw you."

"Yeah? You enjoy being with me?"

"I really do."

"I enjoy being with you, too. I have to kiss you."

Holiday found himself closing his eyes as she made kissing sounds into the phone, calling out each spot her lips touched: his forehead, his eyes, nose, his mouth, chin, his neck. "Mmm… I'm loving it, baby, but I wish it was the real thing."

"It is," she said. "Now roll over on your stomach." When he did, she continued, "Your neck, left shoulder, the center, your right shoulder. My tongue traveling down the crease of your back. How does that feel?"

"Feels damn good."

"Can I go lower?"

"Please do." Holiday couldn't believe how much she could charm him without being in her presence.

"Your skin is the smoothest I've ever felt on a man."

"Oh yeah?" he said, even though this was not the time he wanted to think about her being with another man.

"Are you as sore from the walk today as I am?"

"Oh yeah."

"Let me massage your legs then. But you have to part them a little so I can get the muscle real good on the inside."

He parted his legs.

"It's tight too," she said.

Holiday chuckled. "I can't believe you."

"Shh… just relax. Just a couple minutes on each leg."

Now his mind was on her, wondering what she was wearing and how she'd look once she took it off. About having her in his bed beside him.

"Alright, now turn over."

He turned over onto his back.

"My hands are on your chest, in your hair. I love this. So sexy. I'm going to massage your left thigh now. Is this good?"

"Mmm-hmm."

"I'm gonna move closer to the groin area now okay?"

"Cynthia."

"Yeah?"

He couldn't take it anymore. "What are you trying to do to me?"

"Trying to help you relax so you can go to sleep."

"Well… it's doing the opposite."

"Oh, I see. You want me to stop?"

"Yeah," he said, pulling the bed sheets up to his waist. "Or else you're gonna have me coming to see you for real, knocking on Ms. Genie's door this time of night."

Her cute laugh had him wishing to kiss her mouth.

"Tell me this though before I let you go…"

"What?"

"Tomorrow will you be pretending you didn't say any of this to me?"

She sighed. "Are you gonna hold that against me every time?"

"I just wanna be sure I understand you."

"I meant every word."

He smiled. "I'll see you tomorrow."

She blew a kiss through the phone before she hung up.

THIRTY-FIVE

Cynthia heard when his door slammed shut. She looked forward to that sound every day of the week now. But she did not get up right away and remained there in bed, thinking. She wondered what had come over her in the past couple days. Each time she saw him and every minute she was around him, her resolve weakened. As much as she knew it behooved her to stay away from him she couldn't shake the hold he had on her mind and body.

She checked her phone for messages, and it was the same as every day: no missed calls, no new messages. She pressed the button to turn the phone all the way off and then back on to reboot it. *Just to make sure it's working right.* School began in two weeks and the anxiety was beginning to build since no one was calling. Then she checked her email. There were two messages in her inbox from companies she'd sent her résumé to, which made her sit up in bed. She read the first one out loud: "Thank you for your interest in working with us. However, we are no longer accepting applications for this position. Please continue to check our website for postings."

Then why is the position still posted?! She rolled her eyes and clicked the next email. The next one also thanked her for applying, but stated, regrettably, they sought an applicant with recent experience in the field. She'd written down every single position she applied for, so she grabbed her notebook to scratch the two off her list. She blew out a frustrated breath and got up to go to the bathroom for her morning shower. The summer heat required two a day.

Afterwards, she quickly dressed and went downstairs for breakfast.

"Good morning," she said to Mama Genie.

"Let me guess… you're going next door."

Cynthia laughed. It was exactly what she'd planned to do once she'd finished eating the oatmeal and bacon left for her. Now she had to pretend it wasn't. Not yet anyway.

She sat down on the couch. "What are you watching?" she asked her even though she could clearly hear it from the dining room as she ate. She was just making conversation.

"Family Feud. You know I love me some Steve Harvey. He is so crazy."

Cynthia pulled her legs up into the couch.

She sat through the episode of *Family Feud* and then two episodes of *Judge Joe Brown* before she got up, stretching her arms high above her head. Mama Genie had nodded off, but opened her eyes at the clinking of Cynthia's bracelets.

"I'll be back," she told her. "I'm gonna ask him again about the A/C repairman."

"Alright," Mama Genie responded groggily, and her eyes closed again.

* * *

"Hey, beautiful," he said as she walked in the door. "I was just about to call you." His smile warmed her all over.

"Oh yeah?"

"Yeah, to see what was taking you so long to get over here." She went into the kitchen where he stood and he wrapped his arms around her.

"I didn't know you were expecting me so soon," she smiled up at him.

"You know I can't wait to see you. Especially after all that you was saying last night. I wanna see just how bold you are now that I'm right here in front of your face." She giggled as he dipped his head, bringing his mouth close to hers, his lips brushing lightly against her lips as he spoke. "So now what you wanna say?"

"I wanna say if you don't let me know something about this A/C guy Jesse Lee supposedly knows, it's gonna be hard times for you."

He pulled his face away. "Oh! I am so sorry about that. Damn. I mean… excuse me." He reached into his pocket for his cell phone. "Let me call him right now."

Cynthia smiled and he wrapped his free arm around her shoulder, pulling her body back against him.

"I'm sure he's at work right now, but he might answer."

"Uhn-huh," Cynthia said, feigning skepticism.

Jesse Lee picked up on the first ring. "Hey, man," Holiday said. "I got you on speaker phone. Cynthia is here with me and she say if you don't come with the info on your partner, it's gonna be hard times for you."

Cynthia's eyes widened and she pinched Holiday's side.

"What?! I know she ain't over there talking noise!"

"That is *not* what I said, Jesse Lee. How are you?" She shook her head at Holiday and he smiled and kissed her forehead.

Jesse Lee laughed. "I was just about to say… 'cause *I will* fight a woman."

"He's talking crazy," Holiday assured her. "Don't listen to him. He is one of the softest cats I know when it comes to women."

"Hey!" Jesse Lee yelled. "This between me and Ms. Cynthia."

Cynthia laughed. "Seriously, is he available? I heard he was good and here I am waiting to bring him business, but it seems I have to jump through hoops just to get in contact with him."

"Hey… like I told Holiday: all I can do is call him. He ain't got a voice mail setup, and if he don't hit me back… then ain't much I can do. At this point you might as well get you somebody else."

"Well, I called a tech out and he said we need a whole new unit, so I was hoping to get someone else to look at it and maybe his price will be cheaper."

Holiday said, "Jesse Lee, how about you call him one more time for us? This the last time we trying. And call us right back."

"Yeah, please do Jesse Lee," Cynthia said.

Jesse Lee agreed and hung up.

"Geez," Cynthia sighed, "how does this guy stay in business if he doesn't answer people's calls?"

"That's a good question," Holiday said.

"Had I known it was gonna take all of this I would've just sucked it up and me and Mama Genie would have paid the fourteen hundred dollars between the two of us."

Holiday frowned. "Is that how much he told you it would cost? That can't be right."

"And that was the minimum." She shrugged, not wanting to think about it now. "But anyway… where's Mr. Frank?"

"He stayed home. He wasn't feeling good this morning."

"Oh no. What's wrong?"

"A bad case of indigestion he said. He had some spaghetti pretty late last night."

"Oh. That sucks." She turned to go and take a seat in the nearby fold-up chair, but he pulled her back and wrapped his arms over her shoulders, locking her in his embrace.

"You can't go nowhere until you give me one of those kisses you were telling me about last night."

"Alright," she smiled and pressed her lips into the softness of his.

He slid his tongue into her mouth, raising Cynthia's heart beat as he tasted her with sweet gentleness. His hands traveled from her shoulders down to the curve of her lower back and he pulled her even closer to him as he took a step back to the counter, her pelvis mashing against him, as he explored her mouth. Cynthia wanted him. Damn, she wanted him. She'd come to accept it. And she knew it would only be a matter of time before she could no longer take the heat and give in.

She circled his neck with her arms, surprising herself as she tasted him hungrily, aggressively.

The phone rang and she pulled away.

Holiday chuckled. "Of course he would call back right now," he said and pressed the button to answer Jesse Lee on speaker.

"He say he out of town doing work right now and won't be back until Saturday. I told him it was for your lady friend and he said he can definitely take a look at it for you and see what he can do. But not before Saturday evening around six if y'all wanna wait that long."

Holiday looked at Cynthia for an answer.

"I guess a few more days won't kill us," she said wearily. "Tell him Saturday is good. And thank you so much for calling him for me."

"No problem," Jesse Lee said and Holiday thanked him and ended the call.

Holiday pulled Cynthia to him again. "Now let's pick up right where we left off."

She grinned and wrapped her arms around his waist. "You know you're supposed to be working," she kissed him.

"I'm taking a break right now." He held her face in his hands as he kissed her lips again and again. Cynthia felt like putty with each tender kiss.

He finally let her go and she watched him lick his lips as if to savor that final taste.

She sat down on the chair and only then did she realize the painters tape along the baseboards and ceiling trim and the pails sitting on the floor in the living room. "I thought you had done all of the painting," she said, crossing her legs.

"Oh yeah. The young lady don't want the walls white. Pop found out yesterday."

"What? Y'all didn't have all of that straightened out before you started the job?"

"I don't know what happened with that. Communication got lost between him and his daughter somewhere. Me and Pop just did what we were supposed to do."

Cynthia looked around the rooms. "Well, that was a waste of time."

Holiday shrugged. "It's not so bad. So long as we're getting paid, we'll redo whatever he needs us to. But it shouldn't take us too long." He opened a can of paint and poured the gray liquid into a bucket.

"I'll be glad to give you a hand and help out since Mr. Frank is not here today."

He smiled. "Naw, you don't have to do that. Your company is good enough."

"I am *not* going to just sit here and watch you paint," she laughed, thinking about the very first time he invited her over. It was only a few weeks ago, but being with him felt so right, so natural, it seemed she had known him for a much longer time.

"Well, if you just have to, I guess I can't argue with you. But I don't have nothing for you to cover your hair. And I doubt you wanna get paint all over your dress."

"I'll just go home and change real fast," she said, standing.

"Alright. I'll be right here." He picked up the long-handled brush and made the first stroke of color on the wall.

THIRTY-SIX

"I think you're even sexier in sweatpants," Holiday said when Cynthia entered the house wearing a pair of navy blue sweats and the same bleach-stained T-shirt she'd worn a couple days ago. She'd tucked her braids underneath a plastic shower cap.

"You are so silly," she said, waving him off. "Where do you want me to start?"

"It don't matter. You wanna work in here with me or start in the kitchen?"

"I think I'll work in here with you. I don't wanna risk getting paint all over those new countertops."

"Alright, cool." He gave her the extra brush. "You ever painted before?"

"Not since art class in elementary school."

He demonstrated the technique to ensure a spot would not be missed on the textured walls before picking up his own brush and going to the opposite wall. "Is the music okay? You know you can change it if you want to." He had the local R&B radio station playing.

"Yep. It's fine."

They worked in silence for several minutes before she said, "At first I didn't think this color would look good, but it's actually pretty now that I can see it on the wall. I don't think I've ever seen gray walls in a home."

"Yeah, it ain't too bad," Holiday agreed, "but what's wrong with just white walls? They go with everything, right?"

"White walls are boring. Too barren-looking. It's like living in an emergency room at a hospital."

"Well… I guess I never thought about it that way."

"And they show too much dirt. There's always a dingy ring around every light switch."

He chuckled. "You're right about that. So judging by the bright colors you wear I'm sure your house is full of them."

"Actually, no. When I had the townhouse it was decorated in warm tones. I prefer chocolate browns, tans, beiges, with green or plum accents."

"Oh okay, so you don't have the townhouse now?" He wet his paint roller and slathered the wall again.

"Uhh… no. My landlord took the place back. So I'm rooming temporarily with a friend."

He grunted. "That's what's messed up about renting. As soon as you get comfortable the owner wants to come back and boot you out."

"Well, he had a mistress and children he had to take care of and they needed a place to stay even though he told me the reason he had to take the place back right away was because his mom was having some health issues and he wanted her to live there."

Holiday stopped painting and turned to look at her. "A mistress? For real? How did you find that out?"

"I went over there one day because I was expecting some important mail since he'd only given me a month to move out and my forwarding address request hadn't registered with the post office yet. She answered the door."

"But how did you know she was his mistress and not just a new tenant?"

"Because she referred to him as her fiancé and said she would talk to him to see if he'd picked up any mail that was for me. But I met his *wife*."

"Well… maybe he and his wife divorced and he got engaged."

Cynthia rested her paint brush in the tray. "No. They came by together just a few weeks before he told me I had to move out. And I saw one of those kids there and looking at her was like looking in Mr. Shabani's eyes. He couldn't deny that child if he wanted to."

Holiday shook his head. "That's messed up."

"It's sad, really. I just don't understand men like that. Why the deception? Why play with people's hearts? His wife? Can you imagine what's gonna happen when Mrs. Shabani finds out? How she will feel? And he has the gall to have the woman living in one of their rental properties. Right under Mrs. Shabani's nose!"

Holiday watched Cynthia's beautiful face twist with disgust. He knew she had dealt with betrayal in her own past relationships and she empathized with women like Mrs. Shabani. But he still couldn't understand what would make a man want to stray if he was coming home to a woman as sexy and as sweet as she was. "Maybe the wife know about the other woman," he said. "Something's gotta be up if he's that confident to have his mistress living in one of his houses his wife has access to."

Cynthia narrowed her eyes. "Or maybe he's just that careless. As if he just knows she would be too dumb to suspect he would have something going on with a tenant."

"Yeah, I think men forget sometimes how smart women are when it comes to these things. The real bold one in this situation though is the other woman. It seems she has no shame."

She huffed in reply, "Don't even get me started on women like that. Been there, done that, too."

Holiday was curious. "What you mean?"

"It happened to me. The woman my boyfriend slept with was a friend."

Holiday's eyebrows lifted and his mouth formed an O. "You serious?"

"Yep. She was his coworker, but we all hung out together a lot. She wasn't my best friend, but still…" her voice trailed off and she looked away.

Holiday shook his head. "So what did they have to say when you confronted them about it?"

"I didn't confront them."

"You didn't?"

"No. As much as it hurt I figured it wasn't even worth discussing because what was done was done and I knew there was no going back from that."

"Wow," Holiday said. "So you wouldn't even give the man a chance to explain hisself."

"There was nothing he could explain and I'm sure he knew that. He would show up to my job and call me incessantly, but I didn't want to hear none of it."

"I hear you," he nodded, stroking his goatee. "I don't understand men like that myself. If you got a good woman, why mess that up?"

Cynthia sucked her teeth and rolled her eyes. "Because men are never satisfied."

He chuckled. "Well… it was his loss. And, honestly, I'm kinda glad he did what he did." He let the paint brush handle fall to the floor, attempting to wrap his arms around her shoulders at the stunned look on her face.

She pushed him away. "*What?*"

Laughing, he said, "I don't mean it like that. I'm just saying…

hadn't he did what he did I doubt you would be here right now with me. We probably would've never crossed paths. And I know a good woman when I see one."

She cocked her head and stared up at him. "How did we even get on this conversation?"

"Umm… I don't remember."

They laughed and Cynthia turned to go back to painting her wall, and Holiday picked his brush up from the floor.

They worked for an hour before Holiday recommended they stop to eat some lunch.

He opened his lunch cooler after they washed their hands. Cynthia stood next to him as he pulled foil-covered items out of the bag. "Summer sausage, cheese, fruit, crackers. And some skins. You like summer sausage?"

"I love summer sausage," Cynthia said. "But I don't feel like cold cuts today. I want a hot lunch."

"Oh, well… you want me to run out and get you something?"

"How about you come with me?" she smiled at him. "I owe you a lunch remember?"

He chuckled. "I told you don't worry about that. You don't owe me nothing."

She nodded, taking the shower cap off her head. "It's my treat, now come. Don't resist."

"Man, you are something else." He put everything back into his cooler and turned off the radio.

* * *

"What do you have a taste for?" she asked him as she drove down the county road.

"Hmm… I don't know. It's up to you." He sat in the passenger seat of her compact car because she also insisted on driving him to wherever they were going. It felt strange being so close to the ground and feeling every bump and groove in the road after riding in pick-up trucks and SUVs for so many years. But he loved the fact that she had no problem treating him to lunch and he was just happy to be in her presence.

"Mexican. Chinese. Barbecue. Fish. What?"

He rubbed his stomach. "Oh, I didn't know you wanted to eat heavy like that. I won't have no energy left to finish the other rooms," he laughed.

"Well… you can get something light. But I'm pretty hungry right now, and a salad is not gonna cut it for me."

"Wherever you take me I'm sure I'll find something."

They ended up at a Mexican restaurant on the edge of town, busy with the lunch crowd.

After a fifteen-minute wait they were finally seated and a waiter had come and taken their orders.

Holiday reached across the table for her hands. Cynthia smiled and placed hers in his. "I just wanna say thank you."

"I told you it was the least I could do."

"No, I'm not talking about the lunch. Well, I do thank you for this too, but I'm talking about just allowing me to have your time. For being so cool."

Her eyes lowered as she blushed. "I feel the same way," she said.

Rubbing the backs of her hands with his thumbs, he told her, "I don't know what I'm going to do when it's time for you to go. I hope we can stay in touch for whenever you come back to visit Ms. Genie."

She smiled, but neither confirmed nor denied. His cell phone rang.

It was Annette. He pressed the button to silence the ring and slipped it back into his pocket.

"It wasn't Jesse Lee again was it?" she asked, taking a sip from her water glass.

"Naw, not Jesse Lee."

Holiday glanced around the restaurant.

"So…" he said just as the phone rang again. He took it out, silenced the ring, and placed the phone face down on the table next to the condiments holder.

"Somebody really wants to talk to you," she said.

Holiday shook his head. "It's just Christian's mama."

She frowned. "Then you should definitely answer it because it may be an emergency."

He hadn't even considered an emergency. After everything Annette had said to him last night, he figured she was just calling to continue her rant and get some other things off her chest she'd forgotten to say. She had done it before. "Alright," he pushed the chair back and stood. "I'll be right back," he said, and pressed the button to answer as he walked to the front of the restaurant and out the door.

"I need you to go and pick up Christian from Roxy's house," Annette said without preamble.

"What's up? What's wrong?"

"He called me and said he had a headache and he threw up."

"Wh— What he eat?"

"He said cereal, but I'm sure it was a whole lot of other junk too. Roxy doesn't care what those kids eat and she lets them eat junk all day long. So I need you to pick him up and take him home until I get off."

"I'm working today Annette. I can't leave right now."

"Mason, he's sick. You need to go and see about him."

"Alright, let me call Roxy," he said, and dialed her as soon as Annette hung up.

Roxy answered in her usual, cheerful way. "Hey, Brother-in-Law!" Holiday could hear the television blaring in the background and Genesis banging on her toys and babbling away in baby gibberish.

"How you doing, Roxy? Annette called, telling me Christian is sick."

"Yeah, he had a li'l upset stomach, but he fine now."

"Let me talk to him right quick."

"Well, he in my room laying down. I'm sittin' here folding up these kids' clothes."

Holiday shook his head. He knew she meant her favorite daytime television show was on, she was focused on completing her household task, and she was not getting up unless it was absolutely necessary. Christian was fine now, she'd said.

"Alright, well, I'm out for lunch right now, but I'll stop by later. Call me if anything changes before then."

"Brother-in-Law, you ain't gotta leave work to come and get him. He fine. I gave him some Sprite and a lemon to suck on for his stomach. I'm watching him. I told him he probably just played too hard. Maximillion be up and out of this house as early as eight o' clock sometimes playing. He just need some rest. He all right."

"Alright. Thanks, Roxy. I'll see you later."

Her high-pitched laughter pierced the line, startling him, but then he realized it was the TV she was laughing at as she hung up.

"Everything okay?" Cynthia asked when he returned to the table. Any other woman would probably not have appreciated—much less suggested—he take a phone call from his ex-wife while out with them.

"Yeah, Christian just had a upset stomach. He's with his auntie and she said he's fine. She'll call me if he feels worse." He took a long drink of water.

"That's good," Cynthia smiled.

The waiter finally brought their meals and they dug in. But not even ten minutes later Holiday's phone rang.

"It's her again," he said, and noticed Cynthia's raised brow as he got up from the table to take the call.

"So I hear you're out having lunch," Annette said. "Mason, you take your lunch to work. So this is why you told Roxy you would stop by later? Are you out having lunch with some broad? Your new whore?"

"Annette, don't start that today. Roxy told me Christian is doing fine now. It's no different from any other time he's been there and had to wait until me or you got off work to pick him up. You know if it was something serious I would be there in a heartbeat. But Roxy told me it was nothing to leave work early over."

"So you value Roxy's opinion over mine? *I* am his mother. Roxy doesn't run anything when it comes to me and mine. And I'm pissed that you don't seem to care."

"Annette, you're making this way more serious than it actually is."

"It *is* serious!" she snapped. "Mason, he needs to be home in his own bed where he can rest. Not in Roxy's house with all that damn noise around him. He could be over there dying from heat exhaustion, but all you're concerned about is eating lunch and romancing another bitch?!"

Holiday blew out a breath and slid his hand into his pocket. "Alright, Annette. I'm on my way there now."

Her reply was low, more sinister. "That should've been your *first* response," she said and hung up.

"I'm so sorry. We gotta take this to go," he told Cynthia. "His mama is worried it might be heat exhaustion or something, so I'm gonna go and check on him. I'm sorry."

Cynthia nodded. "No, no. I understand completely. It's not a problem at all."

They waved over a nearby waitress and requested the check and to-go containers. He took out his card to pay for their meal, but Cynthia insisted. "It's my treat, remember?"

"Naw, it's on me this time. I have to pay since I'm the one messing up the date."

She obliged. And he knew it was only because he needed to go and see his son right away.

She drove him back to pick up his truck. "Again, I'm so sorry about this," he said when she pulled into the driveway. "I will make this up to you."

"Don't worry about it," she said and leaned towards him to receive his kiss. "It was just lunch."

"Yeah, but how many more of these will I get before you go?"

She rolled her eyes. "Get out and go and see about your son. I am the last thing you should be worried about right now."

"I'll see you later," he said and got out of the car and walked next door to his truck.

THIRTY-SEVEN

The television was on, but Mama Genie was nowhere in sight when Cynthia entered the house. She went straight to the kitchen to reheat her takeout lunch since it was probably cold by now. It was unlikely Holiday would be returning to work for the day so she went upstairs to change out of her painting clothes.

"You back already?" Mama Genie asked when she made it back downstairs. "And what's that I smell?"

"Mexican food," Cynthia said, going to the microwave. "You want some?" She pulled the container out and opened it. She stirred the sides, tasted one, and then put the container back in, pressing the quick button to heat the platter for another minute.

"You told me y'all was going out for lunch."

"We did, but we had to take it to go. His son got sick, so he had to go and see about him."

"Really? I didn't know he had children. Well... I guess I never asked, but..."

Cynthia nodded. "Yeah, he had two. A boy and a girl, but the girl died."

Mama Genie looked at her with interest. "You don't say?"

"Mmm-hmm. He told me she drowned in the lake. It was the summer before last I think."

"*What?!* I remember that! Me and Sister Nash was settin' right here when it came on the news."

"Oh yeah?" The microwave beeped and Cynthia gathered her plate and took a seat at the dining table.

"Yeah, 'cause we was trying to figure out if we knew who the family was. But I 'member Reverend Moore including them in prayer the next day at service. The girl was no more than about five or six, right?"

Cynthia shook her head. She didn't remember Holiday mentioning how old Laila was when she passed away. "I'm not sure," she replied and Mama Genie fell silent as Cynthia bowed her head to say Grace.

"Oh mercy. I had no idea," Mama Genie said when Cynthia opened her eyes again. "That is so sad. So now he just got that one boy, huh?"

Cynthia nodded. "And she was the first girl grandbaby for his parents since his brother has five boys with his wife. Holiday told me when she came along they were all crazy about her, so imagine how they must've felt."

Mama Genie shook her head in sympathy. "Wait 'til I tell Sister Nash this—"

Frowning, Cynthia said, "Now why you wanna go telling Sister Nash everything, Mama Genie? This happened two years ago."

"Because. I'm sure she wanna know."

Cynthia groaned under her breath. "Please don't. I can see Sister Nash now the next time she's over here and sees him, asking him all kinds of questions. I'm sure he doesn't want to talk about that all the time. Losing her was hard enough."

"Well… I'm just gonna tell her I know who it was now. And maybe we should send a little memorial tree to the family from Saint Emmanuel."

Cynthia wanted to scream. "Mama Genie! Why? What's the

point of doing or saying anything? Just forget I told you, okay?"

Mama Genie laughed. "What you gettin' all upset for? What's it to you anyway?"

Cynthia had to stop herself. As crazy as she was about her Mama Genie, she didn't appreciate how she felt the need to share *everything* with Sister Nash. True, Sister Nash was Mama Genie's closest friend, but Cynthia thought there were certain things that needed to remain between her and her grandmother. Holiday's daughter's passing was something he confided in her and Mama Genie did not need to go sharing it with the church, causing grief for the Holiday family all over again. "I'm just saying, Mama Genie, it happened a long time ago. He thinks about her every day. There's no need to open that wound further."

Mama Genie sighed. "Well... I guess I won't say nothing if you don't want me to. I just hate I didn't know it was him."

"Mama Genie, you didn't even know Holiday two years ago. It doesn't matter. Now... do you want some of my food or not?"

Mama Genie turned up her nose. "Nope. I don't want none of your food you ol' sour puss."

Cynthia cracked up. "Fine then," she said, grinning. "More for me."

* * *

Night fell and Cynthia had not heard from Holiday. She would not call him because she did not want to give the impression she was checking up on him and his whereabouts. They'd spent nearly every day together for the past several weeks, shared many laughs and steamy kisses, but he was not her man. And she was not his woman. In two weeks she would be packing up her things and heading back to Houston.

She powered down her laptop after spending a half-hour perusing job postings. Discouraged after seeing so many ads requiring specific years and experience in the field—and after that email she received—she thought it would be a waste of her time and the company's to even apply to a position seeking certain years of experience even though it was noted as a preference and not a requirement.

Cynthia sighed heavily and lay back on her bed. Her college degree was in business management with a minor in communications. She was one of those students that could not make up her mind what she wanted to do with her degree after graduating, so she'd attended a seminar about a fast-track way to become a teacher in Texas boasting a generous starting salary, great benefits, and every holiday and summer off. She jumped at the opportunity.

But after working for two school districts and one charter school, and after too much work to do on the weekends, she was ready to move on to something new. She loved working with kids, but wished she could find something that would allow her to work with them in another capacity. Somewhere she could help foster their learning and growth in a creative, but less restricted way.

She decided she would take a traditional teaching job for one more year if she had to until she figured out exactly what her next career would be.

THIRTY-EIGHT

"It's been a long time since I came to work with you huh, Daddy?"

"He need to start bringing you every day so I can go on and retire."

Holiday shook his head at Frank's comment. Frank was in one of the guest rooms across the hall while he and Christian worked together in the master bedroom. They'd just finished placing painters tape along the baseboards. "Yeah, son, it's been a while," he said to Christian. "But you know I can't take you all the time for insurance and safety reasons. Only for small jobs like this." He watched as Christian dipped the paint roller into the tray and then made his first stroke on the wall.

"Remember that time you let Maximillion and Solone come with us and Solone stole that lady's candy bar?"

Holiday chuckled. "Yeah, which is why they can't come with us no more."

"And what you talking about, Grandpa," Christian said. "I'm just barely going to middle school, so you can't retire. You gotta stay and help my daddy until I'm old enough to work with him."

"What you mean *help your daddy?*" Frank shot back. "Your daddy is here to *help me*. That's *my* name on that truck outside," he laughed. "Don't get it twisted. Is that what y'all kids say? Twisted?"

Christian giggled. "But my daddy's last name is Holiday, too."

"Hello? Is anybody here? I heard a bunch of racket all the way next door, but I don't see anybody."

Holiday smiled when he heard her voice. He'd taken a chance and called to wish her a good morning as soon as he woke up that morning and to let her know he was thinking about her.

"Who is that?" Frank yelled out. "Is that that Cynthia girl?"

Holiday stepped into the hallway to see Cynthia standing near the front door smiling. He had to restrain himself from pulling her into his arms and kissing her mouth since Christian was in the next room. Instead, his eyes feasted on the beautiful smooth skin of her shoulders and legs dressed in a purple tank top and dark denim shorts. "What's going on, beautiful?"

"The usual nothing. So I've come to interrupt your flow."

"I like the sound of that," he smiled at her. "Pop and Christian are here. We're working the other rooms today." He let her go ahead of him down the hall and his eyes took in the lovely view of her from the back: her small waist, her round bottom, her shapely calves. And maybe it was just his imagination or maybe it was just her sassy way because she knew he would be watching, but there seemed to be an extra sway to her hips.

"Hi Frank," she said as she peered into the guest bedroom.

"Ms. Cynthia! How you doing, dear?"

"Good," she replied.

"Don't tell me my son got you coming over to put you to work again? He told me you helped him with the living room yesterday. Is he paying you for your services?"

Cynthia laughed. "Well—"

"There you go, Pop," Holiday said before she could answer. "She volunteered because I told her you were home with heart burn. See how sweet she is?"

"Yeah, she is because she didn't have to do that. And you know what…" Frank set his paint roller down and reached into his back pocket for his wallet. "I gotta give you something for helping us out yesterday."

Cynthia shook her head and waved her hands. "No, Mr. Frank, you don't have to do that. It was nothing."

"Naw, naw. We gonna pay you something. We gettin' paid to do this, so it's only right that we pay you for your share."

"No. I can't take your money, Mr. Frank. I didn't even do that much. He did most of the work."

Holiday enjoyed watching Cynthia look on in disbelief as Frank pulled two fifty dollar bills off his stash and handed them to her.

"Mr. Frank, I cannot take this. I didn't do one hundred dollars' worth of painting that's for sure."

Frank waved her off. "Go 'head and take it. That come from *his* portion anyway."

"I can't—"

"Ms. Cynthia, if you don't want the hundred dollars, you can give it to me!"

Cynthia turned around to see Christian standing in the hallway behind her as Holiday and Frank laughed.

"You must be Christian," she laughed too.

Christian nodded. "Yes, ma'am."

"So you're feeling better today?" she asked him. "I heard you were sick."

"Yes, ma'am," he replied again.

Holiday said, "Which is why he's hanging out with me today so he can get a break from his auntie's house."

"Oh, okay. So they got you working hard today?" Cynthia said to Christian.

"Yeah, I know how to paint too. My daddy show me a lot of stuff when I go to work with him. He say we gonna build a go-cart and I can paint it whatever color I want."

Cynthia smiled and looked at Holiday. "You teaching him to be a handyman already?"

Holiday nodded. "We try to keep him busy so he's not sittin' around playing video games all day."

"That's cool," she said and followed Holiday and Christian back into the master bedroom.

"See, Ms. Cynthia, this the wall I'm doing now." Christian picked up his paint roller, eager to show her what he could do.

"It looks like you're a pro at this already," she smiled at him. "The whole house will be finished in no time now that they have you here to help."

"Now don't you go filling that boy's head up," Frank chuckled across the hall. "He'll be talking about his arms tired and he ready to go home in a minute."

"No I won't," Christian whined. "I don't say that all the time, Grandpa."

Holiday asked her, "Cynthia, you want a chair?"

"I don't have anything to do today, so I can stay and help if y'all want me to."

"You don't have to—"

"I *know* I don't have to," she grinned at him. "You tell me that all the time, but I don't mind."

Frank interjected, "Yeah, son, go 'head and give her a brush. She done already told us she didn't work for the money she got paid, so this her opportunity to make up for it."

Holiday shook his head and Cynthia laughed out loud.

"Alright, Mr. Frank. You're right."

Holiday let Cynthia takeover the roller he had been using while he began working in the en suite bathroom. And it wasn't long before he heard her engaging in easy chatter with Christian.

"That's a cool hat you got on. So you're a Steelers fan?" she asked Christian.

"Yep. That's my favorite team."

"My best friend is from Pittsburgh. She likes the Steelers too."

"Black and gold is my favorite colors. And I like the coach."

Holiday laughed quietly to himself. He listened as Cynthia and Christian moved on to other topics: Christian looking forward to attending junior high school, his favorite subjects, what he likes to do in his spare time, what he wanted to be when he grew up, how much he liked playing with his cousins, Maximillion and Solone, at their house because they have the coolest toys. In turn, he asked Cynthia what she liked to do and what were her favorite colors, favorite foods, if she liked video games, and if she had a favorite football team.

It touched him to hear her interacting with Christian, and when he peeked in on them at one point it reminded him of what he missed most: having a family.

"So, are you my daddy's new girlfriend?" he asked.

"Alright, son," Holiday said, stepping back into the room.

Cynthia gave him a quizzical look.

Holiday walked over and laid a hand on Christian's shoulder. "Ms. Cynthia here is a friend. Ms. Genie next door is her grandmother who she's here spending time with for the summer. And me and her just been hanging out, having some fun while she's here in town."

"Oh," Christian said, "'cause she is very pretty, Daddy. I thought she was your girlfriend."

Cynthia and Holiday and Frank laughed.

"I agree with you, son. She is quite beautiful. Inside and out," Holiday winked at Cynthia, watching her blush.

* * *

"Well, that was fun," Cynthia said as she and Holiday stepped out onto the porch.

"Even with Christian talking your head off?"

"I loved it," she said, dusting her arms, shirt, and shorts. "He's a sweet kid. And he's charming already. Must've gotten that from you."

Holiday grinned and wrapped his arm around her shoulder. "Thank you for your help. If I didn't have him with me I would take you out for lunch since I owe you one for yesterday."

"It's no big deal. I'm sure you're gonna show up and force me to go out with you at some point. You're good for doing that."

"Aww, man. So now you think I force you to do things with me?"

She nudged his side and grabbed his hand resting on her shoulder. "I'm just teasing. Hey, I've never seen this side of the porch."

Cynthia led Holiday around the other side of the porch with his arm still resting on her shoulders. "Y'all did a really good job with this. It looks like it's been this way the whole time."

"Thanks."

"It's making me want to consider having a wrap-around porch when I buy my first house."

"Oh yeah? So you're getting your own this time, huh? To hell with renting, right?" he laughed.

She sighed. "Well… I have to get a job first."

Holiday frowned. "I thought you were teaching?"

She pulled away from him and leaned against the banister. "I got laid off. The school closed."

"Closed?"

"It was a charter school."

"I didn't know. You told me you were preparing to go back to school in a few weeks." Holiday watched her fold her arms across her chest.

"I know, but it was only because I didn't want to talk about it. These past few months have been absolutely crazy for me."

"Wow," he said and leaned his back against the banister next to her. "But you should've told me. Maybe I could've called around for you to see if somebody know somebody that's hiring."

A smile spread across her face. "Look at you. Wanting to save me from everything."

"Hey, I just wanna help out a friend."

"You're too kind."

"Seriously though… I can talk to Yoauna. She just got a promotion, so maybe her old position is available. Or maybe my other buddies' wives may know something."

Cynthia shook her head. "I appreciate your concern, but I'm searching for a job in Houston, not here. Aside from Mama Genie, there's nothing for me here. I think I've outgrown the small-town life."

"Ouch," Holiday threw a hand to his chest. "Just stab me right in the heart why don't you?"

"What are you talking about?"

"You leave a brotha no hope," he said, shaking his head. He twisted his mouth and took on a feminine voice, mocking her, *"It ain't nothing here for me!"*

She laughed. "I didn't mean it as ugly as you're making it sound. But it's just that all of my life is in Houston. I've been there for almost fourteen years now."

"Mmm-hmm… I get it," he nodded.

"What do you want me to say?" she looked up at him.

Since they were out of sight of Frank and Christian, he moved to stand directly in front of her and wrapped his arms around her shoulders so that her face was just inches away from his. "Nothing more than what you want to say. I just want you to know that I dig you. A lot. And I hope you continue to think about me when you go back home." He kissed her then, and did not stop until she gently pushed him away.

"Christian could walk out here any minute. You need to go back inside."

"See you later," he said, and as he turned to go back into the house he felt a slap on his butt.

THIRTY-NINE

Cynthia lay in bed, her room illuminated by the light of her cell phone screen as she flipped through old photos. She couldn't sleep. The night air was still and humid, rendering the fan standing near the foot of her bed useless. The glass of iced water she'd tiptoed downstairs to get sat on her nightstand, beads of sweat sliding down its sides, staining the oak. She took a long sip just to get the feeling of the cold rush through her body. Her nipples hardened as she lay there wearing only a pair of pink cotton bikini briefs.

She looked at the pictures of old friends and colleagues, of her former students. Tora and her beloved crazy cats. *Why do I even have these?* she wondered. Nights out with Jonathan and the crew or just herself and Tora. Random photos of meals she'd cooked or bought. Of the townhouse she rented from Mr. Shabani. She loved that townhouse. Of both beautiful or weird sights and objects she'd come across while out and about at home in the city.

A door slammed shut and she dropped the phone face down on the bed to block the light—as if no one should know she was awake. The clock on her nightstand showed 12:47 a.m. She got out of bed and went to the window.

Holiday?

She caught sight of him just as he stepped on the porch and went into the house. The kitchen light came on shortly after and she watched him moving about inside. And then the light switched on in the bathroom. Minutes later, in Sister Dunham's old bedroom. *What is he doing?*

Cynthia grabbed her sleeping T-shirt off the foot of the bed and pulled it over her head. She thought of calling him to see what he was up to after several more minutes passed, but then he was on the back porch. He was looking for something.

"What are you doing out so late on this side?" she asked when he reached the side of the porch facing her window.

She surprised him, but his smile let her know he was glad to see her.

He replied back, but Cynthia could not hear him as he tried to maintain a whisper, and she went to turn the fan down to its lowest setting.

"What did you say?" she asked, back at the window.

"I said, another late night for you?"

"I can't sleep. But I asked what are you doing out this late?"

"Oh, just messing around with Jesse Lee. He had me come over and help him with something, and we had a few drinks, and before we knew it, it was late. I just came by here looking for Pop's cell phone," he pointed back at the house. "He can't find it and thinks he left it here."

Cynthia nodded. "Oh, okay."

"I didn't see it nowhere in there though," he said. "Why can't you sleep?" He left the porch and came to stand just beneath her window, looking up at her.

"I don't know. It's hot for one thing."

"I'm so sorry y'all have to deal with that. I could've brought a extra fan for you had I thought about it."

She smiled. "That's sweet. Saturday will be here soon."

"Yeah," he said.

"Come here."

"Huh?"

"Come up here," she repeated.

"Come up there?"

"Yes."

He looked towards the front of the house and then back at her.

"You have to use the ladder," she told him. "Mama Genie is asleep in the front room."

He chuckled. "Cynthia. Are you serious?"

"*Yes*," she hissed. "I want you to see something."

He shook his head all the while smiling his bright smile and went to the truck bed to get the extension ladder. She watched him unfold it and place it gently against the side of the house and ascend the rungs, continuing to shake his head.

"Somebody could pass by and think I'm trying to break in this house and call the police on me."

"Now you know these country folks are in their beds for the night. Nobody's gonna see you," she laughed quietly.

"What is it you want me to see?" he said, once he reached the top, eye to eye with her.

"This," she answered, and pulled his face into hers for a kiss. Delicately, she kissed his top lip, then his bottom, the right corner of his mouth, and then the left. She wrapped her arms around his neck, repeating the pattern all over again. "Come inside," she whispered against his mouth.

He grabbed one of her arms, bringing it down in between them. "Cynthia. What? No. I can't do that."

"Yes, you can. Mama Genie is sleeping. Come in here."

"No. What are we? Fifteen? You're not gonna have your grandmama coming at me with her shotgun." He shook his head stubbornly. "No."

His defiance only made her want him more. She grinned and kissed him again. On his chin, his neck; she nibbled his earlobe. She was hot and she needed him to come inside. She pulled at his arms. "Come on," she said. "Just come in for a few minutes. Only a few minutes."

He tsked, but smiled. "Woman, you are something else," and stepped up another rung.

Cynthia turned the fan back up to High.

It took some effort to get his body through the window and his boot hit the floor with a hard thud as the other got twisted in the curtain. Cynthia threw her arms around him, attempting to steady him, but his weight pushed her back and they stumbled together across the hardwood floor another three or four steps. She buried her face in his chest to stifle her laugh, trying to shush him at the same time.

"This is crazy," he whispered. "I can't believe you got me doing this!"

"Shhh…" she said again, but couldn't stop laughing, and pressed her face into his chest until the rumbling of her insides eventually subsided.

He looked down at her. "Only you."

She grabbed his hand and led him back to her chair next to the window to sit.

She straddled him.

Her mouth was instantly on his. The smokiness of alcohol flavored his lips as she probed inside. His mouth was so warm. She cupped his face in her hands, thrusting her tongue deeper. His fingertips gently caressed her skin as his hands traveled the length of her thighs up to her waist. Cynthia arched her back as he squeezed her ass and pulled her body closer into him. She felt his hardness beneath her and a soft moan escaped her lips when the warm wetness of his tongue stroked her neck.

Holiday slipped his hands underneath her T-shirt and Cynthia gripped the back of his head, running her fingers up through his hair. Her nipples were so hard they hurt as they cut through the thin cotton. He pulled one into his mouth—cotton and all—and then the other.

"Cynthia," he breathed into her chest. "We have to stop."

"But I want to," she said, kissing the sweat beads on his forehead. She kissed his eyes and then his lips.

He pulled away and rested his head on the back of the chair, looking up at her. "Are you sure?"

She nodded and leaned into him to kiss him again, and then got up, pulling him towards the bed.

"Naw," he said. "Not here."

Cynthia climbed on top of the bed, patting the soft spot beside her. "She won't know," she said and tugged him down to lay beside her.

With his boots hanging over the edge of the bed he laid beside her, and she could feel the tension in his body. She kissed his temple and then his cheek.

"Here, just lay with me like this," he said and put his arm around her shoulder, moving her to rest her head on his chest.

She sighed heavily, realizing he would not give in, and settled beside him even though the feeling of fire raged between her thighs.

He was quiet for several long minutes stroking her shoulder. His arousal was clearly evident as she lay looking at the bulge inside his jeans and Cynthia wished she had the gumption to snatch his clothes off and mount his lap.

"What brought this on?" he finally asked.

Cynthia rolled her eyes in the dimness of the room. The glow from the moon cast a soft shadow above them on the wall and headboard. "Must you?"

He chuckled.

She shifted beside him and wrapped her arm across his stomach. It was so unfair she thought. His fine body lying next to her, wanting just as much as hers, but there wasn't a damn thing she could do about it.

They lay in silence and Holiday eventually closed his eyes. Cynthia watched his chest rise and fall as he fell into a gentle sleep.

She was still watching him a couple hours later when his eyes popped open and he looked over at her.

She smiled and kissed his nose.

"I need to go," he said, sitting up.

She sighed and rolled onto her side, propping her head in her hand as he left the bed. Her eyes immediately settled on the center of his jeans when he stood. His arousal had not waned.

"I still can't believe I let you talk me into sneaking in Ms. Genie's house," he laughed quietly, and leaned over the bed, planting a kiss on her lips. "See you later."

"Alright," she said.

He eased out of the window, careful not to make a sound or get his boots caught this time, and it was not until Cynthia heard him start up his truck and leave the driveway and speed down the road that she threw herself on her back and exhaled loudly in frustration.

Her body was on fire.

She didn't want to have to, tried not to, and not since Dorian had her do it in front of him, she hadn't had to, but now her hand moved down her stomach, past her navel, over the Mons pubis, until her fingers dipped into the slickness. Cynthia closed her eyes and her hands became Holiday's hands as one squeezed her left breast while the other caressed and massaged her yoni. Her hips rocked slowly with each stroke of his hand until she fell into a rhythm, sending her body closer and closer to a place of ecstasy. She could smell the masculine scent of him, feel the softness of his lips on her skin, the stubble of his goatee as he kissed her neck. And then a wave of heated sensation began at her core, washing over her with an intensity that shook her from the inside out. A guttural moan erupted from her lips and her body tingled all over.

She lay there breathless and spent until her eyes closed and she went into a deep sleep.

FORTY

Holiday stood underneath the showerhead letting the cool water rush over his body. It was his second shower within a few hours' time. When he made it home from visiting with Cynthia it was just a few minutes before four in the morning and he'd undressed and jumped right into the bath tub in an attempt to cool his body down. Her admission that she wanted to be intimate with him sent his mind into a whirl of thoughts. On one hand he could not forget how adamant she was about letting him know she was not one for casual sex, but on the other he would not deny he'd fantasized about making love to her since the first day he laid eyes on her and to do so would be like a dream come true. What brought on her sudden change of heart he wondered? And she had not been forthcoming when he asked her, so her confession had him just as confused as he was excited at the thought.

He had never been a man to pursue a woman only for casual sex. Savannah Holiday had instilled in him and his brother growing up to never play with a woman's feelings and to always be truthful about his intentions. After the split with Annette he'd gone out on dates with a couple of women, but the chemistry was not there and he let them know it was best they parted ways. It had been a long while since he met a lady that held his interest like Cynthia and he knew sweet-tempered women were hard to come by so, although she claimed there was nothing here for her, he couldn't bear the thought of letting her get away. Yet, he also realized, ultimately it was her decision how far their friendship would go.

Holiday grabbed the soap and wash towel and lathered his body. He then squeezed shampoo onto the top of his head to wash his hair. He smiled at the thought of Cynthia running her fingers through it.

Once finished, he turned off the faucet and stepped out of the tub to towel off. He could hear Frank laughing loudly, talking to someone on the phone.

He dressed and Frank said, "Here he come now just getting out the shower," as he stepped into the living room. He held the phone out towards Holiday. "It's Avery."

Holiday took a seat on the sofa. "What's up, bro?" he answered.

"Hey, man. What's going on? How you doing?"

"Man, just chillin'. What's up with you?"

Frank said, "I was telling him how we wanted to get together for a family vacation for Thanksgiving."

"Just working hard as usual," Avery replied. "The center is thriving so we stay busy with that."

Holiday nodded. "That's good to hear, man. How is Dawn and the boys?"

"They're good. Everybody's doing good. We'll be headed that way soon. Me and Dawn got a conference to attend in The Woodlands, so we plan to swing through and see y'all for a bit on our way back."

"That'll be cool."

"But Pop was telling me he wanna take a vacation instead of having Thanksgiving dinner," Avery said.

Holiday looked over at Frank. "Yeah, he want us to get back to our annual family trips. And he don't wanna wait until next summer. He said we should get together sooner, so I told him we needed to find out if you wanted to first."

Avery said, "That's no problem with me, and I'm sure it won't be a problem for Dawn, either. The boys would like that, too. And actually, Thanksgiving is a better time for us because you know summer is our busiest season at the center. And we like to be around for that. Where are y'all talking about going?"

"We haven't figured that part out yet. But Pop already making plans to invite other people."

"Oh yeah? Like who?"

Holiday glanced at Frank, smiling. "He's hoping he has a girlfriend by that time so he can bring her on the trip with us."

Avery laughed. "What?"

"Yeah, he said he's gonna join a bingo club so he can meet him a young lady," Holiday said, joining Avery in laughter.

"Man, tell Pop to sit down somewhere. He's too old for that."

"Oh, so it's rag on Pop today, is it?" Frank yelled out. "I see y'all doubting my abilities."

Holiday pressed the button to put the call on speaker.

"Tell him we don't mind him getting a girlfriend," Avery said, "but please don't bring anybody around here young enough to be our little sister."

"Now see… that's where you're wrong. I'm not into no young girls. I like me a seasoned woman. A woman my age that know how to do a few thangs."

Holiday and Avery continued to laugh and tease and joke with their father until Avery said he had to get to work before Dawn called looking for him. "I will get with Dawn and see where she wants to go for the trip and will let y'all know what she decides."

"Alright, talk to you later, bro," Holiday said, as Frank added, "Okay, son. Bye."

* * *

Holiday closed all the windows in the house and locked the door on his way out for the day. It was four o' clock in the afternoon and he'd completed his overview of the interior, completing any necessary paint touchups and making sure the cabinets, countertops, bathroom floors and vanities were all cleaned. He thoroughly swept the floors but decided to put off the wax job for another day. Frank had chosen to go and start work on another site on the other side of town.

He looked over to Ms. Genie's place as he descended the steps. He had not heard from Cynthia all day, her car had not been in the driveway, and her phone went straight to voicemail when he'd called her earlier, and he wondered what she was up to and if she was okay. He contemplated knocking on Ms. Genie's door to find out if she knew where Cynthia was, but decided against it and drove down to the lake instead.

Holiday pulled around to his usual side of the lake and that's when he saw her car parked there in his favorite spot. He scanned the area, realizing the car was empty, and he found her several hundred feet away closer to the edge of the lake lying on her stomach on a blanket, flipping through a magazine.

"So this is your favorite spot now, huh?" he said, approaching her.

"How did you know I was here?" she asked, smiling up at him.

"I didn't. I just came down to hang out a little bit. Why? Were you hiding from me today? I called you earlier."

"My phone didn't ring today."

"I called you. You must've had it turned off so I wouldn't call."

"Whatever. I have no reason to do that to you. I get a poor signal out here sometimes."

"Oh, I see. Well… you mind if I join you?"

"Of course not," she said, and moved over to allow him a spot on her blanket.

His eyes swept over the dip in her back leading to the roundness of her butt and all he could think about was what she'd said she wanted to do to him last night.

"So what you been up to all day?" he asked, sitting beside her.

She flipped a page in the magazine. "I went out for breakfast this morning with Mama Genie and Sister Nash, and then we stopped by the mall. The church Revival is next week and Sister Nash wanted to do some shopping. And when we made it back I went for a drive just to get out of the house."

He rubbed a hand across her back. "Everything okay? You seem kinda down today."

She looked at him. "Do I?"

"Kind of… unless I'm wrong."

"Hmm… I'm okay. Just thinking about what I'm going to do."

"About what?"

"Work, mainly," she sighed.

"Have you been looking?"

"Every day," she nodded.

"Come and work with me and Pop. We need a secretary."

She scrunched up her nose. "*Secretary?* That sounds so nineteen-eighty," she laughed.

"Really? Or, you can work side-by-side with us. Be our assistant, maybe. You proved you're pretty good at painting, so we can show you how to do a few more things: install floors, cabinets, lay sheetrock, build a gazebo. Now, I'm sure we won't be able to pay you what you were making teaching, and health benefits, but…"

She shook her head, laughing. "You're talking like you're really serious."

"I am," he said.

She sat up, folded her legs Indian-style, and wrapped her arms around his neck. "You're really trying to get me to stay here? You are crazy." She kissed his lips.

"Well… since nobody's calling in Houston, you probably need to expand your search."

"Umm… no. It's just taking a little longer than I thought."

He shrugged. "Okay. I told you I'm just trying to look out for a friend."

"I appreciate you," she kissed him again.

"What's that you reading? One of those magazines for women?"

She pulled the magazine into her lap. "No, it's a travel magazine I picked up at the mall while I sat in the food court waiting on Sister Nash and Mama Genie. I like to dream."

He took the magazine and flipped it over to the cover. "I was just talking to my brother this morning about our family trip and we were trying to decide where to go."

"Oh yeah? A family trip sounds fun. What did y'all decide?"

"We haven't decided yet. He said he's gonna talk to Dawn and we're gonna let it be her decision."

"That's so cool y'all get together like that."

He nodded, "Yeah, it was something my mama started. We took a big family trip together every year, so we're trying to get back to that."

"I sure could use a getaway myself. Just to relax and forget about it all for a few days. Oh! To be on a cruise, lounging while we sail the high seas…." She closed her eyes and laid back on the blanket, her arms stretched out at her sides onto the grass.

Holiday chuckled. "Is that what you wanna do?"

"Mmm-hmm. I wish."

"Then let's go."

Her eyes popped open. "What?"

"You said you wanna get away."

"What are you talking about?"

"We can do something before you go back home. Maybe a day trip or something like that."

She grinned. "I should start calling you Mr. Dream Maker. I think that's what you're trying to be for me."

"Well… I'd like to think I can be."

Her bashful smile stirred something deep inside him. Her sweetness drove him crazy.

"I'm just being honest. Like you said, I could use a little time away myself. It's been a while for me, too. And I'd rather take you with me."

She hesitated a few seconds and then raised an eyebrow. "When?"

"This weekend?"

"Okay," she agreed quickly, but then, "Wait… the A/C man is coming this weekend."

"That's right," Holiday shook his head. "What about tomorrow?"

"Tomorrow? On a Thursday?"

"Yeah, we can leave tomorrow and come back Saturday morning. The A/C repairman is not coming until late Saturday, remember?"

"Sounds good," she said, but then she squint her eyes at him. "Wait… are you trying to get me alone? You had this whole thing planned out as soon as you made it home last night, didn't you?"

Holiday threw his head back, chuckling. "No, not at all."

She smacked him with the magazine. "You're not slick!"

"I'm serious. I really didn't."

"Uhn-huh, sure."

He wrapped his arm around her shoulders to pull her closer to him. And she squirmed as he whispered in her ear, "I would love to be alone with you."

FORTY-ONE

Cynthia had her outfits laid out on the bed, along with coordinating sandals and accessories, and her toiletries. Holiday had called early that morning and said he would be there to pick her up at twelve noon. He'd made plans for them to have lunch before they reached their weekend destination, but would not tell where they were going. She did not get much sleep last night because her mind would not rest as she mulled over what had become of her life for the past several weeks. If someone had told her she would meet a man that would make her change her mind and throw caution to the wind, she would have called them crazy.

She pulled her luggage from the closet and began to stuff her things inside when her cell phone rang.

Tora?

She glanced at the clock on her nightstand. Holiday would be there in a half-hour. Tora could be quite chatty most times and Cynthia knew she did not have time to indulge her friend and instead wanted to concentrate to make sure she'd packed everything she needed. She let the call ring to voicemail. And Tora always left a voicemail—even if it was just to request she call her back.

Cynthia folded her sun dress as neatly as she could between a kitchen trash bag. She'd read somewhere that it was an easy way to keep certain fabrics from wrinkling and thought it would be the perfect time to test its claim. It was the dress she'd worn to Yoauna's party and the one a lot less casual than the others she'd brought with her; and she'd decided to bring it along in case she and Holiday went somewhere requiring dressier attire.

She zipped the suitcase and rolled it over to the door. As she scanned the room, going over in her head to be certain she had everything, she suddenly remembered she forgot to pack bath towels. The familiar tone alerting her of a voicemail message sounded on her phone as she left the room for the linen closet in the upstairs landing.

That must be one long-ass message, she thought.

Cynthia set the luggage on the bed again, unzipped it, and placed the towels inside. She picked up her cell phone and sat down on the bed, pressing the button to listen to Tora's message.

"Hey, lady! You must be out there having a damn-good time because you haven't called me. At least… I hope you're having a good time. When are you coming back? But I have something to tell you, so you have to call me back right away. I went to Julien's last night with Candace and her cousin. Do you remember Candace, my coworker I was telling you about? The one that's getting married to that fine-ass Nigerian? We went there last night because you know Julien's has the wings and drinks special on Wednesday nights now, right? Wait… Mink! Mink! Stop that! I'm not gonna keep telling you…"

Cynthia shook her head and chuckled. One would swear Tora was a mother of a terrible two-year-old with the way she talked to and tried to discipline her pet cat. Several seconds passed before she was back on the phone and continued the message.

"This darn cat, I swear, she's gonna have this apartment complex charging me all types of fines when I decide to move because she tears up everything. Why can't she be as cool as my baby Silk? He's such a good cat. He never gives me any problems. But anyway… what was I saying? Oh! So, we were at Julien's and guess who I saw? Jonathan and—"

Cynthia pulled the phone away from her ear and pressed the button to end the voicemail. She didn't even want to hear it. And she was suddenly pissed that Tora felt the need to call her with that information. Why would she want to hear about Jonathan being out on a date with Davina? Why would she want to hear about Jonathan at all?

She stood and zipped the suitcase for the final time. She turned off the fan and then grabbed her purse from the rack hanging on the closet door.

Mama Genie looked questioningly at her as she set the luggage near the front door once downstairs.

Cynthia smiled. "What, Grandma?"

"Don't 'what' me. So you decided to go on back home without telling me?"

"No. Of course not. Just gonna get away for the weekend. I'm hanging out with Holiday." Cynthia went to the kitchen for a glass of water. She could feel Mama Genie watching her the entire time as she pulled a glass from the cabinet, rinsed it, filled it with water from the pitcher in the refrigerator, and stood drinking from the glass until all the water was gone and she set it on the counter next to the sink.

"What you mean you hanging out with Holiday for the weekend?" Mama Genie glanced at the luggage. "Are you trying to tell me you spending the night with him?"

"It's just like a mini vacation. He said he hasn't taken a vacation in a while and asked me if I wanted to come with him."

"A mini vacation, huh? To where?"

"Now, that, I don't know. He wouldn't tell me. He said it's a surprise."

"Uhn-huh," Mama Genie huffed. "Does Jonathan know about this?"

Cynthia sighed. She knew it was time. Her grandmother needed to know the truth.

She plopped down on the couch. "Grandma, it's best I go ahead and tell you."

Frowning, Mama Genie said, "Tell me what?"

"Me and Jonathan are no longer together."

"You kidding."

"No."

"When did this happen?"

"Back in May."

"*May?*" Mama Genie looked at her, incredulous. "Why you just now telling me?"

"I didn't wanna talk about. That's all." Cynthia folded her arms across her chest.

"Why? What happened?"

"He wanted to be with somebody else I guess," she shrugged.

Mama Genie said, "Is that what he told you?"

"No. I saw him with her."

Mama Genie picked up the remote to turn down the television. "So you saw him with another woman? That don't mean much of nothing. Didn't you tell me he had girls he go out with as friends? Kinda like what you and Holiday been doing?"

"It was more than that, Mama Genie." She didn't want to go into the details with her grandmother. It had been a few months since the breakup, but the pain and humiliation she felt after what she'd witnessed that day she let herself into Jonathan's house resurfaced every now and then and pierced her heart anew. However, over the past several weeks and spending time with Holiday she noticed thoughts of Jonathan had become few and far between and the hurt did not hurt as much anymore.

"Well… have y'all talked it over?"

"What is there to talk about?"

"Did he apologize? Jonathan is such a nice young man."

"Mama Genie, a nice young man would not cheat on his girlfriend."

"Well, you're right about that," Mama Genie shook her head. "But I can't believe that Jonathan. I'm so disappointed in him. All this time I thought for sure y'all was gonna get married soon and have me some grandbabies."

Cynthia thought their relationship eventually would have led to matrimony, too, but she didn't say it to Mama Genie.

She sighed. "It wasn't meant to be. I would never stay with a man that cheats on me."

"I know that's right," Mama Genie agreed. "Especially a man you don't have no children for."

"Even if I had children I still wouldn't stay. I expect the same level of respect from my man or my husband as I give to him."

Cynthia heard a vehicle pull into the driveway and she stood up. "That's him," she said, and threw her purse over her shoulder. "I'll be back Saturday morning. Oh, and I forgot to tell you the A/C repairman is coming Saturday. But late Saturday, so we will be back before then." She kissed her grandmother's forehead.

Mama Genie got up from her chair and followed her to the screen door.

Cynthia pulled her luggage out to the porch. The sight of Holiday and the thought of spending an entire weekend with him made her heart flutter in her chest.

He smiled as he came up to the porch. "Hello, Ms. Genie," he said.

"Uhn-huh… so you come to kidnap my granddaughter for the weekend I heard," Mama Genie answered.

Holiday chuckled. "Yes, ma'am. For a weekend getaway to have some fun. I hope it's okay with you."

"Fine time to ask. But, she grown, and it's her decision. You just be sure to bring her back here just like you found her standing here now: in one piece and without a scratch."

Cynthia watched Holiday's surprise at Mama Genie's candor.

He nodded. "I can assure you of that, Ms. Genie. She's safe with me."

"Alright," Mama Genie, said. "Y'all be careful and, Cynthia, call me when y'all get to where you're going so I know."

"I will," Cynthia answered and kissed Mama Genie again. Holiday grabbed her bag and she followed him to the truck.

* * *

"Mmm… I hadn't had a good sandwich like that in a long time," Cynthia said from the passenger seat, running her tongue over her teeth. Lunch was sandwiches and potato salad at a deli and café just outside of town.

Holiday nodded as he pulled away from the small eatery. "It was my first time here, too. Pop told me about it a while back and I had been wanting to try it out for a while."

Cynthia nestled in her seat as she felt sleepiness coming on suddenly. If she had to guess, she got only two to two-and-a-half hours of sleep last night. "You still don't wanna tell me where we're going?" she asked him.

Holiday smiled. "Don't you wanna be surprised?"

"Yes, but give me a hint at least."

"It's only about two hours away and it looks like a really nice place to relax."

Cynthia rolled her eyes playfully. "That's not a hint at all. And how do you know about this place?"

"I was up all night trying to find something and, of the ones I narrowed the choices down to, this one was more suitable for couples. So I was glad to get a reservation on such short notice."

"Well I can't wait to get there and do just that… relax," she said, yawning.

"Looks like you're gonna need a nap when we get there. Am I right?"

Cynthia covered her mouth as a second yawn came on. "No, if it's okay with you, I'm gonna take a nap now."

He chuckled. "Alright."

She reclined the seat and closed her eyes.

FORTY-TWO

Holiday looked over at Cynthia resting peacefully in his passenger seat. If he could he would have carried her right up to the hotel room and laid her across the bed so she could continue to sleep undisturbed since it was clear she was very tired as he noticed she did not stir when he cut the engine.

"We're here," he said, and touched her arm.

She opened her eyes and sat up. "It's been two hours already?"

"Yep. It took us no time."

Stretching, she looked around. "Why did you park so far away from the entrance?"

"Because I wanted this to be what you see when you opened your eyes."

She smiled and he watched her look out towards the expanse of blue water on their left and the evergreen golf course on their right. "A premier Lake Conroe resort and spa…" she said, reading a campus direction sign. "It looks nice."

"I hope it lives up to what I saw online," he said, getting out of the truck. He went around to the passenger side to help her out and then grabbed their luggage from the cab.

"Mmm… smells like vanilla," Cynthia inhaled when they entered the lobby.

Holiday was pleased to see the interior of the resort looked as good as it did online. It was the first time he had ever planned a trip by himself or made a reservation for anything and he could only hope he was making a good choice as he browsed the Internet last night.

The woman behind the front desk greeted them with a warm smile. "Checking in? May I have your name, sir?"

"Mason Holiday," he said.

She swiftly punched the information into the computer. "Alright, that's a reservation for two king suites, checking in today, checking out Saturday morning at eleven a.m.?"

"Yes, ma'am." Holiday had decided on getting them separate rooms because, although she had agreed to take this trip with him, he did not want to overstep his boundaries and assume she would be willing to share a space with him the entire weekend.

"I'll just need your credit card and both of your IDs, please."

Holiday and Cynthia handed over their drivers licenses and after the information was confirmed, the clerk handed them back. "Here you are Mr. Holiday and Ms. Williams." She then laid out a folder in front of them on the counter. "In here is everything you need to know about the resort and what we offer. The spa schedule, our dining room and restaurants. The fitness room hours and about our golfing services. We also have a walking trail. A social room, night club, and piano bar. Here is a map of the facility for your convenience. This is a smoke-free resort; however, there are designated areas should you need them. Here are your room keys. You are on the seventeenth floor and your elevator is just right this way to my right. Please call us if you need anything. I hope you enjoy your stay Mr. Holiday and Ms. Williams," she smiled again.

"Ms. Williams, huh?" Holiday said as they stood waiting at the elevator bank. "After all this time I'm just now knowing your last name."

"Really?"

"You never told me."

"I guess the opportunity never came up."

It seemed like forever before the elevator made it down to the lobby floor. The doors swooshed open and Holiday and Cynthia stood back as several men all dressed neatly in khaki or pastel-colored shorts, polo shirts, and caps filed out of the car, talking and laughing gaily.

"Well, we know where they're going," Cynthia said as she stepped into the elevator.

Holiday pressed the button for their floor.

"Do you golf?" she asked him.

"Naw, I never could get into it. That's Avery's game. Pop watches it sometimes, too. Mostly when Tiger is playing though."

Cynthia nodded and they rode the rest of the way in silence.

They reached their floor and located their rooms. Holiday inserted the key for her room first and opened the door.

"Oh, this is *really* nice," she said as she entered.

"I was hoping we could be on the side facing the lake, but they told me those rooms were all sold out," he said as he set her luggage next to the coffee table in the sitting area.

"This is beautiful." She walked over to the window and looked out. "We still have a nice view. A little bit of the golf course, but mostly trees. I can't wait to see what it looks like at night."

"Yeah."

She turned away from the window. "Oh, and this bed!"

Holiday laughed as she threw herself on top of the plush white bedding with mustard yellow and navy blue accent pillows and bed runner.

"You don't understand how good this feels to be able to sleep in a room with A/C. I *know* I'm gonna sleep good tonight."

Holiday wanted to tell her he knew of a way to ensure she would get a good night's sleep, too, but he didn't want to get ahead of himself.

"I see you got the adjoining room," she said, a devilish grin crossing her face.

Holiday smiled. "Yeah, I wasn't expecting that, believe it or not. But I guess it worked out perfectly just in case you need something. You can just come in and get me."

"Are you going to leave it unlocked?"

"I can leave it open if you want me to."

She bit her bottom lip and Holiday knew he had to do something right now to take his mind away from thoughts of climbing in the bed next to her. "So… you rested up? Or do you wanna finish your nap out? I'm gonna go and unpack."

"I am kinda sleepy still, but I also don't want to be a party-pooper. What do you have planned for today?"

"After we unpack, I figured we could go and check out the pool if you want to. I reserved a table for dinner at the restaurant downstairs for seven-thirty."

"Sounds good, but I don't have a bathing suit with me. Had I known we were coming to a resort, I could've bought a cheap one at the mall or something."

"I know, but telling you would've ruined the surprise. I got a pair of shorts you can borrow."

"It's okay. I have my own," she said.

"Cool. Just knock on the door when you're ready. I'll be waiting for you."

FORTY-THREE

Cynthia and Holiday lay poolside in cushioned wicker chaise lounges. An oversized umbrella and small table separated them. She sipped at her frozen daiquiri while he nursed a beer as they sat watching other resort guests in the pool. Thankfully, the sun had retreated behind a cloud allowing for a few minutes of comfort against its blazing rays.

"When you planning on getting in for a swim?" Holiday asked.

Cynthia pushed her shades up the bridge of her nose and looked over at him. "Swim? I can't swim."

"*What?*" He eyed her in disbelief.

She laughed. "I can't."

"Cynthia, are you serious? What you mean you can't swim? I thought you wanted to go on a cruise."

"You don't necessarily have to know how to swim to go on a cruise," she said.

"You don't? So what's gonna happen if something goes wrong with the ship? How will you get out?"

"They have life boats."

He chuckled. "So you telling me I have to swim alone?"

"I may put my feet in in a little while."

"You are something else." He got up from his seat. "I'm going in," he said.

Cynthia smiled as she watched him walk away towards the deep end. He did not dip so much as a toe in the pool to test the water but, instead, wasted no time and dove right in with the quiet precision of an Olympic swimmer. Her eyes followed him as his dark ebony skin resplendent in red swim trunks glided beneath the turquoise blue water all the way to the shallow end.

His head broke the surface and he looked right over at her, flashing that bright smile.

"That's a long time to hold your breath," Cynthia said.

"You have to get in," he said. "It feels good."

"Oh yeah? Is it cold?"

He shook his head. "No, it's not too cold. It feels good. Come on."

Cynthia got up and walked over to where he stood and took a seat on the side of the pool. She eased one foot in and then the other. "Oh yeah, it does feel good."

"You want me to teach you how to swim?"

She laughed. "Umm… no."

"Why not? Don't you want to learn?"

"It's too late. I'm too old."

"You're never too old to learn how to swim. My mama taught my dad."

"Did she really?"

"Yep. He told me she did that shortly after they got married."

"Wow. That's cool."

"Are you afraid of the water?"

"I don't think so. I just can't float."

"Sure you can. Let me show you," he said, reaching for her hand.

It took a few minutes of his coaxing before she gave in and let him lead her into the water. Two hours later she still had not mastered the basics of floating, and it was nearing dinner time, so they got out.

"I told you I can't float," Cynthia said as they toweled off back at their lounge chairs. She appreciated how patient he had been with her in the pool even though she was a ball of frustration after some time. And he would not let her give up and pushed her over and over to keep trying and not worry about being overtaken by the water, which he believed was her difficulty.

"You'll get it eventually. You just need to learn to relax. We'll try again another time."

He threw the towel across his shoulders, working to dry off his back, and Cynthia tried not to stare at the mass of coal black hair on his chest, at the trail of it that began at his navel and disappeared below the waist band of the swim trunks that did little to hide how well-endowed he was.

"Look at you," he said, adjusting the string tie on his shorts.

"What?" Cynthia grinned.

"You know."

She laughed and he wrapped his arms around her shoulders as they exited the swimming pool area and entered the hotel.

* * *

Cynthia spritzed her body with one of her favorite *Bath & Body Works* fragrances—A Thousand Wishes—and checked herself again in the full-length mirror. It was inevitable. She knew what was to come by the end of the night after dinner with Holiday. And she was ready.

She knocked on the door separating their rooms and he opened it within seconds.

"Oh yeah, baby," he said, looking her up and down and shaking his head. "That's that dress I like." He leaned in to kiss her mouth.

"You're looking good yourself. I see you do own more than just cargo jeans and T-shirts," she teased. He was dressed smartly in an olive green button down shirt cuffed at the elbow, dark wash jeans, and black casual shoes.

"I try to clean up every now and then," he said. He placed a hand on her lower back as they left the room for the elevator.

It was a long ride down as the elevator seemed to stop on every floor and more guests piled in.

The ground floor restaurant offered a romantic setting with its low lighting and classical music playing. Round tables were dressed in cream-colored cloths with gold napkins folded to stand in perfect triangles. Flameless candles flickering in ornate cages served as centerpieces. They were seated near the window overlooking Lake Conroe. A waiter soon came over and took their wine and appetizer order.

"This is really beautiful," Cynthia said, looking out of the window.

"Yeah, I'm pretty impressed so far. I was hoping I made a good choice, but I feel kinda bad now," Holiday told her.

"Why?"

"Because I didn't know you can't swim. I reserved a spot for us to go jet skiing tomorrow."

"Oh no! Did you really?"

"Yeah, for tomorrow afternoon."

"I'm so sorry," Cynthia said, sitting back in her chair. "You probably think I'm so lame."

He chuckled. "Because you can't swim? No, I don't think that."

"With as much as I like the beach and cruises you would think I knew how."

"It is kinda strange. But don't worry about it. I'll see if they let me cancel. If not, then you will be watching me jet ski."

"I can ride with you, but you may have to go slow."

His forehead crinkled. "Say what? That's no fun." He laughed quietly again. "You can just go and get your massage while I jet ski."

Cynthia sat straight up. "Massage? What are you talking about?"

"At the spa. I reserved that for you, too. A hot stone massage or something like that and a manicure and pedicure."

Cynthia couldn't believe it. She asked, "What did I do to deserve all this?"

"What you mean? We came here to relax and have a good time, right?"

She nodded, "Well, yeah, but, I wasn't expecting anything extra like a day at the spa. And why aren't you getting a massage, too, if that's the case?"

"A massage for me? No," he shook his head. "That's for women."

"No they're not. Men get massages. They're for anyone wanting to relax and get the muscles ironed out."

"Well, if anybody's gonna be ironing my muscles out I want it to be you," he winked at her.

"Hmm… I bet you wo—" The waiter approached the table then, setting their wine and seafood combo appetizer in front of them. He asked if they were ready to order and they agreed. Cynthia requested lamb chops and Holiday the NY strip steak. She removed her napkin from the table and flattened it across her lap when her cell phone rang.

"Oh shoot! I forgot to call my grandma," she said when she pulled the phone from her purse.

"I'm guessing y'all still on the road," Mama Genie said when she answered.

"No, we made it a while ago. It totally slipped my mind to call you. Sorry about that."

"So you just lose all your good sense when you're out with Holiday, huh? This ain't the first time you done forgot something," Mama Genie laughed.

Cynthia had no rebuttal because it was true. Being with him she lost all sense of time as well. It was nonstop good times and great feelings. He made her feel beautiful and sexy and wanted. She looked across the table at him as he peered out of the window. Whatever initial reservations she had about being with him were all gone.

"Where y'all end up going to?" Mama Genie asked, breaking her thoughts.

"A resort in Conroe. It's really, really nice, too. I didn't know we had something like this just a couple hours away from town. We're sitting here now about to have dinner at the steakhouse with a lovely view of the lake."

"Uhn-huh. Must be nice. But I won't hold you up. I was just calling to make sure you were all right."

"Okay, Grandma. And I'm sorry again I forgot to call you."

"When you say you coming back?"

"Saturday morning," Cynthia said. She and her grandmother said their goodbyes and when Cynthia pressed the button to end the call she noticed she'd missed another call from Tora. She switched the phone to vibration mode and slipped it back into her handbag. "Why aren't you eating?" she asked Holiday and took a crab cake from the appetizer platter, setting it on her saucer.

"I was just waiting for you," he said, and grabbed a shrimp. "Is that a Iphone you have?"

She nodded as she chewed the tasty crab cake. "Yeah. Why?"

"I forgot to pack my charger and I'm at about two percent battery."

"Maybe the front desk has a charging station," she said. "You should ask. I'm sure you're not the first guest to forget your charger."

He waved his hand. "It's cool. I'm here with you, so I'm not gonna worry about it. This is my vacation, so no phones because I'm here to spend time with and focus on you."

Cynthia blushed and took a sip of wine.

Their meals were brought to the table shortly after and they ate.

"You wanna go and check out the rest of the place or are you ready to go back to your room?" Holiday asked once they were finished.

"Okay, we can do that," she said. "Let's go see what else is here."

The waiter came over to clear their table and they both declined when asked if they wanted to top off their meals with dessert. Holiday settled the tab and they exited the restaurant.

Cynthia linked her arm with Holiday's as they strolled through the dimly-lit path of the resort. The night air was warm, stars dotted the sky, and now that they were outside they were no longer in a hurry to check out the rest of place since they would have all day tomorrow to do so. They ambled along the trail with no particular destination in mind.

"Tell me five things I don't know about you," Cynthia said.

"What do you want to know?"

She shook her head at him. "We are not going through this again. You said that the last time. So, come with it. It can be anything."

"Hmm..." he began, thoughtfully. "Five things about me. Like what though? I'm not good at vague questions like this."

"Just do it," she sighed. "Anything."

"Okay. Well... my favorite color's maroon. Favorite food: smoked pork chops. Let's see... you already know what type of music I like so.... I'm a simple man. And by that I mean it doesn't take much to make me happy. I like for the people around me to be happy—my woman, my family."

Cynthia nodded.

"So that's four things, right? One more?"

"No, that was three."

"Just three?"

"Mmm-hmm," Cynthia said, counting them off her fingers. "Your favorite color is maroon, you like barbecued pork chops, and you're a simple man that enjoys making his family happy."

He laughed quietly. "Alright. Uhh… I want a big family. I always dreamed of being married with like six or seven kids."

Cynthia stopped walking. "Are you serious? Six or seven kids?" she asked, staring up at him.

"Yeah," he said. "I would imagine coming home and all of us sitting around the table for dinner. One of those big tables, too, with eight chairs. And all of them would be filled."

Cynthia's mind was spinning at the thought. She couldn't imagine any woman agreeing to such great responsibility. Especially during these times when the cost of living continued to climb while salaries remained stagnate for most people. She had dreams of one day having a family of her own, too, but two or three children were the most she desired. "That's… that's something," she staggered. "So you prefer your wife to be a stay-at-home mom?"

He shrugged. "Not necessarily. It would be her choice."

"She would have no choice because a daycare bill for just one kid is pretty steep, so I can't imagine having to foot the bill for two or more at one time."

He threw his head back, laughing. "You're right about that. I never thought too much about that part of it I guess. It's just what I always dreamed about: having a sweet wife and a house full of kids to come home to every day."

"I see. Was your mom a stay-at-home mom?"

Nodding, he said, "She was. But she went back to work when I turned three and Avery was in first grade."

"Alright," Cynthia said. "One more thing I don't know about you."

He stroked his goatee and several minutes passed as they strolled along and Cynthia began to believe he did not have anything else to offer when he finally said, "I'm trying to come up with a plan to get you to stay here with me."

She laughed. "You are?"

"Yep. Don't you miss Ms. Genie? I'm sure she wants you here with her, too. Somebody to look after her in her golden years."

It was not something she and Mama Genie talked about. Mama Genie had raised her to follow wherever her heart led her and to not worry—that she could take care of herself. And Cynthia knew wherever she decided to settle, it would be no more than a few hours' drive away from her grandmother.

Cynthia said, "We talk on the phone several times a week. And I come down throughout the year to spend time with her. She doesn't care for Houston at all, but every now and then I can convince her to come and hang with me."

Holiday chuckled. "So in other words I need to stop fantasizing, right?"

She linked her arm around his elbow and laid her head on his arm. "I'm sure you will have a new girlfriend or may even be married again when I come back for the holidays. A handsome man like you don't stay single for long."

"Nooo," he shook his head. "No one around here compares to you. These past few weeks together showed me that."

Cynthia had a hard time expressing her feelings when he said things like this to her. How could she tell him she felt the same way? She had definitely fallen for him, but the fact still remained: he lived here and she lived a few hundred miles away. He had a son tying him here and she loved her life in the city.

They came to a beautiful three-tier garden fountain aglow with LED lighting giving the water a golden hue. "Give me a penny," she said. "I want to make a wish."

Chuckling, Holiday reached into his pocket for loose change and came up with a dime. He placed it in her outstretched palm.

Cynthia closed her eyes, mumbled quietly for several seconds, and threw the dime in.

"What did you wish for?" Holiday asked her when she opened her eyes.

"You're not supposed to tell anyone," she smiled.

"Oh, okay."

"Your turn. Do you have another coin?"

"I don't need to wish for nothing. Mine has already come true," he said.

"What is it?"

"I met you."

Cynthia smiled and felt his hands circling her waist, his fingertips caressing the skin exposed through the cutout detail of the dress. He dropped his head and found her lips and kissed her sweetly. She opened her mouth and he slipped his tongue inside. Despite the cool breeze wafting off the water fountain Cynthia felt heat rising from her knees to her chest as Holiday pulled her closer and their tongues intertwined. It didn't matter to Cynthia that they were outside in public and at risk of someone passing at anytime. Some people were put off by public displays of affection, but, in her mind, and at that moment, no one else mattered except the man that held her in his arms. She took back her tongue only to tease his lips again as she tugged gently at the soft flesh. He pulled her into him as his breathing deepened against her mouth. His hands left her waist, traveled over her butt where he squeezed lightly, and then up to her waist and back again.

Cynthia slowly pulled away and looked him in the eye. Her breathing matched his and she knew it was time. She wanted him and she wanted him now.

"Let's go upstairs," she said.

Holiday was sitting on the edge of the bed in his room wearing nothing but a pair of sleep shorts when Cynthia emerged from her bathroom. She had taken her time in the shower as a myriad of thoughts raced through her mind. Mostly thoughts of how bizarre this situation seemed. Just a few weeks ago she had no intentions of spending time with anyone—did not expect to meet someone—and yet here she was on the verge of sharing her body with a man she'd only known a little less than a month. And it would be the first time in her life where she'd make love outside the boundaries of a committed relationship.

But she was taking a chance and following her heart. Holiday was a kind man, a romantic man, and damn sexy and she could no longer maintain her composure around him if she wanted to.

He left the bed and walked over to where she stood outside the bathroom door with the bath towel barely covering her front. He reached for the towel and she let it go and it fell in a soft pile at their feet. He pulled in his bottom lip as he stared at her, slowly shaking his head. That familiar dark and piercing gaze made Cynthia flush with uneasiness and excitement at the same time. He stepped forward and grabbed her waist with one hand as the other lifted her chin to meet his waiting lips.

"Beautiful, baby," he whispered, trailing kisses along her jaw bone down to the curve of her neck.

Cynthia closed her eyes as his goatee caressed her collarbone with each soft kiss planted there. The skin of his strong hands were a little rough, but he touched her with such tenderness that Cynthia thought he might be afraid to touch her at all. He kissed one shoulder and then the other as his hands left her waist to hold her breasts. Her nipples were already hardened by his touch and when his head dipped lower to take one into his mouth Cynthia moaned softly as he gently sucked and licked and flicked his tongue back and forth. He was careful to give the other breast the same attention and Cynthia struggled to remain standing when she felt his free hand stroke the space between her legs.

Holiday lifted her then and carried her over to the bed. Cynthia noticed how solid his penis was beneath the thin sleep shorts and her eyes blinked in wonder as she watched him take them off. It was thick, black, and smooth just like the rest of him, framed by a thatch of hair not unlike the unruly crown above his shoulders.

Cynthia licked her lips.

He tossed the shorts to the side and they landed on the nightstand on the opposite side of the bed. He climbed in next to her and kissed her again before gently pulling her legs apart to position himself between her thighs.

He began at her feet. He kissed the inside of her right ankle, leaving a trail of tender kisses from her ankle to her calf on up to her knee. Cynthia shuddered as his lips brushed and tickled the skin of her inner thigh before his tongue swept over the joint of her pelvis. He was kissing her in places she had never been kissed and her body burned with anticipation of what was to come next.

His mouth covered her lips and Cynthia closed her eyes, anticipating his tongue, but he kissed it instead. So calmly and so gently his lips kissed the delicate folds that Cynthia raised her pelvis to meet his mouth as he began at the top of the split and worked his way to the bottom and back to the top again. Holiday pleasured the other side of her body and it wasn't long before Cynthia was pulling at him to lie on top of her and give her what she craved.

"I'm ready, too," he told her, and reached for his shorts on the nightstand. He pulled a condom from the pocket, ripped the package open, and rolled it down the length of him. Using his knees he parted her legs even further and Cynthia wrapped her arms around him as he covered her body with his. He kissed her lips and her neck and Cynthia took a sharp breath as he entered her. She was wet and warm below, but was not prepared for the size of him and her body tensed around him. Holiday kissed her again, took his time and waited, giving her small pieces of himself until her flesh expanded and she could receive him completely.

He moved slowly and gently above her, sending ripples of heat throughout her body with each sensual stroke. Cynthia fell in rhythm beneath him, rolling her hips to his unhurried grind. She relished in the way he cared for her, the way he spoke tenderly in her ear of how sweet she was, how good she felt. The size and weight of his damp body atop hers, the tease of his chest hair grazing her breasts, and the feel of his swollen flesh gliding in and out of her drove Cynthia to the point of no return. She sucked in a breath and bit her bottom lip as she felt the climax coming on. Gripping his shoulders tight, she raised her hips slightly as he plunged deeper and deeper until every erotic emotion rushed to her center, pushing her over the edge.

She gasped as the feeling overtook her and buried her face in his neck as her body quaked all over. Seconds later a guttural moan escaped Holiday's throat and he surged forward in one deep final thrust, his own orgasm shaking him.

Cynthia clung to him, her legs trembling, her heart beating wildly.

FORTY-FOUR

Holiday discarded the condom and returned to the bed, pulling Cynthia close to him. He licked his lips before kissing hers. "You can't get rid of me now," he said, smiling.

Her eyes brightened and she grinned back at him. "No?"

"Nope," he shook his head. "That was amazing. And I already told you: when I enjoy something, I like to do it again." It had been so long since he'd made love to a woman—and he'd lost count of the number of months in between—but he knew this was worth the wait and definitely with the right woman, the woman lying on her back beside him. He just wasn't sure if he was capable of convincing her.

"So soon?" she said.

He knew she was teasing him. "Give me a few minutes, but yeah."

She raised a hand to his chest, pulling gently at his hair. "I enjoyed you, too," she said quietly.

He smoothed her eyebrows and kissed her forehead. Clearing his throat, he said, "So... Ms. Cynthia... what's your plan?"

Her brows furrowed. "About what?"

"You. From what you've told me... you don't have a job, don't have a place to stay. What are you going to do when you get back home?"

She laughed and he believed it was more so out of nervousness than finding what he said humorous.

"Hmm… maybe I'll work the street corners… like my parents. Do some busking, y'know?" she smiled.

"I told you you got a little bit of them in you."

"Why do you say that?" she asked.

"Because you don't know what you wanna do or where you wanna be."

She laughed again, and for the first time he noticed the small gap between her front teeth—a gap only big enough to see if you were close up on her mouth as he was. It was hard for him to not focus on her kissable lips. "That's not true," she answered. "I'm just trying to find something I like. I'll be back on my feet soon enough. And, as far as my parents go, people may frown at their lifestyle or consider them bums or lowlifes, but they're just two people in love, traveling the world together doing what they love. That's how I look at it."

He nodded. "That's real cool."

"But, why? Why do you keep asking me what I'm going to do?"

"Well… I just think you're a nice lady and I'd like what we have to continue." Now that she had shared the most intimate part of herself with him, he knew he would not be able to let her go. Her face softened and all he could think about was the idea of being able to see that face lying next to him for many more nights.

"Long distance relationships never work," she said.

"You act like you live in California or Washington or something. Houston is just a few hours up the highway."

"Yeah, but, if we do… then what? One of us will have to sacrifice somewhere."

"Of course. And I'm willing." She was quiet for several seconds and he could see her mulling over the situation in her head. He leaned over to kiss her lips after a while, said, "Say yes."

She giggled and squirmed as he kissed her neck, and then her shoulder. Holiday tugged at the sheet, pulling it down just beneath her breasts. At the sight of the huge, raisin-colored areolas he felt himself rising again. He took one into his mouth then, sucking gently until the nipple rose to a peak. He licked the hollow place of her chest before capturing the other breast.

Cynthia moaned softly when his hand slipped beneath the sheet. "Are you ready for me?" He caressed her gently, sliding a finger in and out of her. The slickness of it made him hot all over and he wanted to make love to her again.

But she surprised him when she yelped *No!*, and bolted out of the bed and into the bathroom, slamming the door behind her.

What the hell? He heard the lock click and then her quiet laughter. Seconds later, the shower came on.

He rolled over on his back, clasping his hands behind his head. *So she has a playful side, too?* He chuckled, but was disappointed that she did not invite him to shower with her. Leaving the bed, he got up to go to his room.

He had something for her.

When she emerged from the bathroom minutes later, he was right there waiting, protected and ready. She didn't get a chance to speak because his mouth was on hers, his hands squeezing her hips as he lifted her off the floor. Holiday pushed her back against the wall, sinking into her sweet spot. She groaned into his mouth and he started to pump. Everything about her turned him on and he knew he would not be able to last long. The silky smoothness of her skin as she clung tightly to him, the alluring scent of her body lotion. He felt a soft hand moving up his neck and when she gripped a chunk of his hair he dug deeper. Over and over he plunged into her. The feel of her plush thighs wrapped around him, her flesh slapping against the wall, and the sensation of her body gripping his with each stroke, he was in paradise.

She began to move with him, throwing her body against his to meet his stroke.

Her screams of passion filled the room, and with her skin still moist from the shower he squeezed tighter just to hang on to her as he felt himself weakening from the pleasure of it all. He strained and grunted, taking deep breaths, willing himself to hold off until she peaked first, but his hips seemed to have a mind of their own and drove her into the wall with the fervor of a runaway train. Inside, her body was so hot and so wet he was beyond the edge of delirium.

But she was there, too, he soon learned.

"Here I come," she breathed in his ear, and when her teeth sank into his neck, he lost it.

Everything within him exploded.

"Do you realize we have been up for almost twenty-four hours straight now?" Cynthia drawled. Her back was to his chest, her butt pressed to his pelvis, as they lay in the darkness. After their lovemaking session against the wall, Holiday had carried her over to the bed, where he collapsed beside her. Once they gathered their bearings they eased into light pillow talk. They talked about a little of everything as the hours ticked away, from the most trivial to the absurd. He enjoyed the quiet moment with her, hearing her sweet laughter bounce around the room in the wee hours of the morning. She was so easy to be around and it pained him each time he thought about the small number of days remaining he had to spend time with her.

They made love again—and he was ready for a fourth time—but she'd kissed him, said 'no,' and gently pushed his hand away.

His eyes closed after a while when she fell silent, succumbing to sleep.

"Did you order room service," she asked over her shoulder

sometime later. It took a nudge from her elbow to his chest for Holiday to realize the phone in his room was ringing.

He shifted in bed, kissed her shoulder, "No," he said. "They must got the wrong room." But the ringing stopped only to ring again seconds later. And then the phone on Cynthia's nightstand rang.

"Okay, I'm answering," she said, and reached for the phone.

Holiday planted soft kisses down her spine, wishing to be inside her again. After months of abstinence, being with her had awakened his sexual appetite and he hungered for more of her sweet love.

He stilled when he heard her say, "Yes, he's here."

She put the phone back in its cradle and turned to him. "The front desk said you need to call home. It's an emergency."

Holiday left the bed and went to his room. He searched the dresser and nightstands for his mobile phone, but remembered it was still in the pocket of his jeans, which he'd laid across the back of the desk chair. There were seven missed calls: two from Pop, four from Roxy, and one from Annette. He dialed Annette, and when she didn't answer, he called Pop.

It was about Christian. Pop told him he was in an accident and had been taken to the emergency room and that the situation did not look good. Holiday needed to come home.

His mind racing, Holiday hung up with Pop and stepped back into Cynthia's room. She'd turned on the lamp and was sitting up in bed. "I'm sorry, baby, but how fast can you get your stuff together? We gotta go. Christian's been in an accident."

FORTY-FIVE

Cynthia stole intermittent glances over at Holiday from the passenger seat as he sped down the highway, his speed reaching as high as eighty-five miles per hour at some stretches, and she prayed they would not be pulled over by a state trooper.

"I hope he's okay," she said quietly.

Holiday reached for her hand, linked his fingers with hers, and raised it to his lips to kiss the back of her hand.

Cynthia didn't know how long it took them to make it back to Mama Genie's house, but she knew it was much less than the time it had taken to drive to the resort yesterday afternoon. The two-hour ride seemed more like forty-five minutes.

Holiday got out and came around to her side of the truck to help her with her bag.

She grabbed it from him before he started for the porch. "I got it," she said. "Go and see about Christian." She wrapped her arms around his waist, rose up on her toes and kissed him. "Call me later. I would like to know how he's doing."

"I will," he said. "Thanks, babe."

Mama Genie was standing at the screen door when Cynthia walked up the porch steps. "I knew I heard somebody pull up in the driveway. But I thought y'all wasn't coming back 'til tomorrow morning," she said.

Cynthia moved past her grandmother. Her body was sore from the inside out, her legs like dead weight, and all she wanted was a soothing warm bath and some sleep. "We had to check out of the resort early. Something happened with his son and he's on his way to the hospital to see him."

"Hospital?" Mama Genie exclaimed. "What happened?"

Cynthia looked at the staircase in front of her and, with the way her legs were feeling, was tempted to use the downstairs bath tub and crash in the spare bedroom until her body felt back to normal. "Holiday said he was riding his bike and fell off and hit his head or something. I don't know all the details yet, but he said he would call and let me know."

"Oh Lord, no! I hope that baby's all right," Mama Genie tsked.

"I hope so, too."

"Well, did y'all at least get to enjoy yourself for the time you were there?"

Cynthia thought about all they did not get to see and do. Her body could really use that hot stone massage right now. Then a full night's sleep in A/C. "Yesterday was really nice. And he had fun things planned for us today, but… this happened." Her bed was calling her and she wasn't in the mood for more chatter. "I am dog tired though, Mama Genie, so I'm gonna go up and get some rest." She made her way slowly up the stairs, wincing all the way to the top with each step.

Cynthia rested her head on the cool tiles. She'd filled the bath tub with enough water so that it covered her entire body all the way up to her shoulders. Any exaggerated movement would send water splashing over the rim onto the floor. The warm water and spearmint bubble bath calmed her achy limbs. She closed her eyes, thinking about Holiday. Though her lower half throbbed, she was already missing him and wanted him again. She smiled at the thought. A few hours ago she had had to fight him off because her body could not take anymore of his powerful lovemaking, but now it seemed to pulse with the need for him to come and massage it back to life.

After a good soaking, Cynthia released the stopper to let the water run out of the tub. She patted her body dry and walked across the landing to her bedroom, threw the towel on the dresser, and climbed into bed. No sooner had her head hit the pillow than her cell phone rang. She snatched it off the side table, expecting Holiday, but noticed the phone number was one with a Houston area code.

"Hello?" she answered.

"Hello. Is this Cynthia Williams?"

"Yes, this is Cynthia."

"Cynthia, this is Susan Higginbotham, Vice Principal, calling from Spring Branch ISD…"

Cynthia sat up in bed.

"We received your application for our middle grade Social Studies position. Are you still available?"

"Yes, I am."

"Great! However, I do want to apologize in advance, but another applicant canceled their interview at the last minute, so I am calling to see if you can come in to meet with me today. We are hoping to wrap up all our interviews for the summer, instead of next week as we originally thought we would need to."

Today?! Cynthia's heart began to pound. There was no way she would be able to show up for an interview today. But she also needed this job.

Susan continued, "But since we had to call you on such short notice, we can have you scheduled for our final time slot today at two-thirty? Is two-thirty okay with you?"

Cynthia looked at the clock on her nightstand. It was a few minutes past eleven o' clock. The drive to Houston was three to three-and-a-half hours on a good day. And she still had to dress and find her portfolio. Rather, she knew exactly where the portfolio was, but she needed time to look over her résumé and past lesson plans to prepare herself for any questions she will be asked on how she organizes and manages her classroom. All summer she had been anticipating a call for a job interview, but it was of the notion that she would have at least a day to prepare and make the drive back to Houston. So to get there on time today would be contingent on no highway incidents and no commuters on the road who traveled to nearby cities for their jobs, or people wanting to leave town for a vacation before school starts.

Nevertheless, it was Friday, and Friday meant more people on the roads just because.

But she wasn't going to tell Mrs. Higginbotham that. "Two-thirty is fine," Cynthia answered.

"Great!" Susan's chipper voice sang in her ear. She gave Cynthia the address and instructions on where to go once she was on the campus. "See you at two-thirty," she said.

Cynthia sprang from the bed when the call ended and went to her dresser for undergarments. From the closet she pulled on her navy blue pencil skirt, favorite burnt orange pussy bow blouse, grabbed the skirt's coordinating blazer, and her nude pumps. She sprayed her braids with a moisturizer and smoothed the edges as best she could with oil. She tried piling them atop her head in her signature bun but, because she was in a hurry the look wasn't coming out right, so she let them fall. After retrieving her portfolio from her tote bag in the closet, and grabbing her purse—which was the clutch she carried while out with Holiday last night that did not suit the outfit for her interview, but she did not have time to change it—she bounded down the stairs.

"I have an interview," she said to Mama Genie as she rushed past her standing in the kitchen.

"What?"

"They just called me for an interview later today." With her leather portfolio in one hand, pumps and clutch in the other, Cynthia walked out the door.

"Wait a minute, Cynthia. Come back here," Mama Genie called.

Cynthia said over her shoulder when Mama Genie pushed the screen door open, following her, "I'll call you in a few minutes. Just let me get on the road."

"Lord, have mercy. You be careful, hear?"

FORTY-SIX

Pop, Roxy, Annette, and several other families were in the waiting room when Holiday entered. Pop acknowledged him with a nod, Roxy a worried smile. Annette was seated next to Roxy, wiping tears from her eyes with a balled napkin. Her face set into a scowl when she saw him.

"How you doing, Annette?" he asked quietly. What's going on with Christian?"

"I'm surprised you could make it, seeing as though nobody in town could get a hold of you. Just like the last time." She sniffed. "Why even bother?"

Holiday wouldn't let her words get to him. "How is Christian doing?" he asked again. "Tell me what's going on."

"Do you really care?" she spat, swiping at her red eyes.

"Oh course I care. It's why I'm here."

"I'm sure you would rather be wherever you were."

"C'mon, Nette," Roxy coaxed, placing a hand on Annette's arm, "don't give him a hard time. He's here now."

Annette snatched her arm away. "So what?! My baby is in there fighting for his life!" She stood up suddenly, and before Holiday could react, she banged her fists into his chest.

Roxy jumped up from her seat, attempting to stop her sister's angry blows while the other patrons looked on in bewilderment and surprise.

Holiday held on to her as Annette tried jerking her wrists away from his grip.

"I'm calling security if you all do not settle down," bellowed the woman behind the reception desk.

"Let her go, Brother-in-Law," Roxy whispered. "I got her."

Holiday was hesitant. It wasn't the first time Annette had gotten physical with him during a fit of anger. The last time was a hard slap across his face when he announced he was walking away from their marriage for good.

He released her wrists and Roxy threw her arms around Annette.

"Let's go outside to get some fresh air," Roxy told her.

Annette broke into a hard sob, her whole body shaking as Roxy led her out the door. "I can't lose another one," she cried. "I can't lose another one of my babies!"

Holiday watched them go, the gravity of Annette's words weighing on his chest. He took a seat next to Pop. "What they say happened exactly?" he asked him.

Pop rubbed a hand over his weary face. "Him and Max was out riding bikes down by Crimson Road. You know… where them kids go to ride they bikes up and down those ramps they put out there?"

Holiday nodded. "Yeah."

"Well, supposedly they was popping wheelies, turning flips and crap, and Chris thought he could do what they was doing and his wheel got twisted some kinda way, and he fell. His head clipped the ramp they say. Roxy told me Max told her it was just a freakish way he fell, but they didn't think it was that serious until he didn't get up right away."

"How bad is it? Did they say?" Holiday asked, recalling what Annette had said.

Pop shook his head, a look of despair on his face. "Well… we're still waiting to hear back from the doctor, but Roxy said he didn't look good at all."

Holiday sat back in his seat, trying to remain optimistic and keep the worry at bay. But it was just as Annette had said: they had already lost Laila. He couldn't imagine losing Christian.

FORTY-SEVEN

Cynthia settled comfortably in the driver's seat after talking with Mama Genie. She had waited until her breathing returned to normal, her body had calmed down and ceased perspiring, and she was twenty minutes on the road towards Houston before she dialed her as she promised she would. Mama Genie wished her luck on her job interview and reminded her to not worry, that if the job is meant for her, she will get it.

Cynthia switched off the radio, deciding to rehearse her response to possible interview questions. She knew there was a high chance she would not be asked these exact questions, but wanted to be comfortable forming coherent responses and not stumble over her words. No matter how many she'd had in the past, interviews always frazzled her nerves.

What do you believe are the qualities of a good teacher?

What is your teaching mission statement?

How do you reach those students possessing a lackluster attitude about their education?

Tell us about a time you went above and beyond for one of your students.

In what ways do you believe technology hinders instruction in today's classroom? How do you rectify this and make it work for you?

Half an hour later, her mind began to drift. She had not yet heard from Holiday and she wondered how he was doing, if Christian was okay. Other than his heavy foot on the gas pedal, he appeared calm on the drive back this morning after receiving the news of his son's accident, but she knew it may have been his way of dealing with the unknown.

Cynthia pulled into the campus parking lot fifteen minutes late for the interview. She'd called Susan Higginbotham with a small tale, telling her that she had been on her way out of town to visit her grandmother when she got the call, but was too embarrassed to admit it because she was looking forward to this interview and was willing to do whatever it took to be here. Susan laughed heartily, told her she appreciated her honesty, and that it was not a problem because, after all, it was a last-minute notice.

She swapped her flat sandals for the pumps she'd thrown on the passenger side floor, checked her face in the visor mirror to apply another coat of tinted lip gloss, and then got out. She decided to forgo the blazer and left it hanging in the back seat.

The door to the school's entrance swung open as Cynthia approached. A woman looking as if she took no parts in consuming solid foods stood bearing a Hollywood smile. Cynthia sized her up and determined just one of her thighs was the width of this woman's entire body.

"We're so glad you could make it, Cynthia," she said, extending a bony hand. "I'm Susan."

Cynthia took her hand and apologized again for being late. Susan waved her off and led her inside. It was tough maintaining Susan's brisk pace and Cynthia wondered where they were going as she followed behind her down a long hallway, their heels clicking on the shiny floors.

As if Susan could hear her thoughts she glanced back over her shoulder and said, "Principal Morgan likes to conduct her interviews in the library. She says the atmosphere is a lot less stuffy in there than in her office.

"Oh," Cynthia nodded.

Susan paused, cupped a vascular hand over her mouth, "But if I'm honest," she said in a conspiratorial whisper, "it's because she has so much shit all over her office she doesn't want anyone in there to see what a mess she is." She threw her head back laughing, but her silver bob cut remained in place.

Cynthia pursed her lips and fell in step behind Susan again. She was not going to take the bait if this was a test.

Principal Morgan stood to greet Cynthia as they entered the library and motioned for her to take the seat across from her and Susan at the round table. She wasted no time with formalities and began the process right away, asking Cynthia to tell her why she was interested in working for Spring Branch ISD and what made her the right candidate for the position.

For the next half-hour Cynthia did her best to sell herself, using her nine years of classroom experience to convince them she was highly-qualified and prepared to work with their students and share her passion for learning. Principal Morgan was pretty stiff at the start of the interview, but by the end, their laughter filled the library space as she and Susan shared stories about their times as former teachers, memories of their favorite and not-so-favorite students, ridiculous parents, and the like.

Cynthia exhaled when she made it back to her car. She was confident the interview went well and looked forward to their phone call. Susan assured her she would hear back from them whether she did or did not get the position. She crossed her fingers and hoped she would, even if it was to be her final year working in a classroom.

She rested her head on the headrest and closed her eyes, her body crashing from lack of sleep. It was near time for rush-hour traffic and she cringed at the thought of driving back to Mama Genie's house in the madness.

She called Tora.

"Lady, I *know* you are not just now calling me back. What is going on with you?"

Cynthia had forgotten all about the calls from her friend because she had been so wrapped up in her time with Holiday. "I'm back here in Houston. I just had an interview with Spring Branch."

"What? That's good! How did it go? Do you feel like you got it?"

"I hope I did. It went really well, but I don't want to get my hopes up."

"So what are you doing now? Are you staying the night?"

"No. I'm just gonna wait until traffic dies down before I drive back. But I was calling because I haven't slept and—"

Tora cut her off midsentence, "You are? Then let's meet up somewhere! You wanna get some drinks? Have you had lunch?"

Cynthia massaged her temple. "That sounds good, but I am about to pass out I'm so tired. I have not slept much at all since Wednesday night. I was calling to tell you I'm gonna go to the apartment and crash for a few hours if that's okay with you." The extra key to Tora's apartment dangled on her key chain.

"Tired? Why haven't you slept since Wednesday night? What exactly have you been doing out there in that country?" Tora laughed.

"It's a long story," Cynthia smiled. The remnants of it still lingered. In the tightness of her legs, the soreness of her insides.

"Oooh," Tora crooned. "Do you have something to tell me? You met a cowboy, didn't you?"

Cynthia laughed. "He is not a cowboy, Tora."

"So you *did* meet someone? Oh my god! You *have* to tell me all about him. Where are you now?"

Cynthia shook her head. "I'm still at the school, just sitting here in the parking lot."

"Okay, go to my apartment and wait for me. I'll be there as soon as I get off, which isn't too much longer."

Cynthia started the car and pulled away from the school. *I guess sleep is out of the question*, she thought.

"Tell me *everything*," Tora said. "And you better not leave anything out. I want *all* the details."

Cynthia laughed. They were sitting on the patio at Taco Cabana, eating street tacos, chips and queso. Cynthia was able to get only a couple hours of shuteye before Tora came bustling through the apartment door, squealing about how much she missed her and for her to get up because she needed a margarita and was anxious to hear about her new beau.

"I mean… there really isn't too much to tell," Cynthia smiled. "We've been hanging out since I've been there. He's a nice guy."

Tora twisted her lips. "So you've been hanging out with him every day since you've been there, but there isn't much to tell? Yeah, okay."

Cynthia laughed again. "Alright… he's handsome, he's sexy, romantic. Thoughtful. Has a good relationship with his dad and his son. Family-oriented for sure. Works hard. Everything. Just a kind man."

"What does he do? Does he own a ranch with cows and stuff?"

"No," Cynthia rolled her eyes playfully. "I already told you he is not a cowboy. He doesn't even ride horses."

"So where did you meet him?"

"Next door to my grandmother's house. He's remodeling the home. He and his daddy are in business together."

Tora nodded approvingly, sipping from her margarita. "Go on."

"Go on, what?" Cynthia said.

"With the rest of the details. You said he has a son?"

"Yep. He had a little girl too, but she passed away."

"Oh no," Tora said. "What happened to her?"

"Drowned in a lake."

"That's so sad."

"Very. And now his son is in the hospital. He had a bicycle accident this morning and hit his head, so that's what he was dealing with when I left."

"Wow. So he's been married before?"

"Yeah. For seven years he told me."

Tora said, "That's good. Definitely a plus there. I'll take an ex-husband over a baby daddy any day."

Cynthia laughed. "What?"

"I'm serious. At least you know he was committed to having a family at one point. People these days just have babies, marriage be damned."

Cynthia nodded. "Actually, that's one of the things I love about him. We were just having that conversation last night. He wants a family again. More kids. He's been trying to convince me to move there, work with him and his dad, and everything."

Tora's eyes widened. "Cynthia, are you serious? He *told* you that?"

"Yep. And he's dead serious."

"Wait… so you've been down there for about a month now and you already got a man wanting to move you in with him and marry you? What kinda hoodoo mess did you put on this man, girl? Better yet, you need to teach me your ways. I can't even get a man to ask me for my phone number."

Cynthia laughed until her eyes brimmed with tears. "You are so crazy."

"I'm so serious," Tora countered. "I wanna know."

Once Cynthia gathered herself, she took a sip from her drink. She sighed. "I don't know. He just told me he really enjoys being with me and would like for us to continue."

"And? What did you tell him?"

Cynthia shrugged. "I haven't told him anything yet. I don't know if I want to do a long-distance relationship. I like to be able to see my man whenever I want to. Besides, how will it work? Are we just supposed to continue dating forever with all these miles between us? One of us will have to move eventually if it's supposed to be a serious relationship with marriage somewhere down the road."

Tora lifted a shoulder. "You're worried about the wrong thing if you ask me. Just let things flow. If he's already told you he wants to have a relationship with you then evidently he's willing to do what it takes to make it work, whatever that means for him."

"Hmm… I don't know." Cynthia grabbed a chip from her basket and took a bite.

"Then what's the problem? Does he have a crazy ex-wife or something?"

"He doesn't say much about her, actually."

Tora continued, "Because that is something you have to consider. You don't want to have to deal with a madwoman trying to ruin your relationship."

"Of course," Cynthia nodded. "But it seems like they're cordial. I really don't know to tell you the truth."

"Well it sounds like he knows what he wants."

"Still… it's all so soon, y'know? Plus, look where I am right now. Unemployed. No place to stay. That's what I'm focused on."

Tora rolled her eyes. "So you're in a bad spot right now. Did he say that was an issue for him? Your situation is only temporary."

Cynthia sighed. "You're right. And I do like him a lot. We'll see," she smiled.

"So I guess this means poor Jonathan no longer has a chance?"

Cynthia's eyes narrowed across the table at the mention of him. "What?"

"Didn't you get my message?"

Cynthia got the message of course, but she still hadn't listened to it. "I was so busy I never got around to it. I completely forgot about it."

Tora laughed. "Well now I know why."

"What did the message say? And, honestly, I thought you were calling to tell me some crap about him and Davina." She waved her hand. "I didn't wanna hear that mess."

"Girl, no. Why would I do that? Come on. You should know me better than that." She sipped from her margarita again. "That man is still in love with you, Cynthia."

"What are you talking about?"

"That's what he told me. And you know after what he did to you I don't even like his ass no more, but he seemed pretty sincere that night. He actually warmed *my* heart a little bit, which says a lot."

Cynthia grabbed another chip, dipped it in queso.

"I was going to the bathroom when I heard someone call my name. He was sitting at the bar by himself. He wanted to know if you were there with me because he needed to talk to you since you won't answer any of his phone calls. I had to sit down next to him because he kept going on and on about you. Talking about all the fun you guys had, that no other woman gives him the satisfaction that you do. That he messed up and he's been beating himself up about it since. He really misses you a lot and wishes he could take that day back and start over. The man was practically begging *me* to try to convince *you* to hear him out, give him another chance. I just told him all I could do was let you know when you were back in the city, but other than that, it's definitely your decision whether you call him or not."

Cynthia didn't know what to say. She couldn't fathom even considering giving Jonathan another chance, but just knowing that he was apologetic about what he'd done gave her a sense of satisfaction.

Tora shook her head and sighed. "I don't know what it is, Sis, but I wanna be like you when I grow up."

Cynthia frowned. "What are you talking about?"

"You got one man wanting to move you in after just four weeks of being with you, and another one about to lose his mind trying to get you back." She raised her margarita cup towards Cynthia. "My friend got that fire!"

Cynthia laughed, falling back in her seat. "I don't know about all that."

FORTY-EIGHT

Holiday walked outside to his truck. He needed a cigarette and he also wanted to call Cynthia. The surgeon had finally come into the waiting room to tell them the news: two fractured vertebras. Fortunately, there was no damage to the spinal cord, but Christian would be in the hospital for several days to recover and confined to a neck brace until the bones healed. He told them once Christian was assigned to a room they would be able to go in and see him.

Holiday grabbed the pack of cigarettes from the console, his cell phone, and walked across the parking lot to the area where smoking was permitted. Taking slow drags of his cigarette, his mind began to calm with each inhale. He was afraid to admit the news about Christian's accident petrified him, and when they mentioned head and neck injury it was hard not to take into account the possibility of the worst outcome. He touched the button on his phone to pull up the contacts list.

The battery was dead.

It slipped his mind that he had not had the chance to charge his phone. Pop left the hospital long ago after waiting for several hours, saying although he hated to leave Christian, he had to get to the contract job he'd started. So now Holiday had no access to the extra charger Pop kept in his truck.

A car slowly pulled up to the curb where Holiday stood: a shiny old-school Roadmaster with windows tinted so dark he couldn't see inside.

The window lowered. "I thought that was you," a male voice said. "Mama pointed you out, but I didn't believe it at first." A small head appeared on the other side of him. It was Annette's brother and mother, Marquise and Silvia, the two of which he hadn't seen in a couple years.

Holiday smiled knowingly. "How y'all doing?"

Silvia said, "How are you, baby? How's my grandbaby? I had to wait until Marq got off work to give me a ride down here, otherwise I would've been here sooner. What they do to my boy?"

"They said he broke his neck…"

Marquise and Silvia seemed to gasp and clutch their chests at the same time.

"My God!" Silvia cried out. "How he do that?"

Holiday reiterated the story Pop had gotten from Roxy. "But the doctor said we're lucky he didn't hurt his spine because that would've been much worse for him. Possibly paralyzed him." Holiday shook his head sadly and blew out a breath. "So I'm glad it wasn't that. But he'll be in here for a while," he gestured towards the hospital.

Silvia pursed her lips, shaking her head. "My poor baby. Is Annette up there with him now?"

Holiday nodded. "We're waiting to see him. They're working on a room for him now. Roxy was here earlier too, but she had to get back home to the kids."

"Well, we're gonna go inside so we can see him. I need to put my eyes on him to make sure he's really okay," Silvia said. "And I haven't seen *you* in so long."

Marquise agreed. "Yeah, man. It's been a long time. We need to catch up."

Of Annette's three brothers, Marquise was the one Holiday bonded with the most over the course of their marriage.

"You're not leaving are you?" Silvia asked Holiday.

"No, ma'am. I'll be here every day until they release him."

FORTY-NINE

The rumbling hum of a lawn mower woke Cynthia Saturday morning. She got out of bed and went over to the window, excitement rushing through her at the thought of seeing Holiday. She'd tried to call him last night before bed after she had not heard from him all day. She was concerned and wanted to know about Christian.

After a quick shower, she dressed and went downstairs. Mama Genie was in the kitchen cooking breakfast as usual. "Good morning, Mama Genie," she said. "Be right back."

"Where you going? Breakfast almost done."

"Just next door real quick. I'll be right back," she said over her shoulder as she walked outside.

It wasn't Holiday's truck parked in the driveway. *Must be Frank's truck,* she thought as she walked around to the side of the house, following the sound of the mower. A young man sporting a head full of bantu knots was grooving to music from his oversized headphones and Cynthia wondered how he was able to hear anything over the noise of his equipment. She smiled as she stood watching him bob his head and rock his shoulders to the beat.

He turned around, startled to see Cynthia standing there. He cut the motor and took off his headphones. "Ma'am?"

Cynthia laughed. "I didn't mean to scare you. I came over looking for somebody else. But, man, you were gettin' it!"

He chuckled. "Oh," he said, lifting the waistband of his sagging skinny jeans. "I just be in my own world sometimes. The music make it better."

"I hear you. I wish I had a job that makes me smile like you."

"Are you Mr. Howie's daughter?" he asked. "He the one sent me to cut your grass."

Cynthia remembered the house was a graduation gift for the daughter of Frank's friend. "No," she shook her head. "I live next door. I thought someone else was here… the men that were working on the house. That's why I came over."

"Oh. Ain't nobody else here but me." He shrugged, put the headphones back over his ears, and started the lawn mower.

* * *

Back in her room after eating breakfast, Cynthia dialed Holiday. The call went straight to voicemail as it did last night, but this time she decided to leave a message: "Hey… I'm calling to make sure everything's okay. I haven't heard from you. You said you would call and let me know how Christian is doing, remember? Call me when you get a few minutes."

She stretched out in bed and grabbed the novel from her nightstand. The book club's meeting was next Saturday—the last Saturday of the month—and she was determined to not live up to her reputation this time as the club's weakest link. She forced herself to read five chapters and closed the book an hour later still unmoved by the characters and plot.

Holiday crept into her thoughts. Rather, he moved to the forefront because, lately, he was always somewhere in the recesses of her mind—especially during the most inopportune moments: while searching job postings, conversing with Mama Genie, washing the dishes, cleaning her bath tub. She wished they were still at the resort lying in bed, enjoying quiet conversation in the dark room. Her body throbbed with the memory of him kissing her lips, licking her skin, stroking her insides. It was the start of her last week here for the summer and she didn't want to think about their opportunity to be together and make love again coming to an end.

Mama Genie's calling from downstairs broke into her musings.

"Yeah?" Cynthia said when she made it to the kitchen.

"You mind running to the store for me? I need a bottle of Vanilla Extract. This ain't enough to finish my pie crust," she said, holding up the near-empty bottle. Flour covered the counter next to the stove where Mama Genie mixed and rolled out the thick dough.

"Alright, no problem," Cynthia nodded. She dipped her fingers into a glass bowl, nabbing a fat slice of canned peaches Mama Genie had poured in it. The peach slipped out of her fingers and hit the floor in a mushy splat before she was able to get it to her mouth.

"That's what you get," Mama Genie laughed. "If you keep eating my peaches, there won't be none left for my cobbler."

Cynthia groaned. "One peach is not going to break your cobbler, Grandma." She wet a paper towel to clean up the sticky mess.

"You going to the revival tomorrow?" Mama Genie asked.

"Yeah, but I don't know if I'll make all five days. I'll go tomorrow… and maybe Thursday—the last day."

Mama Genie went over to the blender to start the mix for her pecan pie filling. "Did you remember to invite three friends like Reverend Moore said?"

"No. Who would I invite? Everybody I know is in Houston."

"Anybody. They don't have to be somebody you know personally. When you go to the store, just walk up to some folks and ask them if they wanna come hear a good service tomorrow. The choir gon' be good, too."

Cynthia shook her head. "Mama Genie, I'm not doing that." She imagined Sister Nash had already canvassed the entire town.

"Well… you can ask Holiday and Frank. That'll get you two people at least."

Asking Holiday to attend church with her was definitely out of the question. She was not keen on the idea of any more people knowing their business. She was keeping him to herself. "His son had an accident, remember? I'm sure attending a church revival is the furthest thing from his mind."

"That's right. How is the boy doing anyway?"

"I'm still waiting to hear from him. I hope it's nothing serious, but I don't know," she sighed.

Mama Genie sighed, too. "All you can do is keep the faith and wait and see. But… go 'head on and hurry back so I can finish up in here. I don't wanna be standing in front of this hot stove all day. What time you say the A/C man coming?"

"Sometime after six," Cynthia said and went upstairs for her purse.

* * *

With the bottle of Vanilla Extract in hand, Cynthia stood in front of the shelf trying to decide if she wanted the soft or hard batch of chocolate chip cookies as a snack for later when someone called her name. She turned around and immediately recognized those plump lips and golden feline eyes.

It was Chanel.

Clad in a knee-length black and white stripe bodycon dress with flat gladiator sandals. Her lips were void of the bright red lipstick Cynthia remembered from the night of Yoauna's party, but the same super-sized gold hoops hung from her ears. A single rope of dark wavy hair lay over her bare shoulder. Cynthia noticed a man hovering down the aisle a few feet away, checking out Chanel. She presumed if he was not her boyfriend, then he was just waiting for the opportunity to approach her.

"I heard about what happened to Holiday's stepson," Chanel said.

Cynthia's eyes left the ogling fellow at Chanel's statement. "You mean his son," Cynthia looked at her.

Chanel gave her a look of mild surprise. "Oh, you didn't know that boy ain't his real son?"

The information stumped Cynthia. She thought back to all the time spent with Holiday, their conversations flipping through her mind like a Rolodex. Not once could she recall him referring to Christian as his stepson. "Oh, right," she laughed self-consciously. "What am I talking about?" The smirk on Chanel's face challenged her sincerity.

As if Chanel knew she didn't know the truth, she told Cynthia, "That's the reason why me and him didn't work out… because he was always on-call for that boy's mama. He always stopped whatever he was doing to answer her calls or go and see what she wanted. And everything was always an emergency." She made quotation marks with her long fingers as she said 'emergency'.

"I was talking to my friend just last night about him," Chanel continued. "I didn't even know he was still married, but she told me that's what she heard—that him and his wife are only separated."

A ball of piercing heat settled in Cynthia's chest, slowly moved up her throat as her mind whirled from Chanel's declarations. *Married? Separated?* She shook her head in an attempt to un-cloud her brain.

Chanel added, "Now I know you probably think I'm crazy or trying to be messy, but believe me, messy ain't me. I'm just trying to warn you that this man ain't what he seems. It's nothing against you.

I don't even know you. So, if you call yourself dating him... just understand that it's only temporary because he's still in love with his wife. And he *always* go back to her."

Cynthia swallowed the lump in her throat and nodded. "Thank you for the information." Holding up the bottle of Extract, she said, "I gotta go now. My grandmama needs this for her pies."

The next several hours went by in a blur. The A/C technician showed up a half-hour earlier than he said he would, surprising Cynthia when he appeared on the front porch. The elusive repairman turned out to be one of her former classmates from high school. They shared a tight hug, and he admitted to having a serious crush on her back in the day, but that Tommy had beat him to the punch. Cynthia couldn't even share his enthusiasm as he relished in the memories of those times. She couldn't stop thinking about Holiday. She couldn't stop thinking about the things Chanel said. Instead, she followed behind him, nodding stupidly and laughing half-heartedly as he looked at the A/C unit, checked all the air vents, and climbed into the attic.

"Y'all don't need a new air conditioner," he said after a second look at the unit outside. "Just need a new fan motor. I can replace that for you for about one-fifty. Parts and labor."

"Thank God," Cynthia exhaled.

"Then why that man tell us we need a new one and wanna charge us fourteen-hundred dollars for it?" Mama Genie asked him.

"Ma'am, unfortunately, that's just how some of these people are in the business. He knew you didn't know nothing about that A/C so he was gonna try to stick it to y'all. I'm glad y'all were smart enough to get a second opinion."

"Well, we're glad you were honest with us," Mama Genie replied.

"No problem, ma'am. I'm gonna go to the shop and see if we have the right one for you in stock. If not, I know a couple places I can go to get one. Will y'all still be here? I can have this done for you tonight if you don't mind me coming back a little later."

"We ain't going nowhere," Mama Genie told him. "Bless you."

* * *

Cynthia closed the window and climbed into bed. She pulled the covers up to her waist. The condenser fan motor had been replaced a couple hours ago and the house was slowly cooling as the repairman advised it would. *No more hot and sweaty nights*, she thought, turning over on her side to stare at the wall. But she would miss the sounds of crickets filtering through the open window, lulling her to sleep at night.

Her phone rang on the nightstand and she snatched it up to answer.

"Cynthia, baby? How you doing?"

The sound of his voice made her heart flutter as if she were hearing it for the first time. It had been only thirty-six hours since she last saw and talked to him, but it felt more like three weeks. "Good. How are you?"

He blew out a breath. "Tired, but I'm fine," he answered. "I'm sorry it took me so long to get back to you. We been up here dealing with this—"

Her heart flopped at the mention of 'we'. "How is Christian?" she asked. "I was waiting for your call to tell me what's going on."

"He's okay. Well… as can be expected. He fractured a couple of bones in his neck—"

"Oh my lord," Cynthia whispered.

"—but he's doing good now. Still in a lot of pain. We're trying to keep him calm, but he'll be here for a while in recovery though."

"I'll be praying for his full recovery," Cynthia told him.

"Thanks," he said.

Questions she needed answers to burned in her throat during the seconds of silence. But she felt this was not the right time to ask him about what Chanel had said. She needed to look him in the face as he confirmed it.

"What you do today?" he asked. "I'm missing you already and can't wait to see you again."

Cynthia closed her eyes, wanting to tell him she missed him too, but wondered if it was even worth it. "Not too much. We finally got A/C."

"Oh yeah? What was wrong with it?"

She told him about the faulty fan motor and that it cost less than two hundred dollars to repair.

"So I guess I won't be able to sneak in your window no more, huh?"

Cynthia laughed quietly. "No. I've shut it down and locked it."

A female voice appeared in the background. Holiday said, "I'm gonna go now, baby. Christian don't like being up here by hisself, so if I can get Pop to come and sit with him for a while tomorrow morning, I'll come by to see you. Maybe we can go out for an early lunch or something."

"I'll be in church tomorrow, so just call me," she said.

"Alright. Good night."

Cynthia pressed the button to end the call and settled back on her pillow. *Tell me the things Chanel said is a lie.*

FIFTY

Three quick raps sounded on the door before the nurse entered, wheeling in a cart with Christian's breakfast.

"I'm baaaccckkk," she sang. Christian was sitting upright in bed, but she raised him a couple more notches so he could eat comfortably. She pointed at the items on his tray. "I got your favorite cereal, some fruit, a slice of toast, and some apple juice." She opened the package of cereal and poured the milk. "Is everything okay?"

Christian gave her a thumbs-up.

"Alright. The movie is going to start in a few minutes, okay? And remember you can always just change the channel if you don't like it. We show two movies a day: one in the morning at nine, and the other at six in the evening." "Dad, can I get you anything?" she asked Holiday.

"I'm good. Thank you."

She smiled and touched Christian's arm. "I'll be back in a little while to check on you," she said and left the room.

Holiday watched as Christian ate. He dipped the spoon slowly in the plastic container, and just as slowly brought it to his mouth. He'd told Holiday he was afraid to move too much because he did not want to hurt anything else, but Holiday assured him he would be fine, that the neck brace was going to protect him.

"So I'm gonna miss the first week of sixth grade ain't I'm?" Christian asked about an hour into the movie.

"Well… you heard the doctor say it's gonna take a while, so yeah, more than likely you will."

Christian sucked his teeth. "Man… this is messed up."

Holiday chuckled. "You gotta wait until you get better, son. That's a serious injury you got and you don't want to rush yourself. Your friends will still be there when you get back."

"I know, but… I don't wanna start school after everybody else."

"I understand, but this is the most important thing we have to focus on right now… getting you healthy. You want to be able to hang out and play with them again, right?"

Christian sighed and took a bite of the dry toast. "I guess so."

"You guess so about what?" Annette said, breezing into the room carrying two plastic bags—one being a large take-out from *Denny's*.

"Hey, Mama," Christian smiled. She set the bags on the counter and walked over to plant a long kiss on his forehead.

"How's my baby?"

"Good. I just had cereal."

"I see. And I brought you pancakes. I guess I can save them for you for later if you don't want them now."

"Later is fine."

Annette took a container from the *Denny's* bag, surprising Holiday when she set it on his lap. "I got you something, too," she said. From the other bag she produced his favorite cranberry-grape drink.

He was aware her attitude towards him shifted one-hundred-eighty degrees after her mother showed up for the visit a couple nights ago. As if she had not tried to beat a hole in his chest just a few hours before that.

And he was still waiting for her to acknowledge what she did and apologize, however far-fetched.

Holiday said, "Thanks, but I wish you would've called me. I

would've told you not to get me nothing." There was enough food in the container for two meals and he was saving his appetite for Cynthia.

"Don't worry about it. The treat's on me," she said. She took the platter she bought for herself and sat in the chair against the wall on the other side of Christian's bed. Holiday opened the package of plastic ware and took a few bites of food as Annette engaged Christian. She asked him to tell her about the movie and, when it was over, Christian brought up his disappointment in having to miss the first week of sixth grade again.

At a break in their conversation, Holiday said, "Annette, I'm gonna head out now. I need a shower and I got something to do."

She nodded. "So you'll be back in a few hours then, right?"

"No. Not right away. I just said I got something to do. I'll be a while."

"Then who's going to be here with him? This is month-end for me and I got several reports due this week at work. I need to get started on those tonight."

Holiday shook his head. He was looking forward to spending the remainder of the day with Cynthia. "How long is that gonna take you?"

She shrugged. "It depends on if I have the information I need from the other departments, which almost always is never the case. But… a couple hours at least."

"Then why not go and work on that now? I can stay here if that's all the time you need." He recalled Cynthia saying she would be in church, which allowed him some time until he was able to see her.

Annette said, "I don't feel like it right now. That's why I said later tonight. I just want to spend time with my son."

"Alright," Holiday said. "Well… since you're here I'm gonna go and do what I need to do. Both of us don't have to be here at the same time." He closed the breakfast container and grabbed his drink from the floor next to his chair.

"So I guess you got other more important things to do, huh? I should've known. Is it to go and see that woman? Is that what you mean when you say you got something to do?"

Holiday gathered his things and stood. He was definitely not up to an argument this morning. And definitely not in front of Christian or the hospital staff.

"Huh?" she said again, her voice rising slightly. "Spending time with that woman is more important than being here with your son?"

"Annette…" he shook his head.

"Mason, just tell me. We can solve all this right here. Right now. Does she come before him?"

"What are you even talking about? I been here two days. I can't go home for a few hours to take a shower and lay in my bed? I let you go home and get some rest, to take care of what you needed to take care of. Are you trying to tell me I can't?"

"Of course you can, but you already know we can't leave him here alone and I've got an important project to complete. You know… since it's just me I have to do what I can to make sure I maintain my job. You can work whenever you want to and it won't be a problem if you miss a few days. I can't do that, unfortunately. But if being with that woman is more important to you, then just let me know. I'll have to find somebody else that cares to help me out and look after him—"

Christian said, "Mama, are you talking about Ms. Cynthia?"

Holiday watched Annette's eyes flash and her face seemed to turn three shades browner.

She looked at Christian. "What did you say?" But she didn't wait for his answer as her eyes shot up to Holiday standing on the other side of the bed. "Cynthia? Is that her name, Mason? How does

Christian know who she is?"

"Annette, it don't even make sense to get into this right now." He slid his hand into his pocket.

"Are you trying to tell me Christian knows who she is?" She stood up from her chair. "Is that what I'm hearing?" her voice cracked.

Christian's eyes shifted between the two since he could not turn his head. "I saw her, Mama. She came over to help us paint. She's real nice, too. She told me her friend likes the Steelers and she got Steelers stuff all over her apartment." Christian chattered away so innocently, oblivious to the storm brewing behind his mother's eyes at his disclosure.

Annette's chest began to rise and fall as she looked from Christian to Holiday. "So you got my son hanging out with you when you're with her? Huh? Like y'all just one big happy family?" She shook her head as if in complete disgust. "Tell me you don't have that *bitch* around my son, Mason."

Christian gasped. "Mama? Did you call Ms. Cynthia a—"

"Christian," Holiday started, silencing him. "Watch your mouth, Annette," he told her. She was not in control of his personal life and he needed her to understand that. "She came over while we were painting and offered to help. She's a friend, yeah."

"A friend?" she said, her eyes tight. "What does that mean? Word around town is that every other woman is your *friend*."

Holiday was not going to entertain the gossip. For all he knew it could just be her way of saying things to get a rise out of him. "Annette, I'm not going to stand here and argue with you about what I do and who I'm with. You see I don't worry about what you do or who you're with. I don't care. It's not my business."

She snatched her bottle of orange juice from the tray next to Christian's bed, rearing her arm back.

Holiday raised his hand. "Put it down. Don't you dare."

Her chest heaved as she glared at him, the bottle suspended at her ear.

The door pushed open as the nurse came in singing as cheerfully as she did a couple hours ago. "Christian, I'm baaaccckkk…. Are you okay, honey?"

Annette's eyes never left Holiday's. Through clinched teeth she said, "Get the fuck *out*."

FIFTY-ONE

"That sure was a good service, wasn't it? Pastor Lewis know he can preach. Especially for him being so young."

Cynthia waited for the click of Mama Genie fastening her seatbelt before she pulled away from the church parking lot.

"I told Reverend Moore to make sure he invite him back for next year," Mama Genie continued. "You know he come all the way down from Chicago? And his wife is so friendly. She told me we need to come and visit their church sometime soon, but I told her I don't do no airplanes. And I can't sit too long in the car or my knees would lock up on me. Did you see that dress she had on? Sure was nice."

"Mmm-hmm," Cynthia muttered. "I saw it." She started down the long stretch of road towards home as Mama Genie chattered away in the passenger seat.

"Sister Nash told me she work at one of them high-end stores up there. Always dressed like a first lady even if she just going to check the mailbox. I don't know how Reverend Moore can afford them because Sister Nash told me their church is 'bout five times bigger than ours, so how can we pay him?" Mama Genie smacked her lips. "But I guess Reverend Moore has his way."

Cynthia hit the knob to turn on the windshield wipers as droplets of rain began to fall across the windshield.

Mama Genie chuckled. "I remember Daddy used to tell us when we was kids that if it started raining while the sun was shining it meant The Devil was beating his wife."

Cynthia grunted.

"Looks like we're gonna get some rain today."

"Yeah."

Mama Genie looked over at Cynthia. "You been mighty quiet all day. You worried about something?"

Cynthia sighed. It was Holiday. Ever since the call last night from him she couldn't stop thinking about it. She imagined him at the hospital with Christian's mother. The two of them together, taking care of Christian, bonding over their son. *Her son.* "Just been thinking about that job interview," she told Mama Genie.

"When you supposed to hear back from them?"

"Sometime this week I guess," she shrugged.

"Well… ain't no sense in worrying yourself about it. You know if it's meant for you, you'll get it."

"I *know that*, Mama Genie, but still… I have next to nothing in my bank account. I need something soon."

Mama Genie nodded. "I understand. Believe me I know how it is when your finances ain't what you're used to. But you know everything always work itself out… just when you think it's not. May not be when you want it to, but it always does."

Cynthia said, "I hope so."

* * *

Cynthia was toweling off after a long shower when she heard her cell phone ringing across the hall in the bedroom. She made no effort to hurry so she could answer it. She knew it was Holiday calling. They were supposed to have lunch earlier in the day. It was nearing nine o' clock now and she was getting ready for bed.

Sitting on the edge of her bed she took her time smoothing lotion over her body. Now that the A/C had been repaired she could return to one of her nightly rituals of moisturizing with her favorite bedtime body lotion. It wouldn't be sweated off in the middle of the night now, leaving her skin sticky. She applied Vaseline to the heels of her feet before slipping on a pair of socks. The phone rang again, but she ignored it.

She laid in bed staring at the ceiling, going over the events of the last few days in her head, the things Holiday had said.

She waited until an hour passed before she picked up the phone to return his call.

"Cynthia, baby. I am so sorry."

"I was waiting all day for your call."

"I can't believe I overslept," he said. "Once I made it home I took a shower, said I was gonna lay down for a couple hours, but I woke up and it was eight-something. Guess I was a lot more tired than I thought. How you doing?"

"I'm okay. How is Christian?"

"He's fine. Starting middle school is all that's on his mind. That's all he talked about today."

"I thought maybe something was going on with him… that you and his mom were together and you couldn't get away to call and let me know we wouldn't be able to meet today."

She sensed a hesitation from him before he finally responded. "Naw. It wasn't nothing like that. I slept longer than I planned to." He cleared his throat. "I wanna see you bad though. But it's late and I can't have you walking out your grandmama's house this time of night."

Cynthia looked at the clock on the nightstand.

"How early do you wake up in the mornings?" he asked. "You wanna meet me at Nell's Diner for breakfast? I have to make it up to you."

Cynthia shifted in bed. She couldn't wait another minute. "Why would it need to be a secret that Christian is not your biological son?"

Silence fell on his end of the line and Cynthia felt as though she was holding her breath.

"It's not a secret," he said finally.

"I didn't know. You didn't tell me. All this time I was under the impression he was your son, your blood. Are you and his mom still married?"

Another taunting second of silence passed before he answered, "No. Cynthia, what's wrong, baby? Where are these questions coming from?"

She sat up in bed. "I saw Chanel at the store yesterday. She'd heard the news about your stepson."

"So this is about some more mess Chanel put in your ear?"

Cynthia asked, "Did she lie? Imagine how I felt when I found out I didn't even know something as significant as this. How foolish I looked? Why it needs to be a secret is what I don't get."

"It's just not something I go around telling people. I didn't think I had to. To me he is my son."

"So you and his mom are separated? Chanel told me you're still married."

"No we're not." He let go a sharp breath. "Can you get out for a few minutes? I can come over so we can talk about it. I need to see you."

"After all that you were saying to me back at the resort. Why?" She threw the covers off her legs as she felt her temperature rising suddenly. "What else don't I know? Chanel said you're only single for now, just waiting until she lets you come back." Cynthia's mind rambled on, thinking about their time together. "So is this why you're living with Mr. Frank? Just waiting until you can go back home to her? Is claiming Christian as your son just your way of having an excuse to keep her in your life?"

"Cynthia, do you hear yourself? Why are you listening to some B.S. Chanel told you?"

"But you're not denying any of this—"

"You haven't given me a chance to!"

His tone shocked Cynthia. Up to this point she had not heard him raise his voice even a fourth of an octave about anything. Whether it was out of frustration or anger, she wasn't sure, but it was enough to rile her attention and drive a flash of heat up the back of her neck.

"Now I'm sorry some of the cats in your past screwed your head up, but… is that all it takes? For somebody to tell you something about me and you take it and run with it? Make you doubt who I am? Baby, I thought you were smarter than that."

Cynthia's whole body shook now. "Look, I don't need the condescension from you, okay? I only asked the questions because these are things I believe I should know. I shouldn't've had to ask. All summer you had the opportunity to tell me the truth about your situation, but you chose not to. It seems to me you had something to hide. About Christian. About your relationship with his mama."

"I have nothing to hide," he said. "And by the way you're talking it sounds like you believed what you were told even before coming to me about it."

Cynthia closed her eyes as she pinched the bridge of her nose. Dorian had been dishonest. Jonathan had betrayed her. His not revealing his relation to Christian was just as deceitful in her mind. "Christian is not your son," she said.

He blew out a breath. "So this is a deal breaker for you? That he's not from my seed?"

"I just don't like the idea that you felt the need to keep that from me. When were you going to tell me? Or would I have been the only fool in town? I know it may seem trivial to you, but it's not so trivial to me. You're filling my head up, saying how much you want to be with me, want me to think about moving back here, that you want us to continue our… this… whatever it is. How could I consider all of this now? This is already a lie in your bucket."

"Cynthia," he said tightly, "I did not lie."

"You withheld information."

"He is my son. And the woman I end up with is just going to have to accept that."

It hit Cynthia like a ton of bricks. All their time together over the past month: the many great laughs they shared, the fun-filled outings around town, the late-night conversations, the getaway at the resort, his trying to convince her to take a chance on him and love again, her letting down her guard and giving her body to him. All of it came down to this declaration—an ultimatum.

Cynthia sniffed and cleared her throat. "Well… I'm glad you told me. Now I know for sure."

"And what's that, baby?"

"That it is exactly what I have been saying all along: we can't be together. This probably shouldn't've happened."

FIFTY-TWO

"Can you check again?" Holiday looked on skeptically as the woman behind the desk punched information into the computer. She bobbed her head as she studied the screen. "Yes sir, Mason Holiday? I'm sorry I can't give you a pass to go up. It says it right here his mother—Annette M. Boyd—has requested her ex-husband not be allowed visitation to her son." Her eyes left the screen to meet his. "For safety precautions."

Holiday offered a quiet *Thank you* and walked away from the counter.

In his truck, he pulled out his mobile phone to call Annette. She wasted no time to answer him.

"Mason," she stated with an air of cool annoyance, as if his call was interrupting her beauty sleep.

"So this is what it's come to, Annette?"

"What are you talking about?"

"You know exactly what I am talking about. You barring me from visiting Christian? You fear for his safety? What is this about?"

"Mason, I'm just trying to protect my son."

"Protect him from what?"

"I don't know what you're up to, but I don't want all of these different women around my son. I don't want him being a witness to playboy behavior thinking this is acceptable behavior for men."

Holiday willed himself to assuage the anger rising in his chest. "What are you talking about? There are no *women*."

"You're introducing him to your conquests guised as friends. He doesn't need to be around that. He will be raised to love and respect women."

Holiday could not believe the words coming out of her mouth. "Annette, you can't be serious. So because he happened to see my lady friend I'm all of a sudden a bad man? I'm dangerous?"

"I'm doing what's best for him. You don't see me bringing some random man around him… into his life. The man I introduce him to will be my fiancé, not just some guy I'm fancying for the moment."

Holiday ran a hand over his face. In all of their years together Annette had said some pretty ugly things, had become violent towards him a few times when she was angry, but never had she banned him from seeing Christian. This hurt him more than her attempt to discredit his morals and values. "So what you saying Annette is that I can't come up here to see him? You don't want me to come around no more?"

Without hesitation she said, "That's exactly what I'm saying."

Holiday popped the top on a can of Budweiser as he sat looking out over the lake. Annette's words ran through his mind, traveled to his heart where they encircled it, held it in a chokehold. For ten years Christian had been a part of his life and not until the past year he was with him every single day. He was just a toddler when he and Annette got together, so Holiday was there right alongside her watching him grow up, through the good and the bad. He was there to see him try to feed himself for the first time, comforted him during the restless nights his little body was wrought with a cold or fever, carried him through the doors of his first pre-school. Holiday wiped away his tears at his first day of Kindergarten, was there through every tantrum, fall and skinned arms and knees, bought him his first bike, answered every one of his '*How come?*' questions. He taught him the game of football and encouraged him to dream big, to always be kind and respectful of everyone he meets.

Holiday thought back to the delight on Christian's face when he learned he was going to be a big brother, of seeing him hold his baby sister for the first time once they brought her home. Of how protective Christian was of her, the patience he exuded the times Laila was a tempestuous toddler, taking his toys or just bothering him when he didn't want to be bothered.

Holiday thought back to the day he had to explain to Christian that he would never be able to see his little sister again, of holding him close as they cried for her together.

And now Annette was pushing him away, out of Christian's life.

Holiday took a sip of the cold beer. And this was because of Cynthia. At least… that was what Annette was making this out to be. *I don't want all these different women around my son….* Annette's words echoed in his head again. *You don't see me bringing some random man around him….* Holiday had no control of who Annette allowed in Christian's life because, after all, she was his mother and would always do as she pleased, but one thing he knew for sure was that Cynthia was no random woman. And if there was anyone he had no qualms about letting into Christian's life it was her. He did not expect to meet a lady this summer he immediately connected with and who stirred his emotions like Cynthia did. She had him thinking about what he wanted and needed in life: a woman to spend his time with, a woman to love. She had him thinking about his future.

Holiday swallowed the last of the beer, crushed the can, and threw it over his shoulder into the bed of the truck. Last night Cynthia had told him getting involved with him was a mistake. He regretted raising his voice at her and he regretted not revealing Christian was not his biological son. If he knew not being forthcoming with this information would put doubts in her mind about the type of man he was, he would have made it known early on. But, as he told her, to him Christian was his son. He was the only true father Christian ever had and throughout his marriage to Annette, he never regarded him as a stepson. He was Christian, his son.

Holiday pulled his cell phone out of his pocket. He'd called Cynthia earlier wanting to talk to her to clear the air and because he needed to see her, but the call went unanswered.

He decided he would have to give her time until she was ready to talk to him.

But he hoped she would not keep him waiting too long. He was determined to set things right with her.

FIFTY-THREE

It took several seconds for Cynthia to realize the ringing she heard was not the buzzing of an alarm clock in her dream. She opened her eyes and grabbed the phone from the nightstand.

"Hello, Cynthia?" the familiar female voice said. "Susan Higginbotham, Vice Principal, Spring Branch ISD."

"Good morning, Susan," Cynthia said, trying to clear the sleep from her voice. She propped herself up on one elbow.

"I'm calling to let you know we appreciate your interest in working with our district, but unfortunately, we are going to go with another candidate. However, I will keep your application on file should another position become available because—" she lowered her voice "—honestly I believe you were the better contender for the job, but Principal Morgan chose to hire her friend's son, which is a load of bullshit if you ask me..."

Cynthia listened with disinterest as Susan went into a two-minute spiel about how inept the chosen teacher was. "Thank you," Cynthia said finally and ended the call. She exhaled and lay back on her pillow. *Back to square one*, she thought.

She got out of bed and dressed.

"I'm going to get out of the house for a while," she said to Mama Genie once downstairs. "Do you need anything while I'm out?"

"This early? Where you going?"

Cynthia shrugged. "Just for a drive. I couldn't sleep much and I just want to get out for a few minutes."

Mama Genie lifted a brow. "Something bothering you, honey?"

Yes… I did not get the job, I don't know what I want to do, the man I've fallen for is keeping ties with a woman he has no ties with, I have to go back to Tora's place in a few days and deal with her pesky cats, and my chest is hurting from the anxiety of it all. "I just want to get out to think."

"Well alright. But I don't think I need nothing. I'll call you if I think of something."

"I'll be back later," she said and walked out the door. She noticed the green truck coming down the road as she left the porch headed towards her car and she wished she'd left the house sooner.

She pretended not to see him and quickly settled in the driver's seat and cranked the engine. But he pulled right up to the edge of the driveway as she backed out and got out of the truck.

He appeared at her window and her breath caught in her throat. *God, why? Why must I be tortured all over again?* It was Tuesday morning and she had not seen him since Friday, but all she wanted to do right now was escape and forget she ever met him.

Concern shone on his face and Cynthia reluctantly pressed the button to lower the window.

"Hey. I was just coming over to talk to you. Since you been dodging my calls."

"There is nothing to talk about, really. It was fun while it lasted. I'm going home Monday, back to reality."

He disregarded what she said. "Will you come out and talk to me?"

She looked up at him and into those dark eyes that left her powerless. Fighting it, she turned her attention towards the windshield. "Let's just move on. I told you it didn't make sense for us to get together. You live here, I live someplace else. You got a son—" she couldn't even finish the statement.

"Move on?" he questioned. "I'm not moving on. You didn't appear in my life for nothing."

Cynthia shook her head. "Please. I'm sure it was just like all the others: somebody to help you pass time."

"So you're still taking what Chanel said as truth? You won't even give me a chance to tell you my side. That's not fair at all."

Cynthia had nothing to add.

"You can't keep trying to run away from everything," he continued. "I noticed that about you. Instead of talking about whatever is bothering you, you'd rather push it to the side and pretend it didn't happen. That's not good, baby. At least hear me out."

After several seconds Cynthia placed the car in Park. "I'm listening," she said.

"You can't believe everything you hear around here," Holiday said from Cynthia's passenger seat. "Chanel is a beautiful woman. Me and her went out a few times, but she's not the woman for me and she knows that. So I'm not sure why she's making what happened between us more than what it was. I never led her to believe it was something more. I wouldn't do that to any woman. It was different with Annette because we were married. We divorced, but got back together, yeah. I believed I needed to work harder to make sure we stayed together."

Cynthia asked, "You didn't want the divorce?"

"Things hadn't been right between us for a long time. She wasn't happy, I wasn't happy. I didn't want to be there, but I didn't want to leave either—but only because of the kids. When I married her I thought it would be forever and I knew there would be some ups and downs, but… she made it hard to stay. And after Laila died, I really felt bad and believed I owed it to her to try again."

"What do you mean?"

He blew out a breath and rested his head on the headrest. "Annette didn't want Laila at the party that day. Laila was a handful and hard to deal with sometimes and I don't know if Annette was having a bad day or if Laila was having a bad day, but Annette wanted me to come and take her off her hands. But I was working and told her I couldn't stop what I was doing and be there right away. That I was going to be another hour or so. She didn't want to hear none of that and… she started yelling at me and saying all this crazy stuff. And it was a childish way for me to handle it, but I hung up on her and turned my phone off."

"So she blames you for Laila's death?"

Holiday nodded. "Well… she says it wouldn't've happened if I had come to pick her up as she asked me to."

Cynthia's heart ached for the both of them. She looked in Holiday's face. "You do realize you had no control over that though, right?"

"Well… it just makes me think, 'what if', y'know? Maybe I could have been a bit more understanding that day."

Cynthia glanced out of the window to keep from looking at him.

"And about Christian," he continued, "I can't give up on him. He wasn't even two years old when me and Annette got together. His real daddy stopped coming around right after we got married, so I'm the only dad he knows. I don't think just because me and his mama ain't together I have to put him down too. He's a good kid and… one man's already gave up on him. I can't do that to him."

Cynthia nodded. *Of course you wouldn't do that to him.*

"We had talked about making it official and giving him my last name and everything." He was quiet for several seconds and then touched her hand. "I didn't mean to raise my voice at you the other night. It's just… I was dealing with some things from earlier that day. I will never do that to you again."

"How is he?"

"He's good. I want to see him, but…"

Cynthia turned her attention back to him. "But what?"

His brow furrowed. "Well… his mama put me on the banned list at the hospital. She don't want me around no more."

"Are you serious? Why?"

Holiday shook his head. "Christian told her about you and—"

"About me?" Cynthia cut in. "What do you mean he told her about me?"

"About the day you came over and helped us paint," he gestured towards Sister Dunham's old house. "So now she's saying she don't want any other women around her son."

"Wow. This is sad. All because I came over and happened to meet him? So what are you going to do?"

He sighed. "I don't know."

Cynthia looked out of the window again. The more she found out, the more she realized why they couldn't be. This was too much to deal with and she needed to let him go. "I had a good time these past few weeks," she said, "but I think this is all too soon. Maybe I fell so easily because I was just trying to get through all the stress I've been under lately. I think you're a great guy, but this wouldn't work."

"Cynthia, what are you saying?" He looked at her, his eyes searching hers.

"I'm saying… you two have a special bond, will always be tied together. I can't compete with that."

"Baby, there is no competition. There is nothing between me and Annette." His thumb stroked the back of her hand as he held it.

She gently pulled her hand away. "I don't want to be the reason she's stopping you from seeing Christian."

A gust of air left his chest, as if he was just now realizing the pressure he was under.

The hum of the motor and the air conditioner filled the small space of the car as they sat in silence. Cynthia looked straight ahead through the windshield, but she could feel Holiday's gaze on the side of her head. She didn't want to look at him because her body was trying to fight everything her mind was telling her.

"This weekend is the last weekend for Hot August Nights." His smooth voice broke the quiet. "Since you're leaving Monday, do you wanna go?"

Cynthia chuckled in disbelief before turning to him. "Did you not just hear anything I said?"

"I heard you. Doesn't mean I have to listen to you."

"No," she said pointedly. "We cannot hang out. We cannot be friends. We cannot be anything. So don't even bother calling. Let's just call it what it was: a great summertime fling." Cynthia gripped the steering wheel. "And please, don't show up here again."

"You serious?" he asked.

"Yes." She put the car in Reverse. "I have to go now."

Without a word he opened the passenger side door and got out. Cynthia waited until he cleared the rear end of the car before she lifted her foot from the brake and rolled out of the driveway.

She never looked back at him.

FIFTY-FOUR

Holiday lay in bed, his hands clasped behind his head as he stared into the darkness. He could not believe the turn of events. Right now all he wanted was to be with Cynthia, to have her in his arms, her legs wrapped around him, his mouth on hers. He did not expect for their first time seeing each other after the beautiful, albeit too short, time spent at the resort last weekend to be the last time. Being in her company was the most-relaxing experience and he wanted more of her time. He wanted more of her. But now she wanted nothing to do with him. It was a great summertime fling she had said.

But he knew better.

To him, what they shared was more than a fling. She was the type of woman he wanted in his life. Long-term.

He picked up his phone to call her only to put it back down. He sighed heavily.

As much as it pained him to do so he would respect her wishes and leave her alone.

FIFTY-FIVE

In attempt to move on and keep her mind off Holiday, Cynthia made herself busy. She began in her room, cleaning it from top to bottom. She removed the curtains from the windows and the coverings from her bed to put them in the washer. The ceiling was swept to get rid of any unseen cobwebs. She scrubbed the windows, removing the dust and grit that had settled in the corners. The dresser and nightstands were dusted clean and polished. She swept the hardwood floor, making sure to include the baseboards and to get the dust bunnies underneath her bed. From her room she moved into the upstairs landing to sweep the runners and floor before tackling the bathroom.

She worked her way downstairs, dusting the pictures and whatnots hanging on the walls as she went. Mama Genie had gone to Sister Nash's house to help with tonight's Revival dinner so she went into her room to clean it as well as the guest rooms and bathroom before heading to the kitchen and living room. For three hours Cynthia swept, scrubbed, and cleaned.

Her arms were sore, her back throbbed, and her legs felt as heavy as lead when she settled into the bathtub after the marathon cleaning. She wished the hot, soapy water could wash away the images in her head, the feeling in her chest. No matter how hard she tried and how much she cleaned, Holiday was right there along with her. She could see his handsome face, that bright smile, hear his sultry voice, feel his hands on her skin.

She admonished herself then for thinking about him. It didn't make sense to entertain thoughts of being with him now that she knew what she knew. There was no way they could be together and she accepted their situation for what it was. *Maybe I needed this experience to help me get over Jonathan*, she thought. But she quickly pushed that thought to the back of her mind.

After her bath, she climbed into bed and quickly fell asleep.

Save for the times she went downstairs to eat or to use the bathroom, she remained in her room for the next couple days. She solved every single puzzle in the Seek-n-Find magazine, a few of the puzzles in the Sudoku magazine, and finally completed the book club reading. She'd told Mama Genie she wasn't feeling well and could not make the last night of the summer revival.

She was sick. Heartsick, but sick nonetheless.

Holiday had come into her life when she was vulnerable, seeking solace from everything that had gone wrong over the past few months. And she had been foolish to go against her better judgment, letting her guard down and taking a chance on love again. Experience should have taught her if it appeared to be too good to be true, then it probably was. If Holiday would hide something as significant as the true nature of the connection to his ex-wife he was liable to hide anything else.

And she wanted no parts of that type of relationship again.

* * *

Youth counselor. Zenith Star Academy—A treatment center for at-risk adolescent girls. Cynthia's back straightened as she read parts of the job posting out loud. "…motivate girls towards a positive, healthy future.

Our mission is to prepare our girls to lead responsible and fulfilling lives… provide mentoring… education. …Assist with homework, one-on-one tutoring… computer courses… provide educational games and field trips…"

Cynthia's phone vibrated on the nightstand as she clicked Submit after completing the online application and uploading her résumé for the youth counselor position.

It was Holiday. She quickly dropped the phone onto the bed and left the room to stop herself from answering. *Why is he doing this? Does he not take me seriously? Does he not believe me when I say we need to go our separate ways?*

"You sure missed out on a good service last night," Mama Genie said from the living room. "I guess you're feeling better today, huh?"

"A little," Cynthia said from the kitchen. It was lunchtime. She made herself a sandwich, grabbed the bag of corn chips from the pantry, and took a seat at the dining table.

"Your stomach upset or what?"

My heart she wanted to say. "I think it's just stress. Headache, anxiety."

"You better stop worrying yourself. Ain't nothing to stress over. This is your house too, remember? You already know you can stay here until you get yourself together."

Get yourself together. She grunted at the thought. That's what she had come here to do. But she was no closer to achieving what she set out to do than she was five weeks ago. Holiday had come in and interrupted those plans and now all she wanted was to leave the town so she wouldn't have to see him, to think about him. She had come to heal her heart. And now it was bruised all over again.

She ushered forth a smile despite her sunken mood so Mama Genie wouldn't worry. "I'm fine. Like you said… everything always works itself out. Whatever is meant to be will be."

Mama Genie looked at her. "Do you really believe that?"

Cynthia stopped mid-bite of her sandwich, wondering if Mama Genie could see her faith wavering. "I do," she told her.

He'd left a voice mail. Her body warmed at the sound of Holiday's voice. "Listen… Cynthia, I know you said you didn't wanna see me no more, but I need to see you. I want to see you. One last time. Before you go."

She lay down in bed, wishing she had something to do to keep her mind occupied. She contemplated driving to the plaza, but didn't want to risk running into him. The lake was definitely not a choice either. She dialed the number for the town's cinema to hear a listing of the weekend's showtimes, deciding she could treat herself to a matinee. His name popped up on the phone screen and, before she knew it, she pressed the button to answer.

"Cynthia?" he said, sounding surprised that she accepted the call.

"Yeah?" She wanted to appear unmoved, but the ever-present butterflies whenever she felt his energy returned.

"How you doing?"

"I'm fine." She waited.

"I uh… was calling to see if you wanted to go to Jesse Lee's tonight. It's tournament night—the last Friday night of the month. You wanna go? Yoauna will be there."

"And Chanel will be there too," she retorted.

"Well…" He paused for a second. "I don't know if she will be there or not, but it means nothing to me either way. You'll be there with me."

Cynthia shook her head. "Why are you doing this? Did we not have this discussion just a few days ago?"

"Because I can't let you go."

"You have no choice."

He exhaled. "Will you let me see you?"

"No," she said firmly. "This doesn't make sense. We can't be. We just can't be," she said, and hung up before he had the chance to say anything else.

* * *

She woke up thirsty, her mouth as parched as the county road asphalt. It was near six o' clock in the evening and she did not remember falling asleep. She got out of bed and when she opened the door to go downstairs she heard the voices. Mama Genie and Sister Nash were laughing at the television. But there was a third voice. A male voice.

She descended the steps slowly. *I tell him I do not want to see him, to not come over here again, so he shows up anyway?* Cynthia couldn't believe it, but she should not have been surprised. *Of course he will not take no for an answer.*

Sister Nash asked him a question and his answer halted Cynthia in her tracks. She paused on the third step from the bottom. She swallowed hard, desperate for something to wet her throat when recognition hit her. Although hesitant, she rounded the corner, confirming what she already knew.

Mama Genie and Sister Nash's heads turned to look at her when she entered the room, but Cynthia's eyes fixated on the back of the head of the man sitting on the loveseat.

It was Jonathan.

FIFTY-SIX

A heady scent of citrus filled his nostrils as he bent slightly to give her a hug.

"Hey, sweetie," Yoauna smiled at him. "This is the earliest I've ever seen you show up for the party."

"I know, but I figured I'd come and help Jesse Lee out on the pit today." He walked past Yoauna into the house.

"Where is Cynthia?" she asked, looking out the door as if she was expecting her to walk up behind him.

"She's not here. It's just me."

"Why didn't you bring her?" Yoauna closed the door. "She had a lot of fun last time, dancing her butt off in that dress. She knew she was sexy that night," she laughed.

Holiday chuckled. "Well… she's going back home Monday, so I think she's spending time with her grandmother."

"Oh okay. You want something to drink? Jesse went to the store to get some vinegar. He forgot it for the barbecue sauce."

Holiday followed her towards the kitchen. "A beer is cool if you got it." He took a seat at the bar as she went to the refrigerator.

"When do we *not* have beer in this house?" she laughed. She pushed the bottle across the bar and returned to the sink where she had a batch of raw chicken wings waiting to season. He watched her coat the poultry with flavored powders and Cajun spices. "So what you been up to these past few weeks? Jesse told me you and Cynthia been hanging out all summer. You must really like her because it's been a while since we've seen you with somebody."

Holiday shrugged and put the beer to his lips. "She is a special lady. I was just showing her a good time." And he wanted to continue showing her a good time. For the rest of her life. *Wait… what the hell am I thinking?*

"She seems really nice… and y'all look good together. Will she be coming back soon for a visit?"

He really didn't want to have this conversation. Yoauna was his girl, but Cynthia had told him to get lost and there was nothing more he could do about it. There was nothing more to say. "I'm not sure, but how is Jay doing?" he asked, deftly changing the subject. "I see he didn't come home for the summer."

Yoauna beamed proudly at the mention of her son, Jesse Lee Jr. "He's doing good. Real good. He decided to stay and take a couple of summer classes. He said he's trying to get out of there as soon as possible. But I think he just stayed behind because he met some girl up there. I told him he is not allowed to even *think about* getting serious with someone until he's twenty-six"

Holiday chuckled. "That's not happening that's for sure."

"I know," she laughed. "My baby is smart, but I don't want him to get caught up before he graduates—trying to get married and all that. He's already decided to go straight through to get his doctorate."

"Wow," Holiday said. "That boy's committed. I like that."

"Yep. I thank God every day he didn't turn out like some of these knuckleheads around here, sitting back doing nothing. But me and Jesse worked hard to make sure he didn't."

"For sure."

Yoauna tossed the wings in the sink to ensure the seasonings were evenly coated before transferring them to a foil pan on the counter.

"You want me to start them on the pit for you?"

"If you want to," she said. "I guess there's enough coals out there. I told Jesse we should've just thrown these on the grill since we're starting so late."

Holiday got up from his stool. "Naw, these won't take long at all," he told her.

"You're so helpful," she said, following him out to the patio. "I still don't understand how Annette let you get away."

He grunted. "Well… apparently I wasn't good enough. I did what I could. That's all water under a bridge now though."

"A couple of my girlfriends ask me about you all the time. They say they have no problem taking care of a man like you."

Holiday shook his head. The woman he wanted was Cynthia. The woman who had captured his heart over the summer. The only problem was that she did not want him. And he was having trouble accepting it. "Naw, I'm good. Besides, I know your friends. No offense, but all of them are not like you."

She laughed. "What you mean by that?"

"Just… believe me," he said, thinking about the never-ending gossip that swirled around town, the affirmations that spilled from the mouths of some of Jesse Lee's buddies over the cards tables after their bellies were full of alcohol. "Jesse Lee is a lucky man is all I'm saying. And that's the kind of woman I want."

"Aww… now you're trying to make me cry." She patted him on the back as he worked to get the fire going on the barbecue pit.

He chuckled. "It's the truth. Y'all remind me a lot of my parents. Together since y'all were teenagers and the marriage is still going strong. To this day I still don't know how you put up with Jesse Lee, but it takes a patient woman. A loving woman."

She threw her head back laughing this time. "He's not so bad. I think that's what's kept me here so long. He is a ball of entertainment all day every day. I've been laughing since day one. Now, of course, he gets on my nerves sometimes, but he always has a way of making me feel better at the end of the day. And I realize, if we had nothing, if we stripped all of the material things away—" she glanced around at their grand home "—I know that we will still be fine just to have each other's company. Because that's all we started with."

Holiday nodded. His mind immediately went to the intimate moments he shared with Cynthia.

FIFTY-SEVEN

"Cyndi, believe me. I was stupid. I never meant to hurt you. I've been thinking about this ever since. I seriously messed up and I'm paying for it every day."

Cynthia stood with her arms folded, glaring at Jonathan as they stood on the porch. For an hour she'd listened to him as he pleaded his case, apologizing over and over for disrespecting her and their relationship. Telling her everything that has been going on in his life since she left him, which hasn't been much. According to him, his world has been a giant storm cloud following him around wherever he went.

If Mama Genie and Sister Nash were not on the other side of the wall in the living room Cynthia was sure she would have cussed him thoroughly. "Jonathan, I wasted three years of my life with you—"

"It wasn't a waste."

"Three years for what? Just to be cheated on? With somebody I knew personally?" Her voice cracked.

"Cyndi… I know. I know."

"Why her?" She didn't know why she asked the question because the answer would not matter. And knowing why was not going to make her feel any better.

He sighed. "I don't have a good answer for that, either. All I can say is it happened that one time."

"And you expect me to believe that?"

"It's the truth. We were drinking and she was playing around, dancing on the coffee table and flirting with me and… one thing led to another and…"

"That's all it took, huh? For her to dance for you on the table?" Cynthia chuckled despite the anger churning inside her.

"She transferred to the Greenspoint location. She doesn't work with me anymore."

"And that's supposed to make me feel better? Three years, Jonathan. I gave you my whole heart. I would *never* do something like that to betray you." Cynthia sat down in one of the rocking chairs. She was hurt again, thinking about the memories and how he so easily threw it all away.

He nodded. "I know. I know. You were the perfect girlfriend. That's why I'm here." He eased down to kneel in front of her. "That's why I brought this." He reached into his back pocket and pulled out a slim, wood box. "I want you to know how serious I am about this. About us."

Cynthia looked on in confusion as he reached for her hand.

"What I did to you was the dumbest thing I have ever done in my life. I know you probably don't trust me no more, but this is a promise to you that I am going to do what I have to do to get you to trust me again."

She didn't realize her hand was balled into a fist until she looked down, seeing him try to pry her fingers apart. Her vision blurred and she blinked to keep the tears threatening to spill from her eyes at bay. But she was unlucky.

Crying? Why am I crying?

"This is a promise," she heard Jonathan say again and he slipped the ring on her finger.

It was a beautiful, single solitaire with a rose gold band.

She looked at him. For three years she loved this man. Trusted him. Believed he was the best partner any woman could have. Imagined their relationship was headed to the next level.

"Don't throw what we had away."

But how would she be able to trust him again? Cynthia shook her head, tried pulling her hand away. "Jonathan, there is no way I—"

"Cyndi, I love you. Please. I'll give you some time to think about it. Will you at least think about it?"

Cynthia remained on the porch to regain her composure before she entered the house after Jonathan left.

"Y'all sure had a lot to talk about I see," Mama Genie said.

Cynthia smiled tightly. "Yeah," she answered and headed straight towards the hall for the stairs.

"Cynthia," Sister Nash called after her just as she planted her foot on the bottom step to go up to the privacy of her room. "Come here, darling."

She quietly sucked her teeth and returned to the living room. "Yes ma'am?"

"Isn't there something you want to share with us?"

Cynthia frowned. "Something like what?"

Sister Nash smiled and looked over at Mama Genie. "Do you see what I see, Genie?"

Mama Genie said, "Unh-huh. And she tried to run upstairs real fast, thinking we wouldn't notice."

"So that's why your eyes are red. He asked for your hand? Bring it over here. Let me see what that fine young man got for you."

Cynthia wished she'd tucked the ring out of sight before she entered the house to avoid all this attention. "It's nothing, Sister Nash."

"Nothing?" she questioned. "A man proposes to you and you say it's nothing?" She looked at Mama Genie again.

"It's not an engagement ring, just a promise ring."

"A promise ring? A promise to do what?" her grandmother asked.

"That's a new one for me too," Sister Nash said. She looked up at Cynthia. "Is it a promise that he'll ask you to marry him later?"

"I'm sorry Mama Genie, Sister Nash. I just want to go to my room and lay down."

"Well you don't sound too happy." Mama Genie picked up the remote to lower the volume on the television. "Sit yourself down and tell me what's going on."

Cynthia reluctantly obliged and took a seat on the loveseat. "It's just a promise to work at building my trust in him again."

"Why did you lose trust in him?" Sister Nash asked.

She hoped she wouldn't have to go into specifics, but Mama Genie answered before she could. "He stepped out on her," Mama Genie told Sister Nash.

"Oh?"

Cynthia didn't say anything.

"Well no wonder he was willing to sit here all that time until you woke up from your nap," Sister Nash said. "He had some things to get off his conscience."

Mama Genie said, "He had some nerve driving all the way down here from Houston, too."

"Well it's evident he really cares about her, Sister Genie. A little infidelity don't have to be the end of a relationship."

Cynthia looked at Sister Nash. *Huh?*

"My mama told me if a man don't cheat when he young, he'll cheat when he get older, but so long as he ain't beating on you and he's still taking care of home, you have nothing to worry about."

Mama Genie's head whipped around to look at her friend. "What you say? You have got to be kidding."

"I'm serious. That's what Mama used to tell us. She said if you leave a man for every time you get cheated on, you'll just be going from man to man."

Cynthia couldn't believe the words coming from Sister Nash's righteous mouth. She and Mama Genie shared the same incredulous look.

"No, Sister," Mama Genie said, chuckling.

Sister Nash held up a hand. "Now wait a minute, Sister. I didn't say I agree with Mama. I did not say that," she shook her head sternly, her silver curls bouncing. "But it gave me something to think about when I was dealing with my own marriage."

"What you mean?"

"Mr. Nash had his own weakness for the flesh. He confessed it to me once. So I had to look at him for the man he was beyond that weakness. He was an awesome father, he was a sweet husband, and I didn't have to ask him for anything. Anything I wanted, or anything the kids needed, he provided."

Mama Genie said, "I don't know about that. You know what the Bible says about adultery, coveting thy neighbor's wife or husband."

"I know what the Bible says about forgiveness too," Sister Nash countered. "He who is without sin cast the first..."

Cynthia wanted to escape to her room as Mama Genie and Sister Nash battled back and forth about the Bible and the sanctity of marriage.

When they finally agreed to disagree, Sister Nash turned her attention back to Cynthia. "Now... this is no judgment on my part because I know your generation does things a little different from ours. You and that young man were not legally bound, but if this is the man you want to be with, and you truly believe in your heart he is capable of change, then you might want to consider it. Everybody makes mistakes, darling. Mr. Nash made his but we sought counseling and prayed together and worked on our relationship because we knew we wanted to be together. Talk to God about it," she smiled.

Cynthia forced a smile back, thanked her for the advice, and hurried to her room where she could lay in the dark and be alone with her thoughts.

FIFTY-EIGHT

It was half past four in the morning when Holiday's head hit the pillow. He'd stayed behind after everyone else had left the tournament to help Jesse Lee and Yoauna clean up. The first two hours of the party had been a nerve-racking experience for him as he was asked the same questions over and over when someone arrived: *What happened to your girlfriend?, Why didn't you bring your girlfriend?, Who is this new chick I heard about?, Is your son all right?*

He'd tried to focus on the games and music and enjoy the atmosphere around him, but the more he tried not to, the more he thought about Cynthia. A few times during the games he had to be reminded to stay focused or he would have to forfeit his hand because he was too distracted and ruining the flow of the game.

After the clean up, he and Jesse Lee sat on the patio to talk some more. Mainly about marriage and relationships.

Holiday thought Yoauna had gone to bed inside, but she came out later dressed in her pajamas and night cap and cuddled up next to her husband on the sofa. And it wasn't long before Jesse Lee was sniffing at her neck, telling her how fresh she smelled, causing her to giggle like a school girl. Seeing the two of them together like that always made Holiday smile and think about his lack of a steady relationship in his life. He wanted their kind of love.

He wanted to be able to sit on the patio on a warm night under the stars with his own wife.

So maybe it was the cups of *Crown Royal* he'd had, or maybe it was just his need to talk to someone, but he had no problem at that time telling Yoauna what he was going through with Cynthia when she wanted to know what he and Jesse Lee were talking about. And she listened attentively before offering her opinion about the situation from a woman's perspective. She advised him to consider how Cynthia must have felt when she learned he withheld some important facts about his life and connection to his ex-wife. She encouraged him to be honest with Cynthia regarding his feelings for her, but also warned that he would also have to accept that, as it was for some men, some women were not looking to be a stepparent to anyone's child.

And this is what was on his mind as he lay in bed. He thought back to that time when he first told his parents about Annette and how serious he was about her, that he wanted to marry her. Pop didn't have too much to say about it, but Savannah disapproved right away, asking why he would want to get involved with a woman that already had a child. *Why on earth would you want a ready-made family,* she'd asked. But Annette was the woman he wanted at the time. And he accepted her and everything she came with.

Now Cynthia was the woman he wanted. But how could he expect her to feel the same way about him?

FIFTY-NINE

"Damn, girl… what did you eat?" Tora held her nose as she entered the apartment.

"I had a burger and fries," Cynthia said.

"Smelling like that?" Tora grimaced.

Cynthia rolled her eyes as Tora went to the kitchen for the can of Lysol. "Whatever," she said. "It was the onion."

"Which is why I can't stand them. They are funky," Tora laughed and commenced to spraying the room in a dramatic fashion. And as soon as the disinfectant spray was in the air and up her nose, Cynthia began to choke.

"Are you trying to kill me," she said between fits. "You know you can't spray too much of that!"

Tora began to choke too.

"Open the patio door! Let it out." Cynthia jumped up from her seat on the couch and followed Tora outside for fresh air.

It took a few minutes for them to clear their throats and before the apartment was safe for them to enter.

"Geez… It's my first day back and you're already trying to kill me," Cynthia said, sitting back on the couch.

Tora went to the refrigerator and came back with two bottles of water. "My bad. I was just trying to get that stench out of here." She sat next to Cynthia on the couch.

They sipped at their waters.

"What have you been doing all day?" Tora asked her.

"What I'm doing now. Sitting here."

"How exciting," Tora laughed. "You can at least turn the TV on."

Cynthia pulled her blanket back up to her shoulders. "I didn't feel like watching TV. I didn't want to hear anything."

"Well damn. What's the problem?"

Cynthia couldn't be at her grandmother's house another day where all her thoughts were preoccupied with Holiday. On Saturday morning she'd got up and peeked out of her window out of habit and saw his truck in the driveway next door. She felt trapped in the house the entire day because she did not want to see him. And she was on edge, wondering if he would show up knocking on their door, persuading her to come out and talk to him. As much as she dreaded having to return to Tora's apartment, she packed her bags that night and left for Houston at the same time Mama Genie was leaving for church Sunday morning.

"I feel like I've been hit by a bus," Cynthia said.

"And you look like you've been hit by one," Tora laughed again. "Whatever."

"At least let me redo your top because it's looking a mess."

"No. I don't feel like getting my hair braided again." Cynthia laid her head on the arm of the couch and closed her eyes. She wished to sleep her heartache away.

"Sis, what happened?" Tora coaxed.

A few minutes ticked by before Cynthia opened her eyes again and told her friend everything.

"Wooowww," Tora said after Cynthia gave an account of her summer, beginning with the day she first laid eyes on Holiday and ending with the conversation she'd had with Sister Nash and Mama Genie after Jonathan's promise. "This is like some soap opera type shit. What are you going to do?"

"I'm going to give Jonathan back this ring," Cynthia answered, fingering the band on her left hand.

"So you're in love with Holiday then."

Cynthia looked at her friend. "In love? No."

"I think you are. You just don't want to acknowledge it."

"Tora, a person doesn't fall in love that fast. In deep like? Yes, but not love."

"Oh it can definitely happen. And it's happened to you."

"He lied, Tora. I was just blinded by how good being with him made me feel. From my experience with Jonathan I should have known. He was too good to be true."

"It wasn't a lie. Just an omission like he told you."

"He is claiming Christian as his biological son. He is going to be dealing with his ex-wife for the rest of his life."

"So which part are you upset about? That he didn't tell you he really doesn't have a quote-unquote son or that he has a quote-unquote son?"

Cynthia remained quiet as she considered Tora's question. She had to admit to herself she really had not thought so deeply about it.

Tora finally asked her, "You prefer to date a man without kids?"

Cynthia shrugged. "I mean… I guess it wouldn't be a problem. If it was no more than one."

"No, honestly. Because it matters."

"The older we get the less we are to meet men without kids."

"Exactly, but if it's one of your requirements, just be upfront about it."

Cynthia sighed. "I don't know. It's just not the right time. I'm still—"

"Blah, blah, blah," Tora said, waving off what she had to say. "I don't want to hear it. I believe you're giving up something that has the potential to be great. And for what? Just because he stood up and took on another man's responsibility when that man wouldn't take care of his own?"

"No, it's not about that."

"Then what is it?"

Cynthia sighed again, wanting to change the subject. She said, "I'm sorry I didn't Skype in for the book club meeting Saturday as I said I would. I just didn't feel up to it."

Tora waved her hand. "Don't worry about it. I didn't go myself. I told one of the other ladies they would have to cover for me."

"What? Why not?"

"I didn't finish the book." She got up from the couch to let Mink out on the patio. She liked to sit outside and people-watch.

"What? So you had me suffering through that boring book and you didn't even read it?" Cynthia picked up a pillow from the couch and threw it at Tora.

Tora slinked away from it and it flew by Mink, frightening her to jump six feet in the air it seemed. "My bad. It wasn't one of the author's best ones. I didn't know."

"Is that the real reason why you didn't attend the book club or was it something else that kept you away from home this weekend," Cynthia teased. When she texted Tora Saturday night to tell her she would be heading back to Houston, Tora texted her back and told her to let herself into the apartment, that she was going out and was not sure when she would be home.

"I was just hanging out with Glenn and ended up spending the weekend at his place. He's going through a breakup too, and I was just there to cheer him up. It seems that's all I am these days—a shoulder for my friends to cry on as they go through the trials of love.

Meanwhile, I can only sit back and wish I had someone to love."

"Don't even start that again, Tora," Cynthia rolled her eyes playfully. "You have to bat men away every time we go out."

"Yeah, but they're not men I'm physically attracted to. They're all too short. What is it with these short guys wanting to approach me? I still don't get it."

Cynthia laughed, but she empathized with her friend. Tora was a tall woman, five feet, eleven inches, and when she wore heels, the average man didn't stand a chance next to her. "Well… maybe you should find out where the tall men are. They're out there somewhere."

"Yeah, they're all taken by short women like you."

Cynthia laughed again. "Height isn't everything. It's about how big his heart is."

"Easy for you to say because you've never had to deal with this problem," Tora said. "But I've given up," she sighed. "I'll be the old lady with a house full of cats."

"You will meet him, Tora. And he's going to come into your life when you least expect it. Most likely when you're not even ready for him."

Tora frowned. "Are you saying this for me? Or for you?"

"*For you.*"

"Sounds like something you need to acknowledge yourself. Have you talked to him?"

"To who?"

Tora rolled her eyes this time. "Did I miss something? Who else are we talking about?"

"No. And I'm not going to. He's a great guy, but it just won't work."

"What a shame. You meet a good man and you don't even want him," Tora sucked her teeth.

"It's not the right time."

"When is it ever the right time, Cynthia? Didn't you go through this before with another ex? You told him it wasn't the right time and you ended up regretting it? And, if I remember correctly, you remained single for several years afterward because you believed you needed some time alone to yourself. Then you met Jonathan. But look how that turned out."

Cynthia wasn't following what Tora was saying. "What's your point?"

"My point is… what are you waiting for? In love you have to take chances. You can't throw a good guy away just because he didn't come into your life when you planned for him to. Listening to you talk about how much you admire about him, and seeing the way your face lights up, I think you know this is the man for you."

Cynthia sighed and laid her head back on the arm of the sofa. "I just need some time. And he will be out of my system soon."

SIXTY

Labor Day came and went, as well as Halloween. For Holiday, his days had returned to the mundane: wake up, go to work or look for work, spend a few hours down at the lake, return home and have dinner with Pop, get up the next morning and do it all over again. He was especially bored now that he did not have Christian to spend some of his free time with. It was by word of mouth he found out Christian had been released from the hospital and was recovering well at home. Holiday had been hoping to receive a phone call from Annette giving him permission to stop by to visit with Christian, but a call never came.

And then there was Cynthia.

Every day he had the urge to call her. He wished to hear her voice again, her sweet laughter.

He saw Ms. Genie on the day he went to complete the wax job on the floors next door and they spoke briefly. When asked, Ms. Genie told him Cynthia was doing good, that she had started a new job and was really happy about it.

Holiday was glad to hear the good news because he knew how stressful the job search had been for Cynthia but, at the same time, the news only set in stone that she would be out of his life for good.

Stevie Wonder's *Rocket Love* filtered through the speakers as Holiday sat in the cab of his truck, a bottle of beer nestled between his thighs, his left arm hanging out of the window with a cigarette clasped between his fingers. He pressed the button on the steering wheel to raise the volume. No other song was more fitting than this one to explain exactly what he was feeling at the moment.

Holiday closed his eyes and laid his head on the headrest as the music took him back to the summer days and nights. *I longed for you since I was born… a woman sensitive and warm. And that you were.*

Stevie had to have gone through what he was going through to be able to write such profound lyrics. To meet a woman who embodied everything you wished for in a partner, have her shower you with her goodness, only for her to snatch it away and leave you in a limp stupor.

… At a half a mile from heaven you dropped me back down to this cold, cold world.

SIXTY-ONE

Cynthia grabbed her bag from the passenger seat and got out of the car. She walked over to an empty bench and sat down. The days were cool enough to sit outside and she'd found a small park to spend her lunch hour just minutes away from the campus. It had been several weeks into her new position as Youth Counselor and she was grateful to finally be moving in the right direction career-wise. She knew as soon as she walked through the doors Zenith Star was a place for her—a place focused on motivating and building healthy mindsets for young women. She liked to think it was her strong belief that the position was hers from the beginning, coupled with her prayers, as she waited for a call back from the program director that landed her the job. But maybe it was simply that she was able to convince the director how nine years of classroom experience prepared her to transition into a counseling role because, after all, teachers were more than just educators for their students. Oftentimes they were counselors, inspirational coaches, even second parents.

She pulled the *Essence* magazine she swiped from Tora's book shelf out of her bag and started on her lunch. Although desperate for her own place again, Tora told her it was perfectly fine for her to stay in her apartment for a few months until she was able to rebuild her savings account and have enough available to prevent being caught in a financial bind again if something were to go awry. To make the best of the situation, Cynthia replaced the air mattress with a roll-away cot and hung thick panel curtains for a semblance of privacy in the small den.

The sound of soft laughter made Cynthia look up. An elderly couple walked the sidewalk, hand-in-hand. *Most-likely retired and just enjoying their days together*, she thought. Holiday immediately came to mind. He was always on her mind. She thought about their strolls through the park that summer. Sitting and laughing with him as he worked to restore Sister Dunham's old house, or sitting and laughing with him over platters of take-out food in the bed of his truck. Dancing with him at Jesse Lee and Yoauna's house party. His arm wrapped around her waist as he grooved to the blues at the festival. The softness of his lips when she kissed him the first time. The feel of him, of his hands, on her, and inside her at the resort.

Tora asked every other day it seemed if she'd called 'that good man'. And every other day she would say she did not, and she was not. But Cynthia surely missed him every day. Tora was right. He was a good man. Taking care of and loving Christian as his own flesh and blood was a noble thing to do. For that alone she had great respect for him.

What woman wouldn't want a man like that? Couldn't appreciate a man like that?

Cynthia sighed and gathered her trash to toss in the garbage can as she walked back to her car. *I'm sure he's moved on to somebody else,* she thought. *Probably went back to his wife like Chanel said. Or maybe back to Chanel herself.*

SIXTY-TWO

"Pop, you ready?" Holiday called from the living room.

Frank emerged from his room, pulling his suitcase behind him. "I'm ready," he said.

"You sure you got everything?"

"I'm sure. And whatever I forgot, I'll just have to buy me another one," he grinned and followed Holiday outside.

Holiday loaded their luggage in the back seat of the truck. It was Sunday evening and they were driving to Forth Worth to spend the night with Avery, Dawn, and the boys. Tomorrow morning all of them would get up and go to the airport to start their Thanksgiving vacation in Destin, Florida.

"You sure you got everything?" Holiday asked Frank again as he settled in the driver's seat.

"Yep," Frank nodded.

"Where is your reflux medicine?"

Frank thumbed towards the back seat. "In my bag."

"What about your reading glasses?"

"Right here," he answered, patting the pocket on his jacket.

"Did you turn off the coffee pot?"

Frank grinned. "Go see."

Holiday chuckled and went back inside. The coffee pot was off, but the iron was still on and plugged in in Frank's room. Holiday made his rounds through the house again to make sure everything was off. His phone rang just as he twisted the knob on the back door to check that it was locked too.

"Hello," he answered.

"Hey, Mason," Annette said. "How are you doing?"

"I'm fine," he said, surprised to receive a phone call from her. He had not heard from her since that day she demanded him to leave Christian's room at the hospital—three whole months ago.

"That's good. What about Mr. Frank? Is he doing all right?"

"He's fine too," Holiday said, wondering what was the purpose for her call. "Is Christian all right?" he asked her.

"Yeah, he's doing fine." She cleared her throat. "He keeps asking me about you."

Holiday's heart warmed. He smiled and walked over to the couch in the living room and sat down. He had not heard from Christian either and he guessed Annette barred Christian from contacting him too.

Annette continued, "But he understands now that since we are no longer together he won't be able to see you as much."

Holiday waited, confused, waiting for her to tell him exactly what was the reason for contacting him this Sunday evening.

She said finally, "Paula invited us to her parents' cabin in the Hill Country for Thanksgiving. Their family meets there every year for the holidays. Christian doesn't want to go. He said he would rather stay here with you or with Roxy, but that's not happening, and I've decided I'm not going to force him to go this time. We're leaving Tuesday morning so I'm calling you ahead of time so you can make plans to come by and pick him up tomorrow. Or I can drop him off to you. Either way."

She was speaking to him as if nothing had happened three months ago. As if they were the best of friends, co-parenting with love and respect for each other like mature adults should do. It muddled his mind every time she behaved this way, but he loved the idea of having Christian with him for Thanksgiving. "Well, I wish you would've let me know sooner because we're leaving right now going to Fort Worth to meet Avery. We fly in to Florida tomorrow afternoon."

"Florida? Is that what y'all are doing for Thanksgiving?"

"Yeah, and we'll be back in town Saturday."

She remained quiet a few moments. "I can call to see if I can get him on a flight."

Holiday sat back into the couch. He was sure Pop wouldn't mind if they left a few hours later while Annette worked to get a plane ticket for Christian. They had plenty of time to make it to Fort Worth before their morning flight. "Alright," he told her. He thought about the look of surprise he was sure to see on his nephews' faces when he showed up to their house with Christian after he'd told them Christian could not attend the family vacation.

"But you're not taking anyone else with you, right? It's just you and Mr. Frank there?"

Holiday nodded. "Yeah, it's just me and Pop."

"Good," she said, "because he can't go if you're taking that woman with you. Let me go ahead and call the airlines now and I'll call you right back with the details."

"Hold on, Annette," Holiday said. He was not going to let that comment go over unchecked. "I haven't talked to you since the summer, you said I was a dangerous man and couldn't be around Christian. You calling me out of the blue to come and pick him up and you still have something to say about who I'm with?" Even though Cynthia was not in his life he would not let Annette dictate who he spent his vacation with.

"I'm just letting you know nothing's changed. I still don't want your girlfriend around my son. Now, if you can't respect that then—"

He was really confused now. He wasn't even aware things had changed since she told him she did not want him around anymore. "Annette, you've been knowing me for years. You know I wouldn't have him around somebody I didn't think he should be around. Come on now. But for you to call me, talking to me like you're doing is not right and it's got to stop. *Now*. You cannot tell me what to do."

"I can tell you what to do when it's in regards to my child. I don't mind him being with you, but it's under this condition. And that's how it's going to be from here on out."

Holiday shook his head, anger rising in his chest. As much as he hated to acknowledge it, he knew this time would come. Annette was using Christian as a pawn. She knew he was willing to do whatever she wanted him to do to lessen the guilt he felt for what happened to Laila. And he would do what she wanted him to do just to see Christian.

But he could not continue to allow her to treat him this way.

"Annette," he said calmly. The gravity of what he was about to say weighed heavily on his soul. "You know I've been there for you and him since the beginning. I loved him like he was my own son. To me, he was my son. He became my son when I married you and his daddy left. There is nothing I won't do for him and you know that. But, as much as I hate to say this… that it's even come to this, I think it's best that I stay away."

Annette remained quiet for several minutes and Holiday wondered what was going on in her mind.

She finally said, "Is that what you want to do, Mason?"

"No, it's not what I want to do," he told her, "but it's what I have to do. Christian is not a carrot for you to dangle in my face anytime you want me to do something for you."

"So you're telling me you want nothing to do with him now?"

"Don't twist my words, Annette." Holiday heard the front door open and Frank walk in.

Annette said, "Well, that's what it sounds like to me, which is a shame. I never would have expected this from you."

And he never expected he would have to do this. But, the reality of the situation was that, no matter how much he felt in his heart for Christian and called him his son, he had no legal claims to him. Annette held all the power and the control. "If it's okay with you I would like to have a talk with him to explain all this to him."

Frank looked at him quizzically before taking a seat in his recliner.

"No," Annette said. "That won't be necessary. Have a nice life."

Holiday sighed and dropped the phone on the coffee table.

"Everything okay, son?" Frank asked. "I was wondering what was taking you so long."

He ran his hand over his face, rested his head on the back of the sofa. "That was Annette."

"What she up to now?"

"We won't be seeing Christian ever again." The realization cut Holiday to his very core.

SIXTY-THREE

"Heeeyyy, Mizz Williams."

Cynthia smiled and looked up from her computer to see Camille Ashby standing at her door. Camille was a sophomore, a girl from a broken home with an alcoholic mother and imprisoned father. She was living from house to house, sleeping on the couch or floor of friends' homes before her grandmother took her in. Her grandmother saw the signs and worried Camille was headed down the same path as her parents and enrolled her in Zenith where she could receive the help and treatment she needed to turn her life in the right direction.

Cynthia took an immediate liking to Camille and realized more than anything Camille just wanted to be seen and heard. On the days Cynthia remained on campus for lunch Camille would come into her office and chat while she picked at her own lunch or volunteer to help Cynthia with small tasks: stapling documents or creating file folders.

"How are you, Camille?" Cynthia pushed the student file she was working on to the side and got up to retrieve her lunch from the small refrigerator in the corner of her office.

"I'm good," Camille drawled in that southern accent Cynthia loved. She sat down in one of he chairs in front of Cynthia's desk. "I just came by to say hi before we leave for break." It was Tuesday and the campus would be closed the remainder of the week for the Thanksgiving holiday.

"Oh, that's sweet of you." Cynthia watched her reach over and take the stuffed animal from her desk. It was the small purple elephant Holiday won and gave to her at the festival. She didn't know why she kept it on her desk because seeing it every day only reminded her of him. Or maybe it was because she wanted to be reminded of him—of the good times they shared.

"What you got planned for Thanksgiving, Mizz Williams?" Camilled asked. "Do you cook for your husband and your kids?"

Cynthia chuckled as she bit into a cracker topped with chicken salad. *Kids have no filter*, she thought. "I will be going to have dinner at my grandmother's house. What about you? Are you helping your grandmother cook dinner this year?" She needed the conversation to stay on neutral ground and not into her personal life.

"I don't even know," she said. "I may go to my friend's house. Her mama say I can come over there if I want to."

"That's good," Cynthia nodded. "But tell me about your exam. How do you think you did?"

Camille shrugged and made a face. "I don't know, Mizz Williams."

"What do you mean you don't know? You did prepare, right? Like we talked about and practiced in here together?"

Camille began to tug on the elephant's ear and Cynthia stood to rescue it out of her hands. She placed it on the opposite side of her desk, out of Camille's reach.

"That's how it always is. I be fine in study hall, but as soon as Mrs. Donohue put that test in front of me—" she flashed her hands "—poof! It disappears."

Cynthia nodded again. "I see. So when we return from break we will work on how to deal with anxiety before a test. Having the confidence and knowing because you were well-prepared beforehand you will most-likely do well on the exam."

Camille smiled. "Alright."

Cynthia continued eating as Camille glanced around her office, obviously searching for another conversation starter.

She pulled one of her legs beneath her in the chair. "So you don't have no kids at all, Mizz Williams? Or a husband? I don't see no pictures. Mrs. Donohue got pictures all over her classroom. She even got pictures of her dogs and turtle."

Cynthia laughed as she wiped her mouth with a napkin. "No, Camille. I do not."

"Do you want one? Mr. Trent is single you know. And he's very cute! Do you think he's cute, Mizz Williams?"

Mr. Trent was the Facilities Manager. Cynthia realized her second day on the job why all the staff (and some of the students) swooned over him.

Cynthia sighed, rolling her eyes. She was glad to be saved by the bell as it blared, signaling the end of the student lunch period. "See you later, Camille," she said as Camille rose from her seat. "Have a happy Thanksgiving and be safe during the break, okay?"

"I will. Happy Thanksgiving to you too," she replied as she hurried out the door and down the hall.

Cynthia got up to close the door since she had another half-hour for her lunch break. She picked up her cell phone to call Mama Genie. "I'll be there tomorrow morning," she said after they exchanged pleasantries. "Do you need me to bring anything?"

"Nope. I got everything I need. Dinner gon' be at Sister Nash's this year by the way. She just asked me to do the dressing and the pies."

After a few more minutes of small talk, Cynthia hung up and sat back in her chair. She was already anxious at the thought of being back in town with Holiday. What if she ran into him? What would she say? What would he say? Would he say anything at all since she was the one to end the friendship? What if she saw him with another woman?

She picked up the stuffed elephant and smoothed its ears. Tora said she was in love. Cynthia still denied it. But one thing Cynthia knew for sure was that getting Mason Holiday out of her system was proving to be more difficult a task than she thought.

SIXTY-FOUR

They decided to have dinner early. It was chilly and overcast when they left Dallas Forth Worth airport Monday afternoon, but flew into a breezy and sunny Destin, Florida, and they were anxious to spend more time at the beach—especially the boys. Holiday and Frank were hanging out with them in the backyard when Avery called them all inside.

"Hot dog!" Frank said as they entered the house. "It sure smell good and look good."

As soon as they arrived in Destin Avery found a place to deep fry a turkey and have it ready on Thanksgiving Day. He and Dawn together made the sides. They kept the spread small, but traditional.

Everyone took their seats at the table. Three of the boys ate at the bar since the table only had a place for six. They wasted no time and dug right in, passing dishes around the table and to the bar. Avery asked Frank and Holiday how the business was doing. In turn, Holiday wanted to know the recent news about Avery and Dawn's youth center. They moved from business talk to sports talk. Holiday was worried they were boring Dawn to death until she joined them in conversation when they switched from football to basketball. He'd forgotten she played basketball in high school and was still very active in one of her son's league.

It wasn't long before Frank had them all laughing as he recalled the crazy things Avery and Holiday did when they were kids. He picked up his paper towel to wipe the laugh tears from his eyes. He said, "I just wanna say I'm glad we did this… got together like this. Y'all know this is what it's all about right here: me and my family and all of us getting together." He looked at Avery and then at Holiday. "Savannah would be proud. And I know y'all haven't heard this from me in a long time, but I'm proud of you, too. Hard-working, caring men that love their family." To Dawn he said, "You know you my favorite daughter-in-law, for loving my son and helping raise fine young men."

"I'm your *only* daughter-in-law!" Dawn laughed. "It would be nice to have some more ladies in the family so I'm not stuck here by myself amongst all this testosterone."

They all laughed.

"Well, that's true," Frank agreed. "Hopefully Baby Boy here will meet somebody soon." Frank cleared his throat and briefly touched Holiday's hand. "Son, I just want you to know I'm also proud of how you handled your situation. I know it hurts you, but you did what you had to do. She may not let you see Christian again, but he will always remember you. You can bet on that. He'll always be in your heart. He'll be in our hearts, too. He was our family, too."

Avery and Dawn nodded their agreement.

Holiday took a sip from his water glass, swallowing the lump of sorrow in this throat.

Frank continued, "You will meet you a nice lady one day and have you another family. I believe it."

Meet a nice lady, he thought. He'd already met one.

"Can we please go to the beach now?" one of the boys groaned.

"We sure can," Dawn said, standing to clear the table. "As soon as y'all help Mama clean the kitchen."

The boys sucked their teeth and groaned some more. Holiday, Frank, and Avery laughed.

Dawn said, "Let's just plan to leave in another hour. That gives us time to clean and then get dressed for the beach, use the bathroom before we go, whatever."

"Sounds good," the men said in unison and got up from the table. Frank and Avery went to the living room to sit in front of the television. Holiday went to his room to grab his phone before retreating to the backyard patio. For three months he fought the urge, but now he couldn't fight it anymore. It was Thanksgiving. He needed to call to wish her Happy Thanksgiving.

SIXTY-FIVE

Cynthia sat on the couch, her stomach grumbling. Mama Genie sat next to her, Sister Nash and one of her daughters on the opposite side of Mama Genie. Sister Nash's other children and three members from the church occupied the other sofa and chairs. Her grandkids sat at the small table just outside the dining room she had set up for them. They were all waiting. Sister Nash insisted she could not serve Thanksgiving dinner until Reverend and Lady Moore arrived. And they were out making their holiday rounds visiting the sick and shut-in. Cynthia wished she'd taken Mama Genie's advice and eaten something before they left the house. *'Don't never go to nobody's house hungry,'* Mama Genie always said. *'You never know if the food's gonna be ready when you get there or if you gonna like it.'*

Cynthia reached for her purse sitting at her feet on the floor. She hoped she had a forgotten snack or a piece of gum inside that would tide her over in the meantime.

She had nothing.

She pressed the button on her phone to check the time. Dinner was supposed to start at five-thirty. It was six-thirty. Cynthia froze when she noticed the missed called. Holiday had called her. Her skin began to tingle as excitement rushed through her body. She couldn't believe it. He'd called two hours ago. What was she doing two hours ago to miss the phone call? *Probably helping Mama Genie get stuff together in the kitchen.* Why had he called? Cynthia looked up from her phone to see if anyone noticed she was on the verge of hyperventilation, grinning from ear to ear. No one was looking at her. They were all in their own conversations trying to talk their way through the hunger pangs.

She got up from the sofa, deciding she could step into the bathroom to return his call. But then, what if someone knocked on the door needing to use it?

She headed for the front door to go outside.

"Cynthia?" It was Sister Nash.

"Huh?" she said, turning around.

"How you liking your new job? Sister Genie told me you're a counselor now."

She had no choice but to return to her seat. It would be rude to just say 'I love it' and keep walking. Besides, everyone's attention was on her now. They heard Sister Nash say something and they more than likely thought she was saying dinner is served.

Cynthia sat down. And for the next ten minutes she discussed her job with Sister Nash, answering all of her and her daughter's questions. Someone announced Reverend Moore finally arrived and they all breathed out 'Thank you, Lord,' and headed for the dining room. Cynthia took a seat on the far end, away from Mama Genie and Sister Nash, Lady Moore and The Reverend. She did not want to be involved in any of their church talk. After Reverend Moore led them in a lengthy blessing they began to eat. The food was top notch, but all she could think about was that phone call. What did he want to say to her? Sure, it was Thanksgiving and probably why he called, but still… why? It's been three whole months. Surely he'd met someone else and moved on because men like him don't remain single for long. And then she thought perhaps it was a mistake. He called her by accident. Maybe he was intending to delete her as a contact but dialed her instead. Because if he really wanted to talk to her he would have called again or left a voicemail.

She took a sip from her drink. It was a childish way of thinking and she pushed that logic out of her mind. She knew from their summer spent together whenever he wanted to talk to her he made no mistake about it.

* * *

It was after midnight once Cynthia got ready for bed after her shower. Dinner at Sister Nash's place went on much longer than she anticipated. She could see from her position at the table Mama Genie was very tired but, like all the others, she was not going anywhere until The Reverend and First Lady bid them all a good night.

She sat at her window looking at the house next door. It was more beautiful than the last time she saw it. The sea green exterior had been painted navy blue, the wraparound porch, windows and trim painted white. But what confused her was the FOR RENT sign in the front yard.

Cynthia contemplated whether she should call him this late. What would be the point if he was sleeping? Just to tell him she would call him back later in the morning?

She reached for the phone on the nightstand. At least he would know she did not ignore his phone call.

"You just made me the happiest man in the world," he said after the first ring.

His voice was everything to her. Like hot chocolate on a cold afternoon. Pink lemonade in the springtime. A dip in the pool on the first day of summer. A gentle breeze across her cheek in the Fall. "How are you?" she smiled, wondering if it was possible he could hear the birds flapping away in her stomach. It wasn't butterflies this time. It was birds.

"I'm better now."

She could tell he had been sleeping.

"I was worried I wouldn't hear from you again. I cried myself to sleep."

"Oh, please!" Cynthia laughed softly. "You did not."

He chuckled. "It hurt just the same though." He moved around in the bed. "Thank you for calling me back."

"Hmm…" she sat with her back against the headboard, grinning, feeling like a school girl all over again talking to her boy crush. He had been thinking about her just as she had been thinking about him. "I didn't notice the call until much later. We were at Sister Nash's house for dinner."

"Ah. Okay. So you are back in town? How was the dinner?"

"Yeah. I drove down yesterday. Dinner was good. What about you? How was your Thanksgiving?"

"It was cool. Real nice. We're in Florida right now."

"Oh yeah?"

"Yeah. Dawn and Avery chose Destin, Florida for the family vacation this year, so… we been hanging out on the beach all week. We did have a Thanksgiving dinner earlier today. We rented a five bedroom house not too far from the ocean. It's beautiful out here…"

She enjoyed listening to him talk about spending time relaxing with his family. It was like catching up with an old friend. She didn't realize how much she missed the sound of his voice until now.

"How long will you be in town?" he asked. "You're not going back home tomorrow are you?"

"I was, but Mama Genie wants to go shopping for a Christmas tree. She's thinking there will be a big sale. So… I will most-likely stay until Saturday to help her put it up and decorate. Why?"

"We come back on Saturday. I was hoping for a chance to see you. If you don't mind."

Cynthia's cheeks warmed. She did not mind at all. "That would be cool," she said.

SIXTY-SIX

Holiday could not remember a time when he was ready for a vacation to be over. They spent their final day sightseeing, taking in the local attractions and to purchase souvenirs. He was on cloud nine after talking with Cynthia last night and just wanted to be back in Texas to lay his eyes on her beautiful face. Before she ended their call he made her promise that she would wait for him. So as he and the family sat enjoying dinner on the patio of a local restaurant before heading back to the vacation house to pack, he was counting down the hours.

And this is why Frank laughed at him as he pulled the truck into their driveway. Holiday could not remember any of the conversations the family had at their final dinner in Destin.

"Where was your mind, son?" Frank laughed again.

Holiday shook his head and got out of the truck, retrieving their bags from the back seat.

Frank said once they were inside the house, "I was telling Dawn we definitely have to go there again. I really enjoyed myself."

"Yeah," Holiday agreed, "but in the summertime when the water's not so cold."

"Shoot, you see them boys got in that water like it was a hot tub? It didn't bother them at all," he laughed and plopped down in his recliner. "Ahhh… it's good to be home though."

Holiday put Frank's suitcase in his room then headed to his own room to undress and take a shower.

"I'll be back later, Pop," he said a half-hour later. "I'm going to see Cynthia."

Frank's eyebrows rose. "She back in town?"

"Yeah, she was here visiting for Thanksgiving, but she's going back to Houston this evening."

"Ohhh," Frank grinned. "Now it all make sense."

"What you talking about now, Pop?"

"The reason why you checked out on us yesterday. Your mind was totally gone most of the day. I bet you don't even remember the sights we saw, do you?"

Frank was only half-right. He did remember them, but he imagined how much nicer they would have been had Cynthia been there to experience them with him.

Frank continued, "Now I been keeping to myself about it because I know it's been a little tough for you these past few months… dealing with Annette and the whole Christian situation and all. But, I can see that you really care about Cynthia."

Holiday nodded. "You're right about that, Pop."

"Tell her I said hello."

"I will," he said and walked out the door. He called her once outside to ask if she wanted him to pick her up from Ms. Genie's house and she told him to meet her at the park. Minutes later he backed into his favorite spot. The sky was gray. A light fog enveloped the trees and rested over the lake. With the exception of a few birds chirping, the park was quiet and mostly empty. He saw only three or four cars in the lot when he arrived.

Holiday sat on the tailgate waiting for her. He couldn't believe after all this time he was finally going to see her. He couldn't believe after all this time she was allowing him to see her.

Her silver Toyota pulled into the parking lot and he stood up. She smiled as she took the space right next to his truck and he was at her door before she could pull the handle to open it. Her sweet sexy body mist caressed his senses as soon as she stepped out of the car. He remembered that scent from their night at the resort.

She smiled up at him and said 'Hey' but all he could do was wrap his arms around her. He did it without thinking. He did it before he paused to gauge her mood and attitude towards him. Yes, she had returned his call a couple nights ago, and yes she had been cordial and laughed with him into the predawn hours, and yes she agreed to take time out of her day to see him—to wait for him—but that did not mean she wanted his affection.

But when her arms wrapped around his waist and her hands traveled up to his back, he squeezed a little tighter. He wanted to kiss her. He wanted to make love to her. Damn, he'd missed her.

She slowly pulled away and he reluctantly released her, staring down into the lovely face that filled both his night and daydreams. Cynthia moved past him for the truck bed and his eyes followed. Her hair was different. Instead of the normal-looking braids she wore that summer, to him, these resembled twisted rope. Tiny gold cuffs wrapped around a few of them. She wore a pair of black leggings, long white shirt and denim jacket. The high slits on both sides of the white shirt lent a sexy view of the curve of her hips.

It was torture.

"How've you been?" she asked him. She stood in front of the tailgate but did not sit on it.

He wasn't sure if he should sit or stand too. Maybe she intended to stay only a few minutes. In that case, he had no time to waste and needed her to know how he felt, what was bothering him all this time.

He sat down. "Cynthia, I just want you to know that it was never my intent to lie to you. Like I said… I didn't think I—"

She shook her head, silencing him. "It's all right," she said. "I understand it now and I admire you for it. Not too many men would even consider maintaining that responsibility after a divorce. It's a beautiful thing to me the relationship you have with him."

Her words moved all through Holiday.

"And what is Christian up to these days? Is he back to his old self?" she asked.

Holiday sighed and shifted on the tailgate. "Well… that's the thing… I haven't seen him since that day I last saw him in the hospital. His mama called me out of nowhere the day me and Pop were leaving for vacation, wanting me to take him with us. But then she started questioning me again about who I was with and who all was going to be on the trip. She said he couldn't go if you were there."

Cynthia turned to look at him.

"I realized then that I just have to accept the truth. Annette is his mama—I have no legal claims to him—and she can do whatever she wanna do, let me see him or not let me see him, and what I think or feel about it don't matter." He shrugged and sighed again. "So I just told her it's best that I remain out of his life. I'm not her puppet."

Cynthia moved closer to him and put her hand on his knee. "I'm sorry to hear that."

He covered her hand with his own. "I mean… it is what it is. I hate it ended this way, but that's life. You win some, you lose some. I'm sure I will see Christian around town. My number won't change. And if he ever decide to call—if she let him call—I'll answer it."

"Yeah," Cynthia said. "But it's just sad. I'm sad for you."

He laced his fingers with hers and pulled her over to him to stand between his legs. He held her face with both hands to look at her. "Cynthia, baby, I missed you." He couldn't hold back anymore.

"I missed you too," she whispered.

He pressed his lips to hers. It was the sweetest feeling. For months he had been wanting, yearning to see her face, hold her in his arms, hear her voice. He believed all this time she had moved on, forgotten about him. But the way she arched her body into his, ran her hands up his sides and over his arms to grip his hands holding her face, kissed him with the same yearning let him know she was feeling what he was feeling. Their time apart only fueled the need for each other.

Holiday slipped his hands underneath the denim jacket, seeking to get as close to her as possible. The shirt was thin enough to offer him a small slice of satisfaction, but it wasn't enough.

He trailed her jawbone with tender kisses and gripped her tighter as a soft breath escaped her lips when he reached her neck. Her neck was her weak spot.

She pulled away from him, smiling, she said, "We should go for a walk."

He chuckled and got up, closing the tailgate behind him. They headed towards the trail. "Pop said hello."

"Really? How is he doing?

"He all right. Pop is Pop. Nothing's changed. I'm sure he's knocked out on his recliner now, wore out from the trip."

She smiled. "Hey, I wanted to ask you... I noticed the FOR RENT sign at Mr. Howie's house. What's up with that?"

"Oh. His daughter didn't want it."

"What? Are you serious?" Cynthia stopped walking.

"Yeah. Pop told me Howie said his daughter changed her mind. Said she wasn't ready for a big family house like that just yet. She want something small, a condo somewhere or something where she can have friends over and they hang out at the pool and whatnot."

"You're kidding."

He chuckled. "Naw. That's what he said."

Cynthia shook her head and started walking again. "So she would rather live in something no more than eight-hundred square feet with shared walls versus a three bedroom house with her own yard free of charge?"

Holiday shrugged.

"These kids today, I swear. I wouldn't've known how to act had my parents had something set up like that for me."

"You and me both," Holiday agreed.

"Maybe you should buy it from Mr. Howie," she smiled up at him.

"Buy? Well… that's something I wanna do with my wife. I want us to go and look and pick it out together."

"Oh. I see."

He looked at her. "What about you? It's the perfect spot for you to be next door to Ms. Genie."

She laughed. "Don't even start that kinda talk again. I just started my new job."

He threw his arm around her shoulder. "Yeah, Ms. Genie told me. How is it?"

"Oh I love it," she said. "It's what I was looking for. Something that would allow me to still work with kids, but in a different way. It definitely beats standing in front of a classroom all day. The pay isn't that great, but there is room for advancement. I'm already planning to start my Master's degree."

"Wow. That's cool. I like that. Make that money."

"Yep," she laughed.

They walked the gravel trail beneath trees of red, and yellow, and orange leaves. They walked through the haze talking and laughing like old times. It felt good to have her with him again, walking beside him, enjoying her company. But the idea that she was leaving to go back to Houston in a few hours broke his heart.

Holiday reached for her hand and stopped walking. He moved to stand directly in front of her. "Cynthia," he said, "if somebody had told me a fat piece of salt bacon was going to be the thing to introduce me to the woman of my dreams I would have called them crazy."

Her forehead crinkled as she looked up at him before she let out a giggle. "What?"

"This summer I met a beautiful woman. A woman who came into my life when I wasn't expecting it, wasn't even looking for something..." He watched her face soften but her eyes looked skeptical. "In the short amount of time we were together you showed me how easy love should be, how it can be when it's with the right one. Now, I know you live a few hours away from me, but... I want you. In the right way. And I've already decided I'm just gonna have to make that trip every weekend until we figure something out and can make this thing official. So... Ms. Cynthia Williams... will you have me?"

Those beautiful full lips of hers spread into a smile as she shook her head. She let go of his hands and reached up to wrap her arms around his neck. She rubbed her nose with his before kissing him softly. "You are so crazy," she said. "Of course I will."

He held her for a long time just to relish the moment before taking her hand again to lead her back to their vehicles.

"You don't want to walk no more?" she asked.

"Naw. We need to go to the house so I can pack my bag. I'm following you home."

She laughed, the sound bouncing around the trees. "I'm still staying at Tora's place, remember?"

"I know. We'll find a nice hotel to spend the weekend. You decide."

She laid her head on his arm. "Hmm..."

Dear Reader,

I hope you enjoyed getting to know Cynthia and Holiday. If you have a minute to spare, please leave a review online. You can also share your thoughts with me by sending an email to teneka@tenekawoods.com .

Visit my website to sign up for my newsletter and be in the know of the latest news and book release info.

I look forward to hearing from you.

With love,
Teneka

P.S. Turn the page for a preview of my next book coming soon!

ONE

Nate drummed his fingers on the steering wheel in frustration. He was caught on the 610 West Loop South just before The Galleria, traffic inching forward at a snail's pace, which only reminded him why he avoided this side of Houston at all costs. No matter what day of the week or what time of day there was always a traffic jam. It was Wednesday afternoon. Their lunch date was scheduled for two o' clock and he was already a half-hour late. To her, that half-hour translated to two hours. She was no doubt sitting at the table fuming by now, swallowing down her iced tea as she contemplated calling him a third time to find out his location. He's been on her bad side for several months and he hoped they could enjoy a peaceful lunch together for once without talk about the money.

But she said she had something to tell him. A surprise. And he had no idea what that could have meant.

The address she'd given led him to a small sandwich shop on Westheimer Road with limited parking. Nate knew something was up because a sandwich shop was definitely not her usual style, even if it was located just a few minutes away from her sprawling River Oaks home. He found street parking a couple blocks over and walked back to the restaurant.

Her back was to him as he entered but the mirrored wall facing her table announced his arrival.

"Is this a joke?" he said as he approached.

"Your sister chose this place."

He leaned down to kiss her forehead. "Hey, Mama."

"Hello my son." Her cup of tea was almost empty.

Nate removed his keys and smartphone from his pockets, threw them on the table before sitting down across from her. "Is that why we're here? Is this the surprise? Because you've never been one to partake in an establishment in the business of cold cuts."

She rolled her eyes at his sarcasm. "Of course not, but I let Sunny convince me to try something new today. She said their soups are really good."

Nate scanned the small eatery with its exposed brick walls, kooky art décor, and mix of high and low table seating that gave it a jumbled appearance. With the exception of one cashier, they were the only brown patrons in sight, surrounded by the college student-type crowd. "Where is she anyway?"

"She's in the ladies' room. She'd just left the table right before you walked in."

Nate bobbed his head. "Did y'all order already? I'm starving." He grabbed a menu from the holder at the center of the table.

The corners of his mother's mouth curved. "Now why would we do that? Unlike other folks I know, we have manners and are considerate of other people. We wouldn't dare have lunch without our guest. Even if they show up *extremely* late. To *everything. All the time.* Oh no. We wouldn't do that."

Nate could only laugh as he'd set himself up for that one. "Mama, you know how it is with my clients. I'm there for them. If they need me a few extra minutes beyond their session for some more pep talk and encouragement then I have to stay. It's my gift to them for their support."

She huffed. "Sure, son. It's always the *client's* fault."

It never failed. She stressed the word client because, in her mind, the clients he worked with were not real clients. They were not the type of clients she—Mrs. Victoria Helena Walker—raised him to work with. To her, they were just people lacking common sense and self-control, paying him a few dollars per hour to show them how to eat healthy and exercise. She wanted her son to follow in the family's footsteps and have a successful career in law or science. She wanted her son to have the career she and his father paid for him to have.

And he'd followed their dream and attended law school, passed the bar with flying colors, and worked as an attorney for a couple years. But his heart was never in it. His heart was in fitness and nutrition. Instead of mulling over criminal case files, he would rather demonstrate the different ways to perform a sit-up.

This is what Victoria had a problem with. Sending him to law school was a waste of their money and she would not let him forget. "It's the truth, Mama. It's a valid excuse. I have no reason to lie about anything like this."

"What are you lying about not lying about now?"

It was his sister Sunny. A big, rotund belly suddenly appeared in his peripheral view as she made her way back to the table. She was only six months pregnant but looked as if she should have delivered his niece a month ago. "What's up, baby sis? How are you doing?"

She blew out a breath as she sat down. "How do I look like I'm doing? Fat. Exhausted. Fat." She laughed weakly.

He laughed with her. "I think you look good. Skin glowing. I like your hair." It looked freshly done. The golden ringlets bounced easily with the slightest movement. It reminded him of the curly fries with mustard they loved to share when they were kids.

"Thank you, but now that you're here we can finally eat. Baby Sunny is not happy at all. Mama and I know what we want, and since you were late *again* the bill is on you."

They told him what they wanted from the menu and sent him to the counter to place the order and to refill their drinks at the soda machine. "Alright," he said, once back at the table, "what is this surprise you had for me, Mama?"

"I'll let your sister tell you."

Nate looked from his mother to his sister.

Sunny's mouth spread into a wide grin. "Well… brother, I'm a little disappointed that you didn't notice. I'd expect my best friend, my twin, to know right away the reason my skin is all aglow as you observed." She moved her hand from beneath the table and thrust it towards him. "We're getting married!"

She said it too loud because suddenly it was quiet in the restaurant and everyone was looking their way. And then, slowly, they started clapping. Sunny grinned some more and Victoria nodded, mouthing a quiet 'Thank you' all around the room.

Nate could not share in his sister's excitement. He narrowed his eyes at the two of them, sitting back in his seat. "This is the surprise?"

"Yes," Sunny continued to beam, her hand outstretched in front of her as she stared at the ring. "We're finally doing it."

Victoria said, "Aren't you happy for your sister, son? As you can see she is over the moon about it."

They knew his sister's boyfriend was his least favorite person in the world. A man he believed was not worthy at all of his beautiful and smart sister. He wanted to be happy because being married to the love of her life was a dream come true for his sister, but he wished she was marrying someone else. Someone who truly respected her and his family. "Well, I've never bitten my tongue about anything when it comes to that dude, and I'm not about to bite it now. What made him finally decide to pop the question? This is baby number three. He was making promises to marry you after baby number one." He didn't give her a chance to respond. "Oh, I know. It's to seal the deal now that you've made partner. He can continue to sit on his ass while you bust yours every day."

Sunny's face twisted.

"Nate, looking after children is a full-time job in itself," Victoria said. "If it works for them what do you have to say about it?"

"Mama, I get that, but how many times do we have to hear it from her own mouth about how Levi really is at home? How he does the bare minimum for my niece and nephew? Doesn't even get them dressed for the day, doesn't cook, doesn't clean or take them out to the park for fresh air and play? And he still expects Sunny to cook him a hot meal when she gets home after a long day in the office? Huh? Or about how she can't even make it in the door good and hang up the car keys before he takes off to *go to the gym*?" Sunny dropped her eyes and he knew he hurt her feelings.

"I thought you would be happy for me, Nate," she said.

Nate shook his head. "You can do so much better, baby sis. So much better than that bum dude."

"He told me he's thinking about getting back in school to finally finish his degree. He's been looking into online programs. Maybe law school, too."

Nate grunted. "And I guess you'll be paying for that too."

Victoria asked, "Nate, if the roles were reversed would you be saying the same thing? Would it be a problem if Sunny was the stay-at-home mom and her husband financed her schooling? And you are one to talk about someone paying for another's education. At least Levi's making plans to do better. *He's* considering law school. You know… something promising? Something sustainable?"

"Oh, so now what I do isn't promising or sustainable?" He shook his head and was glad when the waiter came over with their orders. This was not the type of conversation he wanted to have over lunch.

He pushed back from the table. "I'm going to wash my hands." In the restroom he scrubbed his hands clean all the while thinking about this surprise. His sister was everything to him and he wanted her to be happy, but for her to be such a smart woman she made the dumbest choice of a father to her children and a soon-to-be husband. And now he would have to attend a wedding he didn't care to witness.

"We're throwing the engagement party at a ballroom downtown," Victoria said when he returned to the table. "It'll be formal."

Nate rolled his eyes. His mother lived for extravagance. Since they were kids there was always an affair she and his dad had to attend or host in their home. She would dress him and his older brothers in suits, Sunny in a little girl's gown, and introduce them to their colleagues and bask in the compliments about how neatly dressed and well-behaved her children were. If one of the neighbors came over to talk about the weather, it was reason enough for Victoria to pull out her most expensive tea set or dinnerware.

He picked up the pepper shaker to sprinkle some over his salad.

"And this is the bonus surprise," Sunny said, smiling at him, "I invited Kaneesa. She's going to be in the wedding. And she's walking with you."

Nate stared at his sister as he continued to spice up his bowl of mixed greens. Kaneesa was his one-night mistake, although he'd known her for ten years. She was just an intern at the medical center where his mother worked when Victoria invited her to one of their dinner parties and first introduced them. Nate recognized her attraction for him right away and soon after she was showing up to all of their family events. For ten years he ignored her as he was in and out of relationships of his own and, by then, she had become like another sister to him. But one night after one too many drinks at the Christmas party he retreated to a room upstairs to recuperate and when he finally emerged Kaneesa was right there to push him back in. For nearly an hour she did things to him in that room he wasn't aware the nerdy and uptight Kaneesa was capable of.

The next morning he woke up to find her preparing breakfast for him in his apartment. He didn't have the heart to ask her to leave.

That was several months ago. Kaneesa is still looking for a chance to spend another night with him.

"Aren't you supposed to ask people if they want to be in your wedding? You already know I do not approve of the groom, so… you may have to get somebody else to walk with Kaneesa."

Sunny threw down her fork. "Nate, are you serious? You're not coming to my wedding?"

Nate shook his head. "I hate to break it to you, baby sis, but no. Or the engagement party. I don't want to see you make the biggest mistake of your life."

"Son, don't be ridiculous," Victoria said. "It's been five years already and they're on their third child. Why wouldn't they marry?"

His mother's question fell on deaf ears because his attention was stolen by the woman that walked through the doors of the sandwich shop. A tall, statuesque beauty with legs that appeared to go on forever. His eyes followed her as she strutted over to the counter, completely oblivious to the heads turning with curiosity in her path. She removed the oversized sunglasses from her eyes, resting them atop her head as she perused the menu hanging on the wall. The tattoo spanning the length of her torso piqued his interest.

"Now he doesn't have anything to say."

"Obviously because something's got his mind elsewhere."

Nate could not remember the last time he was so taken by a woman at first sight. "Speaking of marriage… I think I see my wife."

"What?" his mother and sister said at the same time. They turned to see for themselves who he was talking about.

Sunny sucked her teeth and turned back around. "Oh God, no."

"You can't be serious, son," Victoria said.

"She is beautiful."

"She is trashy," Sunny replied. "What the hell does she have on? Kaneesa wouldn't be caught dead wearing something like that."

His mother agreed with a nod. "But of course Kaneesa is not the young lady he wants. She's too classy."

The woman wore a pair of short denim shorts, a white shredded T-shirt just long enough to cover her breasts, and shoes that looked like combat boots with a stiletto heel. He knew the long sheer floral jacket she topped the outfit with was called a kimono. His mother wore them often.

The woman smiled at the cashier as she accepted her order number flag, and walked over to the wall next to the soda machine to wait. Nate did not know what he was going to say, but he knew he had to say something to her. "Y'all don't understand," he said as he grabbed his cup, getting up from the table, "that's confidence. There's nothing trashy about it."

He pulled the top off his cup of water and walked to the soda machine. She was looking at her smartphone. He poured out the water and pressed the button to refill it. "Hello," he said.

She looked up from her phone. "Hello."

"I like your tattoo." It was a tribal print of elongated curves and sharp points. Now that he was close up he could see it was shiny, red and puffy around the edges. She'd just gotten it done.

"Thanks," she said, her attention quickly returning to her phone.

Nate studied her profile: short forehead, concave nose and chin. A trio of miniscule moles dotted her right cheekbone. She was perfect.

He grabbed a straw and tapped it against the counter. "How long did that take?"

She looked at him with a slight smile and he wasn't sure if it was a genuine smile or a smile that she was annoyed. "Three, four hours. I don't remember to be honest."

He nodded. "I was thinking about getting a sleeve myself. Those look pretty cool."

Her eyes roved over him. "I can see that. It would look good on you."

He smiled and extended his hand. "I'm Nate Walker. What's your name?"

"Tora," she said as she shook his hand.

"I like that. You come here a lot?"

"No. This is my first time. I just left the tattoo parlor down the street and decided to try it."

Nate took a sip from his cup before setting it on the counter. "It's my first time here, too. Nice vibe."

She nodded, glancing around the room. "Yeah. I love the artwork."

"Tora, do you mind if I give you a call sometime? Maybe we can meet up for lunch one day?"

She dropped the phone in her purse when her order number was called. Smiling, she said, "Thanks, but no. I don't want to waste your time. It was nice talking to you."

He watched her walk away and towards the counter to pick up her meal.

"Did she spit in your face and tell you to get lost?" Sunny laughed when he returned to the table.

"Naw, she said she didn't wanna waste my time."

"Waste your time?" Victoria said. "So, in other words, you're beneath her?"

Nate picked up his fork. "I'm sure she has a man. That's all."

Victoria said, "That's not it. If she had one, she would have said so."

Nate noticed Tora still standing at the counter chatting with the cashier. He couldn't take his eyes off her honey brown complexion, flat stomach, and long legs. She pulled something out of her purse and handed it to the clerk before walking out the door as sexily as she'd walked in.

His mother was probably right. *There goes my wife.*

www.ingramcontent.com/pod-product-compliance
Lightning Source LLC
Chambersburg PA
CBHW022011120726
47898CB00006BA/1670